D0030647

LISA JACKSON

LIGHT OF DAY

HQN™

ISBN-13: 978-0-373-77965-9

Light of Day

Copyright © 2015 by Harlequin Books S.A.

The publisher acknowledges the copyright holder of the individual works as follows:

Mystic
Copyright © 1986 By Lisa Jackson

Renegade Son
Copyright © 1987 By Lisa Jackson

Recycling programs for this product may not exist in your area.

CONTENTS

MYSTIC

PROLOGUE

Beaumont Breeding Farm—Summer

SAVANNAH SLOWED THE mare to a walk and patted Mattie's sweating neck. Her breath was as short as that of the mare; the sprint through the open pastures had been exhilarating. A soft breeze rustled through the branches of trees along the fence and made the July afternoon tolerable as it cooled the trickle of sweat running down her back. She pushed her black hair away from her face and squinted against the hot sun in the northern California sky.

"I guess it's time to go back home," she said reluctantly as she reined the mare toward the gate at the far end of the field. Mattie flicked her ears forward expectantly.

Looking east, Savannah noticed a tall broad-shouldered figure near the gate. She squinted as she approached and tried to place the man repairing the sagging fence. *Must be a new hired hand,* she thought idly, fascinated nonetheless.

She pulled Mattie up short, several yards away from the man, and waited in the dappled shade of an old apple tree. Unable to get through the gate until he was finished with his work, she leaned back in the saddle and observed him.

He was wearing only dusty jeans and boots. His shirt had been tossed over a post, and his deeply muscled back, tanned and glistening with sweat, was straining as he stretched the heavy wire around a new wooden fence post.

I wonder where Dad found him, Savannah mused, admiring the play of rippling muscles and straining tendons of his shoulders and back as he worked. His hair was dark with sweat, and the worn fabric of his jeans stretched taut over lean hips and muscular thighs.

"That should do it," he said, rubbing the small of his back as he straightened and admired his work. His voice was strangely familiar.

Then he dusted his hands together and turned, as if he'd felt her staring at him. Shielding his eyes against the lowering sun, he looked in her direction and every muscle in his body went rigid. "Savannah?"

The sight of Travis's eyes fixed on her made her stomach jump unexpectedly. Savannah urged her horse forward and stopped the mare only a few feet from him. "I...I didn't know you were back on the farm," she replied, blushing slightly at being caught staring at him. *It was Travis for God's sake. Just Travis!*

His amused smile stretched over the angular features of his face. Wiping the sweat from his forehead, he stretched his aching back muscles. "The prodigal son has returned, so to speak."

"So to speak," she whispered, her throat uncomfortably tight as she stared into his steel-gray eyes. The same gray eyes she'd seen most of her life. Only now, they seemed incredibly erotic, and the corded muscles of his chest and shoulders added to his intense masculinity—a sensual virility she'd never noticed before. He'd always just been Travis, almost a brother. "I thought you had a job in L.A."

"I do." He leaned insolently against the post and the hard line of his mouth turned cynical. "But I thought I'd spend the rest of the summer on the farm before I get stuck in the rut of three-piece suits and three-martini lunches."

"So you're staying?" *Why was her heart pounding so wildly?*

"Until September." He glanced around the farm, taking in the whitewashed buildings, the rolling acres of pastureland, and the dusky hills in the distance. "I'm gonna miss this place, though," he admitted, his gaze darkening a bit as it rested on the scampering, long-legged foals in the next field.

"And we'll all miss you," Savannah replied, wondering at the unusual huskiness in her voice.

Travis's head jerked up and he stared at her for a moment. His brows drew together in concentration before he cleared his throat. "Not much to miss, really," he argued. "I haven't been around much."

"That's what happens when you go to school to become a politician."

"Lawyer," he corrected.

Savannah shrugged. "That's not the way I heard it. Dad is already planning a future for you in politics." She cocked her head to the side and smiled. "You know, I wouldn't be surprised if someday you become a senator or something."

"Not on your life, lady!" Travis let out a hollow laugh, but his gray eyes turned stone cold. "Your old man is always scheming, Savannah. But this time he's gone too far." He reached to the ground and picked up a bottle of beer that had been hidden in the dry grass.

"But your father—"

"Was a senator from Colorado, and now according to the press, the old man might not have been as lily-white as the voters thought." Travis scowled, swore under his breath and kicked at the fence post with the toe of his boot. "But then you already knew that." Eyeing her over the top of the bottle, he lifted his chin and took a long swallow of beer, then tossed the empty bottle to the ground. With a sound of disgust, he wiped the back of his hand over his mouth and then raked tense fingers through his hair in frustration. "It seems to be the popular thing to do these days, digging up the dirt on dead politicians."

Savannah didn't know what to say, so she looked away and tried not to notice the way the afternoon sun played in Travis's rich, chestnut-colored hair. Tried not to notice the ripple of his shoulder muscles as he shoveled a last scoop of dirt around the post, or the fact that the curling hairs over his chest were dark with sweat and accentuated the flat contour of his abdomen.

"I can't worry about it, anyway. What's done is done. Right?"

"Right."

He looked up at her again and she couldn't help but stare at his mouth. Thin lips curved slightly downward in vexation as he noticed the intensity of her gaze.

He pretended interest in his work and avoided her eyes. "Still going with that boy…David what's-his-name?" he asked.

"Crandall. And no."

"Why not?"

She lifted one shoulder and shifted uncomfortably in the saddle. For the first time since she could remember, she didn't like Travis poking his nose into her private life. "I don't know. It just didn't work out."

His jaw tightened a bit. "Want to talk about it?"

"No, uh, I don't think so."

"You used to tell me whatever was on your mind."

"Yeah, but I was just a kid then."

"And now?" He slid a glance up her body.

"And now I'm seventeen." She tossed her black hair away from her face and sat up straight in the saddle, shoulders pinned back, unconsciously thrusting her breasts forward.

Travis sucked in his breath and frowned. "Oh, I see; all grown up."

"Just like you were when you were seventeen." She arched a disdainful eyebrow, hoping to appear more sophisticated than she felt sitting astride Mattie. Her T-shirt and cutoff jeans, wild black hair and freshly scrubbed face didn't help the image. She probably looked the same as she did when she was a skinny kid of nine.

"Seventeen. That was so long ago, I can't even remember."

"I do. That's how old you were when you moved in with us."

"You remember that far back?"

"Give me a break, Travis. I was nine, and I've got a great memory. I thought you were so…I think the word they use today is 'awesome.'"

Travis shook his head. "I was a rebellious brat."

"And I was impressed by your total disrespect for anything."

Travis winced. "Reginald wasn't."

"Dad is and always has been the ultimate authoritarian. That's why I thought you were so…brave." She laughed and some of the growing tension between them dissolved. "And now you're an old man of twenty-five."

"Yeah, I guess so." He leaned against the wooden post and crossed his arms over his chest as his smile faded. "And it's time to quit sponging off your dad and try and make a living on my own."

"You've never sponged off Dad!" Indignation colored

Savannah's cheeks. "Maybe some people don't know it, but I do."

"He took me in—"

"And you worked. Hard. On this farm. For nothing. Just like you're doing now! As for your education, you had a trust fund. You didn't exactly come here as a pauper, you know!"

"Whoa!" He laughed deep in his throat. "I didn't know I had such a bulldog in my corner."

"Just stating the facts, counselor." She smiled and blushed a little under his unyielding stare. The warm familiarity that had existed between them just seconds before suddenly vanished.

"You never cease to amaze me, Savvy," Travis said, using the nickname he had given her all those years before. His voice was barely above a whisper as his flinty gaze locked intimately with hers. Savannah's heart began to pound in the thickening silence, and Travis's eyes narrowed.

A stallion whistled in the distance, and Mattie snorted, breaking the silence. Travis gave his head a quick shake, as if to dislodge an unwanted thought. "Remind me to hire you when I'm having trouble getting the jury to see my client's side of the story," he joked, picking up his shirt, empty bottle and shovel and carrying them to a Jeep parked on the other side of the gate.

"I doubt that my testimony would make an impact."

"I don't know," he said, rubbing his square, beard-shadowed chin thoughtfully. His gaze inched up her bare, suntanned legs before lingering slightly on her waist and breasts and then finally reaching her eyes. She felt as if she'd just been stripped bare, and her cheeks burned under his assessing stare. "I just don't know."

Somehow she understood that he wasn't referring to

his fictitious courtroom scenario, and her heart fluttered. To save herself from further embarrassment, she kicked Mattie and the game little mare broke into a gallop. Savannah leaned forward in the saddle and raced away from Travis and the odd feelings he'd unwittingly inspired.

THE NEXT FIVE weeks were torture. Savannah saw Travis every night at dinner. Every night, that is, that he wasn't with Melinda, his fiancée. Why his engagement to Melinda Reaves bothered Savannah now eluded her. Melinda was a nice enough girl—make that woman, she corrected herself—and Travis had dated her for years. It was only natural that someday Travis and Melinda would marry. Right? Then why did she feel sick inside every time she thought about Travis and Melinda together?

During the days, Savannah ran into Travis working around the farm. In the stables, in the tack room, at the lake, in the stallion barn, everywhere. There didn't seem to be a place she could hide without experiencing the sensation that he was watching her. She had even caught him staring openly at her more than once, though he'd always looked quickly away when she caught his gaze. Though Savannah had tried to be discreet, she was fascinated by him. She'd watch him work and her mind would create deliciously wanton fantasies about him.

"Don't do this," she warned herself on more than one occasion when she found herself dressing with more care than was her custom. "This is Travis you're thinking about. Travis!" But the pain in her middle wouldn't go away, nor could she keep her eyes from straying to his face, his hands, his lips, his thighs. Oftentimes she found herself wondering just what it would feel like to have Travis touch her with those large, work-roughened hands, what it would taste like to have his sensual lips brush against hers…how it would feel to become his lover. Just the thought of his hard, male physique pressed hungrily against her body made her break into a nervous sweat and her heart beat savagely.

"You're out of your ever-lovin' mind," she told herself.

"WHAT'S WRONG WITH YOU, Savannah?" David asked as they were driving back to the farm.

The date with David had been a disaster from the start, and she knew now that she never should have agreed to it.

Though she'd tried not to think about Travis, she hadn't even tasted the gourmet food or paid any attention to the movie that David had taken her to.

"Nothing's wrong with me." *Except that I took this date out of spite, because Travis is with Melinda again.* She felt uneasy, and some of the uncomfortable feeling was from guilt. She'd used David to lash back at Travis. Not fair. David was a friend, a good friend. And Travis hadn't even noticed.

"Give me a break. You've been brooding all night. Why?"

"I'm not brooding."

"Look, just tell me, was it something I did?"

Savannah smiled and shook her head. "No, of course not."

David sighed in relief and parked the car behind her house, near the back porch. He cut the engine and switched off the headlights. The breeze that filtered through the open windows of the car was little relief from the stifling night. Savannah felt hot and sticky as she reached for the handle of the door.

"Wait." David's hand touched her on the shoulder and she stopped. His brown eyes searched hers. "There's someone else, isn't there?"

"No," she lied. Her feelings for Travis were just school-girl fantasies and she recognized them as such.

"Then, what, Savannah? Don't you know I love you?"

It was the last thing she wanted to hear. "David, you're a good friend and I like you very much—"

"And I sense a big 'but' coming here," he complained.

"Can't we just be friends?"

"Friends?" he repeated. "Friends. Savannah, for crissake, didn't you hear me?" He placed a finger under her chin and forced her to look into his intense gaze. "I *love* you."

"David—"

But she couldn't stop him as his arms tightened around her and he kissed her with more passion than she'd ever thought possible. When he lifted his head, her lips were throbbing painfully. "David, please, don't," she whispered, trying to pull away from him.

"You used to like me to kiss you," he rasped in disbelief.

"I told you…I just want to be friends."

"Like hell." He pulled her close to him again and this time when he kissed her she felt his tongue press against her teeth and his sweaty hands reach below the hem of her sweater to touch her naked abdomen and inch upward to her breasts.

I can't! she thought desperately. *I just can't let him touch me!* Gathering all her strength, she wrenched one arm free and slapped him across the cheek. It had the effect of a bucket of cold water. He drew back his head and his eyes glittered frightfully. "Don't push me, Savannah," he ground out.

"And don't push *me*!"

He released her then and his face slackened. "I just don't understand. Why did you go out with me?"

"Because I like you. I thought you were my friend."

"There's that word again," he said, rubbing his cheek. "I never thought I would hate being called a friend, but I do." He placed his hands over the steering wheel and let his head fall forward. "There is someone else, isn't there?" She understood his despair. Wasn't she in the same position herself?

"I don't know, David," she said, tenderness softening her voice. "I...do care for someone else...." He flinched. "But believe me, he doesn't know I'm alive.... I'd...I'd better go."

"I'll walk you to the door."

"No! It's okay. Really. I can make it."

This time she got the door open.

"Savannah—"

"Yeah?"

"I'm sorry."

Tears stood in her eyes. "I know, David." She didn't wait for any further confessions from him. All she knew was that she'd probably lost a very good friend and she'd humiliated him in the bargain. She got out of the car and slammed the door shut.

"I can't seem to do anything right," she thought aloud as she climbed the two steps to the porch. She heard David's car start and listened as he drove away. "Thank God," she whispered and realized that she'd started to cry.

Reaching into her purse for her keys, she heard a sound: the heel of a boot scraping against the flagstones. She nearly jumped out of her skin. Swallowing back a small lump of fear she turned and faced Travis, who was sitting in the shadows of the porch in a rocking chair. *Oh, God...*

"You should be more careful about who you go out with," he said, his voice cold.

"And you should be more careful about sitting in the dark. You nearly scared me to death."

"I thought you weren't dating David."

"I'm not."

Silence. Savannah could hear her own heart pounding.

"You're leading him on," he accused.

Savannah heard the irritation in his voice, though she could barely see his face. "You should mind your own business."

"Then maybe next time, you'll have the decency to roll the windows up." With a sinking sensation, Savannah realized that Travis had heard all of her conversation with David. She was mortified and kept rummaging in her purse. *Where was the damned key?*

"Maybe next time *you'll* have the decency to mind your own business and not eavesdrop."

"I wasn't eavesdropping."

"Than what're you doing out here all alone? Where's Melinda?"

"At home." His voice sounded dead.

"Oh."

Her fingers found the key ring, but it was too late. Travis was on his feet and walking toward her. As the gap between them closed, her pulse began to race wildly. He stopped only inches from her, close enough that she could feel the heat radiating from his body, see the pain and concern etched over his harsh features. "I'm serious, Savannah. You shouldn't lead that boy on. And that advice goes for any other man as well."

"I told you, I wasn't leading him on."

"He cares about you, and when a boy, a young man, cares about a woman, sometimes he gets carried away. He can't help himself. He stops using his brain and starts thinking with his— Oh, hell, I'm making a bloody mess of this!"

"You sound as if you're speaking from experience."

His muscles became rigid. "Maybe I am."

Savannah thought of Melinda and felt like crying all over again. Travis leaned a shoulder against the wall and she felt his eyes staring at her mussed hair and flushed face.

"Just be careful, Savannah," he said tenderly, touching the edge of her jaw. "Don't get yourself into a situation that you can't get out of. I won't always be here to take care of you."

The feel of his fingers on her skin made her pulse jump. The heat of his touch seemed to scorch a path to her heart. "A lot of good it did having you here."

"I didn't want to butt in. It really wasn't any of my business. But, believe me, if David hadn't come to his senses when you slapped him, I would have jerked open that car door and beat the living hell out of him."

"David wouldn't hurt me."

"I didn't know that."

The thought of Travis willing to fight to protect her virtue was pleasant and she couldn't help but smile.

"This is serious business, Savannah."

The finger at her jaw moved slowly to her throat and Savannah felt herself melting inside. A warm ache stretched deep inside her and it was hard to keep her mind on anything but Travis's warm finger and his dark, searing gaze. It took her breath away.

"I...I know."

"Just don't make the same mistake Charmaine did."

Savannah felt herself color. Her sister, Charmaine, had gotten pregnant the year before and was now married to

Wade Benson, the father of her little boy. "I don't need a lesson in sex education," she tossed back.

"Good." He let his hand drop and even in the hot night she shivered. "'Cause I'm sure as hell not the one who should be giving you one."

"What's that supposed to mean?"

He closed his eyes. "Oh, Savannah, you just don't have any idea what you do to a man, do you?" Opening his eyes, he looked at her lovingly for a fleeting moment. "Just don't underestimate your effect on men or overestimate a man's self-control."

Her throat was dry, but she had to ask the question. "All men?"

"All men."

"Does that include you?" she whispered.

"All men," he repeated and opened the door to the kitchen. "Now go upstairs to bed and get some sleep before I forget the fact that I'm supposed to be a brother to you, that I should be looking out for your best interests."

"I don't need a keeper, Travis," she said, placing her fingers on his arm.

His eyes were cold and assessing as he measured the innocence in her gaze. "Well, maybe *I* do." He took hold of her wrist and his face became expressionless as he forced her hand away from him. "You've heard the old expression, 'Don't play with fire unless you're ready to get burned'?" he said, his jaw tight. "Think about it."

And then he strode away, into the dark night.

For five days Savannah didn't see Travis, and she discovered that it was more difficult to work on the farm when he was absent than when he was there. Just how much of the conversation with David had he heard, and how much had he pieced together? Had he realized that he was the man she cared for? Savannah wondered.

That she loved Travis McCord came as an unwelcome and painful realization. The fact that he loved another woman made the situation all the more intolerable.

JUST TWO MORE WEEKS, Savannah thought as she lay on the top of her bed, staring at the ceiling, wondering where Travis was at one in the morning. *Just two more weeks and then he'll be gone.*

At the thought of his leaving and marrying Melinda Reaves, Savannah's heart wrenched painfully. She rolled over and looked at the clock, just as she had every two minutes for the past half hour. "This is crazy," she told herself.

For nearly as long as she could remember, Travis had been a part of Beaumont Breeding Farm. When his parents had been killed in a plane crash, her father and mother had taken him in as if he were their own. Savannah had always looked up to the rebellious young man as the older brother she'd never had. Never in her wildest dreams had she imagined that she would fall in love with him. Well, not "in love" exactly. She loved him. He still thought of her as a kid sister and it was probably best that way. If she could just make it through the next two weeks without letting him know how she felt about him, everything would work out. Travis would marry Melinda, and Savannah would go to college. *If she didn't die first!* Her small fist curled and pounded the unused pillow on her bed.

Her restlessness finally got the better of her and she threw off the covers, grabbed her robe, slipped on a pair of thongs and sneaked down the hallway. The only sounds in the house were the soft ticking of the hall clock and the hum of the refrigerator. One of the steps squeaked as she hurried down the staircase. She froze, but no one in the house stirred. Taking a deep breath, Savannah quietly hurried down the rest of the stairs, softly opened the front door, slipped outside and closed the door behind her.

The night was illuminated by a lazy half-moon and a sprinkling of stars that peeked through the wispy, dark clouds. The smell of honeysuckle and lilacs filled the air and the soft croaking of frogs was interrupted by the occasional whinny of a mare calling to her foal. Other than those few noises, the night was still.

Savannah walked down the worn path to the lake almost by instinct. She climbed over the gates rather than risking the noise of unlatching them. When the scrub oak and pine trees gave way to a clearing and the small irregular-shaped lake, Savannah smiled, slipped out of her thongs, tossed her robe to the ground and waded into the water. It felt cool against her skin and she dived to the bottom before surfacing.

She had been swimming about fifteen minutes when she realized that she wasn't alone. Her heart nearly stopped beating and she braced herself for one of her father's stern lectures.

"Dad?" she called unsteadily at the figure of a man leaning against the sturdy trunk of an oak tree. "Dad, is that you?"

FOR THE FIRST time in years, Travis had consumed more alcohol than he could handle, and he intended to clear his head with a long walk. The argument he'd had earlier in the evening with Melinda was still ringing in his mind. She'd accused him of being aloof, disinterested in her, and maybe she was right. Because for the past few damning weeks, he'd been thinking solely of Savannah Beaumont. *Reginald's daughter, for God's sake!* And the thoughts he'd had about her were far from brotherly.

From the first time he'd seen her, half-dressed, her firm breasts straining against a T-shirt, her supple legs wrapped around that bay mare, he'd been out of his mind with lust. The burning desire had tortured him with wildly erotic fantasies that took away his sleep.

He'd even had to leave the farm for a couple of days to get his head back on straight. The last thing he needed was to get involved with a seventeen-year-old girl, the daughter of the man who'd raised him. But it was confusing. Confusing as hell. And he didn't blame Melinda for being angry. Since he'd seen Savannah again, he hadn't been able to concentrate on Melinda at all—to the point that his interest in making love to her had all but disappeared.

He let his shirt gape open, hoping that the cool air would help clear his head. Leaning against an oak tree, he heard the splashing in the lake. His head was spinning crazily, but even in the darkness he recognized Savannah and the fact that she was swimming nude in the inky water. His fingers dug into the rough bark of the oak tree for support. *Oh, God,* he thought, trying to think straight. *Give me strength.*

Then she called to him. "Dad?" Silence. Travis's heart thundered in his chest. "Dad, is that you?"

"What the devil are you doing here?" Travis asked, barely trusting his voice.

Not Travis! Savannah's heartbeat accelerated when she recognized his voice. *Not here!* "Minding my own business," she managed to choke out.

Silvery light from a iridescent moon rippled on the water, alternately shadowing and highlighting the firm white swell of her breasts and the dark tips of her nipples. Her black hair was slicked away from her face and her chin was thrust forward defiantly. Drops of water clung to her lashes and slid down her cheeks and a traitorous ache began to throb in Travis's loins.

"You shouldn't be here," he said, his throat uncomfortably tight. "Someone might see you."

"*Someone* has."

"You know what I mean." Travis fought to clear his head and he battled against the fire radiating from his loins. Shifting against the tree, he willed the natural reaction of his body to subside. And failed. *Leave right now,* he told himself, *before you say or do something foolish.*

"Where's Melinda?" Savannah asked, swimming nearer to him.

He heard the tremor in her voice, saw the quiet suffering in her eyes. *Go away, Savannah, don't look at me like that.* "I don't know." He closed his eyes and tried not to watch the gentle water caress the satin-white skin of her body. "I don't think we'll see each other again."

"But you're engaged."

"Not anymore." He fished in the pocket of his jeans and retrieved the diamond ring. Holding it up to the moonlight, it winked mockingly at him. His fingers curled around the cold metal and stones before he cursed and hurled the ring into the water. It settled into the lake with barely a splash.

"You shouldn't have done that," Savannah reprimanded, edging closer to the bank, but she couldn't hide the pleasure in her voice.

"I should have done it a long time ago."

"You're drunk."

"Not drunk enough."

"Oh, Travis," she said with a shake of her head. "If you're not careful, you'll self-destruct."

The comfort in her voice touched a primitive part of

him and he knew the battle he was alternately fighting and surrendering to was about to be lost.

He saw her robe near the bank and he pushed himself upright to retrieve it. As he stood, he swayed slightly. Righting himself, he walked over to the bank. "You'd better get out of there," he said. "It's the middle of the night, for crying out loud."

She laughed and dipped back into the water. Knowing that he wasn't tied to Melinda made her feel as if a tremendous weight had been lifted from her shoulders.

"Savannah—"

"Don't worry about me," she said, resurfacing and shaking the hair out of her face.

"Does anyone know you're out here?"

"Just you."

"Great," he muttered, his eyes riveted to the fascinating hollow of her throat and the pulse throbbing there. The reaction that Melinda hadn't been able to stir began just at the sight of Savannah's wet body.

"Oh, all right." She swam to where her feet touched the soft silt at the bottom of the lake and began to walk out of the water. Travis, knowing that his duty was done and that he should walk away, stood fascinated as she slowly emerged from the water.

Savannah knew there was no way she could hide her body. The best thing to do was get to the robe and cover up as quickly as possible, but she could feel Travis's eyes upon her, two gray orbs sizzling into her flesh.

Travis sucked in his breath as he watched her. Her white skin contrasted to the black night and droplets of water slid seductively down her throat to her breasts. He watched the gentle sway of her breasts as she walked toward him. Her waist was small and her navel a provocative dimple in her abdomen.

Travis's breath was tight in his lungs as her hips and thighs emerged. He tossed the robe to her.

"Put it on before you catch cold." He was forcing himself to walk away and had taken the first step when Savannah, intent on putting on the robe as quickly as possible, tripped against the root of a tree and fell to the ground.

"Savannah!"

In two steps he was beside her. "I'm okay," she said, holding on to the shin she had banged when she hit the ground.

"Are you sure?"

"Yes, yes." She shook her head and covered herself with the robe. "Aside from being mortified, that is."

His hands were on her upper arms, his fingers lingering against the silky texture of her wet skin. He felt her tremble at his touch and when he kissed her comfortingly on her temple she sighed and didn't draw away.

"I don't know what came over me," she said, thinking back to her wanton behavior and trying to ignore his tender kiss. She'd just walked out of the lake, stark naked, straight at Travis. She hadn't even had the decency to ask him to look the other way. She felt like a complete idiot.

Travis wanted to comfort her...hold her...never stop making love to her. *Push me away,* he thought as his physical needs overcame common sense. She looked at him with wide innocent eyes and the moonlight caught in her dazzling gaze. Travis felt his resolve waver as he tried to keep the robe from falling off her shoulders. Though she tried to knot the belt, her fingers fumbled and the neckline continued to gap despite her efforts to cover herself.

"What—" He cleared his throat and tried not to concentrate on the dusky hollow between the two silken mounds. "What were you doing out here?"

"I couldn't sleep."

"Why not?"

She shook her head and the droplets of water in her hair caught in the moonlight and sparkled like fine diamonds. "I don't know." He was so damned close to her. She could smell the scent of brandy on his breath, read the smoky desire in his eyes. Her heart throbbed with the thought that he wanted her and her skin quivered from the warmth of his breath on the back of her neck.

"I'm having trouble sleeping these nights myself."

"Because of…the problems with Melinda?"

He shook his head. "Because of the problems with you."

"Oh."

His fingers traced the pout on her lips. "I haven't been able to think of much besides you lately. And it's driving me out of my mind." His eyes caressed her face and watched as she swallowed when he touched her throat, his fingers inching lazily up and down the soft white column.

"Travis—"

"Tell me to leave you alone, Savannah."

"I…I can't."

"Tell me to take my hands off you," he suggested, but she shook her head.

"Then do something, anything, slap me the way you did that kid who attacked you the other night."

"I can't, Travis," she moaned as his fingers slid lower to trace the lapels of her robe.

His face inched closer to hers and the weight of his body leaned against hers as he kissed her, tenderly at first and then with such savagery that it tore through her body.

Her lips were chilled from the water but responded

when his mouth settled over hers in a kiss that questioned as much as it claimed. He was asking and taking all at once and she leaned closer to him, her fingers touching the muscles at the base of his neck.

The fires that had started as a dull ache in Travis's loins burned through his bloodstream and destroyed all of his rational thought. When she parted her lips, his kiss became fierce and hungry, his tongue eager as it discovered its waiting mate.

He lifted his head and saw her swollen lips, the seduction in her eyes. "This is crazy," he groaned. "Haven't you had enough?"

"I don't know if I could ever have enough of you," she admitted.

"Don't do this to me, Savannah, I'm not made of stone, for crying out loud! I was just trying to shock some sense into you!" But the painful ache between his legs told him he was lying.

Savannah's arms wrapped around his neck, her fingers touched the sensitive skin over his shoulders and he groaned before lowering himself next to her and kissing her with all the passion that was dominating his mind and body.

She responded in kind. When he rolled atop her, one hand pressing the small of her back upward against him, she felt the hard evidence of his passion. He rubbed anxiously against her and one of his hands slid beneath the lapel of her robe to discover the creamy softness of her breast.

Her body arched up from the ground, molding her flesh to his, fitting against him perfectly.

Stop. Stop me, Savannah, he thought, but he slid lower on her body, his lips kissing and caressing her skin, finding the pulse at her throat, lingering seductively before his hands and mouth parted the robe, inched down her ribs and found the dark, waiting peak of her breast. He rimmed the nipple with his tongue and Savannah moaned his name into the night. Then slowly, with the delicate strokes of a dedicated lover, he licked and suckled at the straining breast until he felt her fingernails digging into his back.

"Oh, God, I should be shot for this," he muttered, attempting to grasp onto some shred of his common sense. But even as he did, he slid his belt through the buckle and kicked off his jeans.

"Just love me," she begged, trembling beneath him.

"I do. Oh, God, Savannah. I do."

He was naked then, his lean body glistening with sweat as he lay upon her. She welcomed the burden of his weight and when he entered her, she felt a sharp jab of pain before she was lost in the brilliant and beautiful bursts of their union. She stroked the hard muscles of his back with her fingers and kissed at his face and chest and heard herself scream as the increasing tempo of his strokes pushed her upward to a precipice and then over the edge in a dazzling climax that sent aftershocks rolling through her body for several minutes. As she fell slowly back to earth, she sighed in a contentment heretofore unknown to her.

With Travis's arms wrapped securely around her, Savannah listened to the sounds of the night—Travis's irregular breathing, the clamoring of her heart, the sound of a fish jumping lazily in the water and, farther away, the sound of a twig snapping.

Travis's body stiffened. He kissed her softly on the forehead and drew the robe around her. "Go back to the house," he whispered against her ear and cut off her questions by pressing a finger to her lips.

"But—"

"Shh." He squinted into the darkness. "I heard something. I don't think we're alone. I'll come to you—soon," he promised.

Then soundlessly, Travis was jerking on his clothes. Savannah didn't argue, but followed his instructions to the letter. Holding her robe closed with one hand, her thongs in the other, she ran barefoot along the path, feeling the sharp stones and twigs that cut into her feet.

Breathlessly she sneaked back into the dark house, hurried up the back staircase to her room and waited in the bed, her heart clamoring, her ears straining for any sound of Travis's arrival. She was sure that he would be true to his word and come to her. It was only a matter of time.

When the first gray light of dawn streaked through the room, she realized that Travis had probably been held up by whomever it was who had come to the lake. It didn't matter. She'd meet him later in the day.

Facing her father—or whoever it was who had stumbled upon Travis and her—wouldn't be a picnic, but Savannah was convinced she could handle it. She drifted off to a heavy sleep and woke up much later—sometime after ten. She showered, dressed and went downstairs to discover her father sitting at the kitchen table, stirring a cup of coffee, and reading the morning paper.

"Good morning," Savannah said, eyeing him. Everything looked normal. Obviously, Reginald had been out to the stables at the crack of dawn as was his usual custom. He was clean shaven, his boots were by the door to the porch, and he'd already finished breakfast. His plate still held a few crumbs of toast, though it had been pushed to the side of the table.

Reginald looked up sharply, frowned and put down his paper. "Morning."

"Good morning, dear," her mother, Virgina, said, when she came breezing through the door to the kitchen from the dining room. Her dark hair was perfectly combed, her makeup looking as if she'd just applied it. "You overslept this morning. It's too bad, too. You weren't here to say goodbye to Travis."

"Goodbye?" Savannah repeated, stunned.

"Yes." Virginia poured herself a cup of coffee and then sat down at the table across from Reginald. "Seems he and Melinda decided to get married as soon as possible—and high time, I say. They've been dating forever. The wedding will probably be next week, so he went to Los Angeles to see if he could rent his apartment earlier than he'd originally planned."

Savannah sagged against the counter, her cup of coffee nearly spilling from her shaking hands.

"I guess he got tired of working here at the farm," Reginald said. "Don't blame him a bit. Since he passed the bar exam, there's no reason for him to be hanging around here, when he could be out chasing ambulances."

"Reginald!" Virginia admonished, but Reginald chuckled to himself and Virginia's blue eyes sparkled at the prospect of a wedding.

Savannah felt the tears burn at the back of her eyes. "I'm surprised no one woke me up so that I could say goodbye," she said.

"No reason to," Reginald said with a shrug. "Travis will be back. Bad penny syndrome, you know. They always have a habit of showing up again."

"Father! Listen to you," Virginia said, but smiled.

"Didn't Travis want to—talk to me?"

"I don't think so. He never mentioned it. Did he, hon?"

"Not to me." Virginia saw the hurt in Savannah's eyes and sent her a kindly smile. "But then he's pretty busy, what with the wedding plans and all. You'll see him then."

Savannah felt a traitorous burn in her heart, but she told herself not to believe anyone—not until she heard from Travis.

The problem was, he never called or came back to the farm. And he married Melinda Reaves two weeks after having made love to Savannah by the lake.

"I'll never speak to him again," Savannah told herself angrily on the morning of the wedding. To her mother's disappointment, she refused to attend the marriage ceremony.

"I can't, Mom," she said when Virginia pressed her for a reason. "I just can't."

"Why not?" Virginia asked, sitting on the edge of the bed and surveying her youngest daughter with concern as Savannah stood at the window of her room and pretended interest in the view.

"Travis…Travis and I had a disagreement."

"All brothers and sisters—"

"He's *not* my brother!"

Virginia arched a knowing brow. "Oh, I see."

"I don't know how you possibly could," Savannah said, feeling wretched inside. No one could possibly understand, least of all her mother. So why didn't they all just leave her alone in her misery?

"How involved with Travis were you?" Virginia asked gently.

"I'm not—" Savannah's voice caught. "Oh, Mom," she whispered, her fingers winding in the soft fabric of the curtains.

"It's all right, honey," Virginia consoled, walking over

to her daughter and placing a comforting arm around Savannah's shoulders.

The tears that had been threatening for two weeks ran down Savannah's face. *It wasn't all right. Never would be.* She turned and sobbed against her mother's shoulder for a few minutes.

"Loving the wrong man is never easy," Virginia said thoughtfully.

"But how could you know?"

"Oh, I know, all right," Virginia said with a sad smile, as if she wanted to confide in her daughter. "I was young once myself. I've…well, I've made a few mistakes."

"With Dad?" Savannah sniffed, eyeing her mother.

Virginia avoided Savannah's eyes. "Yes, honey. With your father." There was something cryptic in Virginia's voice, but Savannah couldn't think about it, or anything else for that matter. Melinda Reaves was going to be Travis McCord's wife! Savannah felt as if her entire world were crumbling at her feet.

"But I love him so much," she admitted.

"And he'll soon be a married man. There's nothing you can do about it. Not now."

"Oh, yes, there is," Savannah said, the tears still streaming down a suddenly thrusting chin. "I'm going to forget about him. I'm never going to speak to him again. And…and I'll never let myself fall for any man again."

Virginia was smiling through her own tears. "Don't be so rash, there's still a few good men out there. David Crandall cares for you."

"Oh, Mom—" Savannah said, rolling her eyes to the ceiling. "David's just a boy…a friend."

"And Travis was more?"

"Yes."

"So it was that way, was it?" Virginia asked quietly. "Are…are you all right?"

"Do I look all right?"

"I mean—"

"I know what you mean," Savannah said softly, reading the worry in her mother's eyes. "You won't be shamed by me."

Virginia sighed. "And you still love him?"

"Not anymore," Savannah vowed, her fist clenching in determination. "Not anymore and *never again*." Whatever it took, she would throw off the shackles of her love for Travis. He would soon be Melinda's husband and Melinda's problem. As far as Savannah was concerned, she didn't care if Travis McCord lived or died.

She had no idea that nine years later she'd still be trying to convince herself that she despised him.

CHAPTER ONE

Beaumont Breeding Farm—Winter, Nine Years Later

SAVANNAH DIDN'T REGRET moving back to the farm. The gently rolling countryside northeast of San Francisco had been a welcome sight to her when she'd returned. She hadn't realized how much she'd missed the hazy purple hills surrounding the farm and the fields of lush green grass and grazing horses.

The bustle of the city had been exciting while she was a college student and for a few years when she worked in San Francisco in an investment firm. But she was glad to be back at the breeding farm even if it meant putting up with her brother-in-law, Wade Benson.

In the past few years Wade had given up most of his accounting practice to manage the farm, and he was being groomed to step into Reginald's boots, whenever her father decided to retire. That might be sooner than he had planned, Savannah thought sadly, considering her mother's poor health.

It was just too bad that Travis hadn't stayed at the farm and followed in Dad's footsteps, she thought idly and then mentally chastised herself. Though it had been nine years since he had left the farm to marry Melinda, Savannah had never really forgiven him—she'd even managed to avoid him most of the time. Now there were rumors that he would run in the next election for governor of the State of California. Hard to believe.

"Hey, Aunt Savvy, want to go riding?" Joshua, Charmaine and Wade's only child, called as he ran up to her.

Savannah smiled as she looked into the nine-year-old's earnest brown eyes. His cheeks were flushed, his brown hair in sad need of a trim. "I'd love to," she said, and the boy broke into a grin.

"Can I ride Mystic?"

Savannah laughed. "Not on your life, buddy! He's Grandpa's prize colt!"

"But he likes me."

"The way I understand it, Mystic doesn't like anyone."

"Hogwash!" The boy kicked the toe of his sneaker at an acorn on the ground in frustration. "I know I can ride him," Josh boasted proudly, his eyes twinkling mischievously.

"Oh you can, can you?" She smiled at the determination in Josh's proud chin. "Well, maybe someday, if Grandpa and Lester think it's okay, but not today." Savannah eyed the graying sky. "Tell ya what, I'll saddle Mattie and Jones, and we'll take a couple of turns around the field before it starts to rain."

"But they're old nags. They're not even Thoroughbreds!"

"Shame on you. Even old non-Thoroughbred-type horses need exercise. Just like obstinate little boys! Come on—" she gave Joshua a good-natured pat between the shoulders "—I'll race ya."

"Okay!" Joshua was off across the wet grass in a flash and Savannah let him win the race. "You're old, too," he said with a laugh once she had crossed the imaginary finish line at the stable gate.

"And you're precocious."

"What's that mean?"

Savannah's eyes gleamed with love for the little boy. "That no one but an aunt could love you."

He immediately sobered and Savannah realized she'd said the wrong thing. "Well, no one but Grandma and Grandpa and your mom and dad and—"

"Dad doesn't love me."

"Of course he does," Savannah said, seeing the sadness in the little boy's eyes and silently cursing her brother-in-law.

"He never does anything with me."

"Your father's very busy—" *Damn, but she hated to make excuses for Wade.*

"He's always busy," Joshua corrected, and Savannah rumpled her nephew's floppy brown hair.

"Managing this farm is a big responsibility."

"But you have time to play with me."

"That's because I'm totally irresponsible." Savannah laughed. "Now, quit feeling sorry for yourself and find the saddle blankets."

Joshua, appeased for the moment, found the required blankets as Savannah bridled the two horses and silently told herself to have it out with her brother-in-law. No father should be so indifferent to his only son.

"Stay here a minute," she told Joshua after tightening the cinch around Jones's girth. "I'll see if there's anything to drink in the office. Wouldn't you like a Coke while we ride?"

"Sure!"

"I'll be right back."

She walked through the stable door, down the cement walk running parallel to the clapboard building, and up the stairs to the office located directly over that part of the stables used as a foaling shed. The door of the office was partially open, and she heard voices within. Her father and Wade were involved in a heated discussion.

"I just don't think you can count on him," Wade was saying. Savannah took a step forward, intent on telling her brother-in-law to pay some attention to his child, but Wade's next words made her hesitate. "McCord's just about over the deep end, and Willis is damned worried about him."

Travis? What was wrong with him? Savannah's heart began to pound with fear.

"Willis Henderson worries about anything that comes along," her father replied calmly.

"Maybe there's a reason for that. He's McCord's law partner, for God's sake. He works with McCord every day."

"And he thinks Travis is—"

"Cracking up."

Savannah stifled a gasp. "Nonsense," Reginald said. "That boy is tough."

"Willis says McCord hasn't been the same since his wife's death."

Reginald sighed. "Look, Wade, I'm telling you that Willis Henderson is jumping at shadows! Lawyers tend to do that. Travis McCord will end up the next governor of this state, just you wait and see."

"I don't know. I certainly don't want to bet on it."

"Of course not," Reginald said with audible disgust. "God, you accountants are all so damned conservative."

"There's nothing wrong with that. If you had been a little more conservative in the last five years, we wouldn't be in this mess."

"It's not a mess!" Reginald roared.

"I call zero cash flow a mess."

"You're as bad as Willis Henderson; always borrowing trouble," Reginald muttered. "Lawyers and accountants cut from the same cloth."

Savannah, feeling guilty about eavesdropping, and yet overcome with worry for Travis, walked into the room. Reginald and Wade, both seated at the table, looked up from their cups of coffee. "What kind of trouble are you talking about?" she asked her father.

Reginald scowled into his cup before sending a warning glance to Wade. "Oh, nothing. Wade's a little concerned about cash flow."

"Is it bad?" Her eyes moved to her brother-in-law.

"Yes," Wade answered, his gaze shifting uncomfortably under her straightforward stare. He tugged nervously at the hairs of his blond moustache.

"No." Reginald shook his graying head and adjusted his plaid cap. "Wade's just being...cautious."

"That's my job," Wade pointed out.

Savannah didn't listen. "What were you saying about Travis?" she asked, walking over to the refrigerator and trying not to look overly interested though she felt a nervous sheen of sweat break out on her palms.

Reginald's jaw worked. "Oh, nothing serious. That partner of his, Henderson, is worried about him. Thinks Travis is...depressed. Probably just let down from that last case he won. Got lots of publicity with that Eldridge decision and we all know how tough it is to get back into the regular office routine after all that hoopla. It's just a letdown. The same way we felt after Mystic won the Preakness."

"So you think he'll still run for governor?"

Reginald smiled. "*I'd* be willing to bet on it," he said, casting Wade a knowing glance.

Savannah grabbed a couple cans of Coke from the refrigerator and closed the door. "Did Willis Henderson call you? Is that how you found out about Travis's 'depression'?"

"No." Her father avoided her eyes.

"I ran into him at the track," Wade said hurriedly. "Just yesterday at Hollywood Park."

Savannah raised a eyebrow skeptically; she could feel that Wade and her father were deliberately hiding something from her, but she couldn't delve into it. Not right now. Joshua was waiting for her in the stables and she wasn't about to disappoint him.

"Since you got back to the farm," she said, looking pointedly at Wade, "have you bothered to talk to Joshua?"

"Huh? Well, no. I just got in last night, and then he got up and went to school this morning. Not much time." Wade squirmed uncomfortably in his chair.

"Maybe he needs a little fatherly attention."

"I'll…I'll talk to him tonight, when I'm not so busy."

"I think it would be a good idea," Savannah said, striding out of the room and feeling an uncomfortable tightening in her stomach. She'd known there were money problems at the farm, of course; there always had been, but she didn't like the sound of the conversation between her father and Wade, especially the part about Travis.

"What's the matter, Aunt Savvy?" Joshua asked when she returned. She led the horses outside and tried to concentrate on anything other than Travis.

"What? Oh, nothing, Josh," she said, mounting Mattie and remembering that she had encountered Travis all those summers ago while riding the very same mare. "Let's take the horses over by the lake today."

"But you never like to go to the lake," the boy pointed out after climbing onto Jones's broad back.

Savannah smiled sadly. "I know. But today is different. Come on." She urged Mattie into a trot, and Joshua followed behind her on the gelding. The path between the trees was overgrown from lack of use, and the lake, usually calm, had taken on the leaden hue of the winter sky.

"Why'd you want to come here?" Joshua asked, sipping his Coke, oblivious to the cold weather that suddenly cut through Savannah's jacket like a knife.

"I don't know," she admitted, staring at the lake, her thoughts lingering on Travis as raindrops began to pelt from the sky and dimple the dark water. "It used to be a place I liked very much."

Joshua looked at the barren trees, exposed rocks and muddy banks surrounding the lake. "If you ask me, it's kinda creepy."

"Yeah, maybe it is," she whispered, shivering from a sudden chill. "Let's go back to the paddocks." *Maybe then I won't think about Travis and wonder what's happening to him....*

It had all started again a little over a month ago, Travis reflected dourly, when he'd seen Reginald Beaumont and Wade Benson at the racetrack. That in itself wasn't so unusual. After all, Reginald's prize three-year-old colt, Mystic, had been running, and Wade was now, under Reginald's guidance, managing the farm. What had been odd was the fact that Reginald was at the racetrack with Willis Henderson, Travis's law partner. Henderson had never mentioned the fact that he was interested in the races and Reginald had no reason to know Willis Henderson, except through Travis. When Travis had questioned his partner, Willis hadn't wanted to discuss his day at the track.

Later, learning that Savannah was now back at the farm with her father and Wade, Travis had begun to think about her.

And now it seemed as if he could think of nothing else.

She just wouldn't leave him alone, even after nine long years. At the most inopportune moments, her image would come vividly to Travis's mind and he would be teased by the memory of her wide, sky-blue eyes, gleaming ebony hair and seductive smile. In the nine years that had passed since he'd found her swimming in the lake, her image still lingered.

"Mr. McCord!" The sharp voice of Eleanor Phillips brought Travis back to the present, and the image of Savannah faded quickly. Travis's eyes focused again on the stylish but overdressed woman sitting on the other side of the desk. "You haven't heard a word I've said!"

Travis offered a slightly apologetic smile and stared directly into her eyes. "Oh, yes, I have." He couldn't hide the cynicism in his voice. "You were talking about the woman your husband met in Mazatlan."

"The girl, you mean. She was barely twenty!" Eleanor Phillips said with self-righteous disgust. "You know she was only interested in Robert for his money—my money."

Travis listened impatiently while Mrs. Phillips continued to rant about her husband's indiscriminate affairs. The way his wife told it, Mr. Phillips had the sexual appetite of a man half his age.

As she went on about Robert Phillips's indiscretions, Travis glanced out the window of his office, noticed that it was getting dark and checked his watch. Five-thirty. So where was Henderson, his partner? And why wasn't he handling Eleanor Phillips? Too many things had been happening in the law firm that didn't add up, and Travis wanted it out with Henderson.

"So you see, Mr. McCord, this divorce is imperative," Mrs. Phillips said in her high-pitched voice. "I want you to work with the best private investigator in Los Angeles and—"

"I don't handle divorces, Mrs. Phillips. I tried to tell you that on the phone, and when you first came into the office today. You deliberately lied to me—said that you wanted to see me about a take-over bid by a competitor."

She colored slightly and Travis knew he had offended her. The trouble was, he really didn't give a damn about Eleanor Phillips, her husband's sex life or Phillips Industries. As Henderson had so often accused, Travis was suffering from a serious case of "bad attitude." Thinking about Savannah only made it worse.

"But I've been with your firm forever. You've handled all my legal work," Eleanor complained, fingering the elegant string of pearls at her throat.

"On corporate matters." Travis tried to remain calm. The woman only wanted a divorce from her philandering husband and that in itself wasn't a crime. In fact, Travis didn't blame her for wanting out of an unhappy marriage, but there was something in her superior attitude that rankled him, and he wondered if Mr. Phillips was as bad as his wife had insisted, or if her cold, money-is-everything way of looking at life had driven him from her bed.

"Oh, I see," Eleanor Phillips said primly, reaching for her purse and looking around the well-appointed office in disgust. "Since that Eldridge decision, you're too big to take on something as simple as my divorce."

"That has nothing to do with it—"

"Hmph."

"I'm sure one of the associates, or perhaps Mr. Henderson himself, can help you." *If I ever find the bastard.* "I'll speak to him."

"I want you, Mr. McCord! And I think you owe it to

me to handle this yourself…after all, I need complete discretion. And you have a reputation that's spotless."

Travis winced at the ridiculous compliment and instead of feeling flattered, he suffered from a twinge of conscience. "I don't handle divorce."

"But you will for me." She smiled knowingly and Travis experienced the unlikely urge to shake some sense into her cash register of a head. *Wealthy women,* he thought cynically, *he'd met enough to last him a lifetime!* He jerked at the knot of his tie. Once again the suite of modern offices seemed confining.

"I've already contributed to your campaign," Eleanor pointed out, raising her brows.

"What!"

"My contribution."

"What the devil are you talking about?" Travis's jaw hardened and his eyes glittered dangerously.

For the first time that afternoon, Eleanor Phillips had gained the advantage in the conversation and she was pleased. "It was a very healthy contribution," she rattled on. Travis's eyes narrowed, but the expensively clad woman only smiled to herself. "Mr. Henderson took care of it and promised me that you would handle this divorce personally. He also said that you would be able to assure me that my husband won't get a dime of my money—and not much of his."

Travis's jaw tightened and his lips curved into a grim smile. "When did you talk to Mr. Henderson?"

"Just last week…no, it was two weeks ago, when I called to make the appointment with you."

Two weeks ago. Just about the time Travis had noticed some discrepancies in the books.

Eleanor Phillips rose to her full five feet two inches and focused her frigid eyes on Travis. "I'll be frank, Mr.

McCord. I want to divorce my husband as quickly as possible, and I expect you to take him to the cleaners." The smile she offered was as chilly as a cold November night.

"Mrs. Phillips," Travis said slowly, as if to a child, as he stood and leaned threateningly over the desk. "I don't handle divorce and I'm not sure what Mr. Henderson told you, but I haven't decided to run for governor."

"Well, I know it's not official—"

"And I haven't seen your…contribution. I wouldn't have taken it if I had." His gray eyes glinted with determination. "But I can assure you of one thing: Willis Henderson will return it to you." *If I have to persuade him by breaking every bone in his feeble little body.*

"Then perhaps you'd better speak with Mr. Henderson. I assure you I gave him a check for five thousand dollars. Good luck, Governor."

Eleanor Phillips walked out of the room, and Travis punched the extension for Henderson's office. There was no answer. "You slimy son of a bitch," Travis muttered, slamming down the receiver, grabbing his coat and thrusting his arms into the sleeves, "what the hell kind of game are you playing?"

Before leaving the room he looked around the office and scowled at the expensive music box on the shelf collecting dust; a gift from Melinda. The desk was polished wood, and leather-bound law books adorned the shelves of a walnut bookcase. The liquor cabinet housed only the finest labels. The carpet had been found in Italy by Henderson's interior decorator. And Travis hated every bloody thing that had to do with L.A. and his partnership with Willis Henderson.

"Today, ol' buddy, you've just gone one step too far," Travis said, shaking his head. "It's over. Done. *Finis!*"

He marched into the reception area. "Where is Henderson?" he demanded of the blond secretary.

"I really don't know." She quickly scanned her calendar. "He had an appointment out of the building today."

"With whom?"

"I don't know," the girl said again, obviously embarrassed. "He didn't say."

"Did you ask him?"

"Oh, yes."

"And?"

The secretary shrugged. "He said it was personal."

"Great." The muscles in the back of Travis's neck began to ache with tension. "Great. Just great." He rubbed at the knotted muscles in his back. "Do you have *any* idea where he might be?"

"I'm sorry—" A negative sweep of the short blond curls.

Where the hell was Henderson, and why did he take Eleanor Phillips's money? "I know it's late, and you're about to leave, but if he comes back here before you go, tell him to call me."

"I will."

"And I want to speak to our accountant. Call Jack and see if he can come into the office later this week."

"Jack Conrad?" The girl looked confused.

Travis held on,to the rags of his thin patience. "Yes, the accountant for the firm."

"But he doesn't handle the books any longer."

Travis had been heading for the door, but he stopped dead in his tracks. The day had just gone from bad to worse. "What do you mean?"

"I, uh, I thought you knew. Wade Benson is handling the books."

"Benson!" Travis felt his fingers curl into tight fists.

"Didn't Mr. Henderson tell you?"

"You're sure about this?"

"Yes." She looked oddly at Travis before reaching into a file drawer. "Here's a copy of the letter from Mr. Benson and the response from Mr. Henderson. Mr. Benson's accounting fees are much lower than Mr. Conrad's were."

"But Mr. Benson doesn't take on any clients. He's working for Reginald Beaumont now, as the manager of the Beaumont Breeding Farm." *With Savannah.* Travis smiled twistedly. Hadn't he been looking for an excuse to see Savannah again? It looked like Willis Henderson had just handed it to him on a silver platter.

The young blonde shrugged. "Maybe he decided to do it as a favor to you. You've known Mr. Benson all your life, haven't you?"

"Most of it," Travis acknowledged. *So why hasn't Henderson told me any of this?*

Travis pushed open the glass doors with the gold lettering and strode into the hall, down three flights of stairs and through the lobby of the building. As he walked to his car, a crisp Southern California breeze rustled through the palms and rumpled his hair, but he didn't notice.

His thoughts were centered on his partner. *Some partner.* Right now Travis would like to wring Willis Henderson's short, Ivy League neck! Accepting a contribution, legal or otherwise, from Eleanor Phillips wasn't the first of Henderson's none-too-subtle attempts to force a decision from Travis, but it was damned well going to be the last! And this business of switching accountants…

Wade Benson, for God's sake! Travis didn't trust the man an inch. It was bad enough that Benson had married Reginald's eldest daughter, Charmaine, Savannah's sister, and become manager of Beaumont Breeding Farm, but now he was encroaching on Travis's domain. *But not for long!* Travis didn't want anything more to do with Wade, Reginald Beaumont or his raven-haired daughter.

Savannah again. Would he ever be able to get her out of his system?

He smiled grimly to himself. "Your own fault," he reminded himself before concentrating on the problem at hand. Travis had already decided what he was going to do with the rest of his life, and it was a far cry from running for governor of California. And if Willis Henderson, Eleanor Phillips and all the other people who were willing to contribute to his campaign for personal favors didn't like it, they could bloody well stuff it!

Henderson's condominium was across town in Malibu Beach. It would take nearly an hour to get there, but Travis didn't hesitate. If Willis wasn't at home, Travis would wait.

Why did Willis want him to run for governor? Prestige for the firm of Henderson and McCord? Maybe. But Travis couldn't help but feel there was something more to it. It was that tiny suspicion that gnawed at him until he made his way through the snarl of L.A. traffic and reached Willis's home.

Willis was outside, in the driveway, with someone. Travis parked on the street and observed his partner. It was too dark to see clearly, but when the visitor stepped into the light from the street, Travis recognized him. An uncanny premonition of dread slithered up his spine as he stared at Wade Benson.

Swearing softly under his breath, Travis watched the two men. Because his first reaction was to corner Henderson and Benson and have it out with them, he reached for the handle of the door. But there was something slightly sinister in the clandestine meeting, and he stayed in the car. "You're losing it, McCord," he whis-

pered to himself, but couldn't take his eyes off the two
men in the driveway.

It was bad enough that Wade had suckered Reginald
Beaumont into his confidence, but Henderson as well?

The whole setup seemed out of place. Wade was the
manager of Beaumont Farm, but the legal work for the
farm was handled by Travis, not Henderson. Or was it?

Quietly, Travis rolled down the window, but his car
was parked too far away from the condominium to hear
any of the conversation.

Wade lit a cigarette and laughed at some comment
uttered by Henderson. *Just like old fraternity brothers,*
Travis thought unkindly. The anger in Travis's blood
was replaced by cold suspicion. He watched as Wade
walked back to his car and tossed his glowing cigarette
butt onto the ground before stamping on it and opening
the car door.

So Wade was involved with Willis. What about Reginald, Savannah's father? Did he know about this meeting? Probably. Travis had seen Reginald and Wade at
Alexander Park with Willis Henderson when Reginald's
colt, Mystic, the favorite, had run and lost. What the hell
was going on?

Everything he had seen and heard could just be an unlikely set of circumstances. Henderson had the right to
fire an accountant and he certainly could go to the races
any time he damned well pleased.

*But Willis couldn't take a campaign contribution for
a campaign that didn't exist!*

Unless, of course, Eleanor Phillips had been lying.
Travis wouldn't put it past her.

An ache settled in the pit of Travis's stomach as he
thought about Reginald Beaumont's Thoroughbred

farm and the fact that Savannah was still there, working with Wade.

"Dammit all to hell," he whispered, watching Wade's car glide out of the driveway.

Pensively rubbing his jaw, he watched as Willis Henderson walked back into his condo and shut out the lights. Then, Travis slowly got out of the car, stretched and walked up the concrete walk to Willis Henderson's front door.

SAVANNAH WAS SEATED at her father's desk in his study, sifting through the mail, when the phone rang. "No one's here," she said to the ringing instrument and eyed the stack of unpaid bills on the corner of the desk. If the caller was another creditor…

"Beaumont Breeding Farm," she answered automatically.

"I'd like to speak with Wade Benson. This is Willis Henderson," an imperious voice requested.

Savannah straightened in the chair. Willis Henderson was Travis's law partner, the man who had talked to Wade at the racetrack. Her fingers curled more tightly around the receiver and she gave her full attention to Travis's partner.

Maybe something had happened to Travis—an accident. She felt a surge of panic wash over her, but managed to keep her voice calm. "I'm sorry, Mr. Benson is out of town."

A pause. "Then maybe I could talk to Reginald."

"He's also gone for the week. Is there something I can do for you, Mr. Henderson?" Savannah could sense the man's hesitancy to confide in her, so she gave him an out. "Or should I have Wade return the call when he gets back next week?" She eyed the calendar. "Wade should be back by the twenty-third." Two days before Christmas.

"Let me talk to…whoever is in charge."

Savannah bristled a bit, but she smiled wryly. "You're speaking to her. I'm overseeing things while Dad and Wade are away."

"Dad?" Henderson repeated. "Oh, you mean Reginald?"

"Yes. I'm Savannah Beaumont." Savannah settled back in the chair, took off her reading glasses and braced herself for the worst. "Now, what can I do for you?"

Only a slight hesitation. "Ah, well, this has to do with Travis McCord."

Savannah felt her spine stiffen slightly. "What about him?"

"There's been a little trouble."

Her pulse jumped and nervous sweat dotted her forehead. *Trouble.* The second time she'd heard that word in connection with Travis. "What kind of 'trouble'?"

Henderson hedged. "Well, that's why I wanted to talk to Wade."

Savannah frowned at the mention of her brother-in-law. Travis and Wade had never been close. But then, Henderson had bumped into Wade at Hollywood Park…. "As I said, Mr. Benson isn't here and he won't be back until next week—just before Christmas. Now, if Travis is in trouble, I'd like to know about it."

"Look, Miss Beaumont—"

"Savannah."

"Yes, well, Savannah then. I don't want to worry you, but Travis…Travis, he's, well, in a bad way."

Savannah's heart nearly stopped beating and a few dots of perspiration broke out on her back. "What do you mean? Has he been in some kind of accident?"

"No—"

Thank God! Her tense muscles relaxed a little and she fell back into the soft leather cushions of the chair.

"—But he's...well, to put it frankly, Miss Beaumont, Travis has checked out. He's lost all interest in the business, doesn't come into the office, refuses to see me. And all that talk about him running for governor in a couple of years; that's gone, too. He's just not interested. In anything." Once the dam was broken, Henderson talked freely, his words spilling out in a gush. "You probably know that he hasn't been the same since his wife died, but I thought he would pull himself out of it. When Melinda passed away he threw himself into his work, especially the Eldridge case, and now that that's over, he seems to have lost his will to live, I guess you'd say." He stopped abruptly, as if having second thoughts about discussing his partner's personal problems to Savannah. "Well, to put it bluntly, Miss Beaumont, I think he's gone over the deep end."

Savannah tried to think clearly, but her worried thoughts were centered on Travis—a man she should hate. "I don't understand, Melinda's been dead for over six months."

"I know. God, don't I know." He let out a long sigh. "At first he seemed to snap out of it, you know. But it was all just an act. He had the Eldridge case, you see. And once he won that decision and got all the publicity, well, there was talk, a lot of talk, about him running for governor, but I think he's about to chuck it all. It's gotten to the point where he doesn't bother to show up at the office at all. So far I've been able to cover for him, but I don't know how long I can. And what with all this talk about him running for the governorship...I just don't think we can hide what's going on."

"We?" she repeated.

"Wade and I."

Wade again. "What's Wade got to do with it?"

"Wade and your father are pushing Travis toward governorship—you knew that?"

"I'd heard," Savannah admitted sarcastically.

"Well, that's why I'm calling. Travis came by to see me the other night, told me to dissolve the partnership, that he would sell his half to me, and that he was leaving on the noon flight to San Francisco today. I thought he was joking, but when he didn't show up at the office or answer his phone the last couple of days, well, I had to assume that he was serious!"

"Did he say why he wanted out?"

"No…not really, he just said that he was going up to Reginald Beaumont's Breeding Farm. He intended to talk to Wade and Reginald. He asked if I'd have Wade pick him up at the airport."

Savannah glanced at the grandfather clock in the foyer. It was after eleven. "What time will he be in?"

"I think he said one-thirty. Yes. Flight number sixty-seven on United. Will you see that someone goes to meet him?"

"Of course."

"And you'll get in touch with Wade?"

"I'll tell my sister, Charmaine. She's Wade's wife. He should be calling tonight and Charmaine will give him the message that you need to speak with him."

There was a sigh on the other end of the phone. "Thank you, Miss Beaumont," Henderson said before hanging up.

Savannah replaced the receiver and thought for a moment. Several of the hands weren't on the farm, and with Reginald and Wade gone, the farm was being run by a skeleton crew. She couldn't afford to let anyone off to drive to the airport.

"It would serve him right if he had to walk here," she muttered, some of the old bitterness she'd felt toward Travis rising to the surface.

"I guess I get to do the honors," she decided before she grabbed her purse, walked out of the den, across the tiled foyer, and pulled her jacket off the coat rack. *So Travis was finally coming home. But why and for how long? And how much of Willis Henderson's story was true?*

She walked out of the two-storied plantation-style house, turned her collar against the chill December rain, and half ran down the brick path to the garage. Taking the steps two at a time, she climbed upward to the loft that her sister, Charmaine, had converted into a studio and ignored her tight stomach.

It was pouring and Savannah shivered as she rapped on the door and then pushed it open to find Charmaine wrist deep in potting clay. Charmaine looked up from her work and slowed the foot treadle. The revolving, undulating and as yet indistinguishable objet d'art folded in upon itself into a lump of sloppy gray clay.

"Sorry about that," Savannah apologized, nervously gesturing to Charmaine's work. She hated being in the loft.

"It's okay. Wasn't turning out anyway. Good Lord, you're soaked!" Charmaine observed.

"Just a little." Savannah wiped the drops of rain from her face and tried to forget that this loft had once been Travis's.

"No such thing as 'just a little' soaked."

"Look, I'm going to the airport," Savannah said.

"Like that?" Charmaine asked, eyeing her sister's casual jeans and sweater in disapproval.

"Like this. Can you keep an eye on Mom?"

Charmaine grimaced slightly at her work. "I suppose." She wiped her hands on her cotton smock and stood up from the potter's wheel. "I've got to stick around and wait for Josh's bus anyway. What's up?"

"Travis is coming home."

Charmaine started visibly. "Here?"

"I guess. Anyway, that's what his partner, Henderson, said on the phone just now. The flight arrives in San Francisco at one-thirty, so I've got to run. If Wade happens to call, tell him to phone Henderson or, better yet, have him call back tonight once Travis gets here."

Charmaine scrutinized her sister thoughtfully. "Why is Travis coming back to the farm? Why now?"

"I don't know. But I think I should tell him about Mom, so warn her. He'll be furious when he finds out that she's been ill."

Charmaine agreed. "Good luck. You're going to need it." She pursed her lips. "Do you think that he heard about Mother and that's why he's coming back?"

Savannah was in too much of a hurry to sit around and conjecture, and thinking about Travis always brought out a lot of feelings she didn't want to examine. Though her hostility had lessened in the past nine years, it was always there, just under the surface, and she hated to admit it. "Beats me. Henderson said something about Travis needing a rest. He's had a rough year."

As for Henderson's story, it bothered her, but she wanted to make sure it was true before she passed it along to Charmaine or anyone else. Besides, Savannah had never trusted Wade, and Charmaine was his wife. Nervously she shoved her chilled hands into the pockets of her jacket.

Charmaine studied her sister suspiciously. "And that's all?"

"That's all that I know," Savannah lied.

"Hmph." After casting Savannah an I-know-you-better-than-that type of glance, Charmaine capitulated. "Well, I suppose you're right. Melinda's death was a blow to Travis. He loved her very much."

Savannah only nodded but her fingers tightened around the keys in her pocket.

"And now all this talk about him running for governor, right on the heels of that Eldridge decision. He probably does need a rest, but I don't think he'll get much of one here." Still slightly disturbed, Charmaine settled back on her stool and began working the clay. "Sure, I'll look in on Mother."

"Thanks." Savannah left the studio and climbed down the steps quickly. She raced into the garage and hopped into her father's car. As she left the farm her thoughts were centered on Travis. She couldn't remember a time in her life when she hadn't loved him, first as a brother, then as a woman loves a man. Wholly, completely.

Then he'd used and betrayed her.

"Well, that was then," Savannah said with determination. "And I was a fool. A stupid, little girl of a fool. But I'm not about to make the same mistake twice, Travis McCord. You taught me too well. I don't care what's bothering you, I'd rather hate you than fall in love with you ever again."

CHAPTER TWO

TRAFFIC WAS THICK near the airport and it took Savannah nearly twenty minutes to park and get into the terminal building. Pushing her cold hands into the pockets of her jacket and telling herself that she had made a big mistake in coming to get Travis, she threaded her way through the crowd until she reached the concourse where Travis's plane was to unload. The seats near the reservation desk were filled with people waiting for their flights. Carry-on luggage, overcoats and brightly wrapped gifts occupied the vacant seats while tired travelers sat reading, smoking or pacing between the rows of uncomfortable chairs. Above the din of the crowd, faint strains of piped-in Christmas music filtered through the terminal.

Peace on earth, good will to men, Savannah thought as she stood at the gate, but she couldn't help feel a premonition of dread. Inside her pockets, her cold hands began to sweat. She tried to relax and forget that Travis had left her without so much as an explanation, that he had married another woman and walked out of her life without bothering to say goodbye, that he had used her because he was angry with himself and Melinda. But the old bitterness still reared its ugly head.

"It's over and done with; you're a grown woman now," she chastised herself. But this was the first time in nine long years that she would be with Travis alone. Whenever she had seen him in the past, there had always been plenty of people around him, and Melinda had been at his side. The crowds had been convenient, and now Savannah wondered if facing him alone was such a good idea.

She looked through the window and watched as the plane pulled into its berth. *Get a grip on yourself, girl.*

Travis was one of the first people off the plane. To her disgust, Savannah's heart pounded traitorously at the sight of him.

He looked older than his thirty-four years; more cynical. Deep lines bracketed the corners of his hard mouth, and smaller lines formed webs at the outside corners of his eyes. His shirt was rumpled, his tie askew, his chin already darkened with five o'clock shadow, though it was early in the day. A black garment bag was slung over one of his shoulders, and he carried a briefcase in his free hand.

It has been two years since Savannah had seen him, but he seemed to have aged ten. Probably due to the loss of Melinda, she told herself. They had been inseparable. No doubt the fatal boating accident that had taken Melinda's life had destroyed a part of Travis as well.

Savannah forced a smile to her face and walked toward him. He stopped dead in his tracks and the look on his face could have turned flesh to stone.

"Hi," she greeted, tilting her face upward and meeting his cold gaze.

"You're the last person I expected to see," he muttered, unable to disguise his surprise.

"Yeah, well, I'm glad to see you, too."

Something flickered in his gray eyes. "You always were quick to rise to the bait."

"Maybe too quick. Willis Henderson called the farm this afternoon. He was looking for Wade or Dad."

Beneath his shirt, Travis's broad shoulders stiffened. His gaze hardened. "Go on."

"They're both gone this week. So—" she eyed him with the same cynicism she saw in his gaze "—whether you like it or not, you're stuck with me."

"Great." The brackets around his mouth tightened.

Refusing to "rise to the bait" again, she nodded toward the long concourse. "The car's in the lot. Do you have any other bags?"

"No." He shifted his garment bag. "Let's go."

Without further conversation, they walked with the flow of people through the main terminal and outside to the parking lot. Sliding a glance in Travis's direction, Savannah found it difficult to believe that the man beside her could have been the man she had fallen in love with so desperately all those years before.

A winter-cold wind sliced through her jacket and blew her hair away from her face, chilling her cheeks. She huddled her shoulders together and wondered if she was shivering from the wind or the ice in Travis's eyes.

Henderson was partially right, Savannah thought uneasily. Travis looked tired and beaten; world-weary. But there was still a spark of life in his gray gaze, a flicker of interest that argued with Henderson's theory that Travis was "ready to chuck it all." Travis seemed bitter and cynical, but far from suicidal. *Thank God for small favors.*

Once they had made it to the silver sports car, Travis took one look at the BMW and frowned. "Is this yours?"

"Dad's."

"Figures." He tossed his garment bag into the back seat and slid into the passenger side of the car. Once there he pushed the seat back as far as it would go, lowered the backrest so that he could recline, jerked at his tie and let it dangle unknotted at his throat and then unbuttoned the top two buttons of his shirt. Savannah pretended interest in starting the car, but found herself fascinated, as always, with him. She saw the tufts of dark hair visible now that the throat of his shirt gaped and noticed the angry thrust of his jaw as he raked his fingers through his thick hair.

As Savannah started the engine and drove out of the parking lot, Travis leaned his head against the headrest and closed his eyes. His breathing became regular, so Savannah decided not to disturb him. *Let him sleep,* she told herself angrily. *Maybe he'll be in a better mood when he wakes up.*

It started to rain again and she flicked on the wipers. When she glanced at Travis, she found him staring at her. His gaze was thoughtful as it moved lazily over the soft planes of her face. "Why did you come to the airport?"

"To get you; Willis Henderson said—"

"I don't care what he said. Why didn't you send one of the hands?"

"We're shorthanded."

He let out a sound of disgust and looked out the window. "Not exactly flattering."

She felt her temper begin to ignite. "What's that supposed to mean?"

"I thought maybe you wanted to see me again."

After nine years! The arrogant, self-centered bastard! "Sorry to disappoint you."

"I doubt that you ever could," he muttered. "It just seems strange that after nine years of avoiding me, you came to the airport. Alone."

"I haven't avoided you."

He turned his knowing gray eyes back to her face, silently accusing her of the lie.

"Every time you were at the house…" Her voice trailed

off and her fingers clenched around the steering wheel. "There were a lot of people around."

"The way you wanted it. You wouldn't let me near you."

"You were married."

A satisfied smile curved his thin lips and Savannah's anger burned again. "I just wanted to talk to you."

"A little too late, don't you think?" she pointed out, gritting her teeth and trying to concentrate on the road ahead. "Look, Travis, let's not argue."

"I'm not."

"No, you're just being damned infuriating."

"I just thought that since we're alone, I should explain a few things."

"I'm not really interested in any excuses, or apologies," she said "No reason to rehash the past."

His gaze darkened angrily and he shook his head. "Fine—if that's the way you want it. I just thought you should know that I never intended to leave you."

"Oh, sure. But it just couldn't be avoided? Right?" She shook her head and her fingers tightened around the steering wheel in a death grip. The pickup in front of her swerved and the driver slammed on his brakes. Savannah stood on hers. The BMW fish-tailed, but stopped before colliding with the red pickup. "Oh, God," Savannah whispered, her heart thudding in her chest from the tense conversation as well as the close call on the road.

"Want me to drive?" he asked, once the cars started to move.

"No!"

"All right. Then, let me explain what happened at the lake."

Savannah's nerves were shattered. She glanced from

Travis to the traffic and back again. "Look, I'd rather not discuss this, not now. Too much time has passed."

"Okay, not now. When?"

"Never would be okay with me."

He cocked a disdainful dark brow and frowned. "I'm too tired to argue. So, have it your way...for now. But we are going to talk this out. I'm tired of being manipulated and forced to live a lie."

"I never—" She started to protest and then snapped her mouth shut. She wasn't ready for a conversation about the past, not yet. She needed time to reassess her feelings for Travis before she let herself get trapped in the pain of that summer. It seemed like eons ago. "So that's the reason you're coming back to the farm."

"One reason," he admitted, staring through the rain-spattered windows to the concrete ribbon of freeway and the clog of traffic. An endless line of red taillights flashed ahead of them and blurred through the wet windshield. "I think it's time to set a few things straight with you—" Savannah's breath caught in her throat "—and the rest of the family. Speaking of which, where is Wade?"

"With Dad in Florida. They're considering stabling some of the two-year-olds there in the spring. When Mystic won the Preakness, Dad thought it might be time to move some of the stronger colts to the East Coast."

"And you disagree?"

"The Preakness was only one race—one moment of glory. After winning at Pimlico, Dad was on cloud nine and he really expected Mystic to go on to win the Belmont." She shook her head sadly. "And the result was that Supreme Court, the winner of the Derby, walked away from the field at Belmont. Mystic finished sixth. He hasn't won since. He's back on the farm now and Dad's trying to decide whether to run him next year, sell him or put him out to stud."

Travis didn't comment. Instead he slid a glance up her body, taking in her scruffy boots, faded jeans, blue cowl-necked sweater and suede jacket. His cold gray eyes seemed to strip her bare. "That still doesn't tell me why you came to the airport."

"When Henderson called, there wasn't much time."

The corners of his mouth turned downward at the thought of his partner. "Good." He leaned back against the headrest again. "Maybe it's better if I don't see your brother-in-law for a while. And, as for you—" he placed a hand on her shoulder, but she didn't flinch; his fingers were strong and gentle, just as they'd always been "—you may as well get used to the idea that we're going to talk about what happened, whether you want to or not."

"I don't."

"And so you came to the airport all alone." He let out an amused laugh before dropping his hand. "You're lying, Savannah, and you never were much good at it."

"I thought you were coming to the farm to talk to Wade," she said.

Travis scowled. "Him, too. But he's not gonna like what I've got to say."

"And what's that?"

Travis slid her a knowing look and there was just the trace of bitterness in his eyes. "I think I'd better tell Wade myself."

She frowned as she turned off the freeway and onto the country road that cut through the hills surrounding the farm. Wet leaves piled against fence posts and rising water ran wildly in the ditches near the road. "Do you honestly think I'd worm something out of you and then call Wade?" The idea was so absurd that she almost laughed.

"Don't you like your brother-in-law?"

She pursed her lips, but shook her head. "It's no secret and the feeling's mutual but there's nothing much I can do. He's Charmaine's husband."

"And your dad's right-hand man."

"Looks that way," she said wryly, considering her sister's husband. A first-class bastard, in Savannah's opinion. Unfortunately no one at the farm agreed with her, except maybe her mother, and Virginia wouldn't say anything against Wade.

"So what about you?" he asked quietly.

"What about me?"

"I thought you were going to marry that Donald character—"

"David," she corrected.

"Right. What happened?"

Her shoulders stiffened. "I had second thoughts."

"And cold feet."

For a moment, she felt her temper start to flare, but when she looked at Travis, she saw a glimmer of amusement in his eyes. The old Travis. The man she had loved. "Yeah, cold feet," she agreed. "David wasn't keen on a wife who liked to work with horses. He said he didn't like the smell of them and always had a sneezing attack whenever he was near the stables."

Travis grinned. "Then what the hell was he doing with you?"

"He thought he could change me," she said.

"I remember," Travis replied, thinking back to the night that he'd wanted to kill David Crandall when the kid had pushed himself onto Savannah in the car, all those years ago. Travis's mood shifted again and he felt tense. "Crandall didn't know you very well, did he?"

Savannah could feel his gaze on her face, but she kept her eyes steady on the road. "I guess not."

"Do you still see him?"

"Occasionally. He's married now. Has a wife and two kids." She smiled to herself. "A proper, respectable wife who gave up her career as a chamber musician to be his bride."

"Ouch."

Still grinning, Savannah shook her head, and her ebony hair brushed across the shoulders of her jacket. "It didn't really hurt. Well, maybe my pride was wounded a bit. He married Brenda just three months after we broke up, but it all worked out for the best."

"You're sure?" Travis eyed her speculatively.

"Yep. Can you imagine me living in San Francisco as the wife of an architect?"

"No."

Neither could she. "Well, there you go."

"So you came back to the farm."

After four years of college and three years of working in an investment firm in San Francisco, she'd longed to return to her family and the breeding farm. "I got tired of the city."

Savannah turned off the main road and drove down the long lane leading to Beaumont Breeding Farm. Barren cottonwoods and oaks lined the asphalt drive leading to the main house and garage.

Once Savannah had parked the car in its reserved spot in the garage, Travis gathered his bags, slid out of the BMW and stared at the house. "Some things don't change much," he observed.

Thinking of Virginia, Savannah was forced to disagree. She touched him lightly on the arm. "Maybe more than you know."

He looked at her and his eyes narrowed suspiciously. "Meaning?"

She cleared her throat. "I think you should know that Mom's...not well." He continued to stare at her and the only evidence that he had heard her at all was the whitening of his lips as his jaw clenched. "She's suffered from a series of heart attacks...small ones, but still, she's not well."

"Heart attacks!" Travis looked as if he didn't believe Savannah, but the gravity of her features convinced him. "Why wasn't I told?" he demanded.

"Because that's the way Mom wanted it."

"Why?" His angry glare burned through her.

"Mom didn't want to bother you. You've had your share of problems, y'know." When he didn't seem convinced, she spelled it out for him. "The first attack happened about a week after Melinda was killed in the boating accident. Mom didn't want to worry you."

"That was over six months ago," he said sharply, his voice edged in steel.

"And the next attacks... A series of small ones happened when you were in the middle of that Eldridge case."

"Someone should have told me. *You* should have told me."

"*Me?* I couldn't!"

He leaned against the car. "Just why the hell not, Savannah?"

"Mother insisted on it and Dad—"

"Your father wanted me kept in the dark?"

Savannah shook her head. "He knew how important that case was for your career, he knew that you had been shattered by Melinda's death. He was just looking out for your best interests."

"Like hell!" he roared, grabbing her shoulders in frustration. "I'm a thirty-four-year old man, Savannah. I don't need protection. Especially from your father!"

"But Mom—"

"Where is she?"

"In the house…probably her room."

He released her and controlled his rage. "So level with me—how bad is it?"

Savannah gritted her teeth and decided that despite her mother's request, she couldn't lie to Travis. "It's not good, Travis. Lots of days Mom doesn't come downstairs."

The skin tightened over his face. "Why isn't she in the hospital?"

"Because they can't do anything for her. A private nurse visits the house every day."

"Great," he said with a sigh. "Just great. And no one bothered to tell me." He rubbed the back of his neck in frustration. "I'm going to see her, y'know."

"She'd kill you if you didn't." Savannah offered him an encouraging smile as they entered the house. He took off his jacket and headed up the stairs, his jaw clenched in determination.

Savannah started to follow him, but paused. Virginia would need time alone with Travis. She'd been a second mother to him and Savannah didn't want to interfere in the private conversation. She went back down the stairs and into her father's study, but couldn't concentrate on the stack of bills she'd been sorting earlier in the day. All of her thoughts returned to Travis and memories of that summer long ago filled her mind. "You're a fool," she muttered to herself and tossed the large pile of invoices back on the desk in exasperation.

After pacing in the den for a few minutes, Savannah decided to walk out to the barns and see that the stable hands were taking care of the horses. With the intention of speaking with Lester Adams, the trainer of the farm, she walked outside and turned her collar against the cold December wind.

Dealing directly with Lester was usually her father's job, but since Reginald was in Florida, Savannah worked with the grizzled old trainer and listened to his complaints about the horses as well as his praise.

"REGINALD SHOULD HAVE sold this one," Lester said for the second time as he leaned over the fence and watched the colt's workout. "He looks good, but he's hell to work with."

"So was Mystic." Savannah smiled and watched Vagabond run with the fluid grace of a champion. He was a beautiful bay colt with dark eyes that glimmered menacingly and a long stride that seemed effortless.

"He's different."

"Same temperament, I'd say. Besides, I thought you were the one who said you liked a colt with fire."

"Fire, yes. An inferno, no!" Lester shook his head and his gray eyebrows drew together in frustration. "This one, he's got a mean streak the likes of which the devil himself has never seen."

"He could be a winner."

"If he doesn't self-destruct." The old man put his boot onto the bottom rail of the fence as he studied Vagabond's long strides. "He's got the speed, all right. And the stamina."

"And the heart."

Lester laughed and shook his head. "Heart, you call

it." He chuckled softly. "Geez, that's kind. I call it blasted stubbornness. Nothing else."

"You'll find a way to turn him into a winner," Savannah predicted as the horse slowed. "Just like Mystic."

The trainer avoided her eyes. "It'll be a challenge."

"Just what you like."

"Hmph." The old man cracked a wise smile. "That's enough, Jake," he called as the exercise boy slowed Vagabond to a canter.

"Good." The small rider slid down from the saddle, and patted Vagabond's muscular shoulder. Sweat and mud covered the colt's sleek coat. "I'll go clean him up now."

Lester nodded his agreement, pushed his fedora down over his eyes and reached into his breast pocket for a crumpled pack of cigarettes.

"So Travis came back today," he said as he lit up and inhaled deeply. Leaning against the fence, he watched Savannah through a cloud of blue smoke.

"He's at the house now."

"Will he be staying long?"

"I don't know, but I doubt it. He only had one bag with him." She looked past the workout track, over the fields surrounding the farm, and studied the craggy mountains in the distance. Snow was visible on the higher slopes, above the timberline. "He wants to talk to Wade."

"About runnin' for governor?"

"I don't know," she admitted. "I never got around to asking."

"I can't figure it out," Lester said.

"What?"

"It just seems strange, that's all. Travis, he always did well with the horses. And I know he liked working with them, it was obvious from the start. I had a feelin' about that boy, that he'd...well, that he'd stay on here at the farm. But I was wrong. Instead he goes off to college and becomes a lawyer—hardly ever sets foot on the place again. It just never made much sense, not to me."

He flicked his cigarette onto the wet ground and ground it out with the sole of his boot.

"To top things off," Lester continued, "that sister of yours marries Wade Benson...well, I guess she had her reasons. But Benson, for God's sake, a man I swear couldn't tell a mustang from a Thoroughbred, gives up his accounting practice to work with the horses. It just don't seem right."

"Wade still does the books for the farm," Savannah said, and then wondered why she was defending the man when she, like Lester, had doubted Wade's motives from time to time.

"Yep, but that ain't all. He's managing the place most of the time."

"I know. Dad's been thinking about retiring, because of Mom's condition."

"A shame about your mother," Lester said quietly. His black eyes darkened with an inner sadness.

"Yes."

"A damned shame," Lester muttered before slapping the top rail of the fence and clearing his throat. "I guess I'd better go check on the boys—make sure they're earning their keep and watching over the yearlings." He started off toward the broodmare barn, and Savannah, her thoughts once again centered on Travis, turned back to the house.

A few minutes later Savannah took off her boots on the back porch, stopped to scratch Archimedes, her father's large Australian sheepdog, behind the ears and went into the house through the kitchen.

Sadie Stinson, who served as housekeeper and cook,

was busy slicing vegetables, and the room was filled with the tantalizing scent of roast pork.

"That smells wonderful," Savannah said, peering into the oven and warming her hands against the glass door. "I missed lunch."

Sadie Stinson clucked her tongue. "Shame on you."

"Oh, I don't know. From the looks of this, it was worth the wait."

"Flattery will get you nowhere," the cook said, but beamed under the praise. She eyed Savannah's red face, stockinged feet, and damp hair. "Now, you go and get cleaned up. I'll have this on the table in half an hour."

"Can't wait," Savannah admitted, her stomach rumbling in agreement.

"You'll have to."

"Spoilsport," she teased and Sadie chuckled. "By the way, have you seen Travis?"

Sadie's mood changed and the smile fell from her face. "That I have. He's in your father's study, pouring himself into a bottle, it looks like." She began slicing the zucchini with a vengeance. "Probably won't even appreciate all the work I've gone to."

"I doubt that," Savannah lied and walked out of the kitchen and down the short hallway to the den. Travis was inside, sitting on the broad ledge of the bay window, his legs braced against the floor, his eyes trained on the gathering darkness. He'd changed out of his suit and into worn cords and a flannel shirt that he hadn't bothered to button. His eyes were narrowed against the encroaching night and he held a half-filled glass in his hand. A fire was crackling in the stone fireplace.

Travis glanced over his shoulder and noticed Savannah in the doorway. Her black hair framed her face in wild curls and her intense blue eyes were focused on him. At her studious stare he experienced a tightening in his gut. He'd forgotten how really beautiful she was. "Come in, join me," he invited with a grimace as he lifted his glass.

"I don't think so."

Shrugging indifferently, he turned toward the window and leaned insolently against the frame. "Suit yourself."

"I will." She walked into the room and closed the door before kneeling at the fireplace and warming her hands near the flames. "Did you see Mom?"

The broad shoulders bunched. "Yes." He took a long swallow from his glass and, once it was empty, walked over to the bar near the fireplace and poured himself another three fingers of Scotch. "You should have told me."

"I couldn't."

"Like hell!"

"Mom thought—"

"She's dying, dammit." He accused her with cold gray eyes. "I thought that I could trust you, Savannah."

"Me?" she repeated, incredulously. "You thought you could trust me?" *What about the trust I put in you nine years ago? The trust you threw away with the morning light?*

"You know what I mean. When we were kids, we had secrets, but we were always straight with each other."

Except once, she thought angrily. *Except for the one night that you told me you loved me and I believed it with all of my heart.*

"We're not kids any longer and Mom asked me not to say anything," she said. "I keep my word, and besides, Mom said that Dad would tell you when the time was right."

"And when was that?"

"How am I supposed to know?" She shot him an angry glare and then started for the door. "I've got to get cleaned up for dinner. If you don't drink yourself into oblivion, I'll see you then."

"Savannah—"

Her hand was on the brass handle of the door, but she turned to look over her shoulder and for a fleeting second she saw honest regret in his eyes before his expression turned hard. "I'll be at dinner," he said.

"Good." With her final remark, she walked out of the room.

DINNER WAS TOLERABLE, but just. Virginia was tired and had her meal in her room, Charmaine was brooding over the fact that Wade hadn't called and Travis showed no interest in the spectacular feast that Sadie Stinson had prepared.

Wonderful, Savannah thought sarcastically. *This is just great!*

The only person who genuinely enjoyed himself was Josh, and Savannah was grateful for the little boy's company and constant chatter. "So how long are you stayin'?" Josh asked Travis.

"I don't know."

"I heard Dad say that you were going to be president or something!"

"Governor, Josh," Charmaine corrected, and Travis winced before leaning back in his chair and smiling at Josh.

It was the first time Travis had really smiled since he'd gotten off the plane, and it had a disastrous effect upon Savannah.

"Is that what he said?" Travis asked.

"Yep." Josh pushed his plate aside and leaned forward eagerly. "Dad thinks that's where you belong, at the... wherever the governor is."

"Sacramento."

"Yeah, he says that it's best if you're anywhere besides here on the farm."

"Is that right?" Travis drawled, his grin widening and pleasure gleaming in his eyes.

"Joshua!" Charmaine said, coloring slightly. "If you're done with your meal go upstairs and do your homework!"

"Am I in trouble?"

"Of course not, Josh," Savannah cut in, giving Travis a warning glance and pushing aside her chair. "Come on, I'll get you started."

"It's math," Josh warned.

Savannah pulled a face. "Not my forte, but I'll give it a shot anyway. Let's go." She waited for the boy and together they climbed the stairs. Once on the landing, she hesitated. "You go and get started," she suggested, "and I'll check on Grandma. Okay?"

"Sure," Josh replied and ran down the hall.

After knocking softly on the door, Savannah entered her mother's bedroom. Virginia smiled. "I wondered when you'd show up," she chided.

"Couldn't stay away." Savannah walked over to the bed and took the tray off the bed.

"And how are you getting along with Travis?"

Savannah let out a sound of disgust and leaned against one of the tall posts of the bed. "As well as can be expected considering the fact that he's got a chip on his shoulder the size of the Rock of Gibraltar."

"He's had a rough year," Virginia said, her brow puckering slightly.

"Maybe you're right," Savannah said, deciding it best not to worry her mother unnecessarily. Travis's problems were of his own making and they didn't concern Virginia.

"Then give him a chance, for Pete's sake."

"A chance?"

"To heal his wounds."

"Did he tell you why he came here?"

Virginia's head moved side to side on the pillow. "As a matter of fact, he was rather vague about it. I got the impression that he had some business to conclude with Reginald and that he was taking a rest. It does him good to be here, you know. He always enjoyed working on the farm, with the horses. He can even have the loft again, for an apartment...." Her voice faded slightly.

"Look, I'll take this tray downstairs and see you later," Savannah said. "Right now I promised Josh I'd help him with his math."

Virginia chuckled. "The blind leading the blind..." Savannah laughed aloud. "No faith in your own daughter. Won't you be surprised when Josh aces his next test?"

"With you tutoring him? That I will be," Virginia said as Savannah carried the dinner tray to the door.

"I'll see ya later," Savannah said before walking down the long hall to Josh's room and finding the boy on the floor, Transformers and Gobots spread out on the carpet in a mock battle.

"Who's winning?" Savannah said with a smile.

"The Decepticons!"

"I thought you were supposed to be working on math."

"Aunt Savvy..." Josh pleaded, turning his bright eyes up at her.

"Right now, mister." She gathered up some of the toys and set them on Josh's already overloaded dresser.

"You could play with me," he suggested.

Savannah sat on the edge of the bed and shook her head. "Maybe later. Right now we've got math to master." She kicked off her shoes and crossed her legs. "Hop to it."

"I hate math," the boy grumbled.

"So do I, but, though I loathe to admit it, arithmetic, geometry, algebra, etcetera are very important. Someday you'll find out."

"Not in a million years." Josh grabbed his book and put it on the desk. Then he took a seat and hunched his shoulders over his homework.

Savannah concentrated on the problems. "This'll be a breeze," she predicted. "Simple multiplication."

A few minutes and several problems later, a soft cough caught her attention and she looked over her shoulder to find Travis lounging in the doorway. One of his shoulders was propped against the frame and his hands were pushed into the pockets of his jeans. How long he had been there, watching her with his slate-colored eyes, she could only guess. "How's it going?"

"It's not," Savannah admitted.

"Horrible!" Josh said.

"Need some help?"

"Yeah!" Josh was more than eager to have Travis help him. Savannah's heart went out to the boy. All Josh wanted was a little positive fatherly attention and he got very little from his own dad.

"Sure. Why not?" Savannah said. "I've got to take this tray down to the kitchen anyway." She stood up and reached for the tray she had set on the nightstand.

"Don't let me scare you away," Travis said, sauntering into the room, his gaze locking with hers.

"You're not."

"And you're lying again," he accused. "Bad habit, Savannah. You'd better break it."

"I guess you just bring out the worst in me," she whispered through clenched teeth, hoping that Travis would take the hint and drop the subject.

"Or the best." His eyes roved down her rigid body to rest on the thrust of her breasts against her sweater.

Under his stripping gaze, anger heated her blood and colored her cheeks, but she kept her tongue still because Josh had turned his head to study her.

"Is something wrong, Aunt Savvy?"

"Nothing," she replied tightly. "I just have a couple of things to do. I'll…I'll see you later." Controlling her anger with Travis took an effort, but she managed to give Josh a genuine smile before leaving the room and telling herself that she would only have to suffer Travis's indignities a few more days, only until Wade and Reginald returned to the farm.

And what would happen then? Savannah grimaced to herself when she realized that she was looking forward to the reunion with both anticipation and dread.

CHAPTER THREE

WADE DIDN'T CALL that night, and Savannah didn't know whether to be thankful or worried.

The next day Savannah tried to avoid Travis, finding it easier to keep out of his way than risk another confrontation with him. It wasn't difficult. Travis spent his time locked in the study, on the phone, or in the loft, which Charmaine had partially cleared out of. Savannah went grocery shopping, then made it a point to work with Lester and the horses during the day, before going up to her room in the evening to shower and change for dinner. She dressed in black slacks and a red sweater and tried to tell herself she wasn't primping as she brushed her hair.

Savannah walked into the dining room and was surprised to see that her mother was already at the table. Seated at the head of the long table and dressed in a rose-colored caftan, Virginia looked healthier than she had in weeks.

Travis sat to the left of Virginia with Charmaine on his other side. His eyes followed Savannah as she walked into the room and took the empty seat across the table from him. Wearing an open-necked shirt and leaning on one elbow, he sipped a glass of wine and appeared relaxed as he talked with Virginia. *Like a vagabond son returning home,* Savannah thought, meeting his interested gaze. Only when she entered the room, did he show any sign of tension.

"Glad you could make it down, Mom," Savannah said, bristling slightly as Travis poured her a glass of wine.

"It's not every day that Travis comes home," Virginia remarked with a pleased smile. "I'm just sorry he didn't tell us he intended to be here earlier so that we could welcome him properly yesterday."

Properly must have meant with silver, linen napkins, a floral centerpiece, flickering candles and shining crystal, Savannah thought, eyeing the table. The chandelier had been appropriately dimmed, the silver polished until it gleamed. Virginia always had liked to put on a show.

"Not necessary," Travis said, his gray eyes moving from Virginia to Savannah and lingering on the proud lift of her chin.

"Of course it is." Virginia laughed. "You haven't been home for nearly two years!"

Small talk carried Savannah through the meal, though she could feel the weight of Travis's gaze as she ate. He leaned back in his chair and observed her with amused, but cynical eyes that seemed to look into the darkest corners of her mind.

Joshua was seated beside Savannah and he appeared preoccupied. His small brow was creased with worry and he barely touched his food. Any attempt to draw the boy into the conversation met with monosyllabic responses.

Despite the formal decorations and the mouth-watering meal, Savannah felt the undercurrents of tension in the room. *Just like the calm before the storm,* she thought uneasily as she shifted her gaze from Josh's brooding expression to Travis's intense gaze.

"Wade called this afternoon," Charmaine announced, setting her fork on her plate after dessert.

The strain in the room exploded.

"What!" Travis's head jerked toward Charmaine, and

he pinned her with his angry glare. "Why didn't you tell me?"

Charmaine met his gaze and lifted her chin. "You were in the stables with Lester. I didn't want to bother you. Mother was resting and Savannah was in Sacramento doing the grocery shopping. So I took the call and told him you were here and anxious to speak with him."

Travis scowled, his impatience mounting. "Maybe I should phone him."

"No. He said he'd be home tomorrow. The plane lands about six, and he and father should be here by seven-thirty at the latest." She placed her napkin on the table and pushed her chair back, but didn't stand. "If it's any consolation, he was as anxious to talk to you as you are to speak with him."

"I'll bet," Travis mocked.

Charmaine overlooked his remark and turned to Josh. Her voice was still tight, but she attempted to appear calm. "So Daddy will be here in plenty of time for Christmas. Isn't that great?"

The boy had been pushing the remains of his apple pie around in his plate. He stopped, looked past his mother and shrugged.

"Joshua?"

"I don't want him to come home," Josh mumbled, glancing at Savannah before pretending interest in his plate.

Charmaine, obviously embarrassed, cleared her throat. "Joshua. Surely you don't mean—"

"I do mean it, Mom." Tears had gathered in his eyes, though he was bravely trying to swallow them back. "Daddy hates me."

Virginia gasped. "Oh, dear," she whispered, trying to think of something to cut short the uncomfortable scene.

Stiffening slightly, Charmaine blushed. "You know that's not true, Josh."

"It is, too. And I finally figured it out," Josh blurted. "Some of the kids were talking at school today…."

"About what?" Charmaine asked, dread tightening the corners of her mouth.

"I know the only reason you married Dad is because of me!" he said miserably, guilt weighing heavily on his small shoulders.

To her credit, Charmaine didn't flinch. "I married your father because I loved him."

"Because you *had* to!" Joshua said brokenly, partially standing, but managing to hold his mother's gaze. "That's what the kids at school said."

"Josh," Savannah cut in, but Charmaine held up her hand.

"This is my problem, Savannah." Then, looking back at her son, she said, "No one *had* to marry anyone."

"Would you have married Dad if you weren't pregnant with me?" He blinked against the tears in his eyes.

Virginia went pale and picked up her water glass with trembling fingers.

"Of course—" Charmaine whispered tenderly.

"No!" Josh screamed, his face red and tear-stained.

Charmaine braced her shoulders. "Joshua, I think you should go up to your room and I'll come talk to you there," she said in measured tones, her voice shaking.

Savannah tried to touch Josh on the shoulder, but he jerked away and Savannah's stomach knotted in pain. "Josh—"

"I don't want to talk," the boy said angrily, his fists balled at his sides. "It's true—it's all true and I don't want Dad to come home! I wish—I wish that I didn't have a father!"

Travis looked from Savannah to the boy and back again, his jaw tight, his eyes filled with understanding for the rebellious youth.

"You don't mean that," Charmaine insisted.

"I do! I do mean it!"

Joshua's chair slid back from the table, scraping the floor. He ran out of the room and clomped noisily up the stairs.

"No," Charmaine murmured, closing her eyes to steady herself.

"I'm sorry," Savannah whispered, knowing there was no way to console her older sister.

"No reason to be," Charmaine said tightly. "This has been coming for a long time. Wade and Josh have never gotten along. Sooner or later Josh was bound to figure out that his dad resents him. I just…never wanted to face it, I guess."

"I'll go," Savannah offered, fighting her own tears.

"No. This is my problem, a mistake I made ten years ago. I'll handle it." With new conviction Charmaine got out of her chair and hurried out of the dining room. "Joshua," Charmaine called and Savannah had to close her eyes to fight her own tears. "Joshua, don't you lock that door!"

When she opened her eyes again, Savannah found Travis staring at her intently. His jaw was rigid, his gray eyes cold. He finished the wine in his glass and rubbed an impatient hand over his jaw.

"I suppose it had to come to this," Virginia said, breaking the silence and throwing her napkin on her plate in disgust. "I just hoped I wouldn't see the day." She stood shakily from her chair and Travis got up to help her. Virginia, though pale, anticipated his move and waved him away. "I'm all right. I just want to go upstairs for a while. I can make it on my own."

"Are you sure?" Savannah asked.

"I've been climbing those stairs for over thirty years," she said with a worried smile. "No reason to stop now."

With a proud set to her shoulders, Virginia walked out of the room and slowly mounted the stairs.

"When I get my hands on Wade Benson," Travis warned, his voice low, his angry eyes focused on Savannah, "he'll wish he'd had the common sense to stay in Florida or wherever the hell he is." Setting his half-empty wineglass on the table, he stood up and walked out of the room. A few seconds later the front door slammed shut.

Still concerned about Joshua, Savannah helped Sadie clear the table and straighten the kitchen to get her mind off Josh as well as Travis. Then, telling herself that she wasn't looking for Travis, Savannah went outside to the stables, checked on the horses and filed some reports in the office over the foaling shed. Travis wasn't in the yard or the office and Savannah felt a twinge of disappointment when she decided to go back to the house.

"You're a fool," she told herself with a frown. "Stay as far away from him as possible." She stretched before locking the door to the office, then climbed down the stairs. The night was bitterly cold and starless. Huddling against the frigid air, she raced across the parking lot and through the back door of the darkened house.

Archimedes stirred on the back porch and thumped his tail loudly as she kicked off her boots and slipped into the kitchen. The only sound disturbing the silence of the house was the hum of the refrigerator and the ticking of the grandfather clock in the hall.

"God, I'm tired," she whispered, opening the refrigerator. She poured a large glass of milk and slowly drank it while staring out the window to the darkened stable-yard. Thoughts of Travis wouldn't leave her alone and she wondered again where he was and why he had come back to the farm.

After putting the empty glass in the sink, she rubbed a hand over her eyes and walked toward the study to put away the mail.

The den was dark, illuminated only by the light of the dying fire. When Savannah entered the room, she found Travis lounging on the hearth, his fingers clasped around a glass, his back to the blood-red embers, his long legs stretched in front of him.

"What're you doing here?" she asked.

"Waiting."

"For?"

"You." He looked up at her, his intense gaze causing her heart to flutter.

"Okay," she whispered. "I'm here." She planted herself in front of him by leaning against the desk and balancing her hips against the smooth, polished wood. She reached for the lamp.

"Leave it off."

"Why?"

"The room seems quieter that way…less hostile."

Savannah let out a soft laugh. "You should know. Lately I think you wrote the book on hostility."

"Not with you," he said, taking a sip from his glass. "Why'd you interfere with Josh?" he asked slowly.

"I didn't."

A crooked grin sliced across his face. "Call it whatever you want, but it's the second time you've done it."

She lifted a shoulder and frowned, her dark brows drawing together as her thoughts returned to her nephew. "I don't think I'm interfering," she argued. "Sometimes I feel that he doesn't get enough attention or credit around here. Everyone points out his faults, but no one ever seems to pat him on the back."

"Except for you?"

"And his grandfather. Despite what you feel about him, Reginald's been a damned good grandfather, just like the kind of stepfather he's been to you. Just in case you've forgotten."

Travis's square jaw hardened. "What about Charmaine? How does she get along with her son?"

"Josh is a difficult child and Charmaine nearly raises him by herself. Obviously Wade doesn't have much time for the boy."

"Obviously," Travis commented dryly.

"As for Charmaine; she tries. But sometimes she has trouble understanding Josh. You know, she expects perfection and won't let him just be a kid."

"So that's when you step in."

"Only when I think Josh needs a little extra support. It's not easy being the only nine-year-old in a house full of grownups, y'know." She crossed her arms under her chest, unconsciously sculpting her sweater over breasts.

"You love him very much."

"Who wouldn't?" she asked, smiling to herself.

"Maybe Wade?"

Savannah's jaw tightened and she couldn't hide the impotent rage she felt every time she thought about Wade's treatment of his son. "I don't know if Wade is capable of loving anyone, even himself," she muttered. "And Josh is right about one thing: Wade should never have become a father." Then, thinking better of confiding in Travis, she tried to let go of her anger and changed the subject. "Do you know that Josh fantasizes about riding Mystic?"

"And what do you fantasize about?" he asked, his gray

eyes focused on the proud lift of her chin, the flush in her cheeks and the elegant column of her throat. Her tousled black curls gleamed against her white skin and brushed the soft red sweater.

"I don't," she replied, slightly unnerved.

He looked as if he didn't believe her. "No dreams, Savvy?" he asked, and his voice caressed the familiar nickname he had given her when he had first come to the farm and she'd been just a skinny kid of nine.

"Not anymore."

He dragged his eyes away from her and stared into his drink. "Because of what happened between us."

"That's part of it," she conceded, feeling the old bittersweet pain in her chest.

He took a long swallow of his Scotch before lifting his eyes to her face. "So tell me, if you're so fond of Josh, why didn't you have any children of your own?"

"Simple. No husband."

"That's always puzzled me."

She shifted her gaze to the fire before returning it to him. His chestnut hair glinted with red highlights in the firelight and his tanned face looked more angular from the shadows. "I thought I explained that. David and I—"

"There were other men. Had to have been. You went to college at Berkeley, worked in San Francisco. You can't expect me to believe that you lived the life of a nun."

She bristled, thinking how close he had come to the truth. "Not quite. But I guess I never found a man that I thought would be right."

"That was probably my fault, too."

"Don't flatter yourself."

Ignoring her bitterness, he crossed his legs before him and finished his drink. "For what it's worth, you would have been one helluva mother."

"I suppose I should take that as a compliment."

"It was intended as one."

She felt an uncomfortable lump in her throat and tried to use the feeling of intimacy that was stealing into the room to her advantage. "A little while ago you said that we used to share secrets."

"We did."

"So why don't you tell me why you're here. Why now? And why is Henderson, your partner, so upset?"

"I'll tell you when—"

"I know. When Wade and Dad get back. Tomorrow. A good thing, too," she added mockingly.

A muscle in the corner of his jaw began to work. "Why? Are you getting tired of me?"

"No, but you couldn't last here, counselor. At the rate you're going, we'll be out of Scotch in two days."

He cocked his head to the side and a laconic smile sliced across his face. "You think I'm a lush."

"You're doing a damned good impersonation." Standing up and stretching her tired muscles, she kept her eyes fixed on Travis. "Why don't you just tell me why you came back? I already know that you're planning to dissolve your partnership with Henderson and I know that you're probably going to give up on the idea of running for governor, despite the current rumors or any grassroots ground swell."

"Henderson talks too much."

"He didn't want to."

"But with your powers of persuasion, you convinced a respected member of the bar, a man who had held his tongue in a courtroom when it was to his client's advantage, to bare his soul," he prodded, the corners of his mouth pinching.

She ignored his blatant sarcasm. "Something like that."

"Like I said, he talks too much." His eyes slid slowly up her body, lingering at the swell of her breasts. "And you're too inquisitive for your own good. Always have been." His gaze continued upward, hesitating a moment at the corner of her mouth before reaching her eyes.

Savannah's throat worked reflexively. There was something inherently male about Travis that reached her on a very sensual level. There always had been.

"Why did you come back?" she asked, hoping to break the thickening tension in the room.

"I don't want to discuss it."

"Why not?"

He grimaced into the remains of his drink. "Because I want to talk to Reginald first. Something's not right."

"With what?"

He rubbed the bridge of his nose and closed his eyes. "Oh, Savvy, with everything—the law practice, the campaign. There're a few things that don't add up and—" He stopped himself, realizing that he was confiding in her. "Just trust me on this one, okay? Once I talk to Wade I'll be able to sort everything out."

"What does Wade have to do with anything?" she asked.

"I think he's involved."

"In what?"

A muscle in the corner of Travis's jaw tightened. "I haven't put it all together," he admitted in disgust. "But frankly, I'm not sure that I want to."

"You're afraid."

Travis smiled grimly and shook his head. "I just don't know if it's worth all the trouble."

"Something's eating at you."

"I don't like to be a pawn. That's all." He got up and paced around the room. "Have you ever wondered *why* it's so damned important to your father that I run for election?"

"I guess I really hadn't thought about it."

"Well, he's pushing, Savannah. He's pushing very hard. And the only reason I could see that it would matter to him at all is for personal gain—his personal gain."

"You really have become a cynic, haven't you?" she tossed back, but the seriousness of his expression made her heart miss a beat.

"Think about it. Why would he care? What's it to him—unless he were expecting something from me."

"Like what?"

"I don't know...." He lifted his hand and then dropped it again. "Maybe you can tell me."

"I don't have an inkling of what you're talking about."

"Don't you? I wonder." He slid a suspicious glance in her direction before staring at the fire. "You could be in on it."

"You're crazy!" she said angrily.

He laughed a little, leaned an elbow on the mantel and raked his fingers through his hair. "Far from it, I'm afraid."

"You can't just come back here, to the man who all but raised you as his son, and start accusing him of God only knows what. You, of all people, should know that, counselor!" Savannah's temper got the better of her and she looked at him with self-righteous eyes.

"I haven't accused anyone of anything."

"Yet!"

Travis leaned back and smiled sarcastically. "Okay, let's use logic. The governor has a lot of responsibilities. Surely you agree."

"So?"

"For example: the governor of California is the supreme power behind the California Horse Racing Board. The Governor appoints members to the board and may remove a board member if it can be proved that he's incompetent or negligent. And that doesn't begin to touch what the governor is responsible for in the case of land use, corporations…you name it. The governor has a lot of power—the kind of power that some people might like to abuse."

"Like Dad?"

"For one. Wade and Willis Henderson wouldn't be standing very far behind him."

Savannah's eyes widened. Travis really believed what he was saying. "Be careful, Travis. You're talking about my father. My father! A man who has only done what he's thought best for you."

"Maybe not always."

"This is all idle speculation—half-baked theories!"

"I don't think so. Four of the board members' terms are up during the next term of governor. Four. Out of seven."

"And you think Dad cares?" Savannah was seething.

"Of course he cares! Everyone who owns a race horse in California cares!" He came up and stood before her. "For all I know, Reginald might want to be on the board himself or try to convince me to appoint the right people, friends of his who could be easily swayed to his point of view."

"But why?"

"Power, Savannah."

"That's crazy—"

"Power and money. The two biggest motives mankind has known."

"Don't forget revenge," she reminded him.

"Oh, I haven't." A ruthless smile curved his lips. "I visited my partner, Henderson, the other night."

"The night that you told him you wanted out of the partnership?"

"Right. The same night that he met with Wade."

Savannah froze. "I don't understand…."

"Wade and Willis Henderson seem to be working together on several schemes."

"Such as?" she asked, breathless.

He considered her a moment and then decided it didn't really matter what she knew. "Such as the fact that Wade Benson is doing the books for the law firm—without my knowledge."

Savannah couldn't hide her surprise. As far as she knew Wade only did the books for the farm. "So what does that have to do with anything?" she asked.

"In itself, not much. But the fact that Henderson admitted that he and Wade have already been taking contributions for my campaign…" Travis shook his head and the thrust of his jaw became more prominent. "That I saw as a problem. Henderson claims that your father was in on it."

"But you haven't announced your candidacy."

Travis's lips twisted cynically. "And won't." He finished his drink. "You can see my point."

"If what you're saying is true…"

Travis squinted into the fire. "Why would I lie?"

"I don't know," she said, "because I don't know you any more."

"Sure you do." His voice was gentle, as gentle as it had been years ago before the bitterness and pain had settled in his eyes.

"You've changed."

He offered a humble smile. "Not for the better, I assume."

"What made you so callous?" she asked. "Melinda's death?"

"I wish it were as simple as all that," he muttered, finishing his drink. "She wouldn't have liked this, y'know. She expected me to run for some political office and she was behind my ambitions...she and your father." He frowned into his empty glass. "And then there was the Eldridge decision," he said bitterly.

"But I thought you won," Savannah said, reflecting on the newsworthy decision. Travis was the lawyer who had successfully brought a major drug company to trial for the family of Eric Eldridge, who had died from taking a contaminated anti-inflammatory drug.

"So did I."

"What changed your mind?" she asked, knowing that he was carrying an unnecessary burden of guilt.

"Everything," he muttered disgustedly as he strode over to the bar and splashed three fingers of Scotch into his glass. "The law firm made money; the Eldridges got an award so large that they sent me a magnum of champagne and bought themselves two new cars and a yacht."

"What they did with the money doesn't matter."

He took a long drink. "But it didn't bring their son back, did it?" he asked, shaking his head and closing his eyes. "Grace Eldridge got up on the stand and wept for her lost son," he said, as if to himself. "A month later she came into the office wearing a new fur coat and a Bermuda tan and asked if I thought there was any way to file another lawsuit against the drug company." He studied the amber liquid in his glass. "It left a bad taste in my mouth."

He walked back to her and placed his glass on the

desk. "That's what I meant when I said all that matters is power and money."

"And revenge," she reminded him.

He was standing in front of her again, his eyes, luminous in the darkened room, drilling into hers. "Right. Revenge." When his hands came up to take hold of her shoulders she didn't move.

The warmth from his fingers permeated her sweater to spread down her arms. She trembled inside, as much from his touch as from the realization that he was, indeed, suspicious of her father's motives. "So that's what you came here to find out," Savannah whispered. "How my father is involved in your 'campaign' or lack thereof."

"Partly," he admitted, his voice husky.

"What else?" Savannah's heart was pounding betrayingly from the feel of his hands on her arms.

"Just this." He lowered his head and gently brushed his lips across hers, tantalizing her with the feel of his mouth against her skin.

"Don't do this to me," she whispered. "Not again." Jerking free, she took an unsteady step backward and stared into his eyes. "Tell me…tell me what you think Dad's up to," she said, not wanting to think about the passion behind his kiss or her immediate reaction.

"I'm not sure; I'll need your help to find out."

"No, Travis," she whispered. "You really can't expect me to go against my own father."

"I haven't asked that."

He was so close, so damned close, and all she could think about was the power of his body over hers. "But you're trying to—"

"Find out the truth. That's all."

"Then talk to Dad!" she said desperately.

"I will. When he gets back. Until then, I may need your cooperation."

"I can't help you, Travis!"

"If it makes you feel any better, I hope that this is all a big misunderstanding. I would like to think that Reginald's motives are as pure as you seem to think."

"But you won't."

"I'm too realistic."

"Jaded," she corrected.

"Prove it," he dared, his eyes glinting in the firelight.

"I don't know—" She cleared her throat and tried to stop the hammering of her heart.

"Prove me wrong, dammit! You were the one who pushed me, lady. I didn't want to tell you any of this, but you insisted."

"But you're asking me to prove to you that my father, a respected horse breeder, is…what? Trying to get you elected so that he can defraud the racing public? Is that what you're suggesting?"

"Maybe you can verify your opinion."

"Of course I can! If Dad's so hell-bent to abuse your powers as governor, if and when you're elected, it would only affect him here, in California. Then why would he bother with stabling the horses in Florida? Tell me that! There wouldn't be much of a point, not when he knew that here, in the Golden State, he could manipulate the racing board at will!"

"You're being sarcastic."

"And you're talking nonsense!" she nearly shouted, angry with herself for even listening to him.

"Prove it," he suggested.

Savannah's blue eyes sparked at the challenge. "I will."

"Good." His grin was filled with ruthless satisfaction as he leaned against the mantel, his narrowed eyes lingering on her lips. "I don't suppose your father ever told you who was at the lake that night nine years ago." He touched her softly on the underside of her chin.

Savannah jerked her head to the side. "He knew?"

"Of course he knew."

"I don't believe it! He would have said something…."

"Why?"

"He wouldn't just forget about it."

"I don't think your father forgets anything."

She took in a steadying breath. "How did he know?"

Travis's smoldering eyes delved into hers. "Because Melinda told him."

"And how did Melinda know? Did you confess?" Savannah asked, hardly daring to breathe as she relived that night so long ago.

"She saw us."

"Oh, God." The memory came back with crystal clarity: a twig snapping, Travis going to investigate. *Melinda had been the intruder at the lake!* Embarrassment poured over Savannah and she started for the door, but Travis reached for her. His hand was incredibly gentle on her arm. "I don't want to hear this," she whispered, refusing to be dragged back to the pain of the past. "It's over—"

"Is it?" In the dim light from the fire, with only the sound of the crackling flames and the wind against the rafters, his gaze scorched through her icy facade and into her heart. "I never stopped wanting you," Travis admitted, self-disgust twisting his mouth cynically.

"There's no reason to lie."

His fingers curled over her arm and he gave her a shake. Raw emotion twisted his face. "Dammit, Savannah. I'm not lying. I hate like hell to admit it, but not one solitary day has gone by that I haven't thought of you… wished to God that I'd never left you that night."

"You could have come back," she whispered, her pulse racing.

"I was married! And you were Reginald's daughter!"

Savannah didn't want to hear the excuses or think about the lies of the past nine years. "There's no reason to discuss this, Travis," she murmured, trying to break free of his embrace, but his fingers tightened painfully.

"I never wanted to love you," he said, his voice rough, his eyes glittering in the fire glow. "In fact, I tried to lie to myself, convince myself that you were nothing to me, but it just didn't work. All the time I was married to another woman, I couldn't forget you. That night at the lake was burned into my mind and my soul like no other memory in my life." He took in a long, ragged breath. "And at night…at night I would lie awake and remember the feel of you and I couldn't stop wanting you, dammit. Melinda was right there, in the bed with me, and all I could think of was you!"

"What's the point of all this?" she asked, her breath tight in her throat and tears threatening her eyes. The words of love she'd longed to hear sounded out of place and disjointed with nine years standing between them.

"The point is that I got used to living a lie. But there's no reason to live it anymore."

Savannah's throat ached, but she lifted her head high and shook her hair out of her face. "Because Melinda is dead?"

"Yes."

She squeezed her eyes against the tears and lifted her chin. "I don't like being second-best, Travis. I never have."

"Don't you even want to know why I married her?"

"No! It really doesn't matter. Not anymore…." Her voice cracked with the lie.

The fingers around her arms gripped into her flesh and he pushed his head down to hers. He was so close that she could feel the angry heat radiating from his body, smell the Scotch on his breath, see the rage in his eyes. "It *does* matter. It all matters. Don't you understand? I've come here to break away from the lies of the past…all of them. Including the lie of marrying the wrong woman." His gray eyes delved into hers, scraping past the indifference she pretended to feel. "I *loved* you, Savannah and damned myself for it. You were the daughter of the man that raised me—and until that summer I'd always thought of you as a kid sister."

In the thick silence that followed, Savannah stared into his flinty eyes and saw the smoldering passion in his gaze. Her heart throbbed with the thought that once, long ago, he had loved her, and that he still wanted her. The fingers around her arms were a gentle manacle, but when she tried to tear away from his grasp, his hands tightened to the strength of steel.

"And you loved me," he finally whispered.

Tears burned her eyes, but she refused to break down. "The man I loved would never have left me," she said, her voice breaking before she took in a long, steadying breath. "He would never have left me without so much as a word of goodbye or an explanation."

Travis's nostrils flared and his eyes narrowed. "I've made more than my share of mistakes, lady. God knows I'm no saint and I should have demanded to see you before I agreed to marry Melinda, but everyone, including your father, thought it would be better if I just left."

Savannah shuddered. "How did Dad find out about us?"

His jaw was tense, the muscles of his body taut. "Melinda went to Reginald with the story that she was pregnant. Or else they worked out the story together."

"I don't understand." Savannah felt her knees grow weak, but the grip on her arms held her upright and Travis's features became harsh.

"She claimed that the only reason she and I had argued earlier in the night was because she was frightened. Afraid that I would leave her and the child. Then, she had second thoughts and tracked me down."

Savannah couldn't believe him. "How did she know you were at the lake?" she asked angrily.

"Just a lucky guess. My car was in the garage, but I wasn't sleeping in the loft, or in the office. Melinda knew that I went to the lake whenever I wanted to think things out, so—"

"She found us," Savannah whispered, her blue eyes flashing with embarrassment and fury.

"Yes."

She felt tears touch the back of her eyelids but refused to release them. "So you married her because she was pregnant."

"Because she *told* me she was pregnant."

"And the baby?" she murmured.

"Probably never existed."

"What!"

A twisted smile contorted the rugged features of his face. "Oh, yes, Melinda claimed to be pregnant. I didn't question her and that was probably a mistake." His steely eyes inched down her face to her breasts before returning to her gaze. "Obviously not my first."

Savannah tried to pull away from him but was no match for his strength.

"Melinda claimed to miscarry about three weeks after the wedding. I didn't doubt her until much later, when

I thought that we should have a child in an attempt to save the marriage." He read the protests in Savannah's eyes. "I know it's a lousy excuse to have a kid, but I was desperate. I wanted to make things right between us because all the time that we were married, she knew that I'd never forgotten you. Do you have any idea what kind of hell she must have put herself through?"

"Or the kind of hell she put you through, because of your guilt," Savannah thought aloud.

"She was my wife, whether I loved her or not. Anyway, Melinda wasn't interested in a baby then and I doubt if she ever was. I think Melinda lied to me, Savannah, to force the marriage." His eyes darkened to the color of slate. "And your father was all for it."

Savannah digested his words slowly. "That doesn't make sense."

"Sure it does. Especially if he believed she was carrying my child."

"I don't see that what happened in the past changes anything. You could have come to me and explained."

"And how would you have felt?" he demanded.

She felt the color explode on her cheeks. "Maybe a little less…used."

He closed his eyes and dropped his forehead until it rested against hers. "Oh, lady, I never wanted you to feel that I used you."

"How was I supposed to feel?" she demanded, her wounded pride resurfacing. "Did you think that one night with you was all I wanted?"

"Of course not! But I thought the less people that knew about what happened between us, the better."

Anger, nine years old and searing, shot through her. She wanted to strike him, lash out against all the pain she had borne, but she couldn't because he was still gripping her arms. "And what would have happened if *I'd* been the one to turn up pregnant?"

"I thought about that. Long and hard."

"And?"

"I would have divorced Melinda."

"And expected me to fall into your arms?" She shook her head and felt every muscle in her body tense. "I would never have married you, Travis," she said through clenched teeth. "Because it would have been a trap, for you and me and the child and in the end we'd end up with a child caught between us, just like Josh is caught between Charmaine and Wade!"

"You don't believe that any more than I do."

"I do," she insisted, stamping a foot to add emphasis to her words. But her gaze was trapped in his magnetic stare. "I would never—"

His head lowered and he smothered her protest by capturing her lips with his. The force of the kiss was undeniable, the passion surging. Savannah wanted to push him away, to walk out of the room with her head held high, but she couldn't resist the sweet pressure on her mouth.

"No," she whispered, but he only drew her closer, crushing her body to his hard, muscular frame. The taste of him lingered on her lips and when his tongue pressed against her teeth, she willingly parted her lips.

The pressure on her arms became gentle and he pulled her body to his. Her breasts crushed against the rock-hard wall of his chest and began to ache for his touch. She felt a warmth invade her body, stealing from the deepest part of her and flowing through her blood.

Travis moaned and the kiss deepened, his moist tongue touching and mating with hers until Savannah felt her knees go weak and her fingers clutch his shoul-

ders. Blood pulsed through her veins in throbbing bursts
that warmed her from the inside out.

She trembled when his mouth left hers to explore the
white skin of her throat and the lobe of her ear. Unconsciously she let her hair fall away from her face and quivered when his tongue slid along her jaw.

"Travis," she whispered, her breathing more labored
with each breath as his hands slipped beneath the hem of
her sweater and his fingers found the soft flesh between
her ribs. She sucked in her abdomen and felt the tips of
his fingers slide beneath the waistband of her jeans before climbing upward to mold around the straining tip
of a breast. She moaned when his fingers captured the
warm mound.

Fire burned within her body and soul as he toyed with
the erect nipple and pressed his anxious lips to her mouth.

Vague thoughts that she should stop what was happening flitted through her mind, but she couldn't concentrate on anything other than the power of his touch.
He leaned against the fireplace, his muscled legs spread
and pulled her to him, forcing her against the hard evidence of desire in his loins, making her all too aware of
the burning lust spreading through him like wildfire.

"Tell me again that you don't want me," he whispered
against her hair.

Savannah was drugged with passion. When Travis
cupped her buttocks and pulled her close she could hear
the hard thudding of his heart. "I don't...I can't..." The
raw ache within her burned traitorously and her thoughts
centered on making love to this one very special man.

"Tell me that you never loved me."

"Travis...please," she gasped, trying to make some
sense of what was happening. She couldn't fall under

Travis's spell again, *wouldn't* love him again, and yet her body refused to push him away.

The arms around her tightened, and he raised his head to stare into the mystery of her eyes. Gone was any trace of passion in his gaze. If their bodies hadn't been entwined so intimately, Savannah would have sworn that she had imagined the entire seduction. "Don't ever be ashamed of anything that's happened between us. Whether you believe the truth or not, the fact is that I loved you more than a sane man would let himself love a woman."

"But it wasn't enough."

"We were caught in a web of lies, Savannah. Lies spun by the people we trusted. Otherwise things would have been different. I swear that to you, and I hope to God you believe me." His face was drawn, his eyes gleaming with the truth as he saw it.

"It doesn't matter," she said, feeling bereft when he released her.

"Oh, but it does," he argued, pushing his hands into the back pockets of his jeans and trying to compose himself. "It matters one helluva lot!" Striding across the room he stopped at the bar and poured himself another stiff shot. "Because I'm back now and things are going to change in a big way. No one—not you, not Henderson, your father or your brother-in-law, is going to manipulate my life any longer. That's over. When I have it out with Reginald, I'm leaving."

"Running away," she accused.

He lifted a shoulder and smiled at a secret irony. "Just the opposite, lady," he said, the muscles in his face tightening in determination. "For the first time in my life I'm doing things exactly as I please. I'm not running *away* from anything, I'm just burying the past and all my mistakes with it."

"Mistakes like me? Well, bully for you," she hurled back at him, stung by his remark. "And just for the record, *I've* never done anything to manipulate you."

He winced. "Not intentionally, I suppose," he acquiesced. "But you sure have a way of turning me inside out!" With a look that cut her to the bone, he walked out of the room, through the foyer, out the front door and into the night. Savannah stood in the den with her arms crossed, hugging herself. *Oh, Travis,* she thought angrily, *why did you even bother coming back? Why didn't you just run away and leave me out of it!*

CHAPTER FOUR

Sleep was nearly impossible that night. Savannah tossed and turned, knowing that Travis was only a short walk away. She thought about everything he'd said about his reasons for leaving her all those years ago and wanted desperately to believe that he was, as she, a victim of fate.

"That's just wishing for the stars," she told herself angrily. "If he'd really wanted you, he'd have come back and at least explained, worked things out with Melinda...." *But how?* He'd really believed that Melinda had been pregnant. Or so he'd claimed.

And what about her father? Travis seemed to be on some vendetta to prove that Reginald was a scheming, conniving, power-hungry old man hell-bent on ruining Travis's life.

Savannah closed her eyes and tried to sleep, but was awake when the first pale streaks of dawn pierced through the windows of her bedroom.

Realizing that she wouldn't accomplish anything by tossing and turning in bed, she threw back the covers, got up, took a hot shower and dressed in warm work clothes. She didn't bother with makeup and tied her hair way from her face with a leather thong.

The morning was wet and cold with the promise of still more frigid air to come. The sky, darkened by gray clouds, seemed foreboding, and Savannah shuddered as she walked across the parking lot, past Lester's pickup and up the stairs to the office over the foaling shed.

Pulling off her gloves, she shouldered her way into the office. The smell of perking coffee mingled with the faint odors of saddle soap and horses when she walked into the small room.

Lester was already inside, sipping a cup of coffee and reading the paper at a small table near the corner window. From his vantage point, he could watch a series of paddocks near the stables.

"Mornin'," he said, rubbing a hand over his chin and looking up at her with worried eyes.

"Is it?" she asked. "You look like something's wrong." She poured a cup of coffee and sat at the table across from the small man. His tanned crowlike features were tight with strain.

"Probably nothin'."

Cradling her cup in her hands, Savannah blew across the hot liquid and arched her black brows inquisitively. "But something's bothering you."

"Yep." The trainer leaned back in his chair and scowled into his cup before glancing up at her. "Just a feeling I've got. Everything was fine when I left here last night."

"I know. I checked the horses after you left."

He brightened. "Did you, now?" Pushing his chair back, he walked over to the wall housing the security alarm. "Then you know about this?"

"What?"

Lester was fingering a loose wire to the control panel. "This must've broken last night."

Savannah felt cold dread slide down her spine and her muscles went rigid. She set her cup on the table and walked over to the alarm system controls. "I didn't touch it last night," she said, studying the broken wire. "I used my key to get into the barns and then I came up here with some files."

"Was the wire broken then?"

"I don't know, I didn't notice." She saw the worry in Lester's eyes and read his thoughts. "You think it might have been cut?"

"Nope."

Savannah relaxed, but her relief was short-lived.

"Pulled maybe, but not cut. The break isn't clean." He rubbed his jaw thoughtfully. "It could've just worn out or it could've been yanked on purpose."

"But why?" She thought about the horses; they were valuable, but it would be difficult to steal any of them. The same was true of the equipment. There was no cash in the office, nor any to speak of on the grounds. And the broken wire wasn't enough damage for vandals. "Have you checked the horses?"

"All safe and accounted for."

"No other damage?"

"None that I've found, and I've looked."

"Then it must have just snapped on its own."

Lester frowned, his lower lip protruding thoughtfully. "But it seems strange it should happen when Reginald is out of town, and just a couple of days after Travis shows up."

Savannah's stomach knotted at the implication. "You think Travis had something to do with this?"

"No." The old man shook his head and scowled. "That boy's straight as an arrow. But there's a lot of people interested in his campaign...or lack thereof."

"I can't believe that a broken wire has anything to do with political intrigue," she said, taking a calming swallow of coffee. Lester came back to the table and stared through the window at the gloomy morning.

"I hope not, missy," he thought aloud. "I sure hope not." His shoulders bowed as he leaned over his luke-warm coffee.

Savannah glanced at the dangling wire. "Maybe it just wore out," she said again, as if to convince herself. "The system's pretty old."

"Maybe." Lester didn't seem to believe a word of it.

"I'll call the people who installed it and see what they come up with."

"Good idea," he muttered, rubbing his scalp.

"Is something else wrong?" Savannah asked.

"Probably nothing, but I just have this feelin'." He laughed at himself. "Maybe I'm just gettin' old. But when I walked into the stallion barn this morning, I sensed, you know, felt that someone was there."

"But no one was?"

"No." He shifted uneasily in his chair. "The stal-lions, well, they seemed different, like they'd already seen someone and then I thought I heard a noise, up in the loft. So I checked." He shrugged his narrow shoul-ders. "Didn't find anything."

"Maybe a mouse?"

"And maybe it was nothin'. I don't hear as well as I used to, y'know."

"Well, just to be on the safe side, have one of the hands search the building for mice, squirrels, rats...and whatever else you can think of. I don't want them eat-ing all the grain."

"Already done," he muttered. "I'll sure be glad when Reginald gets back."

"He'll be home this evening."

"Good."

Lester, who was facing the door, frowned slightly as Travis entered the room. Savannah felt her back go rigid and the argument of the night before echoed in her mind.

"Good morning," Travis drawled, pouring himself a cup of coffee and leaning on a windowsill. He stretched his long legs in front of him and watched Savannah as he took an experimental sip of the hot coffee.

"Mornin', yourself," Lester replied, checking his watch. "I've scheduled Vagabond for a workout in about forty-five minutes. Want to come along?"

"Sure," Travis replied, a leisurely smile stealing across his angular face.

"Savannah?" Lester asked.

She set her empty cup on the table and felt the challenge of Travis's glare. He was watching her every move, expecting her to find a way to avoid being with him.

"Love to," she agreed as pleasantly as possible, meeting his gaze. "Let's see if he's improved any from the last time I saw him run."

"Getting that one to pay attention to the jockey is like trying to tell a rooster to crow at midnight," Lester grumbled. He pushed his fedora onto his head and walked out of the office, leaving Travis and Savannah alone.

Savannah lifted her eyes and stared straight into Travis's amused eyes. He was leaning forward on his elbows, a small smile tugging at the corners of his mouth. "Is something funny?" she demanded.

"I was just wondering if you were still mad?" Travis asked.

"I wasn't mad."

He laughed aloud, surprising Savannah. "And a grizzly bear doesn't have claws."

Ignoring his remark, she stood and walked to the door. It was too early in the morning to be unnerved by Travis's taunting gaze, and Savannah wasn't up to playing word games with him. "I'll see you at the workout track. I'm going to check on the stallions before I watch Vagabond run."

"Any particular reason?"

"I just want to make sure that everything's okay. Lester discovered this." She walked to the alarm control and held up the broken wire and Travis followed. "I just want to double-check on the horses and make sure that the system fell apart on its own and that it wasn't helped along by someone."

He examined the wire carefully. "Do you think it was?"

"No. But I believe in the 'better safe than sorry' theory, especially since Lester thinks he might have heard a noise in the stallion barn this morning." Savannah explained the conversation with Lester to Travis, who listened quietly while he finished his coffee.

The laughter in his eyes faded slightly. "I'll come with you," Travis decided.

"Don't you have anything better to do?"

"Nothing," he said with a lazy grin that cut across his face in a beguiling manner and softened the hard angles, making him seem less distant and allowing a hint of country-boy charm to permeate his tough, touch-me-not exterior. No wonder everyone was anxious to have him run for governor, Savannah thought. If the campaign were decided on looks, virility and charm alone, Travis would win hands down.

"Then let's go," she said a little sharply, angry with herself for the traitorous turn of her thoughts.

"You *are* still mad."

"Just busy." She brushed past him and hurried down the steps to the brick path leading to the stallion barn.

Before she'd gone five steps, Travis had caught up with her and placed a possessive arm around her shoulders. "Lighten up, Savannah," he suggested.

"You should talk."

"At least I don't hold a grudge."

She slid a glance in his direction and found him grinning at her with a smile that melted the ice around her heart. Shivering against the cold air, she tried not to huddle against him. "What're you trying to do?"

"Just prove my undying affection, lady," he quipped, kissing her lightly on the hair.

Just like all the pain of the past nine years didn't exist. Savannah clenched her teeth and walked faster. "So what happened to the outraged, self-righteous lawyer I saw last night?"

"Oh, he's still here," Travis reassured her, "but he's had a good night's sleep and a hot cup of coffee with a beautiful woman."

"I swear, Travis, you could sweet-talk the birds out of the trees one minute, and cook them for dinner the next!"

Travis's laughter rumbled through the early dawn and he hugged her close to his body.

JOSH, HIS SHOULDERS hunched against the rain, was standing at the door of the stallion barn. He'd started toward the house, but stopped when he noticed Savannah and Travis approaching.

"What're you doing here?" Savannah asked when she was close enough for the boy to hear her. "And where's your coat? It's freezing!"

Guilt clouded Josh's young face and Savannah was immediately contrite. Obviously the boy was still brooding about the night before and the last thing he needed was a lecture from her.

"I...I just wanted to see Mystic before I went to school."

"Next time put on a jacket, okay?"

"Okay."

Travis patted Josh firmly between the shoulders. "You like Mystic, don't you?"

"He's great!" Josh said, his dark eyes shining.

"Well, Grandpa would agree with you, and I guess I'd have to, too." Savannah said. "Now, tell me, have you eaten breakfast yet?"

"No."

"I didn't think so. You'd better hurry back to the house and eat something so that you don't miss the bus."

"I don't need breakfast," Josh complained.

Savannah smothered a fond smile for her nephew, forced her features into a hard line and pointed her finger at the house. "Scoot, Josh. You don't want to end up in any more trouble, do ya?"

"I guess not," the boy conceded.

Travis cocked his head toward the house. "Do as your aunt says, and when you get home from school, we'll go cut down a Christmas tree."

Josh, unable to believe his good fortune, looked from Travis to Savannah and back again. "For real?"

"For real," Travis said with a laugh.

"Awesome!" Josh said with a brilliant grin before taking off toward the house at a dead run.

"You won't disappoint him, will you?" Savannah asked, once Josh was out of earshot.

"You know me better than that." Travis hesitated a minute. "Or do you?"

"It's just that I don't want to see Josh disappointed. He's had more than his share of false promises."

"Scout's honor," Travis said, his gray eyes twinkling

in the dim morning light. "I intend to take him looking for a tree this afternoon. You can come along if you like." He pulled her into the circle of his arms and kissed her chilled lips.

Savannah wanted to back away, but couldn't resist the sparkle in his eyes. "I would like. Very much."

"Good, now, why don't you tell me about Josh's fascination with Mystic," Travis suggested, holding the door to the barn open for her.

The scent of warm horses and hay filled the air. The stallions stirred, shifting the straw in their stalls and jingling their halters. Disgusted snorts and a soft nicker filled the long barn as the inquisitive Thoroughbreds poked their heads over the stall doors.

"Maybe it's because Wade wouldn't let him get a dog or a horse of his own. A few years ago, I bought Josh a puppy for his birthday and Wade made him give it away. He called the gift inappropriate for a six-year-old with no sense of responsibility."

Savannah frowned at the memory. "And then, Josh happened to be in the foaling shed when Mystic was born. From that point on, he's had a special feeling for the horse, though it scares Charmaine to death."

Travis closed the door and looked around the barn. Nothing seemed out of place. Graceful horses, shining water buckets, fresh hay and grain stored in barrels filled the long, hall-like room.

"Why is Charmaine afraid of him?"

"Mystic's got what's known as a 'bad rep.'"

"Not the most friendly guy at the track?"

"See for yourself." Savannah was walking to the end of the double row of stalls and Mystic's box. As she walked, she scrutinized the interior of the barn and looked at each of the stallions, talking softly to each one.

The black colt stretched his head over the top rail and snorted at the intrusion. His pointed ears flattened to his head and he nervously paced in his stall. Rippling muscles moved fluidly under a shining black coat.

"I can see why Josh thinks he's special," Travis said, leaning over the rail and looking at the perfect contours of the big ebony colt. Barrel chested, with strong, straight legs and powerful hindquarters, Mystic was a beautifully built Thoroughbred. His dark eyes were sparked by a keen intelligence, his large nostrils flared at the unfamiliar scent. Mystic looked at Travis and shook his head menacingly.

Savannah patted the black nose and Mystic stamped a hoof impatiently. "When Mystic was running, Joshua read the papers every day, out loud, to me. And when Mystic lost to Supreme Court in the Belmont, Josh really took it to heart." Savannah smiled to herself. "To hear Josh tell it, Mystic lost because Supreme Court boxed him in on purpose."

"Is that the truth?"

"My opinion?"

"Yep. And it won't go any further than these—" Travis looked around at the whitewashed barn "—four walls."

"Okay." Savannah folded her arms over the stall door and studied the big colt. "Mystic could have won the race, I think, if the jockey had given him a better ride. However, whether Supreme Court's jockey intentionally boxed Mystic in is neither here nor there. He didn't do anything illegal. Maybe it was strategy, maybe just luck of the draw. The point is, Supreme Court won and Mystic didn't. End of story. Except that everyone expected Mystic to win at Belmont."

Travis slid a glance in Savannah's direction. "Maybe everyone expected too much. Winning the races he had as a two-year-old and topping it off with the Preakness when he was three was no small feat." Travis patted the horse and Mystic backed away. "Sometimes people expect too damned much."

"Are you talking about the horse or yourself?"

He smiled crookedly. "I never could lie to you."

"Only once," she said.

Travis pushed his fingers through his thick hair and shook his head in disgust. "And that was the biggest mistake of my life. I've been paying for it ever since."

Savannah felt her throat become tight. If only she could believe him—just a little. "We can't go back," she said, but Travis turned to face her. His hand reached forward and slid beneath her ponytail to caress her neck.

"Maybe we can, Savannah." His voice was low and intimate and it made her pulse leap. "Maybe we can go back, if we try."

The fingers against her neck were warm and comforting and if she let herself, Savannah could easily remember how desperately she had loved him.

She pulled away from him. "I think it would be best if we forgot what happened between us," she said.

"Do you honestly think that's possible?"

"I don't know." She stared up at him, her gaze entwining in the enigmatic gray of his, before she looked away.

"Why do you keep lying to yourself, Savannah?"

"Do I? Maybe it's easier."

His hand reached forward and twined in the thick rope of her black hair. "You're afraid of me," he accused. He pulled her head back, forcing her to meet the intensity of his gaze.

"Not of you," she whispered. "Of us. The way we feel about each other doesn't make any sense."

"And everything in life has to be rational?"

"Yes."

"Tell me," he said, eyes narrowed, gaze centered on her lips. "How *do* you feel about me?"

"I think I should walk away from you."

Slowly, gently, his fingers caressed her skin. "Okay, that's what you think. Now, answer my question, how do you feel?"

Her breath was shaky, and the feel of his hands against her neck made thinking nearly impossible. "I should hate you," she whispered through clenched teeth.

"But you don't."

"You lied to me! Used me! Left me! And now you're back." He was toying with the edge of her jacket, his fingers grazing the soft skin at the base of her throat. She tried to jerk away, but his fingers took hold of the lapels of her coat. "I should hate you for what you did to me and what you're insinuating about Dad!"

"I don't think you're capable of hate."

"Then you don't know me very well."

"Oh, I know you, Savannah," he said, his face only inches from hers. "I know you better than you do yourself."

And then he kissed her, long and hard. A kiss so filled with passion that it killed all the protests in her mind and held at bay her doubts. The sweet pressure of his lips crushing against hers helped the years and the pain slip away. The hand on her nape explored the neckline of her jacket and her pulse began to throb expectantly.

She felt his tongue slide between her teeth and she welcomed the sweet taste of him. He drew her close and her own hands were fumbling with the buttons of his suede jacket. She touched the soft flannel shirt that covered the corded muscles of his chest. An ache, deep and powerful, began to burn deep within her.

"I've always loved you, Savannah," he whispered against her midnight-black hair. "God help me, I've always loved you," he confessed, "even when I was married to Melinda."

"Don't—"

His lips cut off any further protest as he kissed her with the surging passion of nine lost years. His fingers twined in her hair, pulling her head backward and exposing the gentle curve of her neck. "Being near you is driving me out of my mind," he whispered. "Do you know, can you imagine, how much self-control it took not to follow you into your bedroom last night?"

Easily, she thought, falling against him and returning the fever of his kiss. "This…this can't, it won't work."

"Savannah, listen to me!" His gray eyes were filled with conviction. "Just trust me. For once in your life, trust me."

"I already tried that, nine years ago!"

"And I won't hurt you again." The honesty in his gaze touched the darkest corners of her soul.

Trust him, dear Lord.

Without any further questions, Travis lifted her into his arms and carried her to an empty stall at the end of the barn. He tossed his jacket down on the clean hay, and gently lay her upon it. Slowly, he untied the thong restraining her hair. The black curls tumbled free.

The zipper of her jacket slid easily open and he helped her out of it as he kissed her face and neck.

"Travis, I don't think—"

"Good!" Kissing her hungrily, he molded her body to his, her soft contours fitting against the harder lines of his frame. His breathing was erratic, his heartbeat as wild as her own.

She pressed against him, unaware of anything but the

sweet taste of his tongue sliding over her teeth and the warmth of his hands as they pulled the wide neck of her sweater down her shoulder to expose the white skin of her breast.

He kissed her feverishly and she returned his passion, her fingers working on the buttons of his jacket and sliding it down the length of his muscular arms. He tossed it aside and jerked the sweater over her head to gaze at the rounded swell of her breasts peeking over the lacy fabric of her camisole.

Dark points protruded upward against the lace, inviting the warmth of his mouth. He took one soft mound into his mouth, moistening the sheer fabric and caressing the nipple with his tongue. Savannah writhed beneath him, the sweet torment he was applying to her breast a welcome relief. She curled her fingers into his thick hair, holding on to his head as if to life itself.

"I've missed you," he whispered hoarsely, his breath fanning the wet fabric and the throbbing peak beneath.

And I've missed you.

He slid one of the straps of the camisole over her shoulder, baring the firm breast to him, and he gazed upon the swollen mound hungrily before caressing it with his lips.

Savannah shuddered as he lowered the other strap over her shoulder. She was lying half-naked on the straw, her dark hair billowing away from her face, her blue eyes dusky with passion.

Slowly he unbuttoned his shirt.

Savannah stared upward to watch the ripple of his muscles as he tossed the unwanted garment aside. "This time I'll make it right," he vowed, lowering himself over her and watching as her fingers reached upward to caress the dark hairs on his chest.

"And this time I won't expect more than you can give,"

she whispered, trembling as his lips found hers and his weight fell across her. The hard muscles of his chest rubbed against her breasts, the soft hair teasing her nipples as his hands splayed against the small of her back, pulling her so close that she could hear the erratic beat of his heart. Fingertips brushed past the waistband of her jeans, tantalizing the skin above her buttocks.

Liquid fire began to spread through her body as he touched and caressed her.

"I love you, Savannah," he vowed, his breath fanning the hollow of her throat.

When she didn't respond, he stared into the blue intensity of her eyes. "I love you," he repeated.

"But...but I don't want to fall in love with you," she said, her throat tight. "Not again."

"You're afraid to trust me." It wasn't a question, just a simple, but distasteful, statement of fact. Travis pulled away from her, rubbed his hand behind his neck and muttered a rather unkind oath at himself.

Savannah was left lying on the straw, feeling very naked and vulnerable. "Can't we just leave love out of it?"

He looked disdainfully over his shoulder. "Is that the way you want it? Just sex? No emotion?"

Blushing slightly, Savannah looked away and reached for her sweater.

Travis laughed bitterly and glanced at the rafters. "I didn't think so." He curled his fist and slammed it into the side of the stall next to Mystic. The colt snorted nervously. "Dear God, woman, what am I going to do with you?"

"As if you have any say in my life."

"I sure as hell do," he said. His gray eyes gleamed possessively.

With unsteady fingers, she tugged the sweater over

her head, squared her shoulders, jutted her chin and faced him again. "I think it's time to go watch Vagabond. *If* you're still interested."

"Wouldn't miss it for the world," he said, sliding a bemused glance up her body.

Anger surged through her at the insolence of his stare. Plunging her arms through the sleeves of her jacket, she began to stand, but Travis reached for her wrist and restrained her. "I just hope that someday soon you'll get over your bull-headed pride and realize that you still love me."

"Dreamer."

"Am I?" His gaze slid down her neck, to the pulse jumping at her throat. "I don't think so." The confident smile that crossed his face was nearly a smirk. "Let me know when you change your mind."

"I won't."

He lifted a dubious dark brow. "Then I'll just have to convince you, won't I?" He pulled on her wrist, drawing her closer, but she jerked away and raised her hand to slap him, then thought better of it when she recognized the glittering challenge in his eyes.

"You're an impossible, insufferable, arrogant bastard. You know that, don't you?" she accused, walking toward the door.

"And you've got the cutest behind I've ever seen."

She twirled and faced him, her face suffused with rage. "That's exactly what I mean. What kind of infantile, chauvinistic male remark was that?"

"The kind that gets your attention," he said, sobering as he stood. He picked up his shirt and held it in his hands, his naked chest a silent invitation. The lean muscles of his abdomen and chest, the curling dark hair arrowing below the waistband of his low-slung jeans and the tight muscles of his thighs and hips, hidden only by the worn fabric of his jeans, all worked together to form a bold male image in the harsh lights of the barn. "I'm just waiting for you to realize that I'm not about to make the same mistake I did nine years ago."

Her blue eyes sparked. "Neither am I!" she said over her shoulder, her small fists balling and her heart slamming wildly in her chest. "Neither am I."

VAGABOND WAS ALREADY on the track by the time Savannah met Lester at the railing. It had just begun to rain and Lester was leaning over the top rail of the fence studying a stopwatch as Vagabond raced passed, his graceful strides carrying him effortlessly over the ground. Lester flicked the watch with his thumb and smiled to himself.

"That was a helluva time," he muttered, his gray brows quirking upward in appreciation as his eyes followed the galloping bay. "He's got it in him. Faster than Mystic, he is."

"I thought you were all for selling him," Savannah teased, stuffing her hands into her pockets and hunching her shoulders against the cold drizzle. She knew that Travis had joined them, but refused to look at him or acknowledge his presence. "Or have you changed your mind in the last couple of days?"

"It's controlling him that worries me," Lester remarked.

"Makes your job interesting," Travis observed.

Lester laughed and watched as the colt took one final turn around the track at a slow gallop. "That it does," he agreed, his black eyes never leaving the horse. "That it does." He waved to the rider and called, "Go ahead and take him inside. That's enough for today."

Lester rubbed his hands together and turned toward

the stables before hazarding a glance at Travis. "I always wondered why you didn't stick it out, here on the farm."

"Funny," Travis replied, his gaze shifting to Savannah, "lately I've been wondering the same thing myself."

"We could still use you, y'know. Always need a man who knows horses." He walked toward the stables and Savannah felt Travis's eyes on her back.

"Do you think I should take his advice and stay?" he asked.

Savannah's heart nearly stopped beating. "I think it would be the worst mistake of your life," she lied before turning toward the house and walking away from him.

JOSHUA WAS RELEASED from school early for the holidays. He raced into the house at one-thirty and threw his books on the kitchen table.

"What's the rush?" Savannah asked. She was sitting at the table, trying to balance her checkbook. Deciding that a five-dollar discrepancy with the bank wasn't a life-or-death situation, she stuffed the statement and checks back into the envelope and focused all of her attention on her nephew.

"Don't you remember?" Josh asked. "Travis said we could all go out and cut a Christmas tree today!"

"He said what?" Charmaine asked, walking into the room and frowning at the untidy pile of books on the table.

"That we could go cut a Christmas tree today," Josh repeated, grabbing an apple from a basket on the kitchen counter and biting into the crisp fruit.

"But Grandpa usually buys one in Sacramento," Charmaine said, looking from Savannah to Josh and back again.

"I know," Savannah said. "But Travis did promise."

"When?"

"This morning. Before breakfast at the stallion barn."

"Were you out there again?" Charmaine asked, paling as she turned to the boy.

Josh froze.

"How many times do I have to tell you not to go out there unless you're with Daddy or Grandpa? Those stallions are dangerous!" Charmaine warned.

Travis walked in from the back porch and heard the tail end of the conversation. "It was all right, Charmaine. Savannah and I were out there."

"I don't like it," Charmaine replied. "Mystic almost killed Lester last year, did you know that? And another time he kicked one of his grooms and nearly broke the man's leg."

"He wouldn't kick me, Mom."

"How do you know that? He's an animal, Joshua, and he can't be trusted. Now you don't go out to that barn again without Grandpa. Got it?"

"Got it," Josh mumbled, his eyes downcast and his small jaw firm with rebellion.

"Hey, sport. Come on, let's go get that tree," Travis said, patting the boy on the shoulders. "Want to come?" he asked Charmaine.

Charmaine hesitated, but shook her head. "I'd better not. Someone has to stay with Mother and I've got something I've got to get done in the studio, if you don't mind me up there, Travis."

"No, that's fine," he replied.

"That's okay, I'll go," Savannah said, hoping to ease some of Josh's disappointment.

Charmaine sighed in relief.

A few minutes later, Travis, Savannah, Josh and Archimedes were piled into a pickup and driving along the rutted lane through the back pastures leading to the hills. Snow mixed with rain began to collect on the windshield.

"Maybe it'll snow for Christmas," Josh said excitedly, looking out the window as the wet flakes drifted to the ground and melted.

"I wouldn't count on it," Savannah said.

"Spoilsport," Travis accused, but laughed. "Now, tell me, what's all this nonsense about Mystic nearly killing Lester."

"He didn't!" Josh said. "No way!"

"Lester slipped when he was in Mystic's stall and the horse stepped on him. It was an accident and not very serious."

"You're sure?"

"Lester is and everyone else agrees except Charmaine," Savannah said.

"Mom's just freaked out by Mystic, that's all."

As Travis drove up the lower slopes of the hills, the snow was definitely sticking, and Josh's spirits soared.

The boy continued to search the forested hills for the perfect Christmas tree. "There's one," he said for the fiftieth time as he pointed to a small fir tree.

"Not big enough," Travis thought aloud, but parked the truck to the side of the road near a clearing.

While Travis pulled the hatchet out of the back of the truck, Josh and Savannah, with Archimedes on their heels, scoured the woods. The snow was clinging to the branches of the trees, dusting the evergreens with a fine mantle of white and clinging to the blackened branches of the leafless maples and oaks.

Josh hurried ahead with Archimedes. Travis caught up with Savannah and placed an arm comfortably over her shoulders. "This is how it should be, y'know," he said, watching Archimedes scare a winter bird from the brush. "You, me, a kid or two, a lop-eared dog and Christmas."

Savannah smiled and shook her head. Snowflakes clung to her hair and melted on her face. "The way it should have been, you mean."

"It still could be, Savannah."

Her heart nearly stopped beating. "You're very persuasive, counselor," she said, refusing to argue with him in the wintry afternoon. Snow continued to fall and cling to the branches of the trees. The mountains seemed to disappear in the clouds.

"Along with self-righteous, insufferable, impossible and arrogant?"

Savannah smiled. "All of the above."

"I hope so, lady," he whispered against the melting drops of snow in her ebony hair. "I hope to God that I'm as persuasive as you seem to think."

"Over here!" Josh shouted, and they followed his voice until they came upon him almost dancing around a twelve-foot fir. "It's perfect!"

"I thought the word was 'awesome,'" Savannah said with a smile, and Travis laughed, giving her a hug.

While Travis trimmed off the lower branches and cut the tree, Josh ran through the forest and tossed snowballs at an unsuspecting Archimedes. The spotted sheepdog barked and bounded through the brush.

When Josh's back was turned, Savannah hurled a snowball at him, and it landed on his shoulder. Josh whirled and began throwing snowballs at Savannah so rapidly that she had to dodge behind a tree for protection. When she was brave enough to peek around the protective trunk of the oversize maple, two snowballs whizzed past her nose. Travis had gotten into the game and was quickly packing another frozen missile.

"No fair!" she called. "Two against one."

"You've got Archimedes, remember?" Josh taunted with a grin.

"Four-footed allies don't count. Oh!" A snowball landed in the middle of her back and she turned to face Travis, who had sneaked around the maple tree. "Enough already. I give!"

"Don't I wish," Travis murmured, a smile lurking on his lips before he wrapped his arms around her and kissed her feverishly. Josh continued the assault, and Travis had to let go of Savannah. He switched alliances and began hurling snowballs at the boy until Josh squealed and laughed his surrender.

"Okay, let's call it quits and get the tree into the truck!" Travis suggested, dusting the snow from his jacket as he looked at the sky. "It looks like this storm isn't going to let up, so we'd better get back to the farm while we still can."

Josh's brown eyes were shining with merriment, his grin stretching from one ear to the other, as Travis and Savannah loaded the tree into the back of the pickup for the drive back to the farm.

The rutted lane was slippery, and the truck lurched, pushing Savannah closer to Travis. She tried to keep to her side of the seat, but the warmth of his thigh pressing against her was irresistible. It even felt natural when Travis's fingers grazed her knee as he shifted gears.

With a sinking sensation, she realized that despite her vows to herself, she was falling in love with him all over again.

CHAPTER FIVE

THE LIVING ROOM smelled of fir boughs, scented candles, burning wood and hot chocolate. Savannah was still helping Josh trim the tree, although Charmaine had already taken Virginia upstairs. The night was peaceful and still, with snow collecting in the corners of the windowpanes and the lights from the tree reflecting on the glass. A fire was glowing warmly in the fireplace. It crackled against the pitchy fir log in the grate.

Savannah set her empty mug on the mantel before stepping on the ladder and trying to straighten the star on the top of the tree.

"I wish Travis would come help us," Josh complained, placing a bright ornament on the bough closest to him.

Savannah slanted the boy an affectionate grin. "He will."

"When?"

She shrugged. "Whenever he's finished."

"What's taking him so long?"

"I haven't the foggiest," Savannah replied truthfully. "He said he had some paperwork to finish." Sighing when the star refused to remain upright on the tree, she climbed down the ladder.

"So why is he locked in Grandpa's study?"

"Good question," she admitted, sneaking a glance through the archway, across the foyer to the locked door of the study. "I guess he needs privacy...to concentrate."

"On what?"

"Look, Josh, I really don't know," she admitted.

"Grandpa doesn't like anyone in his study," Josh said.

"I know, but it's all right for Travis to be in there; he's the attorney for the farm."

"Well, I wish he'd get done."

"So do I." Savannah picked up the empty mugs. "What about another cup of cocoa?"

"Sure!"

"You finish with the tree and I'll be back in a flash," she said with a smile as she walked out of the living room and paused at the door of the study. Travis had locked himself inside nearly two hours before. When she'd asked him to stay and trim the tree after he'd placed it in the stand, he'd shaken his head and told her he had something he needed to do before Reginald and Wade returned. His eyes had darkened mysteriously and Savannah had experienced a feathering of dread climb up her spine.

She knocked softly on the door. Travis opened it almost immediately and she couldn't help but smile at him. A rebellious lock of his chestnut-colored hair had fallen over his forehead and the sleeves of his sweater were pushed over his forearms.

"You're a sight for sore eyes," he said, his voice low.

"So why lock yourself away?" She looked past him to the interior of the room. It was obvious that Travis had been working at her father's desk. An untidy stack of papers littered the desktop and the checkbook for the farm was lying open on a nearby chair.

"Business." The lines between his eyebrows deepened and he frowned slightly.

"Can't you even take time out to see the tree? Josh is dying to show it to you."

"In a minute."

She angled her chin up at him and sighed loudly. "Okay, you win. Go ahead and be mysterious. How about a cup of coffee or some hot chocolate?"

He smiled at her, but shook his head. "I'm just about done in here, then I'll join the rest of the family. Okay?"

"Scrooge," she murmured and he kissed her softly on the nose.

"Be sure to put up the mistletoe," he commanded with a suggestive smile teasing his lips. Then he turned back to the study, entered and closed the door behind him.

"Merry Christmas to you, too," Savannah remarked.

Puzzled by Travis's behavior, she walked into the kitchen and refilled the mugs. Why was Travis looking through the books of the farm? An uneasy feeling stole over her, but she tried to forget about it. The day with Travis and Josh had been too wonderful to spoil with unfounded worries or fears. Travis certainly wasn't hurting anything. Besides, Wade and Reginald were due home any minute. Their arrival was enough of a problem for her to deal with.

Carrying the steaming cups back into the living room, she found Josh returning tissue paper into the packing boxes that had housed the ornaments for the past year.

"It's the best tree ever!" Josh exclaimed proudly as he stood and took a cup from Savannah's outstretched hand.

"I think you're right." Savannah laughed.

"We should go get Travis and Mom."

"In a minute, sport. First let's finish and clean up this mess." She gestured to the empty boxes stacked haphazardly around the tree. "You've done a good job, but we've got a lot of work ahead of us."

The sound of a car's engine caught Savannah's attention, and she felt her pulse jump nervously.

"Looks like Grandpa and your dad finally made it,"

she said to Josh, who was carrying a load of empty boxes out of the living room to the closet under the stairs in the foyer. "And only three hours late."

"About time," Josh mumbled.

"They couldn't help the fact that the airport's a mess because of the snow. Even the weathermen weren't pre-pared for a storm like this," she said cautiously when Josh returned. "Come on, let's not borrow trouble, huh?"

"Okay."

Just then the front door opened and Reginald strode into the living room.

"Well, what do we have here?" Reginald asked, eye-ing the tree while pulling off his gloves. He unwrapped the scarf from around his neck and tossed both it and the gloves onto the couch.

"You know, Grandpa! It's the tree!" Josh exclaimed with excitement. "Aunt Savvy and Travis and I went to get it today, up in the hills! We even had a snowball fight!"

"Did you now?" Reginald took off his coat and tossed it over the back of one of the wing chairs before patting the boy on the head and admiring the tree. "Who won?"

"Travis and me!"

Reginald glanced at Savannah. "Two on one?"

"Archimedes was on my team," she said wryly. "He wasn't too much help."

"I'll bet not," Reginald said with a hearty laugh.

"So what do ya think of the tree?" Josh asked.

Walking around the Christmas tree, Reginald sur-veyed it with a practiced eye. "You picked a winner, my boy."

"I found it all by myself, but Travis had to cut it down."

Reginald winked fondly at his grandchild. "Next year you'll probably be able to handle it all by yourself."

"Maybe," Josh agreed.

"So where is everyone?" Reginald asked, facing Savannah.

"Charmaine took Mom upstairs about forty-five minutes ago."

A thoughtful frown pinched the features of Reginald's tanned face and he glanced up the stairs. "Tell me, how's your mother been?"

"Actually, Mom's been a little better since Travis came back to the farm. Having him here seems to have lifted her spirits a bit. She's had dinner downstairs twice and she helped trim the tree until just a little while ago."

"That's good," the older man said with obvious relief. "Maybe I'd better run up and check on her."

"You'd never hear the end of it if you didn't."

As Reginald left the room, Wade entered the house. His leather shoes clicked loudly against the tiled floor of the foyer as he approached the living room. His even-featured face was tight with tension, his taffy-colored hair slightly mussed.

Josh visibly stiffened at the sight of his father.

"Hi, Dad," the boy said. "See the tree? Travis and I cut it down."

At the mention of Travis's name, Wade frowned and tugged on his mustache. "Oh, ah, it looks good," Wade said without much enthusiasm and glanced at the clock. "What're you doing up so late?"

"Josh helped me decorate the tree," Savannah cut in, trying to avoid the argument she felt brewing in the air. "He's done a terrific job, hasn't he?"

"Terrific," Wade repeated without a smile.

"We're just about finished," Savannah explained.

"Good. It's a school night, isn't it?"

Josh shook his head and grinned. "School's out for vacation."

Wade scowled. "Doesn't matter. It's late."

"But Aunt Savvy said—"

"No 'buts' about it, son!" Wade snapped, his short temper flaring. "I'm home now and you'll do as I say." Then, feeling slightly embarrassed, Wade gestured toward the boxes still lying on the floor. "You finish up here right away and go upstairs. I've got business to discuss privately with your grandfather."

Josh wanted to argue, but Savannah wouldn't let him. "We'll be done in no time, right, sport?"

"Right," Josh mumbled, bending over to pick up the loose boxes.

Once Wade was convinced that Josh was going to obey him, he took Savannah's arm and pulled her away from the tree, close to the windows. "Where's McCord?" he demanded.

"In the study. He said he'd be here in a minute."

Wade paled a bit and his eyes hardened. "What the hell's he doing in the study? Dammit, he comes back here one day and just takes the hell over! Why is he in Reginald's den?"

"I don't know. You'll have to ask him." She looked over Wade's shoulder and saw Travis striding across the hall, his hands thrust into the back pockets of his cords, his sleeves still pushed over his forearms. His mouth was pinched into a tight, angry line that softened slightly as he met Savannah's worried gaze.

"What do you think?" Joshua asked, stepping away from the brightly lit tree.

"Best tree I've ever seen," Travis said with a brilliant smile for the boy. "Maybe you should go into the business!"

"And maybe he should go upstairs to bed," Wade grumbled, raising his eyebrows at his son. Then, as if dismissing the child ended that particular conversation, Wade turned all of his attention to Travis. "Now, Mc-Cord, what the hell's going on? What's all this nonsense about you not running for governor?"

"It's not nonsense," Travis replied, helping Josh with a stack of boxes. "Just the facts." He carried them out of the room and stacked them in the closet under the stairs.

"Great!" Wade muttered, swearing under his breath. He pushed himself out of the chair, walked over to the bar at the end of the room and poured himself a stiff drink.

"Dad," Josh interrupted, sensing the growing tension in the air and trying to find some way of easing it. "Travis cut this tree down all by himself."

Wade looked at his son as if seeing him for the first time. In an obvious attempt to control his irritation with the boy, he gripped his glass so tightly his knuckles whitened. "I think you already said that, son, and I told you I liked it."

"Aunt Savvy says it's awesome."

"Well, she's right, isn't she?" Reginald said, walking back into the room, picking up Josh and hugging the boy to his broad chest. "The important thing is that I think Santa Claus will be able to find it."

"There is no Santa Claus," Josh replied, wearing his most grown-up expression.

"No!" Reginald expressed mock horror and both Josh and Savannah laughed. "I'm going into the kitchen to look for a snack—why don't you come, too?" he asked the boy.

Josh smiled but shook his head. "Not until I finish the tree," he said.

"Have it your way," the old man said, beaming at his grandson before heading into the kitchen.

Charmaine came down the stairs and entered the living room. "You did a wonderful job on the tree," she said to her son before noticing the hard line of Wade's jaw and the glittering challenge in Travis's eye. "Come on, Josh, I think it's time you went to bed," she suggested.

"Not yet."

"You heard your mother," Wade said, irritably waving the boy off. "Go upstairs."

Josh mutinously stood his ground. "But I'm not done fixin' the tree."

Wade tensed and his eyes turned cold. "It'll wait."

"Please?"

Oh, Josh, don't push it, Savannah thought, searching for a way to avoid the fight that was in the air.

"No, son! You heard me! Get your butt upstairs right now!"

"But, Dad—"

"Don't argue with me!" Wade snapped, color flooding his face, rage exploding in his eyes.

"It's just one night," Savannah protested, instinctively standing closer to Josh, as if to protect the boy. "We're almost finished, aren't we, Josh?"

Wade's eyes were as frigid as ice. "This is none of your business, Savannah. Josh needs his sleep and I want to talk to Reginald and McCord alone." His stern gaze rested on the boy. "Now go upstairs and don't push it, Josh, or there just might not be a Christmas this year."

"Wade!" Charmaine whispered sharply, but held her tongue when her husband's eyes flashed angrily in her direction.

"There's always a Christmas," Josh said, holding his ground.

"Not if you're bad," Wade warned the boy.

"I'm *not* bad."

"We know that," Travis cut in. "You're a good kid, Josh. Don't let anyone tell you differently." He turned deadly eyes in Wade's direction, slicing through the blond man's angry veneer. "I'm sure you dad didn't quite mean it the way it came out."

Wade glanced around the room, obviously embarrassed, and then finished his drink in a quick swallow before quickly pouring another stiff shot. Though he attempted to control his anger, his seething temper was visible in the muscle working in his jaw. "Sure," he said unsteadily, smoothing his hair with quaking fingers. "You're a good kid, that's why you'll behave and go upstairs."

"Come on, Josh," Savannah said, offering a hand to lead him out of the room.

"Just butt out, Savannah," Wade exploded. His entire body was beginning to shake with the anger he could no longer contain. "Just butt the hell out of my son's life!"

Travis became rigid. "Benson—"

"This is between my son and me!" Wade growled, turning his furious gaze on Josh and spilling some of his drink. The sloshed alcohol infuriated him further. "Now march yourself up those stairs right now, young man!"

"No!"

"I mean it!" Wade's face was red with fury as he set his drink on a table and advanced toward the boy.

"Leave him alone," Travis warned, reaching forward. He caught hold of the back of Wade's jacket, but the incensed man wriggled free of Travis's grip.

"Wade, don't!" Charmain pleaded, hurrying forward, but she was too late.

"I hate you," Josh said, standing proudly before Wade's wrath.

"You need to learn to respect your father," Wade returned. "And I'll teach you!" Quick as a snake striking, Wade raised his hand and slapped the boy across the cheek. The blow had enough force to send Josh reeling into the Christmas tree.

Savannah gasped. Tinsel and glass ornaments clinked on the wobbling tree.

Travis was in time to stop the second blow from landing. He grabbed Wade by the back of the neck and spun him around. Every muscle in Travis's body was bunched, ready to strike, and the fire in his eyes burned with rage. "You dumb bastard," he growled, looking as if he wanted to kill Wade. His hands tightened powerfully over Wade's shoulders. "Leave the boy alone."

"This has nothing to do with you, McCord."

"It does as long as I'm here. Now leave him alone or I'll give you a little of your own."

"He's not your kid," Wade replied, whirling on his heel, fists clenched as he faced Josh again.

"I wish I was!" Josh shouted, his eyes filled with tears, one hand rubbing the bright red mark on his face. "I know you hate me and I wish I wasn't your son."

"You little—"

"Stop it!" Savannah warned, grabbing Josh and pulling him close to her. "Stop it, all of you!" She felt the warmth of the boy's tears against her blouse. "Josh, oh, Josh," she murmured, kissing his hair. "Don't you ever so much as come near him again," she said, her cold eyes clashing with Wade's.

"You've got no say in it. Josh is my son."

Josh held his cheek and glared upward at his father with open hatred in his young, tear-filled eyes. "You never wanted me," he said between sobs. "But that's okay, because I don't want you either!"

"Josh, no," Charmaine whispered, ignoring her husband and walking to the boy. When Wade took a step toward the child again, Charmaine whirled toward her husband. "Don't you touch him," she threatened. "I mean it, Wade, don't you ever lay one finger on my child!" She straightened and took Josh's small hand in hers. Though she was pale, she managed to square her shoulders and lift her chin proudly. "Come on, Josh. Let's go upstairs." Her lips were white when she added, "Daddy's just tired from his long flight!"

Josh looked at Savannah, and she offered him an encouraging smile. "I'll be up in a few minutes to read you a story…or maybe you can read one to me. Okay?"

"Okay," he whispered, his voice breaking.

Once Josh and Charmaine were out of the room, Savannah, her hands shaking with rage, advanced upon her brother-in-law. All of the worry and anger that had been building over the past few months erupted. "If you ever strike that child again, I'll call the police and have you brought up on charges," she warned, pointing a finger at her brother-in-law and wishing she could strangle him.

"Don't go off the deep end, Savannah," Wade said nervously. He finished his drink, walked to the far end of the room, behind the couch to the bar and poured himself a glass of brandy.

"I'll back her up," Travis said.

"The boy was out of line," Wade pointed out.

"He's just a child!" Savannah said. "A very confused child who feels unwanted and unloved!"

"A lot you know about it," Wade threw back at her.

"I know your boy better than you do," she said in a low voice, accusations forming in her eyes. "And I have enough common sense not to humiliate him in front of his family!"

"He was asking for it." Wade tossed back his drink, but some of his determination seemed to dissolve under Savannah's attack. When he lifted his glass to his lips his hands shook.

"You touch that kid again and I'll personally beat the hell out of you," Travis said calmly, walking over to the bar and pouring himself a drink. He leaned close to Wade, grabbed one of the lapels of Wade's suit and tightened his fingers around the polished fabric before smiling with wicked satisfaction. "And don't think I wouldn't enjoy every minute of it."

Wade had trouble swallowing his drink.

Reginald had walked back into the room and heard the last part of the conversation. "He will, you know," he said, nodding his agreement. "When Travis was about eighteen, I saw him beat the tar out of a kid a couple of years older and forty pounds heavier than he was. I'd listen to his threats if I were you."

"Now wait just a minute," Wade admonished, jerking at the knot of his tie and trying to repair some of his bruised dignity. "Don't tell me you're on his—" he hooked a thumb in Travis's direction "—side!"

"We're talking about my only grandson, Wade," Reginald pointed out as he sat uncomfortably on the corner of the stiff velvet couch. "I know Josh has a mouth on him, but you'd better find a way of dealing with it."

"I am."

"Poorly," Travis said, sipping his drink and smiling to himself.

"I didn't fly two thousand miles to hear about how I raise my kid," Wade said, straightening his vest.

"Then you shouldn't have made a public spectacle of yourself," Travis muttered.

Wade shifted his gaze around the room and cleared his throat. "I think it's time we got down to business."

"Not yet." Travis finished his drink and set it on the bar. "First I think I'll check on *your* kid."

With this pointed remark, he walked across the room to Savannah, took her hand and led her up the stairs.

"Bastard," Travis whispered, his jaw thrust forward and his gray eyes dark with anger.

"You'll get no argument from me," Savannah agreed. When they reached the top of the stairs, Savannah could hear Joshua sobbing in his room. "Oh, no," she said with a sigh. She hesitated before knocking softly on his door. "Josh?"

"Yeah?"

"Are you okay?"

Charmaine opened the door and though she was pale and her eyes were red, she managed a thin smile. "We're okay," she said.

"You're sure?" Savannah looked from her sister to Josh, who looked small and vulnerable beneath the covers of his bed.

"Yes."

"Yeah," Josh agreed, sniffing back his tears.

Savannah's heart went out to the brave boy. "You still want me to read you a story?"

Josh shrugged, but seemed to brighten. "Sure."

"Good. Just give me a few minutes, okay?"

"Okay."

Charmaine had come into the hall and Travis touched her lightly on the shoulder. "Will you be all right?"

She swallowed back her tears. "I think so."

"You don't have to take that kind of treatment, you know."

Rolling her eyes to the ceiling she visibly fought the urge to break down. "Are you speaking as a divorce lawyer?"

Travis shook his head and his shoulders slumped a little. "As a friend. There's just no reason to put up with any kind of abuse—mental or physical."

"It won't happen again," Charmaine insisted, though she couldn't meet Travis's concerned gaze. "Just let me have a little time with Josh alone. And...I'll be able to handle Wade."

"You're sure?" Savannah asked.

"Of course." Charmaine wiped away her tears and forced a trembling grin. "I've got that man wrapped around my little finger."

"Oh, Charmaine—"

"Shh. You go on. Maybe you two can find out what's eating at him."

I wish, Savannah thought hopelessly. She left Josh's room with the feeling of impending doom.

"Has it always been this bad?" Travis asked, placing a comforting arm around her.

"Never," she whispered. "I've never seen Wade hit Josh." She shuddered at the memory. "I didn't think it would come to a physical battle."

"You think it was the first time?"

"It better have been," she said, her anger resurfacing and her blue eyes sparking, "and it had damn well better be the last!"

When they entered the living room again, Wade was standing by the fireplace, one arm poised on the Italian marble of the mantel, his other holding a drink. He seemed somewhat calmer as he looked from Travis to Savannah and frowned.

"Okay, McCord," he said, glancing at Reginald before studying the amber liquid in his glass. "I guess I got out of line. I admit it." Shifting from one foot to the other, he sighed and shook his head. "I'm sorry."

"You're apologizing to the wrong person," Travis said coldly.

"Yes. Well, I'll take care of that. Later. Now, why aren't you running for governor?"

"I'm just not interested."

"You can't be serious."

"I am. I told you that before."

Wade pushed the hair from his eyes and looked to Reginald, who was seated in his favorite chair near the window.

"Why do you care?" Travis asked, leaning against the bar.

Savannah took a seat on the couch, not really wanting to be a part of the conversation, but not knowing how to avoid it.

"Because a lot of time, effort, and money has already been spent toward your candidacy."

"Maybe someone should have cleared all that with me."

"You were too busy—or don't you remember?—playing hero with that Eldridge decision. You were thinking about running. Anyway, that's what you told Reginald."

"And you just assumed that I would follow through."

"A natural assumption, I'd say."

"So you already started collecting campaign contributions, working with my partner on the books of the company and God only knows what else." Travis's jaw had hardened and his eyes glittered angrily.

"Reginald was counting on you."

"Were you?" Travis demanded, sliding a glance in the older man's direction.

"Seems a shame to throw away an opportunity like this," Reginald said. "And yes, I'd say I was counting on the fact that you'd run," he admitted, reaching into the pocket of his vest and withdrawing a pipe.

There was a tense silence in the room as Reginald lit the pipe.

"Even if I did run," Travis thought aloud, "there's a damned good chance that I wouldn't win in the primary, much less take the general election! Why's it so damned important?"

"Reginald has plans," Wade said.

"Well, maybe he should have let me in on them!" Travis walked over and stood in front of Reginald. "Ever since I was a seventeen-year-old kid, I've tried to please you, to the point that sometimes what I wanted got tangled up in what you wanted from me. Well, that just doesn't work anymore."

Reginald ran his fingers around the bowl of his pipe, glanced at Wade and scowled at the brightly lit tree.

Travis sighed loudly and rubbed the tired muscles at the base of his neck. "So, I think we should do something about all those contributions Willis Henderson and the rest of you took in my name. I expect them returned to the people who gave you the money. I want it all over by the end of the year. And I'll pay interest on any of the contributions."

"You don't understand—" Wade said.

"And I don't want to." Travis held Reginald's gaze. "I'm out of it. I don't like the feel of politics any better than I like the feel of corporate fighting, divorces, child-custody hearings or any of the rest of the bullshit that goes with being a lawyer."

"You liked the glory from the Eldridge case," Reginald remarked, puffing quietly on his pipe. The smell of the rich smoke wafted through the room.

"Even that went sour," Travis said, finishing his drink.

"But you can't just drop out," Reginald said, lifting a hand.

"I already have. Talk to Henderson. He knows that I'm serious." Travis stretched and set his glass on the mantel before leaning over the back of a velvet sofa and staring at the Christmas tree. "I don't know exactly why it was so damned important that I run for governor of this state, but I'm really not interested."

"I've worked a long time to see that day when you'd take office," Reginald whispered, as if to himself. Disillusion weighed heavily on the old man's face.

Savannah could almost feel her father's disappointment.

Travis smiled cynically. "I'd like to say that I'm sorry if I interrupted any of your plans, but I'm not. I don't like the way all of you have been doing things behind my back, and I've got to assume that even *if* I had managed to get elected, you'd still be calling the shots. I think it's time the people of the state got the kind of a governor they deserve, one that wants to serve them."

"That's horseshit and you know it," Wade said. "Idealistic words don't work in the real world."

Travis looked at Savannah. "And you thought I was cynical?" He laughed bitterly and shook his head. "That's all I have to say about it."

With those final words, he walked out of the room and into the foyer, where he took his coat off the hall tree. Savannah followed him.

"Come on, let's take a walk," Travis muttered. "I need the fresh air."

"I promised Josh that I'd read him a story." Reluctantly she started up the stairs, but stopped on the second step when he called to her.

"Savannah?"

Turning to face him, she read the passion smoldering in his steely gaze. He was standing at the base of the stairs, close enough to touch. Tense lines radiated from the corners of his mouth and eyes, sharpening his angular features.

The burning stare he gave her seared through her clothes and started her heartbeat racing uncontrollably. The thought flashed through her mind that now that Travis had told Reginald he was dropping out of the campaign, there was no reason for him to stay on the farm. Tonight might be their last together. The realization that he would soon be out of her life again settled heavily on Savannah's shoulders.

"I'll be down in a minute," she said, touching him lightly on the shoulder. "Will you wait for me?"

His mocking grin stretched over his face, softening his ruggedly handsome features. "I've waited nine years, lady, I can't see that a few more minutes will hurt." Then he placed his hand around her neck and drew her head to his, the warmth of his lips pressing urgently to hers in a kiss filled with such passion that she was left breathless, her lips throbbing with desire, her senses unbalanced.

I'm lost, she thought, closing her eyes and wrapping her arms around his neck. *I've never stopped loving him and I never will.*

His arms tightened around her, pulling her body against the taut muscles of his. She fit perfectly in his embrace, her softer contours yielding to the hard lines of his body. "Don't be long," he whispered against her ear.

"I won't," she promised. When she opened her eyes she was looking over Travis's shoulder toward the living room, and Reginald was standing in the doorway, watching her eager embrace with a frown creasing his ruddy features. "I'll be right down."

Travis smiled and then walked out of the house, leaving Savannah on the second step, holding on to the rail to support her unsteady legs.

"That's a mistake, y'know," Reginald commented, drawing deeply on his pipe and walking into the foyer. "Gettin' involved with him again will only hurt you, Savannah."

So Reginald did know! Travis had been telling the truth! The knowledge left her exhilarated and disappointed all at once. Though Travis had been honest, her father had been lying to her for nine long years.

"I'm not a seventeen-year-old child any longer," she said, her fingers digging into the wood of the banister. From her position she could see Wade. He was lying on the couch, staring at the fire, his back to the foyer and apparently lost in his own drunken thoughts.

"Maybe not, but you're still my daughter." His bushy gray eyebrows arched. "And Travis McCord is not the man for you."

"Why not?"

"He's always loved Melinda."

Savannah paled and fought the urge to scream and shout that it didn't matter. Instead she said quietly, "But Melinda's gone."

"Maybe to you and me, but never to Travis. She was his first love, Savannah. You'd better face that."

"Why didn't you tell me that you knew I was involved with Travis?" she asked. "You've known for a long time."

Reginald smiled sadly and studied the bowl of his pipe. "Because it was over. He'd hurt you, but it was over."

"And now?"

Sighing, Reginald offered her a fatherly smile. "You're not right for each other. You want to live on the farm, work with the horses, get married and raise a family. But Travis, well, he's…different, cut out of another piece of cloth. He needs the glamour of the courtroom, the glitter of politics—"

"Didn't you hear a word he said?" she asked, incredulous that her father still saw Travis as a politician.

"He's just disillusioned right now. He's tired. Melinda's death and the Eldridge case, they took a lot out of him." Reginald's faded eyes glimmered. "That'll change. You'll see."

"I don't think so."

"Ah, but you have a habit of misreading him, don't you? You thought he and Melinda had broken up nine years ago."

Savannah came down the two steps to the foyer so that she could stand level with her father. "Travis thought she was pregnant," Savannah said. "You backed her up."

"I believed her."

"It was a lie."

Reginald frowned. "I don't know about that—is that what he told you? Well, yes, I suppose he would." The older man sighed loudly. "You have to remember, Savannah, that nobody put a gun to his head and told him he had to marry Melinda, baby or no. He married her of his own volition and they managed to stay married for nearly nine years. Nine years! This day and age that's quite a record.

"Oh, I'll grant you that he was attracted to you. Always has been. But it's just a physical thing—the difference between lust and love, a mistress and a wife." He patted her gently on the arm when he read the stricken look in her eyes. "I'm only looking out for your best interests, y'know."

"Are you, Dad?" she said, barely controlling her anger. "I wonder. The least you could have done is tell me that you knew about Travis and me."

Reginald shrugged. "Why? What would have been the point? Your affair with him was over and he was married. If you're smart, you'll let well enough alone."

"When are you going to understand that you can't manipulate my life any more than you can force him into running for governor?" she said.

Reginald looked suddenly weary. "I'm not trying to manipulate you, Savannah. I'm just trying to help you make the right decisions."

"And the right one would be to forget about Travis?"

"I just don't want to see you hurt again," he whispered, brushing her cheek with his lips. "Isn't one rocky marriage in this family enough?"

"But you and Wade—"

"Are good business partners, don't get me wrong," Reginald said, looking into the living room where Wade was still draped over the couch. "But he should never have married Charmaine and he's a lousy father to his son." He offered her a tight smile. "Just use your head, Savannah. You've got a good brain, don't let it get all confused by your heart."

Reginald turned and went into his study, and Savannah tried to ignore his advice as she climbed the stairs and walked down the short hallway to Josh's room.

CHAPTER SIX

THE SECURITY LIGHTS cast an ethereal blue sheen on the white ground and surrounding buildings.

Travis was waiting by the stables. His tall, dark figure stood out against the stark white walls and snow-covered roof of the barns and snow-laden trees.

Savannah pushed her father's warnings out of her mind and approached him, shivering a little from the cold.

"So how was Josh?" he asked once she was in earshot.

"All right, I guess."

"You're not sure?"

She shook her head, disturbing the snowflakes resting in her ebony hair. "How would you feel if your father had humiliated you in front of the rest of the family?"

"Not so great."

"You got it," she said with a sigh. "Josh is definitely feeling 'not so great.'"

Travis took her hand, wrapped his fingers around hers, and pushed their entwined hands into the pocket of his jacket. "You can't solve all the problems of the world, you know."

"Is that what they taught you in law school?"

"No." Shaking his head, he led her around the building to the overgrown path leading to the lake. "Believe it or not, I learned a lot of things on my own."

"And I don't want to solve the problems of the world, just those of one little boy."

"He's not your son."

"I know," she whispered. "That's the problem."

"One of them," Travis agreed.

Frosty branches leaned across the trail, brushing her face and clothes with their brittle, icy leaves as she walked. Both pairs of boots crunched in the new-fallen snow.

The mud at the bank of the lake was covered with ice, and the naked trees surrounding the black body of water looked like twisted sentinels guarding a private sanctuary—a sanctuary where a feeble love had flickered to life nine years before.

Travis stopped near the old oak where he had been sitting so long ago. "It's been a long time," he said, staring at the inky water.

The pain of the past embraced her. "Too long to go back."

"You were the most beautiful woman I'd ever seen," he said. "And it scared me. It scared the hell out of me." He shook his head in wonder at the vivid memory. "I'd just spent two days trying to convince myself that you were off limits, barely seventeen, Reginald's youngest daughter, for God's sake! And then you walked out of the lake, without a stitch of clothes on, your eyes filled with challenge." He leaned one shoulder against the oak. "It did me in. All of my resolve went right out the window."

"You were drunk," she reminded him.

"I honestly don't think it would have mattered." He wrapped his free arm around her and traced the curve of her jaw with his finger. His hand was cold but inviting, and she shivered.

His gray eyes delved into hers, noticing the way the

snow clung to her thick, curling lashes. "I was hooked, Savannah. I didn't want to be. God knows, I fought it, but I was hooked." He smiled cynically and added, "I still am."

When his chilled lips touched hers she heard a thousand warnings in her mind, but ignored them all. The feel of his body pressed against hers was as drugging as it had been nine years before, in the summer, in that very spot.

Strong arms held her, moist lips claimed hers and she could smell and taste the man she had never quit loving. She felt pangs of regret as well as happiness build inside.

Lifting his head, he gazed into her eyes. "I want you to stay with me tonight," he whispered, his warm breath caressing her face. "You don't have to promise me the future; just spend one night with me and we'll take it from there."

The difference between lust and love, a mistress and a wife.

"Travis—"

"Just say yes."

Delving into his kind eyes, she swallowed and blinked back her tears. "Yes."

Travis took her hand again and led her back down the path toward the buildings of the farm. He was staying in the loft over the garage, and Savannah didn't argue when he helped her climb the stairs to Charmaine's studio.

After shutting the door behind them, Travis rubbed his hands together and blew on them for warmth. The temperature in the dark room was barely above freezing; Savannah could see her breath misting in the half-light.

Savannah stared at her sister's private domain. Pale light from the reflection of the security lamps on the snow filtered through the windows. Charmaine's draped

artwork was scattered around the room, looking like life-
less ghosts propped in the corners of the studio.

"It's changed a little in nine years," Travis observed,
not bothering to switch on the lights.

Originally the second story over the garage had been
one large apartment, and Travis had lived in the three
sloped-ceilinged rooms whenever he was on the farm.
A few years before, Charmaine had converted what had
been his living room and kitchen into an artist's studio.

The bedroom was still in the back. Travis had been
using it since he arrived at the farm and now, in the darkness of the frigid night, he tugged on Savannah's hand
and pulled her down the short hallway to what was left
of his quarters.

Savannah hadn't been in the room in years. It held too
many memories of Travis, too much pain. She leaned
against the tall post of the bed and felt the old, angry de-
ception stir in her heart. Looking into his night-darkened
eyes she wanted to trust him, but his betrayal was as fresh
as it had been on the night he'd left her all those years ago.

"Try to forget the past," he said, as if reading her
mind. His hand reached forward and he cupped her chin.
"Trust me again."

Savannah's breath caught in her throat when she felt
his arms surround her and tasted the warmth of his lips
against hers. She told herself to push him away, pay attention to her father's advice, but she couldn't. Instead,
her pulse quickened and her blood heated with desire.

He groaned when she responded. "We don't have any
more excuses, Savannah," he whispered against her hair.
"Tonight there's nothing and no one to stand in our way."

And we're running out of time, she added silently to
herself. *Tomorrow you'll probably leave.* Desperation
gripped her heart and she wound her arms around his

neck, returning the passion of his kiss with the fierce need of a woman who'd been held away from the man she'd loved for far too long.

She felt the warmth of his mouth against her lips, her eyes, her cheeks. His tongue slipped through her parted lips to search and dance with its anxious mate.

His hard body, covered by straining, bothersome clothing, pushed against hers, and she felt the volatile tension of taut tendons, corded muscles and unbridled desire pressing against her flesh. His lips caressed her, his fingers explored and stroked her neck and face.

"I've waited a long time for you," he said, anxiously unbuttoning her coat and pushing it off her shoulders to fall to the floor.

"And I for you," she agreed, her voice low, her fingers working at his clothes.

Slowly the cloth barriers slid to the floor, until finally there was nothing to separate their bodies but the pain of nine lost years.

He stood before her, a naked man silhouetted in the night. His hand reached upward and his fingers shook a little as he touched one dark-tipped breast.

Savannah quivered beneath his touch. The gentle probe was light at first, a sensual stroking of the breast that made her knees weaken and the warmth within her turn liquid. "Travis," she whispered.

"Shh." His fingers continued to work their magic and Savannah leaned backward against the cold polished wood of the four-poster. Travis pressed harder against her, the warmth of his body contrasting to the smooth, cool post at her back.

His mouth was hungry, his tongue plundering as he tasted the soft skin at the base of her throat, and one of his strong hands reached downward to fit over her buttocks and pull her against his thighs. Hot, tense muscles fitted against her softer flesh, melting away the memory of betrayal.

His hands molded her body as lovingly as those of a sculptor shaping clay, and Savannah's doubts escaped into the night. "I've never wanted a woman the way I want you," he admitted, kneeling and kissing first one ripened breast and then the other. The wet impression left on her nipples made the dark points stand erect, as he stroked them with his thumbs. "God, you're beautiful," he whispered, his breath fanning her navel.

Involuntarily her abdomen tightened, and when he rimmed her navel with his tongue, she moaned and her knees sagged. She would have slid to the floor, but he caught her, forcing her back to the bedpost as he kissed the soft skin of her abdomen and hips. Her fingers twined in his thick hair, and dampness broke out upon her skin. The ache deep within her became more intense. She was twisting and writhing with an emptiness that only he could fill.

"Please," she whispered somewhere between pain and ecstasy. "Travis…please…"

"What do you want?" he asked, his tongue and teeth tantalizing her skin.

"Everything."

When he picked her up, letting her knees drape over one arm while cradling her head with the other, she couldn't resist—wouldn't, even if she had the strength. Black hair spilled over his arm as he gently placed her on the bed. The patchwork quilt was ice-cold against her back and goose bumps rose on her flesh, but the fire in her eyes burned brightly.

"I'm glad you decided to stay with me tonight," he admitted, looking into her blue gaze and tracing the pout on her lips with one finger.

Trembling with anticipation, Savannah's fingers wrapped around the back of his neck and she pulled his head to hers. Her eager, open lips fused to his.

The weight of his body fell over her, flattening her breasts with the hard muscles of his chest. His dark, swirling hair rubbed erotically against her nipples. A soft sheen of sweat oiled the corded muscles of his back and chest.

Savannah moaned as Travis's legs entwined with hers. She felt the exquisite torment of his tongue and teeth playing with her nipples before his lips once again claimed hers and he positioned his body above her.

"I love you, Savannah," he admitted, closing his eyes against the truth. "I always have."

Moving below him, she stared into the steely depths of his eyes as he slowly pressed her knees apart and entered her. She felt the heat of his body begin to fill her as his strokes, slow at first, increased in tempo until she was forced to move with him, join him in the ancient dance of love.

She clung to him, tasted his sweat, stared into his fathomless gray eyes as he rocked them both with the fever of his passion until at last the shimmering lights in her mind exploded into a thousand tiny fragments of that very same light and she nearly screamed his name. A moment later he stiffened and fell upon her, cradling her shoulders and resting his head on her breasts.

"God, I love you," he said, still fondling her breast before falling asleep in her arms.

Do. Oh, please, Travis do love me, let me believe you, she silently prayed as tears burned her eyes. *Tell me it's more than just one final night together!*

She listened to the regular tempo of his breathing, thought she should return to the house, but created a thousand excuses to stay with him, and fell asleep entwined in his arms.

Hours later, Savannah awakened. One of Travis's tanned arms was draped protectively across her breasts. She rolled over to kiss him and found that he was already awake and staring at her.

"Good morning," he drawled, his gray eyes delving deep into hers, and his fingers pushing the tousled black hair from her eyes.

Savannah smiled and stretched. "Good morning yourself."

She tried to toss off the covers and hop out of bed, but Travis restrained her by placing his hands over her wrists. "Where do you think you're going?" he asked.

"I realize that you're on vacation, early retirement, or whatever else you want to call it," she teased, "but the rest of us poor working stiffs have jobs to do."

He chuckled to himself. "Your father's back; you can relax."

"Not quite yet," she said, trying to wriggle free, but his hands continued to hold her down and she gave up with an exasperated sigh. "What's so important?" she asked.

"I think we should clear up a few things before you high-tail it out of here."

"Such as?"

"Like what we're going to do if you're pregnant."

Disappointment burned in her heart. There were no options as far as she was concerned; she would bear Travis's child and raise it—alone if she had to. Unfortunately, she didn't even have to worry. "I'm not."

He smiled seductively. "Too early to be sure?"

She did a quick calculation in her head. "Let's just say it would be highly unlikely, counselor."

"Oh?"

"I work with brood mares every day, remember? I think I can figure out when I'm able to conceive and when I'm not. Last night we were lucky."

"Lucky? Well, maybe," he said with a frown.

"Now, unless you have something that can't wait, I've got to get up."

"But that's the problem, don't you see?" he teased, still holding her wrists to her sides and sliding his naked body erotically over hers. "There is something that can't wait, something bothering me a lot."

Her breath caught in her throat. "Travis—"

He pulled her hands over her head and positioned himself over her, softly kissing her lips while rubbing against her.

Savannah found it impossible to think. The warm sensations cascading over her body made everything else seem unimportant.

"I really should go to work—"

"In time," he promised, dipping his head and kissing her gently on the swell of her breasts. He watched in fascination as her nipples hardened expectantly and the fires deep within her began to rage. "In time…"

TRAVIS HAD FALLEN back to sleep and Savannah was finally able to slip from the bed, throw on her clothes and head downstairs. It was nearly dawn, sometime after six, and Lester would be arriving at the farm soon.

As quietly as a cat slinking through the night, Savannah sneaked out of the room, through the studio, and down the stairs outside of the garage. The snow had quit falling, but the sky overhead was threatening to spill more powdery flakes onto the earth. She smiled when she noticed that the double set of footprints that she and Travis had made was nearly covered. Snow must have fallen most of the night.

Maybe we'll have a white Christmas this year, she thought with a smile as she pushed her hands into the pockets of her suede jacket and headed toward the stables. *Josh would love it!* This much snow was nearly unheard of in this part of the country.

Her spirits lifted as she walked through the backyard. Spending a night alone with Travis and listening to his words of love had made her think there was a chance that all would be right with the world. Perhaps loving him was the right thing to do, she thought. Even if his words of love had been whispered at the height of passion, he hadn't been forced to say them. So why fight it? She almost had herself convinced that the barriers of the past nine years had been destroyed in one night. Almost.

Humming to herself, she let Archimedes out of the back porch and started on her early-morning rounds. Archimedes bounded along beside her, romping in the snow and breaking a trail in the soft white powder.

Savannah's breath clouded in the air, and her boots crunched through the five-inch layer of snow. Intermittent flakes fell from the sky and clung to her shoulders and hair as she headed toward the stables.

The brood mares, their swollen bellies protruding prominently, snorted and nickered when she arrived. After checking the water and the feed of each of the mares, she walked back outside and crossed the parking lot to the brick path that led to the stallion barn. "That's odd," she thought, noticing the set of footprints leading to the barn from the front of the house. The prints were smaller than her own and softened by a fine dusting of snow.

"What is?" Travis's voice broke through the still morning air.

Savannah nearly jumped out of her skin and turned to face him. He was walking toward her from the direction of the garage. A Stetson was pulled low over his eyes and his hands were jammed into the pockets of his jeans. "Boy, I could use a pair of gloves," he muttered.

"I thought you were still asleep."

"I was, until someone rattled around and made so much noise that I woke up."

"What!" She'd been as quiet as a mouse. She looked into his eyes and saw the sparkle of amusement in his intriguing gaze. "Give me a break."

He leaned over and kissed the tip of her nose. "I missed you, Savvy."

Savannah's heart jumped. *God, how she loved this man.* "Good, I could use the company, as well as the muscle power. You can help me feed the stallions."

"I can think of better things to do."

Savannah laughed merrily. It felt good to throw off the chains of the past. "Not right now, mister," she said. "I told you; I've got work to do." They walked together in the snow. "Speaking of which, are you going to tell me what you were doing in Dad's study last night? Wade nearly fell through the floor when I told him you were in the den."

"I'll bet," Travis muttered, hunching his shoulders against another blast of arctic wind. "I just wanted to do some checking."

"On what?"

"The books."

"Of the farm?"

He nodded and a shiver of dread slid down Savannah's spine. "Why?"

"Curiosity." He kept his eyes to the ground and noticed the other set of tracks in the snow.

"Whose are these?" he asked, then continued without pausing, "Lester's usually the first one around, but they're too small for him." He frowned. "And look at the tread. Definitely not boots. More like running shoes."

Savannah's heart nearly stopped beating. Snowflakes clung to her ebony hair, and her cheeks were flushed from the cold. Her blue eyes darkened with dread in spite of the light from the security lamps and the first hint of dawn.

"Like Josh's shoes?" she whispered.

"Like Josh's," Travis agreed as his eyes followed the arrow-straight path of the footsteps that led from the house to the stallion barn. The crease in his forehead deepened.

A premonition of disaster tightened Savannah's chest and made it hard to breathe. "But what would he be doing here this early?" she asked, as they approached the barn.

"That's what we're about to find out."

Travis opened the door to the barn, flipped on the lights, and began striding down the double row of stalls. Savannah walked more slowly, her eyes scanning the interior of the barn.

"Mornin', fellas," she said, patting Night Magic fondly on his nose as Travis walked down the parallel row of stalls. "It doesn't look like anyone's here," she said. "Just like yesterday morning. Lester heard a noise, but no one was there."

"Strange, isn't it?"

"Creepy," she agreed.

Several of the younger stallions snorted their contempt, while Night Magic whinnied softly. "You're a pushover, aren't you?" Savannah asked, petting the coal-black muzzle again.

Travis stopped at the far end of the stalls. "Where's Mystic?" he asked.

"What do you mean? He's here. The end stall—" The meaning of his question suddenly struck home and Savannah ran down the length of the barn, her boots clattering against the concrete floor, her heart thudding wildly in her rib cage. Once near Travis she stared into the empty box and fear took a stranglehold of her throat.

"Where else could he be?" Travis demanded.

"Nowhere…." Her heart thudding with dread, she slowly went down the double aisle and counted the stallions. All seven stallions and colts were in their proper stalls. Except for Mystic. He was gone, vanished into the night.

"Didn't Joshua say he could ride Mystic?" Travis asked.

Savannah had all but lost her voice. "But he wouldn't… couldn't take him." She leaned against the stall door for support.

"Why not?"

"He's just a boy—"

"An angry, humiliated boy."

Fear tightened her chest. "Oh, God. I don't think Josh would take off like that. Not in the middle of a snowstorm. Not on *Mystic*, for God's sake." But even to her own ears, her protests sounded weak.

"Wade pushed Josh into a corner last night," Travis said. "I know, I've been there myself." He started walking down the row of boxes again, his fists balled at his sides, his jaw jutted forward angrily, and Savannah was reminded of the rebel Travis had been as a teenager. "I'll kill him," Travis swore. "So help me, if that boy is hurt I'll kill Benson and be glad to do it!"

"Wait! Before we go to the house, I think we should check the other barns and the paddocks. Maybe Mystic got out by himself."

"Do you really believe that?" Travis asked, his anger flushing his face.

"Look, I just want to make sure, that's all," she said, nearly screaming at him. "You check the other barns and I'll call Lester."

Travis walked out of the building and headed for the main stables. Savannah used the extension in the stallion barn and dialed Lester's number. While it rang she tapped her fingers nervously on the wall and eyed the interior of the barn.

"Answer the phone," she whispered on the fourth ring.

"Hello?"

"Lester!" she said with relief.

"I was just on my way over," the trainer replied. "What's up?"

"It's Mystic. He's not in the stallion barn."

"What!"

"He's gone."

The old man whistled softly and then swore. "I locked him up myself last night."

"You're sure?"

"Course I am," Lester snapped.

Savannah's knees went weak and she leaned against the wall for support.

"Any other clues?"

"Just another set of tracks coming to the barn. Smaller ones. Maybe Josh might know something about this."

"Well, ask him."

"I will," she promised. *If he's here.* "I'll be over in

about twenty minutes. Have you told Reginald what happened yet?"

"No. Travis is still checking to make sure Mystic didn't get in with the mares or yearlings by mistake...."

"I shut him up myself, missy. If he's gone, it's because someone let him out."

Someone like Joshua, Savannah thought miserably.

Travis came back into the barn just as she hung up the phone. His expression was grim, the set of his jaw determined. "No luck," he said, walking back to Mystic's stall.

"Lester locked him up himself."

"Then it looks like Josh took him." Travis slid open the door at the opposite end of the barn. It was used rarely, only for grain delivery. "And this confirms it." In the freshly fallen snow were two sets of tracks: those of a horse and those matching the tracks at the other end of the barn.

"Oh, God," Savannah whispered. Her small fists clenched when she saw the trampled snow and mud where the horse had shied. At that point, near the fence, the rider had to have mounted Mystic. And then the hoofprints became a single file that led through the gate, across the field and toward the hills. "He'll freeze," she whispered, tears beginning to build in her eyes and fear clenching her heart.

"Not if I can help it," Travis said. "Let's go."

After securing the stallion barn, they half ran back to the house. Savannah didn't bother taking off her boots as she mounted the stairs and raced to Joshua's room. She knocked quietly once and then again when there was no answer.

"Josh!" she called through the door.

Charmaine's door opened. Her dark hair was mussed,

her eyes still blurred with sleep. "Savannah, what's going on?"

"I don't know," Savannah replied, her hand on the doorknob. Until she was sure of the facts, she didn't want to worry her older sister.

"Savannah?" Charmaine whispered, her eyes widening.

Ignoring her sister, Savannah opened the door to Josh's room and sank against the wall when she saw that the room was empty. The covers of the bed were strewn on the floor. A quick check in the closet indicated that Josh's jacket was missing, as were his favorite shoes and hat.

Charmaine walked into the room. "Where's Josh?" she asked, nearly choking with fear. "Where is he?"

"I don't know," Savannah admitted. Her shoulders slumped in defeat as she thought about the child braving the elements. "But we think he took Mystic."

"Mystic!" Charmaine leaned against the dresser for support and knocked over a stack of comic books. "What do you mean?"

"That's a good question," Travis said. "All we know is that Mystic is missing. There're small footsteps from the house to the stallion barn and then it looks like someone took Mystic from his stall, led him outside and rode him into the hills."

"Not Josh," Charmaine whispered, shaking her head. "He wouldn't have done that. He's got to be here on the farm somewhere. Someone else let the horse out of his stall or rode him away but Josh is here…. He's just hiding…."

"He told me he could ride Mystic," Savannah said.

"What the hell is going on here?" Wade demanded, running his fingers through his unruly hair as he entered the room. "Where's the boy?"

"They think Josh is missing," Charmaine whispered miserably.

"Missing?"

"Gone, Wade." She gestured feebly toward Savannah and Travis. "They think he took Mystic."

"Josh took Mystic? That's impossible. That demon of a horse won't let anyone near him...." Wade's angry words died as he surveyed the tense faces in the room. "My God, you're serious, aren't you?" The sleep left his eyes.

"Dead serious," Travis muttered.

"I don't believe it. He's just here somewhere," Charmaine insisted, looking frantically around the boy's room. "Josh? Josh!"

Travis caught her by the arm. "We're pretty certain about this. Otherwise we wouldn't have alarmed you."

Charmaine jerked her arm free. "It's freezing outside. Josh wouldn't go out in the cold...not away from the house. And he wouldn't take the horse...." The reality of the situation finally caught up with her. "Oh, God, it just can't be." She moaned, letting her face fall into her hands and finally releasing the sobs she had been fighting since entering the room.

"Listen, I'll call the sheriff," Savannah offered.

"The sheriff!" Charmaine was horrified. "What good will that do?" Her pale face was terror-stricken and she lashed out at the first person she saw. "Savannah, if what you're saying is true, this is all your fault, you know. You're the one who took him riding, you're the one who planted all those damned horse-loving ideas in his head, you're the one who let him think about riding that horrible horse!"

Travis stood between Charmaine and Savannah. "We're not getting anywhere by pointing fingers! We've got to find Josh."

"We are talking about my son," Charmaine said, tears sliding down her white cheeks. "My son, dammit! He's gone!"

"This is insane," Wade said, shaking his head as if trying to shake out a bad dream. "Josh wouldn't take Mystic. Why in the world would a boy want a racehorse?"

"Maybe he thought it was the only friend he had," Savannah said, fighting her own hot tears.

"You're wrong!" Wade said, pacing the small room and rubbing the golden stubble on his chin. "Josh is probably just pulling one of his rebellious stunts. No doubt he's hiding somewhere on the farm and having a good laugh over this."

"He's only a nine-year-old boy," Charmaine wailed.

"That you mortified last night!" Savannah said, staring at Wade through tear-glazed eyes.

"Oh, give me a break," Wade mumbled, but he was sweating. "Charmaine's right, you know, Savannah. You've been filling that boy's head with all sorts of idiotic ideas. You should never have encouraged Josh to have anything to do with the horses. Especially Mystic. If anything happens to my boy, I'll hold you personally responsible!"

Travis's eyes glinted like newly forged steel. "And if anything happens to either Savannah or Josh, you'll have to answer to me, Benson," he threatened, his voice becoming ruthless. "Now let's quit arguing about it and get to work. Savannah, you call the sheriff. Charmaine will stay here with Virginia in case anyone calls. The rest of us will start searching the farm by following the tracks as far as we can."

"I'm coming with you," Savannah insisted, trying to pull herself together.

"Not on your life. You stay and wait for Lester and the

rest of the hands. Someone's got to run the farm and take care of Charmaine. Besides, I want you to talk to that repairman, make sure that the broken wire was just a case of the alarm wearing out. If we get moving now, there's a good chance that we can catch up to the boy by noon."

Travis was walking out of the room and toward the stairs. Wade was only two steps behind him. Before Travis descended, he turned to Wade and his cold eyes bored through Josh's father. "I think you'd better tell Reginald what's happened—that he's missing a valuable colt as well as his only grandson."

Wade nodded curtly and walked toward Reginald's room.

Savannah had followed Travis and Wade. At the top of the stairs she brushed her tears aside and held her chin defiantly while holding Travis's severe glare. "I'm coming with you," she announced. "Josh is my nephew."

"No way, lady."

"You can't talk me out of it."

Travis let out an exasperated sigh and hurried down the stairs. Savannah was on his heels. "Use your head, Savannah. You're needed here," Travis said.

"But I know Josh; I know where he might go."

"We'll find him. You stay with your sister. Whether she knows it or not, she needs you."

"I can't stay here! Not while Josh is out…wherever!"

Travis looked up at the ceiling. "Don't we have enough problems without you trying to add to them?"

"I only want to help."

"Then stay here and be sensible!" he snapped before turning to face her and seeing the tears in her eyes. He wrapped his arms around her and sighed. "Listen, Savannah, you're the only one on this whole damned farm that I can count on. Stay here. Help your mother and the police."

"But—"

"And quit blaming yourself! If Joshua left it was because of his father."

"I did encourage him to take an interest in the horses," she whispered, her throat raw.

"Because you're his friend." Travis's face softened. "And right now, Josh needs all the friends he can get. So hang in here, okay? Help me."

The sound of Lester's pickup spurred Travis into action. He released Savannah and went outside. A few minutes later, Wade and a pale-looking Reginald, who was still stuffing his shirt into his pants, joined Travis and Lester. The men formed a search party on horseback and in four-wheel-drive vehicles.

It had begun to snow heavily again, showering the valley with white powder and making it impossible to see any distance. Finding a nine-year-old and a runaway horse would be difficult.

Savannah stood near the fence by the stallion barn, her arms huddled around herself. She felt absolutely helpless.

"I'll see you later," Travis promised as he climbed into the saddle on Jones. The chestnut gelding swished his tail and flattened his ears impatiently.

Travis's plan was to follow Mystic's footprints on horseback. Reginald and Wade were driving ahead in a Jeep, but Travis insisted on taking the horse just in case Josh rode Mystic through the trees and the vehicle was unable to follow the Thoroughbred's prints in the snow.

Lester and Johnny, one of the stable hands, were searching the other areas of the farm in a pickup. They were hoping to come across Josh's hiding place…if he had one.

Then Travis and the others were gone.

The sounds of engines rumbling up the hills made Savannah shiver inside and she said a silent prayer for the lost boy. *Come home, Josh,* she thought desperately. *Please come home!*

Savannah watched the tall man on horseback for as long as she could. Travis rode past the stallion barn, through the enclosed field and up the hillside, carefully following the slowly disappearing tracks in the snow and the roaring Jeep.

Standing on the fence, Savannah squinted and stared after him until he finally vanished from her sight.

With cold dread settling in her heart, she climbed off the fence, turned back to the house and worked up the courage to face Charmaine and call the sheriff.

CHAPTER SEVEN

SAVANNAH LEANED ON her father's desk, closing her eyes while trying to hear the voice on the other end of the phone. Listening was difficult as the wires crackled and the background noise in the sheriff's department was nearly as loud as the deputy's voice. Deputy Smith sounded weary, as if he'd been on the job all night, and the words he gave Savannah were far from encouraging.

"It's not that I don't appreciate your problem, Ms. Beaumont," he said in a sincere voice, "and we'll do what we can. But you have to understand that the storm is causing a lot of problems for other people as well as you folks. Several cities are without power and I don't have to tell you about the conditions of the roads. We've got two trucks jackknifed on the freeway and traffic backed up for six miles." He paused for a minute and Savannah heard him talking in a muffled voice to another officer. He was back to her within a minute. "We'll send someone out to the farm as soon as possible."

"Thank you," Savannah said before hanging up the phone and feeling the energy drain from her body. *So Travis and the rest of the men couldn't count on anyone but themselves.* Travis. She should have ignored his anger and logic and gone with him. At least that way she would feel as if she were accomplishing something, doing something useful.

She picked up a cold cup of coffee, took a sip, frowned and set the cup back on the desk.

Taking in a steadying breath, she dialed all of the neighbors within a three-mile radius of the breeding farm. It was another waste of time. No one had seen Josh or Mystic.

"Well, what did you expect?" she asked herself after hanging up and staring through the window at the white flakes falling from a leaden sky. "Oh, Josh, where are you?" She stood transfixed at the window of the study and watched with mounting dread as the small silvery flakes continued to fall. Maybe it was a good sign that none of the neighbors had seen Josh. Maybe he was still on Beaumont property. *And maybe the neighbors were just too busy taking care of themselves in the snowstorm to notice the boy or his horse,* she thought grimly.

Pushing the hair from her eyes, she tried not to think about either Travis or Josh, but found it impossible. No matter what she did to try to keep busy, her thoughts always returned to Travis. He'd been in the storm on horseback for nearly two hours, following a mere shadow of a trail in the snow. The longer the snow continued to fall, the less able he would be to track Mystic. God, how long had Josh been braving the elements? Was he still on the horse or was he curled up in the snow freezing to death?

Tears pricked the back of her eyes, and she leaned her head against the cool panes of the window. "Use your head, sport," Savannah whispered, as if the boy were standing next to her instead of somewhere outdoors in the cold. "Use your head and come home."

Shaking off her fears and fighting back tears, Savannah went into the kitchen and made coffee. When she let Archimedes into the house from the back porch, she eyed the snow. The storm hadn't let up and white powder was drifting against the sides of the stables and garage.

Somewhere out in the near blizzard Josh was alone. And so was Travis. Savannah shivered as she came back inside. Archimedes, from his favorite position under the kitchen table, thumped his tail against the floor.

"You're not worried, are you?" she asked the dog, who lifted his head and cocked his ears expectantly.

She prayed when the lights flickered twice. If the power went out now, running the farm would be nearly impossible. She switched on the small black-and-white television in the kitchen. After listening to the news for a few minutes and discovering that the intensity of the storm wasn't about to let up, she snapped off the set, poured two cups of coffee, put them on a tray and carried them upstairs to Virginia's room.

Knocking softly on the bedroom door, Savannah entered. Virginia was sitting in the bed, her pale hands folded over her lap, her eyes fastened on the floor-to-ceiling window at the far end of the room. Through the glass was a view of the hills surrounding the farm.

"Any news?" Virginia asked quietly.

Savannah shook her head. "Not yet."

With a loud sigh, Virginia slumped lower into the mound of pillows supporting her back. "What about the police?"

"I called the sheriff's department. They're pretty busy right now."

"Yes, I imagine so," Virginia said distractedly. One of her hands lifted and she fingered a small cross hanging from a gold chain at her throat. "And the storm. Who would have thought that we'd get so much snow? It's unusual…. Can't the sheriff come over?"

"The deputy said he would send a man over as soon as possible."

"For what good it will do—"

"Mom," Savannah gently reproached.

Virginia sighed before stiffening her shoulders. "I know, I know. And I haven't given up hope. Really. I…I just can't help but think about Josh and that horse lost in the mountains or God only knows where…." Her voice faded and she swallowed hard. "He's such a dear, dear boy."

"I won't argue with that," Savannah said kindly. "But you know that Travis will find him." Her own throat was nearly swollen shut and the conviction in her voice wavered, so she changed the subject. "Here, I brought you some coffee. What about something to eat?"

Virginia waved the cup aside. "Not hungry," she mumbled, shaking her head against the pillows.

"You're sure?"

"Yes."

"Okay. Suit yourself." Savannah left the cup and saucer on the night table near her mother. Then she took the remaining cup of coffee and stood. "I'm going to see how Charmaine is, and then I'll check on the horses. If you need anything, I'll be back in about an hour."

"I won't need a thing," Virginia whispered. "But as for Charmaine…" Pain crossed Virginia's eyes and she raised her hand in a feeble gesture. "Maybe it would be best if you let her alone—let her sort out her feelings."

"She still blames me," Savannah deduced, leaning a shoulder against the wall.

"She's not thinking clearly. Josh is the only thing she has in her life. Even Wade…" Virginia lifted her shoulders. "Well, it's different when you have a child of your own."

"I think I'd better see her."

"Just remember that she's under a horrible strain."

"I will." Savannah started down the hallway to Charmaine's room, but stopped when she came to the open door of Josh's bedroom and saw her sister. Charmaine, still in her bathrobe, was seated cross-legged on the braided rug and softly crying to herself.

"How about a cup of coffee or some company?" Savannah offered, setting the cup on the dresser before folding her arms over her chest and leaning a shoulder against the doorjamb.

"No, thanks."

"Charmaine, I know what you're going through—"

Savannah's sister took in a long, deep breath, as if trying to calm herself. "You know what I'm going through," she repeated incredulously. "Do you? You couldn't!" Charmaine lifted red-rimmed eyes and stared at Savannah as if she wanted to kill her. "How could you understand—you don't even have a child!"

Savannah felt the sting of the bitter words, but tried to rise above Charmaine's anger. "But I love Josh. Very much."

Charmaine's throat worked convulsively. "Too much. You treat him as if he were your child, not mine!"

"I just wanted to be his friend."

"Like hell!" Charmaine tossed her head back angrily and her dark hair fell around her shaking shoulders. "You tried to be his mother, Savannah. And you allowed him, *encouraged* him to hang around the horses."

"The same way we were encouraged when we were children."

Charmaine just shook her head, and tears tracked down her cheeks. "You don't understand, do you? Because you don't have a child. Those horses are dangerous, and Mystic…Mystic, he's so mean-tempered that even Lester has trouble handling him. And you let a boy, *my* boy work with him. Now look what's happened. He's out there, with that demon of a horse, probably hurt… maybe…maybe dead. All because you wanted to be his friend." She began sobbing again, raking her fingers through her hair in frustration.

"Have you ever thought that the reason Josh ran away was because of his argument with Wade?"

"Ran away!" Charmaine repeated, her face draining of color. "Ran away?" She shook her head. "Josh did *not* run away! Sure, he was mad at his father, but he just took the horse for a ride, that's all. He didn't have any intention of running away!" Charmaine's fingers trembled when they cinched the belt of her robe around her waist.

"I hope you're right," Savannah whispered, wanting to stand up for herself, but knowing there was nothing she could say in her own defense. Charmaine was beyond reason, too distraught to be comforted, and she was lashing out at the easiest target. In this case, the easiest mark was Savannah.

"Of course I am. I'm his mother…. I…I understand him." She stood on quivering legs. "Now, just leave me alone." Looking around the boy's room, noticing the posters of football players, rock stars and running horses as if for the first time, Charmaine cleared her throat. "I can't stand being in this house another minute. If Travis or Wade gets back, or you hear anything about Josh, I'll be in the studio."

"You'll be the first to know."

Charmaine walked past Savannah without a glance in her sister's direction, and in a few minutes the door to her room closed shut with a thud that echoed in Savannah's mind.

Swallowing against the sense of desperation and fear that parched her throat, Savannah braced herself and walked out of Josh's room. Surely Travis would find Josh and within a couple of hours they would all be together again. It was just a matter of time.

Savannah looked in on her mother again and found that Virginia was sleeping. She removed the cup of untouched coffee from the night table, went downstairs, and placed the cup in the sink. Then, on an impulse, she dialed Sadie Stinson's number. The housekeeper lived several miles away in the opposite direction of Mystic's hoofprints, but there was a slim chance that Josh had sought solace with Sadie. The phone rang several times, but no one answered.

Trying to disregard a feeling of impending doom, Savannah grabbed her coat and continued trying to convince herself that everything would be all right as she walked outside and headed for the brood mare barn. There was work to be done, the first of which was to draw water and make sure that the reserve tank was full. Electricity the farm could do without, but water was another story altogether.

A DEPUTY FOR the sheriff's department, a young red-haired man with sober brown eyes and a hard smile, made it to the farm later in the morning. After several apologies for not being able to respond earlier, and excuses ranging from jackknifed trucks on the freeway to power outages all over the state, he took a statement from everyone at the house before following Savannah to the office over the foaling shed.

"So you don't think the horse was stolen?" he queried, his dark eyes searching Savannah's. She gave him a cup of coffee and sat at the table near the window.

"No, it looks as if Joshua took the horse."

"Any note from the boy?"

She shook her head and frowned into her cup. "None that we've found."

"And he didn't bother to say goodbye to anyone."

"No."

The young deputy lifted his hat and rubbed his head before scratching a note to himself on his clipboard. "Now, the colt: Mystic. This the same horse that won the Preakness earlier in the year?"

"Yes."

"So he's valuable?"

"Very."

"And insured?"

"Of course." Savannah impaled the young officer with her intense gaze. "What are you getting at?"

"Just checking all the angles. Would you say that this Mystic was the most valuable horse on the farm?"

"No doubt about it."

"And would it be easy for another person, say one that wasn't familiar with the farm, to recognize him?"

"You mean someone that didn't work with him?"

The deputy nodded and took a sip from his cup. "Right."

Savannah thought for a moment. "I don't know. He was pure black, that in itself is striking, I suppose. Most Thoroughbreds are bays or chestnuts."

"How about the other stallions?"

"We have one other black horse, Black Magic, but he's quite a bit older than Mystic; his sire, in fact."

The deputy looked up from his clipboard. "His what?"

"Black Magic is Mystic's sire…you know, father."

"Oh. But could anyone tell them apart?"

"Temperamentally the two are night and day. Black

Magic is fairly docile and Mystic is difficult to handle. Magic is slightly larger and has one white stocking. Both horses are registered with the jockey club so their identifying numbers are tattooed inside their upper lips. Anyone who knew what he was doing could make sure that he had the right horse," she mused, "but I don't think we have to worry about that. Josh is missing; he loved the horse, and the boy had a horrid fight with his father last night."

"So you think he just took off in the middle of the biggest snowstorm we've had in fifteen years with the most valuable horse in your stable?" Deputy Smith was clearly dubious.

"He's only nine and he was angry, so, yes."

Scratching the reddish stubble on his chin the deputy stared at the broken wire on the security alarm. "Don't you think it's quite a coincidence that the horse would be taken just when the alarm appeared to be broken?"

"I don't know about that."

"Okay." He shoved the clipboard under his arm and took a final swallow of coffee. "Let's have a look at the barn where the missing horse was taken from."

Savannah led the officer down the path to the barn. Most of the footprints she and Travis had made earlier were covered with snow, just as Mystic's trail was probably covered.

Opening the door of the stallion barn, Savannah stood aside while Deputy Smith peered inside the building, scrutinized every horse and continued to make notes to himself. After searching the barn completely, Mystic's stall thoroughly, and asking Savannah again why Lester thought he'd heard someone in the barn the morning before, he scoured the outside of the buildings. By the time he was finished with his search and was driving away from the house it was almost three in the afternoon, and Savannah felt bone tired and discouraged.

"You'd think they could do more than just poke around and ask a few questions," Charmaine said bitterly when Savannah walked into the kitchen. Charmaine had returned to the house when the young deputy sherrif had arrived, although she hadn't had much to tell him.

"He promised to watch all the roads and inform all the state and county officers about Josh and Mystic," Savannah said quietly, shivering slightly as she took off her coat and hung it on a hook near the door to the back porch. "And when they have more men free, they'll be back. I don't know what more they can do."

"I just thought Josh would be home by now," Charmaine whispered.

"So did I."

Charmaine bit at her lower lip and studied the floor. "I know I've been a bitch, Savannah. I really didn't mean to blame you."

"I know."

"I said some pretty awful things earlier."

"You always do when you get angry."

"So why do you put up with it?" Charmaine asked, her chin quivering.

"Because I know you're doing the best you can and you're sick with worry about Josh. And—" she hesitated, but decided to say what she felt "—and you don't want to blame Wade."

Charmaine closed her eyes. "You're right," she admitted, shaking her head and frowning. "Thanks for understanding."

Shrugging, Savannah forced a smile. "What are sisters for?"

Charmaine thought a minute. "Well, I don't think they

were meant to be whipping posts and I'm sorry that I lost control."

"It's okay."

"We all owe you something for holding this place together today."

"Don't thank me yet," Savannah said, watching through the window as the wind buffeted the wires near the barn. "We're not out of the woods, not by a long shot." Savannah gazed out the kitchen window to the stallion barn and beyond. Her thoughts were with Travis and Josh…wherever they were.

TRAVIS STUDIED THE tracks in the snow again and cursed. Mystic's hoofprints had become less defined until they all but disappeared in a stand of birch near a frozen creek.

"Son of a bitch," he muttered to himself, dismounting and eyeing the ground more closely. After tying Jones to a tree, in order to keep the hoofprints from crossing, he slowly circled the area again. Keeping his eyes on the frozen earth and trying to imagine where the kid had decided to go, he walked carefully, oblivious to the icy wind that cut through his clothes.

The tracks had faded near the edge of Beaumont land. On the other side of the ridge the property belonged to the federal government, and Travis hoped that Josh hadn't been stupid enough to leave Beaumont property. Dealing with the government only meant more red tape and more time lost. "He couldn't have gotten over there," he told himself for the third time. "No gate, and Mystic is smarter than to attempt to hurdle a fence. At least I hope he is."

Frowning at the dim prints, he thought about the boy. By now Josh had to be scared out of his wits. "Where the hell are you?" Travis muttered, as if the boy could hear him.

Maybe Reginald and Wade had found Josh. Two hours ago, they had doubled back to the house, still looking for Josh. Lord, he hoped that the boy was already back at the farm. This was no weather for man or beast. The wind had picked up and the snow was falling in small, hard crystals, somewhere between sleet and hail. A nine-year-old kid wouldn't last long out here.

Travis rubbed the tired muscles of his back and thought about Savannah. He envisioned her beautiful face and intriguing blue eyes. Less than twelve hours before, she had been in his arms, naked, warm and filled with passion. She would be devastated if the boy wasn't found.

With a frown, Travis remounted and tried to pick up the trail again. "Josh!" he yelled, cupping his gloved hands over his mouth and listening as his voice echoed through the hills. "Josh!"

The only answer was the whistle of the wind. *Damn it all to hell,* he thought angrily and reined Jones in the direction that Mystic's hoofprints had taken. *If something's happened to Josh, Wade Benson is going to pay and pay dearly.* Travis's steel-gray eyes concentrated on the frozen earth and he tried once again to read the puzzle in the snow.

FOR SEVERAL HOURS Savannah tried to keep herself busy in the house. Fortunately, when Savannah had finally gotten through to Sadie Stinson and told her about Josh, the housekeeper had insisted on braving the elements and driving to the farm. Though Savannah had protested, the housekeeper hadn't been deterred. Now Savannah was glad that Sadie was in the house. Just the familiar sound of clattering pans and the warm scent of Irish stew filling the house relaxed her a bit.

"When that boy get's home, he'll be hungry," Sadie had said when she'd removed her coat and scarf and donned her favorite apron. "And the men, you can bet they'll expect something on the table!"

"You don't have to—"

"Hush, child, and do whatever it is you do around here," the housekeeper had said, shooing Savannah out of the kitchen with a good-natured grin. "And you, too," she'd ordered, when she had spotted Archimedes under the kitchen table. "The kitchen's no place for a sorry mutt like you." Then with a wink, Sadie had extracted a soup bone and handed it to the dog as she'd opened the door to the porch. Archimedes had slid through the portal with his treasure clamped firmly between his jaws.

"Now don't you worry, Savannah," Sadie had cautioned, when Savannah was almost out of the room. "Josh is a smart lad; he'll be all right. And Travis, you can count on that one. He'll find the boy and the horse."

Though Savannah knew the older woman's optimism was more of a show than anything else, she was grateful for the cheer. The gloom that had settled in the house was oppressive. She was glad for the familiar sight of Sadie's happy face and her constant off-tune whistling as she rattled around in the kitchen.

Savannah glanced outside and noticed that there was a slight break in the weather. *Maybe the storm is finally letting up,* she thought without much hope. The sky was still dark and foreboding, but at least the falling snow had eased. Deciding that it was now or never, she went to the barns and talked to the few hands left on the farm, instructing them to let the horses out of their stalls for a little exercise. "Just keep them in the paddocks close to the barns," she told one of the hands. "I want to give them all a chance to stretch their legs." She glanced up at the cloud-covered sky and frowned. "No telling when this will let up, and if it ices over the horses will be stuck inside."

And what about Josh? she wondered grimly.

Not daring to think about what was happening to the boy, she concentrated on the horses. Watching the yearlings as they came out of the barn made her smile. Most of the young horses had never seen snow before, and they pranced gingerly in the white powder as the stable boys walked them around the paddock. Savannah led a chestnut colt around the small fenced area, and nearly laughed when the sleek animal tried to shake the clinging white flakes from his eyelashes.

"Careful now," she cautioned, leading the frisky colt back to the barn as he tossed his head and pulled on the lead rope.

The sound of an engine splitting the silence caught Savannah's attention, and her heart squeezed in apprehension.

It had to be news of Josh and Travis, she thought, quickly instructing the stable hands to finish walking each of the horses as she sprinted over the snow-covered parking lot.

A silver Blazer was parked near the house. Savannah didn't recognize the vehicle, but it could belong to one of the neighbors. *Maybe someone had seen Josh!*

She nearly slipped as she climbed up the back steps. Quickly kicking off her boots and sliding into a pair of loafers she kept on the back porch, she hurried through the kitchen and down the hall following the sound of unfamiliar voices.

Her heart was in her throat by the time she rounded

the corner by the staircase and walked into the living room. Charmaine was standing nervously near the fireplace, her thin face pale and drawn. She seemed relieved to see Savannah.

Two young men whom Savannah had never seen before were sitting on the couch. One of the men, the shorter blond man, had a camera. The taller man held a tape recorder in his hand.

Charmaine made hasty introductions. "This is John Herman and Ed Cook from the *Register*, Savannah." Both men stood, and John stretched out his hand. "My sister, Savannah Beaumont."

"How do you do?" Savannah responded automatically, her eyes narrowing as she shook the reporter's hand.

"Fine," the tall man replied with a grin. "And the pleasure's all mine, Miss Beaumont."

"They've heard about Mystic and Josh," Charmaine said, her voice barely above a whisper. She was leaning against the mantel for support.

"I don't think there's much we can tell you," Savannah admitted, offering what she hoped would appear a sincere smile. *What the devil was the press doing here and who had sent them?* "Not yet."

"But surely you can confirm the rumor that Mystic is missing," John suggested.

"That's true," Savannah stated, wondering why she felt so nervous. "He's been gone since sometime last night."

"And he was stolen—"

"He was not stolen," Charmaine interrupted. "It looks as if my son, Josh, took him for a ride."

John Herman arched his eyebrows skeptically. "In this storm?" Shaking his head as if he didn't believe a word she was telling him, he adjusted his recorder. "But you must be worried; otherwise you wouldn't have called the police."

"Sheriff's department."

"Yeah." He checked his notes and then looked straight at Savannah. "What's the real story?"

"That's about all there is to it."

"So where do you think your son would take a horse like that?" the reporter asked, turning to Charmaine.

"I have no idea."

"Was he running away?"

"No!" Charmaine said, the features of her white face pinching together angrily. She paced from the fireplace to the window, as if by staring into the dark afternoon she could bring Josh back.

"So who's out looking for him?" Herman asked.

"Some of the people here on the ranch. We've called the neighbors, of course, as well as the sheriff's office."

"Maybe we can help."

"How?"

"If you give us a picture of Josh, we'll run it in the paper. There's a chance that someone who's seen the kid will recognize his picture. As for the horse, we've got a lot of photos on file, don't we, Ed?"

Ed nodded. "Yeah, about thirty, I'd guess."

"Good."

John smiled crookedly. "It's a long shot, but worth it, don't you think?"

"Yes," Charmaine said. "I've got a picture of Josh— it's recent; his school picture. It's upstairs, I'll get it." Glad for an excuse to leave the room, and buoyed at the thought of another avenue to locate her son, Charmaine hurried up the stairs.

"I'd appreciate any help you can offer," Savannah said, relaxing a little.

"Good. Then maybe you can explain a few things."

"Such as?"

"Why is Travis McCord back here? This is where he grew up, right?"

Savannah's chest tightened. "He came to live with us when he was seventeen."

"And now he's back. There are a couple of rumors circulating about him."

Savannah felt cold inside and her eyes sparked angrily. "Are there?"

"People are claiming that he's dropping out of the race for governor."

"I didn't know that he'd even announced his candidacy," she replied stiffly, her fingers curling over the back of a velvet chair.

"He hadn't. Not officially. But there's some controversy there, too. A couple of people, especially one lady by the name of Eleanor Phillips, claimed they made contributions to his campaign."

"Even though he hadn't announced his candidacy?" Savannah returned, her voice even, her heart cold with dread. "That doesn't sound too smart. Are you sure you have the story straight?"

The reporter slid her an uneasy smile. "I've got it straight, all right. But I sure would like a chance to interview Mr. McCord."

"He's not here right now."

"Then maybe you or someone else can tell us what the real story is. You know, why he came here from L.A. and threatened to give up practicing law as well as drop out of a primary that he might easily win."

"I can't even guess," Savannah lied. "And I wouldn't want to. What Travis McCord does with his life is his business."

"Here it is!" Charmaine announced, returning to the room and handing the man a picture of Josh. "I really appreciate the fact that you're trying to help," she said.

"No problem," the reporter replied, meeting Savannah's frosty stare. "And if you change your mind or have anything to add to the story…" He handed Savannah one of his business cards. "Tell McCord that I'll call him."

"I will," Savannah promised tightly as Charmaine escorted the two men out the front door. After the reporters were out of the house and Savannah saw the silver Blazer slide out of the driveway, she crumpled John Herman's card in her fist and threw it into the fireplace.

Charmaine paused in the archway of the living room before heading upstairs. "Do you think that running Josh's picture in the paper will help?"

"I don't know," Savannah said, "but it certainly couldn't hurt. Let's just hope by the time that the *Register* is on the stands, Josh and Mystic are home."

"Oh, God, yes," Charmaine whispered desperately. "If he's not home by tonight…" She looked out the window to the darkening skies.

"He will be," Savannah promised, hearing the hollow sound of her own words.

LESTER AND THE stablehand arrived back at the house at nightfall to report that they hadn't seen hide nor hair of the horse or boy. As Lester checked on the horses, Savannah walked with him and explained about the events of the day at the house.

"Why didn't that blasted repairman show up to fix the security system?" Lester asked.

"Problems with the weather, or so he claimed when he called," Savannah replied.

"Just what we need. How's your mother takin' all this?" the grizzled trainer asked Savannah.

"Not well," she admitted. "Josh is pretty special to her."

"Ain't he to all of us?" the older man asked, and then scowled. "Except maybe for that dad of his. Y'know, I can't understand it, the way that man treats his kid. If I were Reginald, I'd—" He caught himself and the hard angles of his face slackened. "Well, I suppose your father knows what he's doing. Just because a man ain't much of a father doesn't mean he can't run the farm, and though I'd never have thought I'd admit it, Wade does a passable job."

"But not great. Right?"

Lester's jaw worked angrily. "Like I said, the man was an accountant, and a decent one, I guess. Just never thought he'd want to work with the horses, that's all."

He opened the door to the stallion barn and let out a long sigh. "Why on earth did that boy take Mystic?" Lester wondered aloud.

"That's the sixty-four-dollar question," Savannah replied with a frown.

Lester slapped her affectionately on the shoulders. "Don't you worry about Josh. Travis will find him."

"I hope so," Savannah replied, close to tears again. She patted Vagabond's silken muzzle and stared at Mystic's empty stall. "I hope so."

An hour later Savannah was in the house, looking through the books of the farm and wondering what Travis had been checking into the night before. She never had been one to work with figures, and this day, while her mind was filled with worried thoughts, she couldn't concentrate on the balances. She slapped the checkbook closed and leaned back in her chair.

Just the night before she had slept in the protective circle of Travis's arms. Never had she felt more secure, more loved. And now he was searching the darkness for Josh.

She stood just as a distant rumble caught her attention. Recognizing the sound of her father's Jeep, her heart began to thud, and she grabbed her coat before racing through the kitchen and outside. It was late evening and the sky was dark, and in the distance she could hear the sound of the Jeep as it roared through the fields closer to the house.

Please God, let Josh be with them, Savannah silently prayed as she searched the night for the welcome beams of the vehicle.

Charmaine was standing on the back porch in an instant. "Oh, God," she whispered, just as the Jeep came into view. "Oh, God. Is he with them?" Running out of the porch and down the slippery steps, she hurried to the garage.

Savannah was only a step behind her sister.

Reginald cut the engine and emerged from the truck. He looked exhausted. His weary eyes sought those of his elder daughter. "I guess this means that Josh hasn't shown up."

Charmaine nearly collapsed. "You didn't find him?" she asked, her face ghostly with anguish.

Wade got out of the passenger side of the Jeep and tried to place a comforting arm around his wife, but Charmaine backed away from him. Stiffening, he sent Savannah a silent glare. "Now I suppose you're blaming me," he said to his wife.

"I'm not blaming anyone," Charmaine whispered, her fists clenching as she pounded the fender of the Jeep. "I just want Josh home and safe!"

"What about Travis?" Savannah asked. Her heart was

beating wildly with worry for her nephew as well as Travis. *Where were they and why hadn't Travis returned?*

Reginald just shook his head. "Last we saw of him, he'd had no luck. He was going to keep following the tracks as far as he could. We had to turn back when it seemed as if the horse had gone into a thicket of oak."

"I don't even think that was Mystic's trail," Wade said, pulling nervously on his moustache and looking scared. "The damned part of it is, Travis won't find him, not tonight. Those hoofprints were nearly invisible. Now that it's dark, searching any longer would be a waste of time. We'll have to call the police, ask for choppers in the morning."

"No!" Charmaine nearly screamed, shaking her head violently and impaling her husband with furious green eyes. "We've got to find him! Tonight! He'll freeze if he stays out there all night!"

Savannah couldn't help but agree. She was anxious to join the search herself. Travis and Joshua were somewhere in the wilderness, possibly hurt, and she couldn't wait through a long, lonely night just hoping that they would be safe in the morning. She kept her thoughts to herself and just told her father the important facts. "We talked to the sheriff's office earlier today," she said, once they were all walking back to the house.

"I think we'd better call again," Reginald thought aloud.

Once inside the house, Savannah called Deputy Smith and told him that the search party had returned without Josh or Mystic. Charmaine, trying to control herself, told Reginald and Wade about the reporters, the deputy, and the fact that Lester hadn't seen any sign of Josh.

"Where could he be?" Wade asked angrily, stalking

to the bar in the living room and pouring himself a stiff drink.

"He's got to be somewhere on the farm," Reginald said.

"We searched every square inch of this place," Wade reminded him, tossing back his bourbon.

"Except where the Jeep couldn't go."

"The rest of it is up to McCord," Wade said, pouring himself another shot. "He and that horse will have to ride down the ravines and through the forests. Like I said, our only hope is police helicopters in the morning."

Savannah walked into the room and heard only the tail-end of the conversation, but she could see from the fear in Charmaine's wide eyes that nothing of consequence had been decided.

"I'd better go upstairs and talk to your mother," Reginald said, looking as if he dreaded the conversation. "How's she been?"

"Remote," Savannah admitted.

"Worried sick, I'll bet," Reginald muttered. "Well, hell, aren't we all?"

Sadie came into the living room and tried to liven up the crowd. "Dinner's on. Now, come on, all of you. We'll eat and make some plans about finding the boy. None of us can think on an empty stomach."

"I'm not hungry," Charmaine said, but Sadie only offered her a stern look.

"I've set the dining room table, including a place for Virginia. I think a hot meal would do all of us a world of good!" Sadie reprimanded.

After much cajoling on Sadie's part everyone sat down at the dinner table. The conversation was strained, and though the meal was superb, Savannah barely tasted it. Her thoughts were moving furiously forward, and she nearly jumped when she heard the grandfather clock chime nine o'clock, just as Sadie served an elegant lemon mousse.

Savannah spooned the light dessert into her mouth, but didn't taste it. She was too busy thinking ahead. If Travis didn't return within the hour, Savannah decided, she would go out and find him. Her father would be furious, of course, so she would have to leave the house behind his back and then argue with the security guard posted at the stables. But she couldn't stay cooped up in the house another minute. Come hell or high water, she intended to find Travis and Josh, and she intended to find them before morning!

CHAPTER EIGHT

AT ELEVEN O'CLOCK that night, Savannah was alone. The house was quiet as everyone had watched the ten-o'clock news and then gone to bed, but Savannah's thoughts were screaming inside her head.

Exhausted from the nerve-wracking day, she sat on the edge of her bed and considered trying to sleep, but she knew that despite her weariness she was too restless and worried. Her mind was turning in endless circles of anxiety about Josh and Travis.

Staring out the window, she silently cursed the snowfall then slapped her palm against the cool sill. She was tired of waiting, tired of worrying and had to do something before she went stark, raving mad!

With renewed determination, she walked to the closet, jerked on her warmest riding clothes and silently went downstairs. Once through the hallway she paused in the kitchen at the pantry and grabbed a box of matches, two flares and a flashlight from the small closet.

"What else will I need?" she asked herself and tapped her fingers on the open pantry door. "Lord only knows." With a frown she took a couple of candy bars and stuffed them into her jacket pocket. "So much for nutrition," she muttered wryly.

Going out in this weather is insane, she thought to herself as she pulled on her gloves and wound a scarf around her neck before slipping out the back door. The cold night air cut through her suede jacket as easily as a knife. *Travis will kill you if he catches you,* she cautioned herself, but kept walking, through the backyard, down the path past the garage and across the parking lot to the stables.

The wind whistled and howled through the trees, and the icy snow stung her cheeks, but she had her mind set. She had to find Travis and Josh and there was no time to waste. The news reports indicated that the storm wouldn't let up for several days. *It's now or never,* she thought as she marched through the snow.

"Wait a minute," a male voice called to her just as she reached for the handle on the door to the main stables. "What're you doing?" Johnny, one of the stable hands who had appointed himself security guard when he found out that Joshua and Mystic were missing, placed a hand on Savannah's shoulder. She whirled around to face him and saw the confusion cross his face in the darkness. "Miss Beaumont? What're you doing out here?"

"I'm going looking for Josh."

"Tonight? Are you crazy?"

"Maybe, but I can't stand being cooped up another minute."

The young man was obviously nervous. He dropped his hand from her shoulder and rubbed his jaw pensively. Johnny was used to taking orders from Savannah, but he couldn't believe that she actually planned to light out in the middle of a cold, wintry night like this one. "Reginald said that none of the horses were to leave the stables and no one was to go in."

"I know, Johnny, but Mattie is *my* mare."

Johnny's small eyes moved from Savannah to the cold, dark night and the constantly falling snow. "I don't see that you can do any good out on a horse in the middle of all this," he said, gesturing helplessly at the frozen surroundings.

"As much good as I'll do if I stay in the house."

"Except that tomorrow morning we might have to send a search party after you."

"Tomorrow morning the storm is supposed to get worse."

"I don't know…."

"I'll be careful," she promised, reaching for the door.

"Really, Miss Beaumont—"

She offered him her most disarming smile. "You're off the hook with my dad. I'm taking full responsibility for my actions."

He was wavering, but didn't seem convinced. Savannah pushed a little harder.

"Look, I promise I'll stay on Beaumont land and if the storm gets any worse, I'll come right back. You know Mattie, she could find her way back to the barn in an earthquake."

"It's not the horse I'm worried about."

"Well, don't worry about me. I'm twenty-six. I can take care of myself, and I'll absolutely go out of my mind if I have to stay cooped up a minute longer."

The poor man looked caught between the proverbial rock and a hard place. "You're the boss," he finally admitted. "But I think I should tell Wade or Reginald."

"And worry them further?" she asked. "Because whether they like it or not, I'm going after Josh." Feeling less strong than her words, Savannah turned back to the door of the stables and walked inside the barn without any further protest from Johnny. *Maybe he will tell Reginald,* Savannah thought as she pulled down the saddle and placed it on Mattie's broad back. If Johnny went

through with his threat, she'd deal with her father when
Reginald came roaring out of the house.

The little bay mare snorted and stamped her foot at
the interruption in her sleep and several other horses
looked inquisitively at Savannah, their dark ears pricked
forward expectantly.

"It's okay, girl," Savannah whispered, tightening the
cinch and slipping a bridle over the nervous mare's head.
"So far, so good."

Obviously Johnny had decided against waking Reginald with the news that his youngest daughter had her
mind set on taking a cold ride through a snowstorm.
Otherwise Reginald would already have come storming
to the barn in a rage. *Thank God for small favors,* Savannah thought.

Leading the mare out the back door and through the
series of paddocks surrounding the stables, Savannah
braced herself against the rising wind. She walked Mattie past the stallion barn and heard the quiet whinny of
one of the horses that had been awakened by the unusual
noises in the night.

The snow all but covered the hoofprints that had been
visible earlier in the day. Only the deep ruts of the Jeep
remained in the crystalline powder, but even the double
tire tracks were disappearing rapidly. Her lips tightening
as she tried to read the trails in the soft snow, Savannah
climbed into the saddle and pressed her heels into Mattie's warm flanks. "Let's go," she said encouragingly,
then wondered if she was talking to herself or the mare.

Deciding to work on intuition rather than fact, Savannah ignored the direction of Mystic's tracks and headed
the little mare to the lake. As Mattie slowly circled the
dark water, Savannah scanned the darkness and called
Josh's name.

No response.

Reining in the horse to a stop and straining to hear over the roar of the wind, she tried shouting again, but still there was no answer.

"Strike one," Savannah muttered to herself. With a deepening sense of dread, she circled the lake and skirted the center of the farm until she came to a field with an old apple tree and a tree house that Josh had constructed the previous summer.

Tying Mattie to the thick trunk of the tree, Savannah climbed up the makeshift ladder of loose boards nailed into the bark and trained the beam of her flashlight inside the rough structure. The interior of the tree house was deserted, snow covering the dirty floorboards as it slipped through the cracks in the roof.

Savannah directed the thin beam of light around the crude shack in the branches and then, from her perch in the doorway, moved the light to the snow-covered earth. Again there was no sign of the boy or his horse.

"Great," she muttered under her breath as she snapped off the flashlight. *This isn't getting us anywhere,* she thought with a sigh. How many times last summer had she had to track down Josh for dinner and found him in his favorite spot, hidden in the branches of the gnarled old apple tree? *But not tonight.*

As Savannah climbed down the ladder, untied Mattie and pulled herself into the saddle, another image crossed her mind. The picture in her mind was of herself as a seventeen-year-old girl, sitting upon a much younger Mattie under the umbrella of the protective apple tree while secretively watching Travis as he strung the wire over a broken fence.

Don't torture yourself, she reprimanded herself, but thoughts of Travis and Josh spurred her into action. She turned Mattie's head and urged the little mare toward the fields surrounding the stallion barn. Having checked all of Josh's favorite hiding spots, she decided to follow Mystic's almost nonexistent trail into the hills.

As long as the double ruts of Reginald's four-wheel-drive unit were still visible, Savannah was able to follow Mystic's path. The journey was long and cold, but she bent her head against the wind and kept riding, silently promising herself that if she ever saw Travis and Joshua again, she would never let them out of her sight.

Don't think like that, she thought angrily. *Be positive.* But the cold blast of the wind and the silence around her made the doubts in her mind loom like foreboding ghosts that couldn't be driven away.

TRAVIS SWORE UNDER his breath. *Not one damned sign of the boy!* Where the devil had he gone? Josh couldn't have vanished into thin air. Of course, there was the remote possibility that Josh had returned to the house, but Travis didn't think so. Reginald had promised to send off flares and fire a rifle shot three times in succession if the boy had been located. Neither signal had reached Travis and despite the fact that he distrusted Reginald's politics, Travis was certain the old man would be true to his word and let him know about Josh's safety.

Huddling against the wind, he scowled and considered stopping to build a fire. He was cold to the bone, his face raw from the bite of the frigid air, and Jones, game as the gelding was, needed a rest. Trudging through the snow with a two-hundred-pound man on his back had tired the horse.

"Well, let's see what we've got here," Travis said to himself. Dismounting, he let Jones drink a small amount of water from a near-frozen stream.

His eyes trained on the ground, Travis walked to the edge of the clearing, plowing through half a foot of snow. He stretched his legs and tired back muscles; it had been years since he'd spent so much time in the saddle, and his thighs and lower back were already beginning to ache and cramp.

To Travis, the rest of the night looked bleak. In the morning, he'd have no choice but to return to the farm. Both he and the horse would have to rest. Maybe the roads would be more passable and maybe in the light of a new day, the boy would be found.

The creases near the corners of his eyes deepened as he squinted through the darkened pines. A slight movement caught his eye and he focused all of his attention through the thick curtain of snow.

Nothing stirred. He wondered if he was beginning to imagine things in his desperation to find the child.

Where the hell was Josh? Travis had scoured every inch of Beaumont land and there had been no trace of the boy or the fiery black colt. When Travis had lost Mystic's tracks just before nightfall, he hadn't been able to find any clue as to Josh's whereabouts. He paled beneath his tan when he thought about what might have happened on the more rugged federal land that bordered the farm.

Was the boy lying unconscious somewhere with snow piling over him, or did the kid have enough sense to seek shelter for himself and his horse? The bitter thought that Josh might not be alive crossed his mind again. Travis's jaw hardened with renewed determination. The longer the boy was on his own in the wilderness, the slimmer were his chances of survival.

After walking back to his horse, Travis lifted his Stetson from his head, scratched his head and then replaced the hat. "Let's go," he muttered angrily as he swung into the saddle, lifted the reins and directed the horse across the slippery rocks of the stream before shouting Josh's name into the darkness.

Again he saw a movement through the trees. This time he didn't hesitate, but dug his heels into Jones's sides and took out after whatever was hiding in the shadows.

SAVANNAH'S TOES FELT as if they would fall off. Even though she was wearing riding gloves, her fingers were stiff. *Maybe Johnny was right,* she thought angrily. *Maybe riding out here was nothing more than a fiasco. If I'm not home by morning, Mom and Dad will be worried out of their minds!* Still, the idea of turning back stuck in her throat. At least she was trying to find Josh rather than lying in a warm bed hoping the boy was all right.

She bit at her lower lip as she studied the ground. For over an hour, since the point where the tire tracks had turned back in the direction of the house, she'd seen no sign of Josh or Travis. If there had been hoofprints in the snow, they had long been covered with the drifting white powder.

Travis. Had it only been last night that she had slept in the strength of his arms? It seemed like an eternity had passed without him. *God, where was he? Was he all right?*

Her voice was raw from shouting Josh's name over the whistle of the wind. Her own words echoed back to her unanswered and the silence filled her heart with dread. "Merry Christmas," she whispered sarcastically, tears from both the stinging wind and her tortured thoughts filling her eyes.

She shivered as she came to the clearing where she, Josh and Travis had cut down the Christmas tree only two days before. Urging Mattie forward, she ignored her pleasant memories of cutting the tree, the snowball fight, decorating the room and making love to Travis…. It all seemed so long ago.

The storm continued to rage, and Savannah bent her head against the wind. Mattie was laboring through the drifts, and snow was falling so thickly that it was almost impossible to see.

Savannah was almost on the verge of giving up her search and starting back to the house when a slight movement in the surrounding trees caught her attention. Mattie shied and nickered nervously, and Savannah's skin crawled in fear before she recognized the big black colt.

"Mystic!" she cried, her heart leaping at the sight of him. "Josh?"

Then she froze as she realized Mystic's saddle was missing, and the reins to his bridle were loose and dragging on the ground. "Oh, Lord," she moaned, dismounting and tying an anxious Mattie to a scrub oak. "Josh! Josh, can you hear me?" *Please let him be all right.*

She approached the black colt cautiously, but Mystic sidestepped, rearing on unsteady hind legs and slashing in the air with his forelegs. He tossed his head menacingly and snorted. His dark eyes were wild looking; rimmed in white from fear. As he reared he stumbled backward and let out an anguished squeal.

"It's all right, boy," Savannah whispered, knowing that the horse was more than frightened. It was obvious from Mystic's erratic behavior that he was in severe pain. She walked up to the colt confidently, hoping to instill some calm into the overwrought animal.

"Be careful!" a voice warned, and Savannah turned to see Travis, leading Jones, step out of the trees. Relief swept through her body at the sight of him. Both he and his horse looked past exhaustion.

"Thank God you're all right!" she whispered, running to Travis, throwing her arms around his neck and warming just at the feel of his arms around her. "I've been worried sick about you!" She couldn't help the tears of relief that pooled in her eyes as she clung to him and kissed his beard-roughened cheek. The smell and taste of him was wonderful, but the feeling of joy was short-lived. "Where's Josh?" she asked, when she felt the restraint in his embrace.

"I don't know," he said softly. "I haven't seen him."

Savannah's heart squeezed in fear. "But Mystic…"

Travis slowly released her and wearily rubbed the back of his forehead. "I know," he admitted, "I thought when I found the horse, I'd find the boy. But I didn't. And right now we've got to catch this one and calm him down." He fixed his eyes on the skittish colt while he tied Jones to a branch of a tree next to Mattie. "And you be careful around him," Travis warned Savannah, keeping his voice low and calm. "He's hurt and scared out of his wits. I've been following him for about a couple of hundred yards. There's something wrong with his right foreleg."

"No—"

"Shh…" Travis continued to advance slowly on the nervous horse. "Steady, boy," he whispered, slowly extending his hand toward Mystic's head.

The frightened animal bolted out of the clearing. "Son of a bitch," Travis muttered. "This is what happened when I came across him a couple of hours ago, but he can't go far…." Travis trained the beam of the flashlight onto the snow, displaying Mystic's tracks as well as bloody splotches where the colt had stood.

"Oh, God," Savannah moaned. "What do you think happened? Where's Josh?"

"I wish I knew," Travis replied, starting out after the horse. "Come on. Let's go."

Slowly, with the quiet determination and ruthlessness of a predator stalking prey, Travis followed the colt. Mystic was standing under a naked maple tree, his ebony coat wet with sweat, his glistening muscles shivering with apprehension. Wild-eyed and ready to bolt, he watched Savannah and Travis as they approached.

"It's all right," Savannah said to the horse.

The colt moaned, tried to rear and finally stood still as Travis, moving with quiet deliberation, took hold of the bridle and wrapped the reins firmly around his right hand.

"Oh, no," Savannah whispered, coming close to the horse and seeing the frozen lather clinging to the big colt's body. She held her breath while Travis ran experienced hands down Mystic's shoulders and legs.

When Travis's fingers touched a sensitive spot on Mystic's foreleg, Mystic reared and jerked his black head upward with such force that the movement nearly wrenched Travis's right arm out of its socket.

"Whoa," Travis ordered, wincing and forcing the colt's head back down in order to continue his examination. "Damn!" He felt the distinctive bump near Mystic's ankle when his fingers touched the horse's foreleg and Mystic tried to rear again.

"What?"

Travis sighed and shook his head. "I think it's broken. The leg's swollen and he's favoring it. When I touch the area over his sesamoid bones, he nearly jumps out of his skin."

Travis tied Mystic's reins to the nearby tree, then trained the beam of his flashlight on the wound. Savannah felt her stomach turn over at the sight of the bloodied gash. She examined Mystic's leg and swallowed back the urge to scream in frustration. "Maybe it's just sprained," she whispered hopefully.

"Maybe." Travis didn't sound convinced.

"So, what now?"

Travis's jaw hardened and his eyes flashed with determination when he turned them upon her. "First we find a way to get him back to the barn, then we find Josh, and then maybe you could give me a quick explanation as to why you're out here."

"There's no time right now," she hedged, eyeing Mystic.

Travis studied the big black colt and sighed when he realized that she was right. They had to work fast to avoid injuring the horse any further. And then there was Josh to find…. "Okay, you win. For now. But when this is all over, you can bet your hide that I'll want an explanation from you and it had better be good."

"It will be," she said frostily, then turned her attention back to the horse. "I don't think he should walk any farther than absolutely necessary."

"Agreed." Travis ran a hand over his stubbled chin. "If you ride Mattie, it will only take an hour, maybe less, to cut through the fields and get back to the house." Travis studied the big colt with a practiced eye. "I'll stay here with him until you can get Lester or Reginald to drive the truck up the federal road…I think it cuts through the land on the other side of the fence, about four hundred yards north."

"It does."

"Then bring wire cutters. We'll have to cut open the fence to get Mystic through."

Savannah hesitated. "I don't want to leave you."

Travis managed a weary, but rakish smile. "Just for

a little longer," he promised, "until we can get the horse back to the farm. Oh, and call the vet."

"I will."

"And bring up a fresh horse and a couple of rugs for these two." He motioned toward Mystic and Jones.

"Why the extra horse?" she asked, dreading the answer.

"Jones is tired."

"And you want to keep looking for Josh?" she surmised, not knowing whether to feel glad or worried.

"I found the horse, didn't I? The boy couldn't be far away."

"Only miles," she speculated.

"Not if he fell off when Mystic hurt his leg. I can't believe that Mystic would try to travel that far when he was in as much pain as I think he feels. Anyway, let's hope not, for Josh's sake."

There was logic to Travis's thoughts and for the first time that night, Savannah felt a glimmer of hope that they would be able to find Josh and bring him home. *Unless he was dead,* she thought, her heart fluttering with panic.

"Don't think like that," Travis said, his gray eyes delving into hers as he seemed to read her morbid thoughts. "We'll find him and he'll be all right."

"Oh, God, I hope so."

Travis's arms surrounded her. "Come on," he urged, pressing his cold lips to her forehead and hugging her fiercely. "Don't lose the faith; not now. Josh, Mystic and I are counting on you."

"Okay," Savannah whispered, then sniffed, pushing her worries aside and bracing herself for what promised to be a long, tiring night.

"I knew I could count on you," Travis said, slowly releasing her.

She mounted Mattie reluctantly, unable to tear herself away from Travis. There was something in the cold night air that seemed to warn her that leaving him would cause certain disaster.

Travis noticed her hesitation and he looked up and forced a tired smile. "Buck up, will ya? It's only a little while longer," he whispered, reaching up and stroking her trembling chin with his gloved hand. "And then it will be over."

"And Josh?"

"I'll find him," Travis promised, hoping that he sounded more sure of himself than he felt. "I won't give up until I do."

His fingers wrapped around the nape of her neck, and he pulled her head slowly downward until his lips brushed hers. "Don't you know there's nothing that can keep me away from you?"

Savannah's raw throat went dry. "I hope so," she whispered as he kissed her chilled lips, and she realized how desperately she loved him. Her heart seemed to bleed at the prospect of leaving him.

"Now, go on. Get out of here," he commanded, once the kiss had ended. He squared his shoulders and looked directly into her eyes. "You'd better hustle because I'm going to give you about a forty-minute head start and then I'm going to fire rifle shots into the air. That should wake everyone up at the house. Then I'll send up my flares. By that time, you should be getting back and everyone will be ready to go. Have Lester bring the truck with the fresh horse."

"And the wire cutters."

"Right."

"I'll throw in a thermos of coffee and a sandwich," she said, and then as a sudden thought struck her, she dug into her pockets for the candy bars. "It's not much, but here." She tossed him the snack.

Travis smiled and caught the candy. "You're an angel of mercy."

"I doubt it," she said, her eyes scanning the darkened landscape as she thought about Travis staying up there alone. "Do you really think that staying out here tonight looking for Josh will do any good?"

Travis stared straight into her eyes, his face suddenly solemn. "I don't think I have any choice. Do you?"

"No, I guess not," she admitted, gazing longingly into his eyes before reining Mattie toward the farm.

Travis watched her leave the clearing before striding through the snow to Jones, taking off the horse's saddle and blanket and placing the blanket over Mystic's quivering shoulders.

"I don't know how much good this will do, old boy, but it's better than nothing." He patted Mystic and then walked back to Jones and frowned, rubbing the gelding's neck. "Hardly seems fair, does it? Unfortunately, that's the way life is."

SAVANNAH RELUCTANTLY LEFT Travis, calling Josh's name as she started back to the farm. She listened but heard nothing other than the steady crunch of Mattie's hooves in the snow. The wind whipped at her face and pushed her hair away from her neck while her thoughts lingered on Travis standing guard over Mystic.

"Josh," she screamed again, cupping her gloved hands to her mouth. "Josh! Where are you?" There was no response other than the rustle of the wind through brittle leaves and the mournful cry of a winter bird disturbed from his sleep. *"Dear Lord, let me find him,"* she whispered to herself. Where was he? Was he still alive, or lying half-frozen somewhere nearby?

Mattie came to an unexpected halt and sidestepped.

Savannah's eyes pierced the darkness, but she saw nothing. Knowing it was futile, she called one last time to Josh and waited for a response.

Somewhere in the distance, she heard a faint reply, a small groan in the darkness. Savannah's heart skipped a beat, and she told herself that she was probably just imagining what she'd heard. As loudly as possible, she called again. Not daring to breathe, she waited. This time the reply was more distinct.

Her heart in her throat, she urged Mattie forward, following the sound of Josh's voice and calling to him continually. "I'm coming," she yelled over the shriek of the wind, praying silently that Josh could hear her. To her relief, she saw Travis riding Jones through the trees.

"I heard you," he said, "I would have been here sooner but I had to resaddle old Jones here." Then he shouted Josh's name as loudly as possible.

The boy's groans sounded closer.

"He's alive," Savannah whispered, tears of relief threatening her eyes as Mattie plowed through the snow until they came to the edge of a steep ridge and they could ride no farther. "Josh, where are you?" she called, her voice echoing in the snow-drifted canyon.

"Here…help me…." The boy's feeble voice came from somewhere below.

"I'm here, Josh," Savannah replied, nearly jumping off Mattie and racing to the edge of the ravine. *Oh, God, it was so dark and so far down.* She could barely make out Josh's inert form in the snow. "We'll get you out of there in no time," she said, with more conviction than she felt. "You just hang in there."

Travis was at her side, his narrowed eyes surveying the snow for the quickest path to the boy. "I think I'd better handle this," he said.

"But he needs me," she protested.

"And how're you going to carry him?" Without waiting for her response, he took a rope from his saddle bag and anchored it around the trunk of a sturdy pine.

"Let me go after him," she pleaded.

"Just this once, Savannah, do as you're told, okay? If I need help, I'll yell, but the last thing I need is to have you get yourself hurt trying to help the boy. Now, I don't have time to argue with you."

Gritting her teeth, Savannah backed down. "Just get him up here."

"I will."

After securing the other end of the rope around his waist, Travis carefully picked his way down the steep hillside. Savannah watched from the top of the ridge.

The boy was huddled under the relative protection of a small pine tree. "How're ya doin'?" Travis asked, once he was near enough to talk to Josh.

Josh didn't answer. His teeth were chattering, and he was shaking from head to foot.

"Come on, let's check you out and see if I can carry you out of here." Carefully Travis examined the boy, feeling for any broken bones. "I know this is going to hurt, Josh, but we've got to get you home. Can you make it?"

Josh nodded weakly, but he didn't attempt to stand.

Travis threw his coat over the boy and gently lifted him from the hard ground. He considered his options. Either he could take the boy out of there now, or wait until Savannah went for help. But that could take hours. "Look, Josh, I'm going to try and carry you out of here. Do you think you can make it?"

"Don't know," the boy admitted, and groaned as Travis shifted his weight.

"It won't be long now," Travis encouraged, starting up the steep hillside, the boy pressed to his chest.

Savannah watched as Travis slowly climbed up the snow-covered incline. It seemed to take hours. He slipped twice and she gasped as she watched him fall, then regain his footing, until he finally made it to the top of the ridge.

"Oh, Josh," she whispered, kissing the boy on the head and crying softly. "Thank God you're alive." Tears were streaming down her face as she touched Josh's cold skin. "He's freezing."

"We've got to get him back, but I don't think he can ride alone, and Jones is too worn out to carry two of us. Can you hold him in the saddle with you?"

"Of course."

"Good." After Savannah mounted Mattie, Travis helped Josh into the saddle.

"Where's Mystic?" Josh asked faintly once they were moving. He was pressed against her body, quivering from pain.

"I've got him tied; we'll send a truck for him when we get down the hill," Travis assured the boy.

"Shh. Don't worry about Mystic," Savannah said, her voice soothing as she helped hold Josh in the saddle. "We'll get him home. You just take care of yourself."

The journey back to the house seemed to take forever. Savannah's arms ached from the strain of holding Josh while trying to balance on Mattie. Josh didn't talk, but only groaned during the ride.

Savannah could hardly take her eyes off Josh, and she held him until she thought her arms might break. By the time the buildings of the farm came into view, the first

streaks of dawn were lighting the sky, and Savannah recognized Lester's pickup in the parking lot.

They had barely gotten into the paddock near the stables when Lester spotted them. His grizzled face spread
into a wide grin, and he told Johnny to wake everyone
in the house to let them know that Josh had been found.

"You're a sight for sore eyes, child," Lester said to Josh
as he and Travis carefully got the boy out of the saddle.

Charmaine and Wade met the ragged party just as
they approached the house. Charmaine was dressed in
her nightgown, bathrobe and boots. "Josh," she called,
tears streaming down her face. "Oh, honey, are you all
right? Let me look at you."

"I think I'd better take him inside," Travis said.

"No. Give him to me." She took the boy in her arms
and held him tightly to her breast before raising tear-filled
eyes to Travis. "Thank God you found him!"

"You'd better call an ambulance," Travis replied. "He's
hurt and nearly frozen."

"Oh, baby," Charmaine whispered, turning to the
house. Josh clung to his mother as if to life itself. Charmaine was sobbing and Savannah felt her own tears tightening her throat.

"Let's get him inside," Wade suggested, unable to do
anything other than appear worried. "What the devil were
you doing out there?" he asked Savannah, but she didn't
bother to respond.

"What about Mystic?" Lester asked.

"We've got to go back to get him," Travis said, watching as Charmaine walked through the back door with
Josh. "He's hurt and it looks bad. Right foreleg, probably his ankle."

Lester scowled. "I'll get the truck." He was off in a
minute.

Travis turned to Savannah. His countenance was grave, his silvery eyes narrowed with worry and shadowed from lack of sleep. "I've got to go back for the horse, but you take care of Josh. Make sure an ambulance is on the way, and don't forget to call the vet."

"I won't," she said, running to the house.

Slipping her boots off on the back porch, she entered the kitchen and smiled at the sight of Archimedes under the table. "Sadie will skin you alive if she catches you," she murmured to the dog, who responded with a sigh.

The warmth of the house made her skin tingle, and she jerked off her gloves with her teeth and set them on the counter.

Rubbing her hands together, she walked through the kitchen and down the short hallway to the den. Wade was just hanging up the phone.

"Ambulance?" she asked.

"It's on its way."

"Good. What about Josh?"

Wade frowned. His blond hair was stringing over his eyes and his skin was white with worry. "Charmaine's got him upstairs in his room. He…he doesn't look all that good," Wade said nervously.

"He was thrown from a horse, fell down a mountainside and spent over twenty-four hours outside in a snowstorm the likes of which we hardly ever get around here. He probably feels terrible!"

"I hope he'll be all right."

Savannah's eyes narrowed on her brother-in-law, and all of her anger and frustration exploded. "He'd be a lot more 'all right' if you'd treated him like your son, like you care about him, instead of acting like he's just one big bother!"

"I try—"

"Bull!"

"I don't relate to children very well."

"He's your son, dammit. Don't give me any excuses, Wade, or college buzzwords like 'relate.' Just give the kid a chance; that's all he wants. The bottom line is he needs your love!"

"I know, I know," Wade admitted, his fingers rubbing anxiously together. "But I can't help it if he gets on my nerves."

"My God, you almost lost a child and all you can say is that he gets on your nerves. That's disgusting, Wade. Think of what he's been through! Maybe it's time you showed him some compassion!" Savannah's cheeks were flushed, and she didn't bother to hide the rage and loathing she felt for her brother-in-law.

Wade paled slightly but didn't move. He had no response to her outburst. "God, Savannah, this is no time to get angry. What about Mystic? Where is he?"

"Still on the mountain. Travis and Lester are going to get him." She turned away from Wade in disgust, grabbed the telephone receiver and punched out the number of the local veterinarian, Steve Anderson. When he answered, Savannah explained about Mystic's condition and the vet assured her that he'd be over as quickly as possible, considering the conditions of the roads.

Just as she hung up, Reginald entered the room. He looked as if he hadn't slept all night. "What's this I hear about you taking off last night?" he asked.

"I couldn't sleep."

Reginald paled and ran his fingers over his head. "I was just up in Josh's room with Charmaine. That boy's been through hell and back. And you, taking off in that storm; that was a foolish thing to do. Good Lord, Savannah, we could have lost you, too!"

She shook her head and waved off her father's fears. "But you didn't and Josh is safe."

"Thank God. I think I need a drink."

"Me, too," Wade agreed, starting for the liquor cabinet.

"Why aren't you with your son?" Reginald demanded.

Stopping dead in his tracks, Wade turned to face his father-in-law. "I just got through calling the ambulance."

"Hmph."

Wade's back stiffened. "I'm as worried as you are about Josh, but I thought it would be better if he spent a little time alone with his mother."

Savannah didn't want to hear any of Wade's feeble excuses. She sighed and faced Reginald. "Travis and Lester are going to get Mystic."

"I'll go with them," Reginald decided.

"You should know something first," she said quietly. "Mystic's injured, Dad."

Reginald went ashen at the grim expression on her features. "Seriously?"

"I don't know, but it's his foreleg, around the ankle... well, you can judge for yourself. I've already called the vet."

"The horse will be all right," Wade said, looking to Savannah for support.

"I hope so," she replied, before walking toward the foyer. "I want to see Josh before the ambulance gets here."

"And you'll look after your mother, won't you?" Reginald asked, as he walked into the foyer, grabbed his coat from the closet and placed a warm cap on his head. "She's been worried sick about the boy."

"Of course."

"Tell Josh that I'll be up in a minute," Wade said,

following Reginald. "I just want to see that they've got enough men to get the horse."

"Sure," Savannah said with a weary sigh. *Put your kid last again,* she thought as she hurried up the stairs to Josh's room. He was lying in bed, Charmaine huddling over him.

"How're ya feelin', sport?" Savannah asked.

Josh tried to smile, but couldn't.

Savannah's heart wrenched for the child. "The ambulance will be here in a minute. They'll fix you up, good as new. I promise."

Josh's worried brows drew together and when he spoke his voice was only a rough whisper. "What about Mystic?"

"Grandpa and Travis are going to get him right now," Savannah said. "Now don't think about him, you just take care of yourself, okay?"

Josh turned away from her and closed his eyes, letting exhaustion carry him away.

Am ambulance arrived a little later, and two attendants put Josh on a stretcher before carrying him downstairs. Savannah watched as Wade nervously paced the foyer between the den and the living room.

"Aunt Savvy?" Josh whispered to her as the attendants stopped in the hallway.

She walked over to the stretcher and took hold of the boy's hand. "What is it?"

"Will you come with me?"

"Of course I will," she answered, but Wade held up his hands in protest.

"No dice, Savannah," he whispered loudly. "I want you to leave Josh alone. If you hadn't encouraged him to ride that horse in the first place, we wouldn't be in this position, would we?"

"Dad—"

Savannah gave Josh a silent glance that warned him to be quiet. "I only want what's best for Josh."

"Please," the boy begged, his voice cracking. "Come with me."

Swallowing back the urge to cry, Savannah looked at Josh's drawn face and shook her head. "I'll come visit you later, but right now I think I'd better made sure the vet gets here to check on Mystic."

"Is he hurt?"

"We don't know, but he's had a pretty wild twenty-four hours. I promise to let you know how he is, okay?"

"Okay," Josh replied with obvious effort, wincing at a stab of pain.

"Good. And the minute you get home, we'll have Christmas."

"But Christmas is tomorrow."

"We'll wait for you," Savannah said.

"Promise?"

"Promise!"

She let go of Josh's hand and fought her tears.

"We'll be at the hospital," Charmaine told Savannah as she came hurrying down the stairs with an overnight bag. "I'm riding with Josh, and Wade will bring the car."

"Not alone, he won't," Virginia stated from the top of the stairs. She was dressed and holding on to the banister as she slowly descended. "I'm coming, too."

"You don't have to be there," Charmaine said.

"I know I don't, but Josh is my grandson and I intend to be at the hospital with him."

"Lady?" One of the attendants prodded Charmaine.

"I'm coming," Charmaine replied. "You two fight this out," she said to Wade and Virginia, as she followed the attendants outside and shut the door behind her.

"There isn't going to be a fight and that's that," Virginia stated evenly.

"Mom?" Savannah asked, but saw the look of defiance in Virginia's proud stare.

"Are you sure you're up to this?" Wade asked skeptically. "I think you should rest—"

"I'm going to the hospital. I think this is a good chance for you and me to have a little talk about your relationship with Josh."

"I don't think—"

"That we have much time," Virginia finished for him. "Let's go."

"All right," Wade said tightly, but turned his eyes to Savannah. "I want you to call me when the vet examines Mystic."

"And I'll expect the same from you when the doctor checks Josh."

Wearing a pained expression, Wade walked briskly out the door after Virginia, leaving Savannah to wait for news of Mystic.

Travis and Lester returned within the hour.

Steve Anderson, the local veterinarian for the farm, was already waiting in the office over the stables when the big truck slowly drove into the stable yard.

"Well, let's see how bad it is," the vet said, getting up from the table and setting down his coffee cup. He and Savannah quickly put on their jackets before going outside to meet the truck.

Travis was the first man out of the cab, and from the expression on his face, Savannah guessed that returning Mystic to the farm had been more difficult than expected. The strain was obvious in his eyes.

"It doesn't look good," Travis admitted, placing a

strong arm around Savannah's shoulders for support. "Lester agrees with me; he thinks Mystic's broken his sesamoids."

"Maybe not," Savannah said hopefully, but grim lines deepened beside Travis's mouth.

Lester and Reginald had opened the back of the truck and were attempting to lead Mystic outside.

The horse was in a state of shock. Wild-eyed and flailing his hooves at anything that moved, Mystic tried to bolt when the veterinarian bent to look at him.

"I think he's broken his leg, sesamoid bones," Lester said as Steve tried to examine Mystic's ankle. The vet frowned at the sight of the frenzied animal's wound.

"Maybe." He shook his head and worked to place an inflatable cast on Mystic's leg, but the frightened colt tried to thwart all Steve's attempts to help him.

Savannah felt her insides shred at the sight of Mystic. Unless the veterinarian was able to calm him, the horse would be his own worst enemy and wouldn't survive the effects of the anesthesia.

"We'd better take him right to the hospital," Steve thought out loud. "I'll need X-rays and I'll probably have to perform surgery—unless we get lucky."

"He's not stable enough for surgery," Savannah said.

Steve nodded. "I'll sedate him and maybe we'll get lucky and nothing'll be broken. But I think that's being optimistic. It looks like Lester is right."

Savannah felt herself slump, but Travis's arms tightened around her shoulders.

"We'd better get moving," Steve said.

"Then let's do it," Reginald replied, looking at the agonized colt and shaking his head. "Travis, can you drive the truck?"

With a frown, Travis nodded. "Sure."

"I'm coming, too," Savannah said firmly. "This time you're not leaving me here alone."

"Don't you think you'd better get some rest?" Travis asked.

"No."

"You have to stay here," Reginald pointed out.

"Why?"

"Don't ask foolish questions," her father said irritably. "You need your rest."

"I'm fine!"

Reginald's face flushed with anger. "Okay, so you played the heroine and helped find Josh; now let it lie. You're needed here. Think about it. What if Charmaine calls about Josh? He's not exactly out of the woods yet, you know. Won't you want to take the message?"

Savannah looked helplessly from her father to Travis and then to Mystic as Lester led him back into the truck. "I suppose so," she agreed reluctantly. "But this has shades of a conspiracy, you know."

"Nothing all that sinister," her father assured her. "I just need someone I can depend upon to stay here and look after things. As soon as we know Mystic's condition, we'll call."

Steve was already walking to his van. Reginald and Lester had climbed into the cab of the truck.

Travis looked dead tired and his eyes held hers in silent promise. "I'll be back," he promised, "and soon."

She forced a weary smile and caressed the stubble on his chin. "I'll be waiting."

Managing a smile he said, "That makes it all worthwhile, you know." Then, as if to make up for lost time, he climbed into the truck, started the engine and drove out of the frozen stable yard to follow the path of Steve Anderson's van.

Savannah watched as the truck rumbled out the drive, and she felt more alone than she had in years. Josh was on his way to the hospital with the rest of the family, Travis and Lester were taking Mystic to a fate she didn't want to think about and she was left with the responsibility of the farm.

Shivering, she walked back to the house and let Archimedes inside for what little company he could provide. "Well," she said, making a cup of hot chocolate, "I guess all we have left to do is wait."

Looking out at the early-morning light she shook her head sadly and silently wished for the strength of Travis's arms.

CHAPTER NINE

TIME HAD NEVER moved so slowly for Savannah as she waited for word on Josh and Mystic. It was nearly dark when the phone finally rang. Savannah answered and heard the exhaustion in Charmaine's voice.

"Josh will be all right," Charmaine assured her.

Savannah sank against the wall of the kitchen in relief. "Thank God!"

"But he has to stay here a few days. He's got a broken collarbone and several fractured ribs, as well as a lot of cuts and bruises. Fortunately there's no evidence of internal bleeding or damage to any of his organs. He should be out of the hospital in two or three days."

"I'm just glad it wasn't any worse," Savannah said.

"My sentiments exactly." Charmaine hesitated and then sighed. "So...have you heard anything about Mystic? Josh keeps asking about that damned creature."

Savannah winced at Charmaine's harsh words, but managed to hold her tongue. Charmaine was under a lot of strain. "There's nothing to tell him yet. The vet was here and he took Mystic to the equine hospital near Sacramento. Everyone, including Steve, seems to think that Mystic may have broken the sesamoid bone in his right foreleg."

There was a pause at the other end of the line and Charmaine sighed. "What bone? I think you'd better talk in layman's terms, okay? Even though I've lived on the farm all these years, I've tried to avoid most of the talk about horses—especially when it came to anatomy," she admitted. "How serious is it?"

"Serious."

"I see," Charmaine whispered. "But he will pull through, be all right even if he can't race again, right?"

"I don't really know. Lots of horses do," Savannah thought aloud. "It all depends upon the horse, his mental condition at the time of the surgery, the skill of the vet and luck, I guess. The problem is that Mystic's temperament is against him and he was overwrought before the surgery. That's not good."

"But surely they can save him," Charmaine persisted.

"I hope so, for all our sakes," Savannah said, knowing that if Mystic didn't survive, Josh would be devastated with guilt.

"I guess we can only hope for the best. Look, I'll call you if our plans change," Charmaine said. "But at least for tonight, Wade and I are staying in town."

"How's Wade taking it?" Savannah asked.

"Not too good. Josh admitted that he took the horse because he was angry with his father. He also said that he had intended on running away. And, oh, that's how the security wire broke. Josh was using a key he had 'borrowed' from his father one morning when he wanted to see Mystic, and the wire snapped."

Savannah let out a weary sigh. Josh had managed to dig himself into a deeper and deeper hole of trouble.

"And now Josh is petrified that Wade will punish him—not let him see Mystic again. It's a horrible mess."

"Is there anything I can do?"

"Not now."

"I'll call Josh in the morning, when he's feeling better," Savannah said.

"He'd love it."

"How's Mom doing?" Savannah asked.

"Fine. She's staying here with us."

Savannah thought about her mother's frail health. Worrying about Josh and Mystic wouldn't help Virginia's condition. "How's she taking all this?"

"Like a trooper. Hard to believe, isn't it?" Charmaine replied, and then she rattled off the name and number of the hotel in which she and Wade were staying. "Call me if you hear anything about Mystic."

"I will," Savannah promised. "And give Josh my love."

After hanging up the phone, Savannah glanced at the clock. Four-thirty. She'd spent the past six hours making sure that all the horses were comfortable and cared for, especially Mattie and Jones, and that the stalls had been cleaned, the water was running and the heat was working.

Exhaustion had finally taken its toll on her. Even a quick snack of cheese and crackers didn't give her the energy to stay on her feet.

Worried about Mystic and Josh, she went upstairs, took a long, hot shower and then tumbled into bed and fell asleep just after her head hit the pillow.

WHEN SAVANNAH AWOKE it was completely dark. A glance at the bedside clock told her that another four hours had passed. Still tired, she forced herself out of bed and was about to call the veterinarian's number when she heard the sound of familiar voices drifting up the stairs. Travis's low voice made her heart leap expectantly. *He's home! Maybe Mystic was already in the stallion barn!*

Shoving her arms through the sleeves of her robe, Savannah hurried down the stairs, through the hall and into the kitchen, where Travis and Lester were talking. Both men looked as if they hadn't slept for over a week.

Travis was sitting on the counter, his long legs dangling down the cupboards, his elbows supported by his knees. The lines of strain on his rugged face had become deep grooves and his gray eyes had lost their spark. His wrinkled shirt was stretched tautly over his broad shoulders, which were slumped in defeat, and his jaw was dark with his unshaven beard. All in all he looked completely worn out.

Lester, too, appeared fatigued. The wiry little trainer seemed bent with age as he sat at the kitchen table slowly sipping coffee and smoking a cigarette. His eyelids folded over disenchanted dark eyes and his cheeks were hollow. Gray smoke curled lazily to the ceiling.

Instinctively, Savannah prepared herself for the worst.

"How's Mystic?" she asked without preamble as she walked over to Travis and stood next to him.

The men exchanged worried glances and then Travis looked at her with pained gray eyes. "He's gone," he said. "Never had a chance." With a sound of disgust, he lowered himself from the counter and angrily tossed the dregs of his coffee into the sink.

"Gone?" she echoed blankly but she knew exactly what he meant. Steadying herself against the refrigerator she fought the dryness in her throat. "Oh, no...."

Lester stared into the black liquid in his cup. "Your father had him put down, missy. It was the only thing to do." Taking a drag from his cigarette, he blew out the smoke and then crushed the cigarette out in disgust.

"But why?" she asked, slowly sinking into one of the chairs at the table and staring at the little old trainer.

"It wasn't anyone's fault, and Steve, he tried his damnedest to save Mystic's leg," Lester said, rubbing his chin and fishing into his jacket pocket for another crumpled pack. "I thought he'd do it, too, but..." The old man shook his head and lit up again, blowing smoke through his nose. "Mystic, he just couldn't handle it."

"What happened?" she asked, though it really didn't matter. Mystic was dead and that was that. But the thought of the proud black colt brought tears to her eyes. Mystic had been the finest horse ever bred at Beaumont farms. A hellion, yes, but also a gallant Thoroughbred with the speed and endurance of the best. Savannah had to clear her throat against a painful lump that blocked her voice.

Travis stretched his shoulders and rubbed his hands over his dark chin. "The way I understand it, the operation on his ankle was a success. After Mystic had been sedated, Steve had been able to clean the wound, remove some of the bone chips, repair the torn ligaments, set the bones and put a cast on the leg."

"Then what went wrong?" Savannah asked, but knowing Mystic's high-strung temperament, she had already guessed the answer.

"Mystic was in a frenzy when he came out of the anesthesia," Lester explained, drawing on his cigarette and staring through the window into the black night. "We couldn't control him."

"He was frantic, kicking and rearing. No one could hold him down. He managed to kick off his special shoe as well as his cast and he even landed a blow on Lester's thigh."

Lester just shook his head and stared blankly through the window.

"So couldn't Steve have set the leg again, put him in a sling? They do wonderful things these days."

"Maybe," Lester admitted, "but your dad, well, he did the most humane thing possible. The horse was out of his mind as it was; more anesthesia and surgery would have been too traumatic for him. It was doubtful if he would have survived a second operation. It's a shame," Lester said softly. "A goddamned shame."

Fighting the constriction in her chest Savannah stared at her hands. "So what about Josh? What're we going to tell him?"

"I don't know," Travis said. "Your father went straight from the equine hospital to Mercy hospital, where Josh is, but I don't think he's going to tell the boy about Mystic until Josh is on the mend."

"Do you…do you think that lying to him is a good idea?"

Travis took the chair next to her and took hold of her hands. "I wish I knew. I've been asking myself a lot of questions today, and I haven't had much luck finding any answers."

"Well," Savannah said, taking in a steadying breath and telling herself not to grieve for the big, black colt. At least Mystic was out of pain and there was nothing she or anyone else could do for him now. And Josh was going to be well. She explained about Charmaine's phone call to both Lester and Travis. As she told the men of Josh's condition and prognosis, both Travis and Lester relaxed a little. "Now, how about something to eat?" she asked, forcing false cheer into her voice. "I made some soup earlier."

"Not for me, thanks," Lester said, stubbing his cigarette in an ashtray on the counter. "It's been a long day. I think I'll go home."

"You're sure?"

"As sure as I am about anything, missy." He reached for his hat, which was sitting on the corner of the table, pushed it onto his head and walked out the back door.

A few minutes later his pickup rumbled down the drive toward the main road.

"What about you?"

"I'm starved," Travis admitted, gazing affectionately at her. But his gray eyes were clouded with a silent agony. "I just hope I don't have to go through another day like this one," he admitted, stretching his tired back muscles. "There just wasn't a damned thing anyone could do to help the horse."

"Then it's over."

"Except for Josh."

"Except for Josh," she repeated hoarsely. "It won't be easy for him."

Seeing the defeat on her soft features, he squeezed her shoulders and then placed his larger hands over hers. "Well, we'll just have to help him through it, won't we? Now, didn't you promise me something to eat?"

"Oh. Yes. It'll only take a few minutes to warm."

"Do I have time for a shower?"

"Sure." She tried to shake off her black mood and offered him a tentative smile.

Still holding her hand in his, he pulled her closer to him, so that his face was just a few inches from hers.

"It's been one helluva thirty-six hours," he said, his voice low, a finger from his free hand reaching forward to the point where the lapels of her robe crossed. The finger brushed her skin and her heartbeat accelerated rapidly.

His eyes lowered to the seductive hollow of her breasts. "And throughout it all, the one thing that kept me going was the thought that eventually, when it was all over and the smoke had cleared, I'd be with you."

The lump in Savannah's throat swelled. "I've been waiting a long time to hear just those words, counselor," she admitted with a weary sigh.

His hands drifted downward to the belt cinching the soft velour fabric together, and his long fingers worked at the knot.

Savannah's breath caught in her throat as his fingers grazed the sensitive skin between her breasts.

"There's one thing I'd like better than a hot shower," he admitted, his voice rough, his eyes meeting hers in a silent, sizzling message.

Savannah's blood was already racing through her body in anticipation. "And what is that?"

"A hot shower *with you*."

The robe slid open to reveal Savannah's scanty silk-and-lace nightgown, and Travis, his teeth flashing beneath the dark stubble of his beard, smiled wickedly. "Looks like you were expecting me."

She laughed unexpectedly at the seductive gleam in his eyes. "You're flattering yourself."

"I deserve it."

Smiling shyly and observing him through the sweep of dark lashes, she had to agree. "Yes, I suppose you do," she said, gasping when his fingers slid downward to outline the point of her nipple beneath the pink silk.

His other hand slipped upward, behind her neck, and his strong fingers twined familiarly in the black silk of her hair as he gently drew her face closer to his.

Savannah's heartbeat quickened. When his warm lips molded to hers hungrily and a gray spark of seduction lighted his gaze, she felt warmth spread through her body in rippling waves of desire that started deep within her and flooded all of her senses.

Travis groaned and buried his rough chin against her neck as the breast in his hand swelled, and the firm dark peak pressed taut beneath his palm. He felt Savannah quiver beneath his touch. His loins began to ache with the need to make love to her, the desire to wipe away the strain of the past two days by burying himself in the soft, liquid warmth of her and the yearning to be comforted by her tender hands.

He squeezed his eyes tightly shut and kissed her almost angrily, as if by releasing his leashed fury in passion he could forget that he had just spent two days in the wilderness to save a boy and a horse and that he had failed.

"Just love me, sweet lady," he insisted, wanting to think of nothing other than the yielding woman in his embrace, the smell of her hair, the feel of her pliant muscles, the taste of her skin. "Make love to me until there's nothing left but you and me."

Her answering moan was all the encouragement he needed. Without another word, Travis picked her up and carried her lithely up the stairs to her bedroom.

Then he placed her on the bed and stared down at her with night-darkened eyes that studied every curve of her body.

The pink silk shimmered in the semidarkness. Beneath the fragile cloth, dark nipples stood erect. Her tousled ebony hair splayed against the white pillow, framing the oval of her face in billowing, black clouds. A soft flush colored her creamy skin and her deep blue eyes, glazed with longing, delved deep into his soul.

A powerful swelling in Travis's loins pressed painfully against his jeans as he watched the gentle rise and fall of her breasts. It was all he could do to go slow, take it easy, draw out the sweetness of making love to her.

"I couldn't forget you," he admitted roughly, slowly unbuttoning and removing his shirt only to let it fall onto the floor.

She watched in fascination as he started on the wide buckle of his belt.

"I tried, y'know," he admitted, as if remembering an unpleasant thought. "For nine years I tried to tell myself that you were just a summer fling, one night in a lost world that didn't really count." He slid the jeans off his hips and kicked his boots into the corner of the room. "But I couldn't. Damn it, I couldn't forget you."

"And you regret that?"

A crooked smile slashed white across his face. "Never!" Sliding next to her on the bed, his fingers fitting familiarly around her waist, he let out a long, ragged breath. "We should have stayed together; it would have saved everyone a whole lot of grief."

"We're together now," she whispered.

"And that's all that matters," he said with that same wicked smile, his fingers inching upward to stroke the underside of a breast through the lace and silk.

"You're so right," she agreed with a sigh as she arched upward, fitting her body against his and kissing him passionately, her tongue slipping familiarly between his teeth.

Travis moaned and slid one hand under the hem of her nightgown as he moved against her. "About that shower?" he asked.

"Later..." she whispered, listening to the thudding of his heart and feeling the wiry hair of his chest brush against her cheeks. "Much later."

VAGUELY AWARE OF someone saying something to her, Savannah woke up. She rolled over in the bed and groaned before she felt a warm hand reach over and brush her hair away from her cheek.

"Merry Christmas," Travis whispered.

Opening her eyes and blinking as she stretched, Savannah smiled into Travis's silvery eyes. "It is Christmas morning, isn't it?"

"Christmas afternoon."

Savannah's groggy mind snapped, and she levered herself up on one elbow in order to see the clock on the nightstand. Twelve-thirty! Without another thought she swung her legs over the side of the bed. "Oh, my God! The horses—"

Travis's long arm encircled her waist. "Hold on a minute, will ya? Lester's already been here and looked in on them. Everything's fine. Even Mattie and Jones survived without you. Lester said he'll be back later this afternoon."

"And I slept through it?" she asked, unbelieving.

"Like a baby."

"I can't believe it!" She pushed the hair out of her eyes and let out a sigh. "I haven't slept like that in years."

"Nine years, maybe?" he asked softly, nuzzling her ear.

She remembered back to that morning long ago. She had woken late and learned that Travis was going to marry Melinda without even offering an explanation. The old needle of betrayal pricked at her heart and she had to ignore the painful sensation. "Maybe," she admitted, her voice rough.

"Well, lady, you'd better get used to sleeping in, I guess," Travis said with a twinkle in his eye. "Because I never intend to let you get away from me again and I expect that last night was just a preview of what's ahead."

She blushed a little as she thought about the shameless passion that had overtaken her just hours before. Her hunger for Travis had been all-consuming to the point that she had finally fallen asleep from sheer physical exhaustion.

Looking at him lovingly and affectionately stroking his chin, she asked a question that had been in the back of her mind for the past two days. "What is ahead, for you and me?"

"Before or after we're married?"

Her heart nearly stopped beating. *Married? To Travis?* It was almost too good to be true.

He nibbled at her ear, but she pushed him away. She needed to clear her mind and force him to become serious.

"Both," she finally replied, thoughtfully.

"You're no fun," he accused. Then when his thoughts revolved back to what had occurred between them just hours before, he grinned roguishly. "At least you're not much fun this morning."

"And you're ducking the issue."

"Make me some breakfast and I promise to confide in you," he suggested, burying his face in her hair and playfully running his fingers up her spine. "Or maybe you have a better idea...."

She laughed as his fingers slid against her skin, tickling her lightly. "Okay, okay, I guess it's the least I can do," she muttered, realizing that he hadn't eaten much for the better part of two days.

She slid out of bed and started dressing in front of the bureau, aware that his eyes never left her as she took her clothes out of the drawers. Though she was facing away from him, she could see his reflection in the mirror. After tugging her sweater over her head and pulling her thick hair out of the neck opening, she shook the black strands away from her face and arched a brow in his direction. He was still draped across the bed, the sheets covering only the lower half of his body.

"I'm not about to bring you breakfast in bed, you know," she pointed out.

"Like I said, 'no fun in the morning.'" He reached behind his head, grabbed one of the plump pillows and hurled it across the room.

Savannah sidestepped, managed to dodge the soft torpedo and laughed merrily. "Watch it, buster, or you'll end up with dry toast and water instead of crepes and salmon pâté," she warned.

He arched a thick, dark brow and smiled. "Thank God."

"You'll be sorry," she warned.

"I don't think so. As long as I'm here with you, I really don't care." His gray eyes were serious.

"Give me a break," she muttered, but smiled all the same as she left the room.

A half hour later, the kitchen was filled with the tantalizing scents of sizzling bacon, warm apple muffins and hot coffee. Travis was pulling a sweater over his head as he walked into the kitchen. He eyed the table with a Cheshire-cat-sized smile.

"For me?" he asked, looking at the small table decorated with brass candlesticks, a Christmas-red cloth and dainty sprigs of holly.

"For you, counselor," Savannah admitted, pouring two glasses of champagne and setting them on the table near the plates before lighting the candles.

"Champagne?"

"It's Christmas, isn't it?"

"Maybe the best one of my life," he thought aloud.

She was standing at the sink cutting fresh fruit, when he came up behind her and rested his chin against her shoulder, his long arms wrapping possessively around her waist, his fingertips pressed against her abdomen. "I love you, you know."

Savannah felt tears of joy build behind her eyes. "And I love you."

"I can't think of a better way to spend Christmas than with you," he said, his voice low, his clean-shaven cheek warm against her skin. "Domesticity becomes you."

"Does it? I'm not sure I like the sound of that."

"It's a compliment, and you'd better get used to it," he suggested. "I think I want to wake up with you every morning to pamper me."

"I'm not pampering you." She slid him a sly glance, but grinned at her obvious lie.

"No?"

Smiling, she thought for a minute. "Well, maybe a little. But I really just wanted to say thanks for finding Josh. If you hadn't been out there looking for him…" Her voice drifted off and she shivered.

Travis's strong arms tightened around her. "But I was," he remarked. "I just wish we could have done something to save Mystic."

"So do I," she whispered, thinking of Josh and how devastated the boy would be when he learned that Mystic had been put down.

She'd called Charmaine with the bad news while Travis was still upstairs. Charmaine had been adamant that Josh wasn't to be told about Mystic, at least not right away. When Savannah had spoken to Josh, she'd found it difficult to sidestep the truth about his beloved horse. Josh had sounded tired, but anxious to come home to celebrate Christmas and see Mystic. Savannah had hung up with mixed feelings.

Now, she frowned and pushed those unhappy thoughts aside. It was Christmas, she was alone with Travis and she wouldn't let the rest of the world intrude. Not today. "Come on, let's eat and then I intend to put you to work."

"That sounds interesting," he drawled, kissing the back of her neck.

"Not that kind of work," she quipped. "I'm talking about the back-breaking work on the farm."

"Even on Christmas?"

"Especially on Christmas. No one else is here."

"Precisely my point," he said, his lips brushing her ear sensually.

She trembled beneath the gentle assault of his tongue on her ear. He smelled so clean and masculine and the feel of his fingers moving against the flat muscles of her abdomen started igniting the tiny sparks of passion in her blood all over again. It was all she could do to concentrate on the apple she was slicing.

"Travis," she whispered huskily, "if you don't stop this, I might cut myself...or you."

"Spoilsport," he accused with a soft chuckle, but kissed the top of her head and finally released her.

The meal was perfect. They ate in the kitchen and finished the bottle of champagne in the living room between a warm fire and the decorated Christmas tree.

"Two nights ago I never thought I'd be warm again," Travis said, setting his empty glass on a nearby table. He was lying on the thick carpet and lazily watching Savannah.

"And I wondered if I'd ever see you again."

"Well, that's behind us," he said, propped on one elbow near the tree and staring up at her as she sat on her knees and adjusted a misplaced ornament. "And now you'll have one helluva time getting rid of me."

"Promise?" she asked.

"Promise!" He leaned closer to her and kissed her neck until she tumbled willingly into his arms.

They spent the rest of the day taking inventory of the feed and supplies in the barns. It was tiring work and, coupled with the usual routine, Savannah was dead tired by the time she returned to the house.

Sadie Stinson had come by earlier in the day and put a stuffed goose in the oven, a platter of cinnamon cookies on the counter and a molded salad in the refrigerator.

"It's not much," the older woman had said as she was leaving.

"What do you mean? It's a feast and it'll save my life! I didn't have anything planned," Savannah had replied.

"Well, I'd rather have stayed and helped."

"Forget it!" Savannah had waved off the older woman's apologies. "I won't hear any excuses! You have your family to worry about. It's Christmas!"

The housekeeper had finally agreed and left with a gift from Savannah tucked under her arm and a promise to return and fix "that child the best beef Wellington this side of the Rocky Mountains" when Josh was released from the hospital.

"I'll hold you to it," Savannah had replied, waving as Sadie drove carefully down the snow-covered lane.

Now, hours later, as Savannah opened the door to the kitchen, the scent of roasting goose filled her nostrils. "Thank you, Sadie Stinson," Savannah murmured to herself while kicking off her boots and walking through the kitchen in her stocking feet.

She dashed upstairs for a quick shower and hurried back down to the kitchen to put the finishing touches on the meal just as Travis returned from the barns.

"I'd forgotten what it's like to work with the horses," he said, raking his fingers through his hair. "I've spent so many hours behind a desk or in the law library that I can't remember the last time I cut open a bale of hay."

"And how did it feel?"

"It felt good," he admitted with a bemused frown as his eyes searched hers. "But maybe that was because of the company. What do you think?"

"I think you're addled from overwork, counselor." She laughed.

Travis built a fire in the living room while Savannah set the table. They ate by candlelight in the dining room and finally had brandied coffee in the darkened living room. The flickering fire and lighted Christmas tree cast colorful shadows on the walls and windowpanes.

Savannah sat with Travis on the floor, her back propped against the couch, Travis's head resting in her lap. He had taken off his shoes and was warming his stockinged feet by the fire while her fingers played in the dark chestnut curls falling over his forehead.

"I want you to marry me," he said at last, moving slightly to get a better view of her face.

She arched a slim, dark brow. "Just like that?"

He chuckled. "This isn't all that quick, you know. I've known you most of my life—well, at least most of yours," he said with a smile. "I don't think we're exactly rushing into it, do you?"

"No…"

"But?"

"A lot of 'buts,' I guess," she admitted.

"Name one."

"Melinda."

Savannah felt the muscles in Travis's back tighten. "Melinda's gone," he said, his jaw clenching and anger smoldering in his eyes.

"But if she were still alive?"

"That's a tough one," he admitted, rolling over and sitting up so that his eyes were level with hers. "And it's not really fair. While she was alive I tried to be the best husband I could to her. Maybe I failed, but I damned well gave it my best shot. Now it's over. She's gone. Don't get me wrong, I didn't wish her dead, but I can't bring her back, either."

Savannah's throat felt raw. "You loved her."

"Yes," he admitted, his eyes seeming distant as he gazed into the fire. "I did. It was a long, long time ago. But I loved her very much."

Even an admission that she had expected tore a hole in Savannah's heart. She tried to tell herself that what happened in the past didn't matter; it was the future that counted, but doubts still nagged her mind. Loving Travis as much as she did, she couldn't bear the thought of him having cared for another woman.

"But I fell in love with you," he said, his lips twisting downward at the corners as if he had read her thoughts. "I think I fell in love with you on the very day I saw you riding Mattie in the fields. You were watching me from under the apple tree and trying to look very grown up and sophisticated. Remember?"

How could she ever forget? "I remember."

"From that day on I couldn't get you out of my mind." He turned his solemn gaze in her direction, and his eyes caressed the soft contours of her face. "You have to believe that I would never have married Melinda, never, except that I believed she was carrying my child. I couldn't very well marry you knowing that Melinda was going to have my baby, could I?"

"I suppose not. But Dad seems to think… Oh, I guess it doesn't matter."

He became rigid and his back teeth ground together

in frustration. His thick brows drew downward over his eyes. "Of course it matters. Tell me, what does Reginald think?"

"He warned me to stay away from you, that you weren't the man for me, that you've always loved Melinda and she'll always be between us."

Travis's face hardened. "Do you believe that?"

"No..."

"Then?" he snapped.

"I just wanted to be sure."

"Good Lord, Savannah," he said with a loud moan. "Haven't you heard a word I've said this past week? Don't you know that your father is still trying to manipulate us both?"

"That, I don't believe. My father is only concerned about my happiness."

"Is that why he didn't tell you that he knew about our affair?" he argued.

Savannah's temper flared. "You mean our one-night stand, don't you? It was only once, by the lake, remember?"

Travis softened a little. "Oh, I remember all right. That night has haunted me for the past nine years, and for the first time since then I'm going to do something about it. I'm going to marry you, lady, and you're not going to come up with any more excuses."

The argument should have ended there, but Savannah couldn't let it lie. Instead, she got to her feet, walked to the fireplace and turned to face him. "Suppose we do get married Travis. What then?"

"We'll move to Colorado."

"Colorado!" she repeated. "Why Colorado?"

"I have some land there; my parents left it to me. I

thought we could make a clean, fresh start away from everything and everyone."

"You're talking about running away and dropping out, right?"

The corners of his mouth twisted downward. "No. What I mean is that we could raise horses, if that's what you want to do. But we wouldn't have Reginald looking over our shoulders, and I'd be rid of the law practice for good."

She could feel her stomach quivering, but the anger in his eyes gave her pause. "Is that what you want?"

"What I want is you. It's that simple. I've got enough money to get started somewhere else and I want to get away from lawsuits, political schemes and the past." He looked her squarely in the eye. "I'm not running away from anything, Savannah, I'm running *to* a home, a private, safe place for my wife and my children and I'm asking you to come with me."

"I want to, Travis, but I have a family here, a family that I love very much. My mother's not well, my father depends on me, my sister needs me and then there's Josh. He's more than a nephew to me, he's almost like my own son."

"I'm not asking you to give them up, not entirely."

She raised her hands in the air and let them fall to her sides. The argument was futile, but couldn't be ignored. "I understand that you're dissatisfied with your work and your life, but I'm not. I love it here. It's my home. Working with the horses is what I do. I tried working and living in the city once and it didn't work out. This house, this land, these horses…" She gestured around the room and toward the windows. "They might belong to Dad, but they're mine."

"You're not coming with me, are you?" he asked.

She felt the tears threatening her eyes. *Why was she arguing?* All she ever wanted was to be with Travis, and he was offering her a lifetime of love, if only she could give up the family that meant so much to her. "You know that I love you," she said. "I always have. But I need a little time to think about all this."

"I can't wait forever," he said slowly.

"And I wouldn't expect you to." She shrugged her shoulders and tried to think clearly. "Would it be possible for you to stay here on the farm?"

"Live here with your family?"

"Yes."

"No," he replied tersely. "I'm not about to live my life like Wade and Charmaine. I want my own place, my independence, my own home. I came here to cut the ties with Reginald, Savannah, and I still mean to do it."

A slow burn crept up her cheeks at Travis's ingratitude to her father. "You're going to forget that he raised you?" she asked, sarcasm tainting her words. "When no one wanted you because you were such a problem, my father gave you a home!"

Travis pushed himself upright and his shoulders bunched angrily. "I'll always owe your father a debt, no doubt about it, but I'm not paying for it with my life. I'm going to try and forget that he's tried to run my life— to the point of going behind my back with my partner, Henderson. I'm not about to be anyone's pawn, not even Reginald Beaumont's!"

"You'd better watch it," she snapped, her blue eyes sparking. "Or that chip you're wearing on your shoulder might just fall off and create another Grand Canyon!"

"Cheap shot, Savannah."

"But true."

A glimmer of revenge flickered in his eyes. "Then while we're taking shots…"

"Be my guest."

"At least I'm not afraid to face the past or take a chance and be my own person. I'm not tied like a calf ready for branding to a father and mother because I'm afraid of stepping out on my own for fear of failure."

"I haven't failed!"

"Because you haven't even tried. We all fail, Savannah."

She was so angry her fingers curled around the edge of the mantel. "The only time I've ever failed was when I trusted you nine years ago," she said, shaking with raw emotion. "I trusted you and loved you, and you made a mockery of that love. And you! You were such a coward that you didn't even bother saying goodbye before you married another woman!"

Stripped of all pretenses, alone in the house, Travis walked over to Savannah and gripped her shoulders. His eyes were bright with challenge, his jaw hard with anger. "I made a mistake," he said between clenched teeth. "And I'll be damned if I'll make another. I've lived with the love I felt for you burning my skin, ruining my wife's self-worth, and I've paid over and over again. Now I'm through paying and lying, and so are you. You can hide from me, Savannah, but I'll find you, and sooner or later you're going to have to face the fact that the past is dead and gone. Buried, just like Melinda and Mystic. We've got a future, damn it, and we're going to have it together."

He pulled her roughly to him and kissed her angrily, his lips hard and bruising, his tongue plundering. She tried to resist but couldn't. Traitorous desire burned brightly in her breast, and she leaned against him and let her tears of frustration run down her cheeks.

"Tell me you love me," he demanded, his hands spreading on the small of her back, pushing her tight against the hard evidence of his desire, possessively claiming her as his.

"You know I do—"

"Say it!"

"I love you," she whispered, her voice catching.

His glittering eyes softened a little. "Then don't let all the bullshit get in our way. I love you and I'm not about to let anything or anyone stand between us!" His shoulders slackened a little as the fury seeped from his body. "Oh, Savannah, we've come too far to turn back and hide. We're going to face the future and we're going to face it together!"

He kissed her again, more gently this time, and she wound her arms around his neck. And then, by the warmth of the fire, with the colored lights from the tree winking seductively, he slowly undressed her and made love to her long into the night.

CHAPTER TEN

FOR THE REMAINDER of the week, Savannah and Travis lived with an unspoken truce. The subject of the future was pushed aside while Savannah concentrated on keeping the farm running smoothly.

The snow had finally begun to melt the third day after Christmas, and life on the farm returned to a more normal schedule.

Travis seemed to thrive on the physical labor of the farm, and Lester was pleased to have him around. From time to time, Savannah caught the trainer smiling to himself and nodding as he watched Travis working with the animals.

Saturday afternoon, Lester was watching Vagabond and a few other other colts stretch their legs in the paddock when Savannah and Travis joined him. Only a few patches of snow remained on the ground, and the horses were making the most of their freedom.

Vagabond, his tail and head held high, raced from one end of the field to the other while snorting and bucking.

"Sure beats all that Perry Mason law business, doesn't it?" Lester remarked, watching the frisky colt's easy strides.

Travis threw back his head and laughed aloud. "If only my cases were as interesting as Perry's. If they had been, I might not have given up law." He leaned against a fence post and rubbed his cramped shoulders. "Most of the time I was in the library reading decisions regarding corporate law."

Lester's older eyes sparkled. "Not exactly your cup of tea."

"Not exactly," Travis commented dryly, his lips thinning as he watched the animals romp.

"But you've got a way with the horses," Lester pointed out.

"That's right," Savannah added, smiling slyly in Travis's direction. "You've got Vagabond eating out of your hand."

"That'll be the day," Travis replied, cocking his head in the direction of the bay colt. "Just yesterday he tried to take a piece out of my arm."

"He's a little temperamental," Savannah admitted with a teasing smile.

"High-strung," Lester added.

"Temperamental?" Travis echoed. "High-strung? I'd call it downright miserable and mean," Travis said before chuckling to himself.

"But you've got to admit he's got charisma," Savannah said.

"And speed," Lester added, watching the bay colt kick up his heels in the west pasture. The bay's smooth coat and rippling muscles glistened in the pale morning sunlight. "Let's just hope he has a little luck as well!"

"That, we all could use," Savannah agreed.

Later in the morning Charmaine called to say that Josh was about to be released from the hospital. Reginald and Virginia as well as Wade, Charmaine and Joshua would be home late in the afternoon.

"Worried?" Travis asked, resting on the handle of the pitchfork in the hayloft over the stallion barn and staring into Savannah's troubled blue eyes.

"A little," she admitted. "These past few days I'd for-gotten about all the problems, I guess." She smiled faintly and climbed down the ladder to find herself standing in front of Mystic's empty stall. It had been cleaned and now was waiting for another one of Beaumont Breeding Farm's colts to claim it as his own. She felt empty inside at the loss of Mystic.

"And now all the trouble is coming home?" Travis fol-lowed her down the ladder and hopped off the final rung.

"Yeah, I guess."

"Don't worry about it," he suggested with a patient smile.

"Easier said than done." Leaning over the gate to Mys-tic's stall, she thought about the magnificent black colt.

"You can't bring him back, y'know," Travis said softly.

Savannah sighed and nodded. "I know, but I can't help but worry about Josh and Wade…."

"Wade is Josh's father."

"Unfortunately," she whispered. "I wish to God that I could take that kid away from Wade Benson."

"He's the boy's father whether you like it or not."

Her throat ached and her frustration made her angry. She turned around to face the tenderness in Travis's eyes. "Is it as simple as all that?" she asked. "Is the law so cut-and-dried that a man who should never have become a father in the first place can browbeat a child until he has no self-esteem left?"

Travis tugged pensively on his lower lip. "Unless you can prove abuse—"

"Physical abuse, you mean," she snapped, her jaw jut-ting forward angrily. "But it doesn't matter what kind of mental cruelty a child like Josh is put through."

"That's Charmaine's problem," Travis pointed out,

steadying Savannah with his hands by placing his palms firmly over her shoulders.

"According to the law! But I feel responsible for that child. It's just so damned unfair!" She crossed her arms over her chest and tried to turn away from him.

"Hey, slow down. Come into the house…. I'll buy you a cup of coffee. Josh will be home soon and you can shower him with all that pent-up auntly love."

"Auntly?"

"That's what you are, aren't you?" he asked, pulling on her shoulders and hugging her body next to his before kissing her tenderly on the top of the head.

She had to smile despite her anger. "I suppose so."

"And I'd guess that you bought out the stores with all sorts of those ugly creatures and robots that he likes."

"Not quite."

Travis laughed. "Then buck up, will ya? Josh's coming home tonight and you promised him that we'd celebrate Christmas together. So you'd better put on one helluva show or you'll disappoint that nephew you love so much. I've got to run into town for a while, so you can fiddle in the kitchen with Sadie."

"She'd kill me. When she's here, the kitchen is her domain. Even Archimedes isn't welcome."

"Then go and string popcorn, hang mistletoe, sing carols or whatever it is you do around this time of the year, and while you're at it put a smile on that beautiful face."

"Sing carols?" she repeated, laughing a little. "I don't think so."

He sobered slightly and squeezed her shoulders. "Just be happy, love; that's all."

The depth of her feelings for him was reflected in her eyes as she forced a small grin. "And where will you be?"

He winked broadly. "I'm gonna get Josh a present that will knock his socks off."

"Are you?" Savannah was delighted.

"You bet."

"So who's going to take care of the horses while I'm, uh, singing carols?"

"I will, when I get back."

"You?"

"Sure, what's wrong with that?"

"Nothing," she said with a wicked twinkle in her eyes. "You're on." She chuckled as she handed him a bucket and a brush. "First you can clean the stalls and then—"

Setting the tools aside, he glared at Savannah in mock anger. "And then I'll come into the house and show you who's boss."

"Promises, promises," she quipped as she slipped out of his arms, through the door of the stallion barn, running back to the house with Travis on her heels.

"I thought you were going into town," she laughed when he caught up with her and jerked her roughly against him.

"I am, but when I get back…" He pressed warm lips to hers and held her as if afraid to let go.

"What?" she coaxed with a knowing smile.

"I'll deal with you then."

"I can hardly wait." She extricated herself from his arms and heard him swear under his breath as he started toward the pickup in the parking lot.

SAVANNAH, HER HEAD bent while tucking a pin in her hair, started down the stairs. After helping Sadie in the kitchen, she'd spent the past hour showering, dressing, pinning her hair into a chignon and wondering when Travis would return. Josh would be home any minute and Travis hadn't come back from town.

The doorbell caught her by surprise.

"I'll get it," she called downstairs toward the kitchen, where Sadie was still fussing. She hurried down the remaining steps and across the foyer.

Jerking open the door, Savannah found herself face to face with the reporter from the *Register*. Her heart nearly stopped beating and her smile froze on her face. *Not now,* she thought wildly, *not when Josh is due home within the hour!*

"Good afternoon," John Herman said, extending his hand.

"Good afternoon. What can I do for you?" she asked warily.

"I'd like to talk to you about Mystic, for starters," the reporter responded, a full smile sliding easily over his face. "I'd like to do a story about a great horse, you know, from the time he was a foal to the present."

She blocked his passage into the house and met his inquiring gaze. "I thought the *Register* already ran an article on Mystic."

"Right, but I'd like to do a bigger piece on the horse. You know, more of a human-interest story. I'd need to find out where he was raised, who worked with him, interview his trainer and the jockey who rode him, bring up all of his races, especially the Preakness, and slant the story for the local readers."

"I don't think so."

"It could be good publicity for the farm," John Herman persisted. "We'd be glad to include anything new, say, about the other horses. You've got another horse, a—" he checked his notes "—Vagabond, isn't it?"

"Yes. He's a two-year-old."

"I've heard people compare him to Mystic."

"The same temperament," Savannah said, forcing a tight smile. "But that's about it. And, as for Mystic, I'm not ready to give you a story about him, not yet, anyway." *Not until Josh is told the truth.* "I'm sorry you made the trip for nothing, maybe next time you'll call," she apologized, when she heard the sound of a pickup coming down the lane and realized with a sinking feeling that Travis had finally returned.

"Then maybe I could speak to Mr. McCord," the reporter persisted.

"He's...he's not here at the moment."

The screen door to the back porch banged shut. Savannah heard Travis walk through the kitchen and toward the hall.

"I'll tell him you were here to see him," she said hurriedly.

"Savannah," Travis called out, stopping when he walked into the hall and saw her wedged between the door and the doorjamb. "What the devil?"

"Mr. McCord!" John Herman said with enthusiasm, looking over Savannah's shoulder and smiling broadly.

There was nothing she could do about it. Reluctantly Savannah let the man inside. It was obvious from the spark of interest in John Herman's eyes that the main purpose for his visit to the farm had been to question Travis.

"John Herman," the reporter said, extending his hand. Travis took the man's outstretched palm, but didn't hide his skepticism. "I'm a reporter for the *Register*."

"I see." Travis smiled cynically. "Why don't you come into the living room where we can talk?" He glanced at Savannah and mildly inquired, "Savannah?"

Stunned at Travis's polite reaction to the press, Savannah realized she had completely forgotten her manners. "Yes, please come into the living room and I'll get some coffee." Casting Travis a I-hope-you-know-what-you're-getting-yourself-into look, she went to the kitchen, grabbed the blue enamel coffeepot and several empty cups and quickly explained to Sadie what was happening.

"Lord have mercy," Sadie prayed, rolling her eyes to the ceiling before preparing a tray of cookies. "Just make sure that reporter is gone before the boy arrives. His folks haven't told him about the horse, you know."

"I know," Savannah muttered angrily.

Sadie noticed Savannah's trembling fingers and placed her hand over the younger woman's wrist. "You go in there and keep Travis out of trouble. I'll bring the coffee in when it's brewed."

"You're sure?"

"Go on…go on."

"All right," Savannah replied as she walked out of the kitchen.

There was something about John Herman's attitude that rankled and unnerved her. The reporter tended to write a biting column that was filled with sharp wit, a smattering of truth and more rumors than fact.

Don't worry, she told herself as she started back to the living room, *Travis can handle himself. He's a lawyer and was almost a politician. He can deal with the press.*

"So you really are dropping out of the race?" Herman asked, his tape recorder poised by his side on the arm of the couch.

Travis, looking calm and nearly disinterested, leaned against the fireplace. Only the tiny muscle working in the corner of his jaw gave any sign of his inner tension. "I was never in it."

"But you did take contributions?"

"Never."

Herman's mouth tightened and he quickly scanned his notes. "There are several people who would dispute that. One of the most prominent is a Mrs. Eleanor Phillips. She charges that she gave you five thousand dollars."

"She didn't give me a dime," Travis replied. "And I wouldn't have taken it if she'd tried to give it to me."

"She claims she has a cancelled check to prove it."

"If so, I've never seen it."

John Herman held out his hand, as if to prevent Travis from lying. "Mr. McCord—"

"There may have been a few people working for me who were...overzealous in thinking that I would run. And they may have taken contributions in my name, but they did it without my knowledge, and I've instructed them to return the money with interest."

"So you're saying that you can't be persuaded to run for governor."

"That's right."

Flipping his notebook to a clean page, and making sure that his recorder was working properly, the reporter turned to Savannah just as Sadie brought in the coffee.

"Now, what can you tell me about Mystic?" he asked, while accepting a cup of coffee from a cool Sadie.

"Nothing you don't already know."

Herman wasn't about to be dissuaded. "We got the official story from the veterinarian, Steve Anderson, but we'd like to know exactly what happened to the horse to cause the break in his leg."

"I really don't know," Savannah replied.

"Well, how did he get out? Did the kid really take him?"

"Joshua took him," she admitted.

"But why? Where was he going? Did he have an accomplice?"

"I think that's enough questions," Travis cut in, the smile on his face deadly. "Josh took the horse out for a ride and got caught in the storm. Subsequently, Mystic was injured and unfortunately couldn't be saved. It was a very unfortunate and tragic situation for everyone involved."

"Yes, but—"

"Now, if you'll excuse us," Travis said calmly. "Ms. Beaumont and I have work to get done."

Begrudgingly taking the hint, John Herman stood from his position on the couch, shut off his recorder and stuffed it, as well as his notepad, under his arm.

"It's been a pleasure, Mr. McCord," he said and nodded curtly to Savannah. "Thank you, Ms. Beaumont."

"You're welcome," she lied.

Travis escorted the reporter to the door and Savannah sank into the cushions of the couch.

"Vultures," Travis muttered once the reporter was gone. Taking a cup of coffee from the table, he balanced on the arm of the couch and patted Savannah on the knee. "The good news is I don't think he'll be back."

"Impossible," Savannah replied, threading her fingers through Travis's strong ones. "You know what they say about bad pennies?"

Nodding, Travis waved off her worries. "Well, we can't be too concerned about John Herman; he writes what he wants to. We'll just have to hope that the editor of the *Register* makes him stick to the facts." He cocked his wrist and checked his watch before finishing his coffee. "Everyone will be home soon and we still have Christmas to celebrate."

"Speaking of which, what did you get Josh?"

A broad smile crept over Travis's face. "Something that he'll positively adore."

"I hate to ask."

"Then don't. I'm going to get cleaned up and then I have some work I have to finish in the den," Travis said.

"Again?" Savannah's fine brows drew together in confusion.

"It wont take long," he promised, kissing her lightly on the cheek.

"What is it you do in there?"

"Accounting," he replied cryptically.

"Why?"

His smile grew. "For peace of mind."

"I don't believe you."

"You asked," he said, standing and stretching, "and I told you. Now, why don't you get this couch fixed up for Josh? That way he can be down here with the tree before we have to put him in his room for the night."

"That's a good idea, even if you only offered it because you wanted to change the subject."

"Stick with me," he said, his eyes gleaming seductively and his voice lowering as he touched her cheek. "I've got lots of good ideas, some of which I'll be glad to personally demonstrate later."

She laughed in spite of herself. "That's a terrible line, counselor," she said, chuckling. "It's a good thing I love you or I'd never let you get away with it."

Deciding to bring down warm blankets and a thick quilt for Josh, she left the room and smiled to herself. The love in her heart swelled until she could almost feel it.

JOSH LOOKED SO SMALL. He was pale and in a brace that covered most of his upper body. His usually bright eyes were dull, and his hair had lost some of its sheen.

"You look like you've been to the wars and back," Savannah said as she finished tucking the blankets around the cushions of the couch.

"I feel like it, too."

"Tell me about it," Savannah suggested, helping the boy onto the sofa and tugging a Christmas quilt around his slim pajama-clad legs.

"I'm okay, I guess," he said bravely looking at the room full of adults.

"Are you ready for Christmas?"

"You bet," he replied, his eyes dancing a little and color coming back to his cheeks.

"Good. Just wait here, and I'll move this table in front of the couch, and you can eat right in here."

"Will you eat with me?" he asked shyly.

"Wouldn't hear of anything else," she agreed, smiling fondly at the boy and pulling up a chair near him.

While the rest of the family changed for dinner, Savannah spent her time spoiling Josh. "I missed you around here," she said, once the small table was covered with more food than an entire battalion of soldiers could eat.

"Really?"

"Really."

"I missed you, too," Josh admitted. "And I missed Mystic. Do you think you can take me out to see him?"

Savannah had thought she'd prepared herself for the question, but her carefully formed response felt like the lie it was and it stuck in her throat. She forced herself to meet Josh's worried gaze. "No, Josh, I can't. You know that. You've got to stay in the house and rest. At least until the brace is off."

"That might be weeks," he whined.

"Well, for the time being the stables and the stallion barn are definitely off limits." Turning to her plate, Savannah made a big show of starting the meal, hoping Josh would follow her lead and quit asking about Mystic.

Josh studied the platter of food before him but didn't touch it. "I think something's wrong with Mystic," he finally said.

Savannah's palms had begun to sweat. "Wrong? Why?"

He eyed her speculatively, with the cunning of a boy twice his age. "Everyone gets real jumpy when I talk about him."

"It's just because we're worried about you."

He shook his head and winced at a sudden stab of pain. "I don't think so," he said paling slightly. "Dad and Mom, even Grandpa, they act like they're hiding something from me."

"Maybe they're just sharing Christmas secrets."

"Aunt Savvy?"

Here it comes, she thought.

"You wouldn't lie to me, would you?"

Savannah felt her heart constrict, but she managed to meet his concerned gaze. "I wouldn't do anything to hurt you, Josh."

"That's not what I asked."

"Have I ever lied before?"

He was quiet for a moment. "No."

"Then why would I start now?"

"Because something bad happened. Something that nobody wants me to find out about."

Savannah forced a smile. "You know what I think, don't ya?"

"No, what?" Earnest boyish eyes pierced hers.

"That you've been lying in that hospital bed with too much to think about and too little to do. Well, sport, we're about to change all that right now. Eat your dinner and we'll open some presents, what do ya say?"

"All right!" Josh exclaimed enthusiastically, but slid a questioning look through the window toward the stallion barn.

JOSH WENT TO bed early, and he was so besotted with the cross-breed cocker spaniel puppy that Travis had given him, he didn't ask about Mystic again.

The evening had been strained and Savannah was grateful that it was over. *But there's still tomorrow and the next day,* she thought angrily to herself. *Sooner or later someone will have to tell Josh the truth!*

Savannah and Travis were just pushing the used wrapping paper into a cardboard box when Charmaine came back down the stairs. She was dressed in her bathrobe and slippers and she looked tired enough to drop through the floor.

"I just came down to say good-night," she explained, leaning one shoulder against the archway between the foyer and the living room. "And to say thanks, Travis, for the puppy."

"I figured that Josh might need a special friend when he finds out about Mystic."

"I know, I know," Charmaine said, shaking her head. "I should have told him before now, but I just couldn't. Strange as it was, he loved that foul-tempered horse. It'll kill him when he finds out that Mystic's gone."

"He'll know sooner or later," Travis said. "Reporters were here earlier today. There's bound to be another story in the paper. Even if that doesn't happen, one of Josh's friends might call and ask him about the horse."

Charmaine paled. "You're right, of course, but it's just not that easy."

"It's better if he hears it from you," Savannah said, pushing the last piece of paper into the box before straightening. "That way the lie will seem smaller."

"Maybe we'll tell him tomorrow," Charmaine said. "I just can't think about it right now, I'm too tired." She smiled sadly and left the room.

"Someone's got to tell him," Savannah said, crossing her arms over her chest.

"But not you, remember?" Travis reminded her. He took her hand and pulled her into the archway. "That's a job for his parents."

"Then they'd better do it and soon."

"I've got no argument with that," Travis said, "but let's trust Charmaine and Wade to handle it their way. Like it or not, you're not his mother."

"So you keep reminding me. But I am his aunt and his friend, and I can't stand lying to him."

"Then don't. Just avoid the subject of Mystic."

"That sounds like a lawyer talking," she said caustically. "And even if I do avoid the subject, it won't matter. Josh can read me like a book."

"Come on, lady," he cajoled, unplugging the Christmas tree and then pinning her against the wall with the length of his body. "You can worry about that tomorrow. Tonight you've got enough on your hands just keeping me happy."

"Is that so?" she asked.

The darkened room cast intriguing shadows over Travis's handsome features. His eyes stared deep into hers, and the kiss he gave her made her insides quiver. "There is something else I've been meaning to discuss with you," he murmured into her ear.

"Such as?"

"Something I've wanted to do for a long time." He

reached into his pocket and extracted a white-gold ring with a large, pear-shaped diamond. The exquisite stone shimmered in the firelight, reflecting the red and orange flames. "Merry Christmas," he whispered against her hair.

Savannah stared at the ring and fought the urge to cry. "But when did you get this?"

"It came with the dog."

"Sure." She laughed, tears gathering in her eyes.

"Honest."

"I never dreamed..." she whispered.

"Dream. With me." His lips brushed over hers and his slumberous gray eyes looked past her tears and deep into her soul. "Just know that whatever happens, I love you."

"What's that supposed to mean?"

"Just that the fireworks are about to begin."

She swallowed hard. "You're going to confront Dad again, aren't you?" she accused. "Oh, Lord, Travis. What is it? What have you found out?"

"Nothing," he said. "Nothing yet."

"But you expect to."

"Just trust me." He placed the ring in her palm and gently folded her fingers around it. "I'm giving this ring to you because I love you and I want you to marry me. No matter what else happens, remember that."

"You act as if you're going to leave," she said.

"I am, for a little while. But I'll be back."

"And then?"

"And then I'll expect you to come with me."

"To Colorado," she guessed, feeling a weight upon her slim shoulders.

"Wherever. I really don't think it will matter."

Savannah sensed that things were about to change, that all she had known was about to be destroyed by the one man she loved with a desperation that took her breath away. "What're you going to do?" she asked, her fingers clutching his shirt.

"Bait a trap," he said with a sad smile.

"And you're leaving tonight?"

"In the morning." Travis saw the anxiety in her eyes and kissed her forehead. "Don't worry. I'll be back, and when I am, you'll be free to come with me."

Ignoring the dread that feathered down her spine, she responded to the gentle pressure of his hands against her back and the warmth of his lips over hers.

"We only have one night together for a while," he murmured. "Let's make the most of it." Without waiting for her response, he gently tugged on her hand, led her through the kitchen to collect their coats, and out the back door, to the loft.

As she had worried it would, Savannah's life changed drastically the next morning.

"What the hell is all of this about?" Reginald roared as he kicked off his boots on the back porch. He'd already made his rounds and had come back into the kitchen with the morning paper tucked under his arm. Seeing Travis and Savannah together obviously made his blood boil.

He slapped the open paper onto the table. Bold black letters across the front page of the *Register* made Travis's withdrawal from the governor's race official.

"I told you I wasn't planning on running," Travis said, a lazy grin slanting across his face.

"But I thought you'd change your mind. A man just doesn't throw away an opportunity like this! We're talking about the governorship of California—one of the most powerful positions on the West Coast! Why in God's name wouldn't you want it?" Reginald looked stunned and perplexed, as if Travis were a creature he couldn't begin to understand.

"I explained all that before."

Reginald slid into the nearest chair and Savannah poured him a glass of orange juice. "I thought you'd change your mind, that you just needed a change of scenery to recover after the Eldridge case as well as Melinda's death."

"I haven't and I won't."

"You should have waited before you told the press," Reginald said dejectedly.

"No reason."

"But there's a chance you will reverse your position."

"No way. I'm out." Travis finished his glass of juice and reached for a cup of coffee.

"So what do you plan to do? Willis Henderson said you wanted to sell your half of the law partnership to him."

"That's right. I'm going back to L.A. today to sign the papers and tie up a few loose ends."

"And then?"

"And then I'll be back. For Savannah." The smile on Travis's face hardened around the corners of his mouth. "I've asked her to marry me."

"You what!" Reginald paled. He slumped lower in the chair and sighed before looking at Savannah. "You're really not seriously thinking about marriage are you?"

Savannah laughed. "I'm twenty-six, Dad."

"But your feelings for him are all turned around. They have been since that summer that he came back to the farm." He rubbed a tired hand over his face and then impaled Travis with his cold eyes. "And after the marriage, what then?"

"Colorado."

"Colorado? Oh, God, why?"

"A new start."

Reginald reached into his jacket pocket for his pipe. "Well, I can't say as I blame you, I guess," he said wearily. "From the looks of this," he tapped his pipe on the paper, "you'll need one."

Savannah picked up the paper and her stomach twisted as she read the article. Though most of the facts were accurate, the slant of the report was that Travis was leaving the race because of a reported scandal in which he had been accused of taking contributions for a nonexistent campaign.

Later in the article it was mentioned that Travis may have been involved in the controversy surrounding Mystic's death.

Savannah, white and shaking after reading the article, lifted her eyes to meet the concerned gaze of her father. "What controversy?" she asked.

"There are those who think Mystic could have been saved," Reginald said. "I heard about it when I stayed in Sacramento to be near Josh."

"But Steve did everything possible."

"There are always some people who will second-guess." Reginald studied his pipe. "I considered another surgery on the horse, but it just didn't seem fair to Mystic. The odds that he would have survived were minimal and we—Lester, Steve and I—agreed it would be best to put him out of his agony. I explained that to the press, but of course, other people, including some in the racing industry, disagreed."

"So what does that have to do with Travis?"

"Nothing, really," Travis explained with a grimace. "But right now it makes for an interesting story, especially since I've been staying here at the farm and was involved in finding Mystic."

"You should stay here and fight," Reginald said, his face suddenly suffusing with color. "You should run for the governorship and win, damn it. That would stop all the wagging tongues...."

Travis took a seat opposite Reginald at the table. "But that's not what you're worried about, is it? You have other reasons for wanting me involved in politics."

"Of course I do."

"Name one."

"I think it would be a great accomplishment for you."

"I said, '"name one' and I meant a real reason."

Reginald's eyes flickered from Travis to Savannah and back again. "You know it would be a feather in my cap," he said nervously.

"How?" Travis leaned forward on his elbows and stared straight at Reginald with a look that could cut through steel.

"I practically raised you as my own son and—"

"And that has nothing to do with it except for the fact that you've always tried to use me." He pointed one long finger on the table and tapped it against the polished wood. "Now, give me specifics."

"I don't have any."

Travis frowned and settled back in his chair, crossing his arms over his chest. Then he smiled cynically and his eyes remained cold.

"What's this all about?" Savannah asked, surveying the confrontation between the two men with mounting dread.

"I think it all started with a piece of property just outside of San Francisco."

"You mean Dad's land?" Savannah asked, noticing that Reginald's stiff shoulders fell. "I don't understand."

"You would if you snooped through his office and did some digging in the checkbook."

"Oh, Travis, you didn't," she murmured.

"Why don't you let your father explain?"

Reginald's thick brows lifted. "Wade was worried that you'd been looking where you shouldn't have."

"He had good cause to worry," Travis said angrily.

"What's wrong with the property?" Savannah asked.

"Nothing. Not yet. But plans are already being made."

"What kind of plans?" she asked, leaning against the counter and staring at her father with wide, disbelieving eyes.

"It's not all that big a deal," her father said with a frown. "You know, I've always thought that Travis should go into politics."

Savannah nodded and Travis's eyes narrowed. "Go on," Savannah coaxed.

"Two years ago I had this opportunity to buy some land near San Francisco at a good price. The company that owned it was going bankrupt. I heard of the distress sale and bought the acreage. It was just a case of being in the right place at the right time. Anyway, I had it surveyed and decided that I'd want to build a racetrack, a kind of memorial to myself and the horses we've raised, name it Beaumont Park." His eyes slid to Travis. "There's no crime in that, is there?"

"I didn't know this," Savannah said incredulously. "So what does that have to do with Travis?"

"Red tape," Travis explained. "The land was zoned all wrong and there was bound to be some protest from the farms bordering Reginald's land if he decided that he wanted to build a racetrack."

"But Travis wasn't even elected," she said to her father.

"I know. It was kind of a long shot, but when I couldn't

get a straight answer from Travis, I talked to Melinda and she told me that he was setting his sights for the next governor's race. I knew that as governor he could be influential and help me build the park."

"As well as make a ton of money," Travis cut in.

"That, too, of course."

"Of course," Travis repeated. "You know, Reginald, that's taking a helluva lot for granted. Especially since I hadn't announced any intention of running."

"But I knew Melinda and how influential she was in your life." Reginald looked at his daughter. "She managed to get you to marry her, when you were attracted to Savannah, didn't she?"

Savannah felt her face color in the ensuing silence.

"And she held on to you, helped you make career decisions as well as personal ones. I knew that you relied on her judgment, Travis, and if she said you were going to run, it was good enough for me."

"All behind my back."

"You were busy."

"So what happened when Melinda died?" Travis wanted to know.

"There was the Eldridge case, which you won with flying colors. You were the hero of the hour after winning that decision against the drug company...."

Travis glared at the older man. "What if I had run and lost? That was a distinct possibility, you know."

"Not according to the pollsters."

"A lot could have happened between now and then; besides, the public does happen to change its mind on occasion."

"I'd considered that," Reginald admitted. "I could still sell that land at a substantial profit. But of course, it would be a lot less than I'd make if I sold to a consortium of investors who were interested in building Beaumont Park."

"I don't believe this," Savannah said.

"There's more," Travis thought aloud. "You expected me to appoint you to the board, didn't you?"

Reginald frowned thoughtfully. "I'd hoped," he admitted.

"You expected one helluva lot, didn't you?" Travis said, swearing angrily. "Good God, man, not only did you bet that I'd win a race I wasn't running in, but then you wanted personal favors from me as well." Travis's face colored as he became more incensed. "I just want you to know here and now, for the record, if I ever decide to go into politics, I'll never owe any man anything!"

"This is insane," Savannah thought aloud. "Travis hadn't even announced his candidacy!"

Reginald offered his daughter a humbling grin. "I still have dreams, you know, dreams I haven't fulfilled, and I'm running out of time. I'm not the kind of man who can just retire…." He lifted his palms, hoping she would understand.

"But you don't have to."

Lighting his pipe, Reginald shook his head. A thick cloud of scented smoke rose to the ceiling. "I'm afraid I do. I need to move your mother into town, so she's closer to the things she likes to do. She needs to be near a hospital, but I'd be bored to death in the city. You know that."

"Yes," Savannah replied, remembering her own brief career in San Francisco. All the while, she'd been itching to return to the farm. Working outside with the horses was in her blood, as it was in her father's.

Reginald stood and walked to the door. "Then try and understand and be patient with me."

She watched in disbelief as Reginald, attempting to

straighten his shoulders, walked out the door. "So you were right," she whispered to Travis. Through the window Savannah watched her father walk through the wet grass toward the stables. Archimedes was tagging along behind him.

"Does that change things?" Travis asked.

She offered a faltering smile. "A little, I guess."

He looked down at her hand and the diamond sparkling on her finger. "Come with me to L.A."

"I can't." She shook her head and smiled. "Too much is unsteady here at the farm. Josh is still laid up, Charmaine's worried, Dad's still despondent about Mystic and Wade…"

"Yeah, I've noticed. He's holed himself up with a bottle every night." Travis sighed wearily and looked deep into her eyes. "So what happens when I come back for you? Will you be able to leave with me?"

"I hope so," she said, her eyes sliding over the familiar rolling hills and fields that were so dear to her.

"But you can't say for sure."

"No, not yet."

"I was afraid it would come to this, but maybe I can help you make up your mind." His smile became hard. "Like I told you last night, I'm going to L.A. to bait a trap, and when I come back, maybe this whole mess will be straightened out."

"I don't see how," she whispered.

"Trust me," he said, kissing her softly on the lips. "I told you that I wasn't about to let you go again and that's a promise I intend to keep!"

CHAPTER ELEVEN

TRAVIS HAD BEEN gone for over a week, and Josh was beginning to heal. So far, Charmaine had been able to screen Josh's friends' calls, and no one had let Josh know that Mystic had been destroyed.

Savannah was more on edge with each passing day, afraid that she or someone else on the farm would experience an inadvertent slip of the tongue around the boy. She'd even tried to talk to both Wade and Charmaine, but no amount of persuading could convince Josh's parents to tell their son about the dead colt.

She missed Travis more than she thought was humanly possible and reluctantly agreed that he had been right all along. It was time for her to make a life for herself, a life with him. But walking away from the family she loved and the farm she held dear would be like tearing a huge hole out of her heart and leaving a dark empty chasm in her life.

"Don't be foolish," she'd told herself, but couldn't fight the pangs of regret she was already feeling.

She walked slowly from the main stables toward the stallion barn and wondered when Travis would return. Though he'd called once, their telephone conversation had been brief and stilted.

The engagement ring around her finger continued to sparkle and remind her that soon, after so many years apart, she would be Travis's wife, able to start a new life, perhaps have a child of her own. *Travis's child.*

With that warming thought she hurried to the stallion barn but stopped dead in her tracks when she saw Josh near the barn door.

"Hey, sport," she called, and Josh jumped and whirled to face her. "What're you doing out here?" she asked softly. "I thought you gave up your early-morning rounds."

"I just wanted to see Mystic," Josh replied, turning earnest eyes upward to meet her loving gaze.

"Does your mom know you're here?"

Josh pushed his toe into the mud. "No."

"Or your dad or grandpa?"

"No one but you, Aunt Savvy. You're not going to tell on me, are you?"

Savannah shook her head and smiled. Bending her head to be on eye level with the boy, she winked at him. "I wouldn't dream of it."

Josh took advantage of her good nature. "Then you'll let me into the barn?"

She leaned a shoulder against the door and weighed the alternatives. In another week Josh would get his brace off and would be returning to school. He needed time to adjust and grieve for the horse he'd loved before he faced his friends.

"I'd be in big trouble with your folks," she said.

"They'll never know," Josh pressed.

"They'd know." Her smile slowly fell from her face.

"How?" His question was so innocent. It ripped through her heart.

Breathing deeply, she placed a comforting hand on Josh's shoulder. "First of all, let me explain something."

"Why?"

"For once, you just listen, okay?"

The boy swallowed and stuck out his chin. "Okay."

"You know that we all love you very much." When he tried to interrupt, she held up her hand and kept talking very quickly. "And everything that we've done is to protect you and keep you safe."

"Like what?"

"Josh, I really don't know how to tell you this, but I wish I'd done it a long time ago. Come on." She pushed open the door to the barn. It creaked on old hinges and let a little daylight into the darkened interior. Several stallions nickered softly as Savannah snapped on the lights and braced herself for Josh's despair.

"What's wrong?" Josh asked, his gaze wandering to Mystic's empty stall. "Where's Mystic?"

"He's gone, Josh," Savannah said softly, touching the boy on the shoulder.

"Gone?" he repeated, his face pinching with fear as he twisted away from her. "Gone where?" The boy raced down the aisle and stood at Mystic's empty stall. "Where is he?" he asked, tears in his eyes. "Grandpa didn't sell him did he? He wouldn't!"

"No," Savannah said calmly. "But Grandpa did have to have Mystic put down. He was hurt and the vet couldn't help him."

"Hurt!" the boy screamed, losing all of his color, his eyes widening in horror. Several of the horses began to shift warily within their stalls. "What do you mean?"

"His leg was broken," she said as calmly as possible.

Josh's small features contorted in grief, and tears drizzled down his cheeks. "Because of when I took him away from here during the storm, right?"

Savannah's stomach knotted painfully. "That's when it happened."

"Then it's all my fault!"

"Of course not." Slowly she advanced toward her nephew, offering him an encouraging smile as well as her understanding gaze.

"How can you say that?" Josh demanded, his voice cracking. "I took him, didn't I? I rode him when I wasn't supposed to! Oh, Aunt Savvy, I killed him! I killed Mystic!"

"Mystic hurt himself. It was an accident."

"Then why didn't anybody tell me?" Josh asked, wiping his eyes with his sleeve.

"Because the doctors were afraid that you'd be upset. Once you got home it was difficult to tell you about Mystic because you loved him so much."

"I should never have taken him," he said, sobbing.

"That's right, you shouldn't have. But it happened and you can't blame yourself for the accident. You loved the horse; no one blames you for his death. Now, come on. Let's go into the house and I'll fix you some breakfast."

"No!" Josh stepped away from her and angrily pushed her arm away from his shoulders. "You lied to me! All of you lied to me! You let me think that Mystic was alive and all the time he was dead!"

Josh began to run from the barn.

"Josh, wait!" Savannah yelled after him, and watched as he disappeared through the door. "Damn!" Her fist balled and she slammed it against the top of the gate to Mystic's stall. Vagabond snorted and tossed his head, but Savannah, her thoughts centered on her nephew, ignored the horse. "You made a fine mess out of this, Beaumont," she chastised herself before running after Josh to the house.

When she walked into the kitchen, she found that the entire household was awake.

"You told him about Mystic, didn't you?" Wade demanded. He was sipping from a cup of coffee and impaling her with his cruel eyes.

"Josh was already at the barn. What else could I do?"

"March him back here and have him talk to me. I'm his father."

"Then I suggest you start acting like it and quit lying to the kid. You had plenty of opportunities to talk to him about Mystic."

"And since I didn't you took it upon your shoulders to handle the situation."

"Don't push this off on me, Wade. Face it, you blew it." She started through the kitchen in an effort to go up to Josh's room and try to console him, but Wade's hand restrained her.

"Stay away from him, Savannah. He's with Charmaine. She'll handle him. As far as I'm concerned you can leave my boy alone and just butt the hell out of my life."

"I love Josh, Wade."

"But he already has a mother." He dropped her arm and ran an unsteady hand through his hair. "And as for Travis McCord, you can tell him to leave me alone as well."

Savannah bristled. "What's Travis got to do with you?"

Eyeing her speculatively, Wade pressed his fingers against his temples as if trying to forestall a headache. "Nothing. Forget it."

"Forget what?" she asked. "Have you talked to him?"

"Of course not!" Wade snapped.

"Then—"

"I said, 'forget it,'" Wade grumbled, taking his coat from a peg near the back door and storming out of the house toward the garage.

"What was that all about?" she whispered to herself as she watched Wade walk angrily to his car. A few minutes later he drove away from the farm at a breakneck speed.

Knowing that something had happened between her brother-in-law and Travis, she tried to dial Travis's apartment in L.A. Though she let the phone ring for several minutes, Travis didn't answer. "Where are you?" she wondered aloud, hanging up the receiver and realizing just how much she depended upon him.

Taking a deep breath, Savannah climbed the stairs and found Charmaine walking out of Josh's room.

"I let the cat out of the bag," Savannah admitted.

"I know. It's all right. I should have told him when it first happened," Charmaine said with a weary smile. "He just wants to be left alone for a while."

"Do you think that's okay?"

"Yeah. He's okay. And Banjo's with him."

"Thank God Travis gave him the puppy."

Charmaine slid a conspiratorial glance in her sister's direction. "I had to do some fast talking to get Wade to agree to the dog," she admitted.

"I imagine. Wade just left."

"I heard," Charmaine said as if it didn't really matter one way or the other.

"How're things…between you two?"

"No worse than they ever were, I suppose, but it's hard to say. He's been a basket case ever since Travis showed up here a few weeks ago, and I'm about ready to call it quits." She ran a trembling hand over her eyes.

"Charmaine—"

"I'm okay. Really. I just don't understand Wade anymore. And his reaction to Travis…it's scary, he almost acts paranoid."

"Because of the governor's race?"

Charmaine shook her head and bit pensively on her lip. "There's more to it than that, I think. I just don't exactly know what it is." Looking Savannah squarely in the eye, she said, "But the whole thing scares me; it scares me to death."

"Why?"

"I don't know. I feel like Wade is worried about something—something big. But he won't confide in me."

"Maybe you're just imagining it," Savannah offered. "We've all been on edge ever since the accident with Mystic."

"I wish I could believe that was all it was," Charmaine replied grimly. "But I don't think so."

TWO DAYS LATER Travis returned to the farm. Savannah was standing near the exercise track with Lester when she heard footsteps behind her. She turned and found Travis, his eyes sparkling silver-gray in the morning light, walking toward her.

"I was beginning to think that you'd changed your mind," she accused with a laugh.

"About you? Never!" Travis took her into his arms and twirled her off the ground. "God, it's good to see you," he said, lowering his head and capturing her lips with his.

"You could've called," she accused.

"Too impersonal. I didn't want to waste any time. The faster I got done in L.A., the quicker I could get back to you!" He kissed her again, and this time the kiss deepened, igniting the dormant fires in her blood and sending her senses reeling.

Savannah blushed when she looked up and saw Lester staring at her.

"Don't mind me, missy." Lester grinned. "I always knew you two were right for each other."

"How?"

The older man grinned. "I was younger once myself, y'know. Had myself a wonderful lady, but things didn't work out."

Savannah was dumbfounded. "Why not?"

The older man smiled wistfully. "Turned out that she was married. And to a good man, too." He shrugged. "Water under the bridge. But with you two, that's a whole other story."

Vagabond finished his workout and Lester studied the colt with narrowed eyes. "This one, he might just do it this year."

"Do what?"

"Win 'em all!"

Savannah laughed and shoved her hands into her pockets. "That's what you said about Mystic."

"Ah, well, some things just don't work out as ya would have liked, don't ya know?" he said wistfully.

Lester walked over to the horse, and Travis and Savannah turned back to the house.

"You think you can ever really leave this place?" Travis asked suddenly.

"With you? Yes."

"But you wouldn't be happy." It was a simple statement and one Savannah couldn't really deny as she looked at the wet, green hills and the carefully maintained buildings of the farm. In a few months the brood mares would be delivering their foals and the spindly-legged newborns would get their first breath of life on the farm.

"I'll miss it," she admitted.

"Even if we start again?"

"In Colorado?"

"Wherever."

She angled her head and looked up at him. Light from

a wintry sun warmed her face. "This farm is special to me. For you it represents my father and the fact that he tried to mold you into something he wanted. So, to you, it's a prison. But to me, it represents freedom to do exactly as I please."

"Which is work with the horses."

"And be near my family."

"I see," he said tersely, his teeth clenching together just as they reached the back porch. "I think it's time I talked to Reginald in person."

"Oh, God, haven't you quarreled enough already?"

"That's behind us."

"I don't understand."

"Oh, but you will. I've been doing a lot of thinking lately and I've talked to Reginald every day."

"You called here and didn't talk to me?" she demanded, confusion clouding her eyes. *What was going on?*

"Guilty as charged," he conceded with a rakish smile.

"I'll get you for that, you know."

A grin sliced across his tanned face. "I can't wait."

They walked into the den and found Reginald, his glasses perched on the end of his nose, sitting at his desk and carefully making marks on invoices as well as ledger entries.

"So you finally got here," Reginald said, all the old animosity out of his voice.

"Just a few minutes ago."

"You knew he was coming?" Savannah asked in surprise.

"Didn't you? Oh, I see." Reginald pushed the papers on his desk to the side and motioned for Savannah to take a seat in his recliner. "Well, I thought you'd want to know that I've decided to retire."

"Right away?"

"Yes. As soon as possible."

"What!"

He tapped a pencil to his lips and smiled at his daughter. "I've given a lot of thought to it, ever since the tragedy with Mystic and then with what Travis has discovered, it just seemed like the right time to turn over the farm to you."

"To me?" Savannah repeated, stunned. "Wait a minute. What about Wade?"

Reginald frowned and looked at Travis. "So you haven't told her anything, have you?"

"I figured it was your responsibility."

"What responsibility?" Savannah demanded. "What's been going on?" Then Travis's cold words came back to her. *I'm going to bait a trap.* What had happened?

"I've decided to sell that piece of property near San Francisco, take your mother and move to a warmer climate, somewhere south near San Diego, I think."

"But why now?"

"I told you that your mother needs to be closer to town and a hospital, and I'd been giving some thought to retiring anyway. When Travis discovered that Wade had skimmed money from the farm, I double-checked. Unfortunately, he was right. In the past six years, Wade has taken Beaumont Breeding Farm for nearly a quarter of a million dollars."

Savannah blanched and dropped into the nearest chair. "No!" But the expression on her father's face remained grim.

"Yes," Travis interjected. "Also, much to my partner, Willis Henderson's, embarrassment, Wade has been skimming money out of the law firm with phony invoices and receipts."

"Same here," Reginald said, gesturing to a stack of bills. "Dummy companies, who supposedly charged us for anything from paper clips to alfalfa to stud services." Reginald picked up his pipe and began cleaning the bowl. "I guess I'm getting too old to oversee everything. A few years ago this never would have happened. I would have caught it." He sighed heavily. "I just can't afford to make mistakes like that, not even for my own son-in-law."

"I can't believe any of this," Savannah whispered, but Travis's stony gaze convinced her that it was true. *Wade? A thief?*

"So I'm counting on you to keep the farm going," Reginald said with a sad smile. "Charmaine has no use for the horses, but you, you've had a feel for them ever since you were a little girl."

Savannah looked from her father to Travis. "You knew all about this, didn't you? And yet you let me think we were still going to Colorado."

"Just checking," he replied, his eyes lighting mischievously. "I had to know that you were serious about marrying me."

"Nothing will ever change my mind," she vowed, standing next to the man she loved with all of her heart.

"What the hell's going on here?" Wade demanded, bursting into the room. His face was flushed, his eyes wild and he was shaking from head to foot. "Charmaine just gave me some cock-and-bull story about you retiring and leaving the management of the farm to Savannah."

"That's right," Reginald said quietly.

"But—" His voice dropped when he saw the stack of invoices on the corner of the desk.

"I think you'd better call a good lawyer," Reginald said. "We've found you out, Wade."

"And don't bother contacting Willis Henderson," Travis added. "He's on to you."

"What's that supposed to mean?"

Travis sighed loudly. "Give it up, Benson," he suggested, his voice cold. "Not only do we know about the phony receipts and how much money you've embezzled to the penny, but we also know about the gambling debts that you've had to repay."

Wade blanched and stumbled backward, leaning against the wall for support. "Lies," he choked out. "All a pack of lies."

"I don't think so."

Gesturing wildly, Wade pointed a condemning finger at Travis. "And I suppose you've spread all these lies to Charmaine, haven't you! Haven't you?"

"She knows all about it. If you want, you can try and explain your side of the story," Travis said. "But she's got all the facts and figures."

Wade's eyes narrowed and his fist curled at his side. "This is all your fault, McCord. You've spent the last few weeks of your life trying to destroy me. Well, I'm going to fight it. Tooth and nail. Just because you're a big hotshot attorney, you're not going to force me into going to jail for something I didn't do!"

He stomped out of the room and thundered up the stairs.

"Well, that's that," Reginald said wearily. "Can't say that I like it much." He lit his pipe and sighed as the smoke billowed around his face. "It will probably kill your mother."

"She's stronger than you think," Savannah whispered.

"I hope so." Reginald shook his head and put his hands on the desk to rise to his full height. "Oh, and Savannah, you may as well know that I told Travis I expect him to help you with the farm."

"That's right," Travis said. "The old man is still trying to manipulate me."

"And you let him?" Savannah asked.

Travis's smile stole from one side of his face to the other. "Maybe it's because he told me he wanted us to fill this house with his grandchildren."

She lifted her confused eyes to her father. "Wait a minute. Are you saying that after all your warnings you *want* me to marry Travis?"

Reginald snorted. "I would have preferred him to become governor; I wouldn't even have opposed having a daughter who's the first lady of this state, but I guess I'll just have to settle for a son-in-law who will run this farm with care and integrity."

"And what about Wade?" Savannah asked.

"I don't know," Reginald said, obviously tired. "But he's made his own bed; now he'll have to lie in it." Reginald walked out of the room and trudged up the stairs to talk to Virginia.

"So what happens to Wade now?" Savannah asked.

"I suppose Wade will be prosecuted, if Willis Henderson and your father have their way," Travis replied.

"And Charmaine?"

"She's taking it in stride, but she could probably use a little support from you."

Savannah's heart twisted and her voice was only the barest of whispers. "And what about Josh?"

"Charmaine's already talked to him. The boy seemed to handle it fairly well. Remember, he and his father didn't get along very well, anyway."

"He and Charmaine have become a lot closer since Mystic's death," Savannah said.

Travis leaned against the desk with his hips and drew Savannah into the circle of his arms. "The way I figure it, we'll live here until we can build a house of our own. And your father has promised not to try and run our lives."

"I can't believe you've buried the hatchet."

"Face it, the man is your father. I'm stuck with him and he's stuck with me. Because of you, we're trying to work things out."

"Unbelievable," she murmured. "Now, tell me what's wrong with this house."

"Nothing, except that it belongs to Reginald and Virginia. Charmaine and Josh will probably stay here."

"So what was all this song and dance about filling up this house with children?" she asked, turning to face him, a sparkle lighting her blue eyes.

"Just that. The house I intend to fill with children will have to be twice this size just to hold them all."

"You're out of your mind, counselor," she said, but tossed her hair away from her face and laughed at the thought.

"Only with love for you." He pulled her closer, so that her ear was pressed to his chest and she could hear the steady pounding of his heart. "Don't worry about anything, we can have it all."

"And Wade?"

"He'll probably be sent to prison, and I think that's a good place for him. He won't be around for the next few years, and by the time he gets back, if Charmaine doesn't decide to divorce him, Josh will be old enough to stand up for himself."

"You've got it all figured out, don't you?"

"Except for one thing."

"Oh?" She lifted her head and traced the seductive curve of his lips with her finger. "What's that?"

"How I'm going to get you to marry me before to-night."

"Impossible."

"Reno's not that far away...."

She laughed merrily. "Oh, no, you don't. I'm not set-tling for a quick ten-minute speech in front of some jus-tice of the peace I've never met before. You're going to have to go the whole nine yards on this one. You know, big church, long white gown, stiff uncomfortable tuxedo and at least four attendants."

Travis squeezed her. "You're really out for blood, aren't you?"

"I've waited a long time."

"And it was worth it, wasn't it?" Without waiting for a response, he pressed his hungry lips to hers and deftly swept her off her feet. "Don't answer that question," he whispered against her ear. "We have much more impor-tant things to do right now."

Without a word of protest, Savannah stared into his eyes and locked her arms around his neck. "And for the rest of our lives," she added.

Travis smiled and carried her out of the den, down the hallway and into the kitchen.

"Hey, where are you taking me?" she asked.

"To some place where we can be alone." He crossed the parking lot to the garage and climbed the stairs to his loft. Once inside, he set her on the floor, kicked the door shut and locked it. "Now, Ms. Beaumont," he said, with a twinkle in his eyes. "I think it's time we spent the next few days locked away from the rest of the world."

"Is that possible?" she asked.

"Probably not, but we can try." Grinning wickedly, he extracted a gold key from his pocket and dangled it in front of her nose. "Face it, lady, you can't get away from me."

"I wouldn't have it any other way," she agreed, as he folded her into his arms and carried her into the bedroom.

* * * * *

RENEGADE SON

PROLOGUE

Boise, Idaho
April 18, 1985

CHASE MCENROE STARED down at the cashier's check, greatly annoyed. Distrust darkened his clear blue eyes. Two hundred thousand dollars. More money than he'd made in all of his thirty-two years and it was being handed to him on a silver platter. *Or with strings attached.*

"So what's the catch?" he asked cautiously as he dropped the slip of paper onto his letter strewn desk. Ironically the check settled on a stack of invoices that were already sixty days past due.

"No catch," Caleb Johnson replied with a satisfied smile. "We've been over all this before, and everything's spelled out in the contract." The older man grinned encouragingly and thumped the partnership agreement with his fingers. "I trust you had your attorney go over it."

Chase stared straight at Caleb's ruddy face and nodded, but still he frowned and his chiseled features didn't relax. His tanned skin was drawn tight over angular cheekbones, square jaw and hollow cheeks.

"Let's just say that I don't trust strangers bearing gifts."

"It's not a gift. I own fifty percent of your company if you take the money."

Ah, there it was: the trap!

Rubbing a hand wearily over his beard-roughened jaw, Chase stood and walked over to the window of his small office, which was little more than a used construction trailer. He poured a cup of coffee from the glass pot sitting on a hot plate beneath the window.

"I don't like partners," Chase said almost to himself as he glared through the dusty glass to the empty parking lot. Sagebrush and grass were growing through the cracks of the splitting asphalt, as if to remind him how much he needed Caleb Johnson's money.

"The way I understand it, you could use a partner right now."

"How's that?"

"Didn't most of your staff walk off the job five weeks ago?"

Chase didn't answer. Instead he frowned into his chipped coffee cup. But Caleb's point had struck home; the unconscious tightening of Chase's jaw gave his anger away.

"And aren't they planning to start a rival company in Twin Falls with a man named Eric Conway as president?" Johnson added.

"There's a rumor to that effect," Chase replied tightly.

"So they've got the expertise, the money to back their project, the manpower to work efficiently and all the contracts that you worked ten years to develop. Right?"

"Maybe." Chase felt his muscles bunch with tension. The deceit of his best friend still felt like a ball of lead in his stomach. He'd trusted Eric Conway with his life, and the man had kicked him in the gut.

"So, the way I see it, you're just about out of options."

"Not quite." Chase took a long swallow from his coffee and set the cup on the windowsill. "I still like being the boss."

"You would be." Caleb smiled and shrugged his broad shoulders. "Think of me as a silent partner."

"So what's in it for you?"

"Your guarantee that when I'm ready with the resort—"

"Summer Ridge?"

"Right. I'll let you know, then you can come up to Martinville and make Grizzly Creek viable for trout. When the job's complete, I'll pay you by returning twenty-five percent of Relive, Inc., just the way it's outlined in the agreement." Satisfied that he'd taken care of everything, Caleb pointed a fleshy finger at the document.

"And what about the final twenty-five percent?" Chase asked, his blue eyes narrowing.

"Oh, that you'll have to buy back."

"For a substantial profit over what you paid," Chase guessed.

"Market value. Whatever that is."

"Sounds fair enough," Chase thought aloud. Not only had he looked for catches in the agreement, but he'd had his attorney poring over the documents for two weeks. Everything appeared legal. *And too good to be true.*

He returned to his chair, glanced again at the check on the thick pile of invoices and then studied the slightly heavyset man in front of him. He'd never laid eyes on Johnson before in his life, and suddenly the man was here, in his office, offering him a godsend.

"So why me?" Chase finally asked. "Why not go with Conway's outfit?"

The easy Montana smile widened across Caleb Johnson's face. "Two reasons I suppose—you've got a track record and, even though you're slightly overextended right now, you plow all of your money back into the operation of Relive. Unless Conway was the brains behind this operation, you're the best in the business."

"And the other reason?"

Caleb Johnson's eyes glittered a watery blue. "I knew your mother," he said with a reflective grin.

Something in the older man's voice brought Chase's head up. His gaze narrowed speculatively on the big man. "I never heard her speak of you," he drawled.

"It was a long time ago," Caleb replied. He tugged thoughtfully on his lower lip and gauged Chase's reaction. "Before you were born."

"And that was enough to convince you?"

"Any son of Ella Simpson had to be a scrapper."

"Her name was Ella McEnroe," Chase said slowly.

"Not when I knew her…"

The wistful ring in Caleb's voice rankled Chase. How had this slightly unsavory man been connected with his mother? The thought that she'd even known Caleb Johnson bothered Chase more than he'd like to admit.

In the distance the sound of a freight train whistle pierced the air as the boxcars clattered on ancient tracks. The noise broke the mounting tension in the room. Caleb glanced at his watch and then, shrugging off the memories of a distant past, stood abruptly. "Look, I've got a plane to catch. Do we have a deal?"

Chase glanced down at the check. Two hundred grand. Damn, but that money could make the difference between making it or not, especially with Conway intent on ruining him. With a nagging feeling that he was making the worst decision of his life, Chase clasped Caleb Johnson's outstretched hand.

"Deal," he said and then reached into the drawer of his desk for a pen and signed all four copies of the partnership agreement.

"You've made the right decision."

Chase doubted it but tried not to second-guess himself. Caleb stuffed his copies of the paperwork into the pocket of his expensive, Western-style jacket and smiled in satisfaction. "Oh, there's one other thing," he said, walking to the door.

Here it comes, Chase thought, bracing himself for the elusive catch in the agreement. "What's that?"

"One of my neighbors is fighting me about developing Summer Ridge."

"Just one?"

"So far...oh, well, it'll all be cleared up by the time you come to Martinville. There's always a way to get people to come 'round to your way of thinking, y'know."

Yeah, like two-hundred-thousand dollars, Chase thought cynically.

Caleb waved a big hand and opened the door of the trailer before walking down the three worn steps to the parking lot.

Chase watched the big man from Montana drive off in a rented white Cadillac and tried to ignore the absurd feeling that he had just sold his soul to the devil; the same devil who had known his mother all those years ago.

CHAPTER ONE

Hawthorne Farm
Martinville, Montana
August 16, 1987

THE SUN BLAZED hot in the summer sky. Dry grass crackled and grasshoppers flew from the path of the buckskin gelding and its rider as the horse headed toward the clear stream slicing through the arid field.

Sweat beaded on Dani's forehead and slid down her spine. She lifted the rifle to her shoulder and cocked it, her eyes squinting through the sight at the target: a tall, blond man with broad shoulders, a tanned, muscular torso, slim hips and the nerve to trespass on her property by wading in Grizzly Creek. No doubt this stranger was another one of Caleb Johnson's men.

The element of surprise was on her side and definitely to her advantage. The stranger's back was to her, his sweat-glistened muscles rippling as he waded in the mountain stream, his eyes scouring the clear ice-cold water. It didn't appear that he had heard the warning click of the hammer of her Winchester or seen the horse and rider approach.

Dani's elegant jaw hardened with determination and her lips tightened though her hands shook as she took aim. "Move it, mister!" she shouted.

The target looked up and visibly started, the muscles

of his naked back bunching as he spun around to face her. Water sprayed upward from his sudden movement.

"Get the hell off my property!"

The stranger just stood in the middle of the creek as if dumbstruck, his eyes narrowing against the bright Montana sun and his body poised as if to run. But there was nowhere to hide. Aside from a few scraggly oaks, the fields of brittle sun-dried grass offered no cover. The gently sloping land was barren and dry as a bone.

Dani softly kicked the buckskin and advanced on the object of her outrage. When she was near enough to see the man clearly, she smiled at the mixture of indignation, horror and fury in his sky-blue eyes.

"I said, move it," she repeated, stopping the gelding a few feet from the creek and cocking her head in the direction of the bank where a pile of his belongings—shirt, fishing creel, and worn boots—lay on the grass.

His square jaw was thrust forward, his tanned skin nearly white over his face as he slowly waded out of Grizzly Creek. He kept his gaze on the barrel of the rifle as she moved forward. The steel glinted a threatening blue in the afternoon sun. Dani kept the Winchester trained on the stranger's every move as he bent down, picked up a plaid work shirt and angrily stuffed his sinewy arms through the sleeves.

She placed the rifle across her thighs. "Why don't you tell me what you're doing on my land?" she suggested, breathing once again when she realized that this man was complying with her orders. Some of Caleb Johnson's thugs hadn't been so easily buffaloed.

The intruder didn't flinch, but slowly buttoned his shirt. His lips were tight over his teeth, making his mouth seem little more than an angry line. "I was told this land belonged to Daniel Summers."

"*Danielle* Summers," she corrected.

"And you're she," he deduced.

"That's right." Dani almost grinned at his reaction. "Now, suppose you tell me just who you are and what you think you're doing on my property?"

"Why not?" he asked rhetorically and then muttered an angry oath under his breath.

"I'm waiting."

He shook his head and looked up at the cloudless sky. "How do I get myself into these things?" he muttered with a grimace before letting out a long, angry sigh and dropping his gaze from the heavens to horse and rider. "Okay, if you want to play out the bad B Western scenario, I'll state my name and business."

"Good." She stared down at him without a smile, her eyes glued to his chiseled features. She guessed him to be around thirty-five, give or take a couple of years. From the looks of him, the poor bastard had probably been on Caleb Johnson's payroll less than a week. Otherwise he wouldn't appear so clean-cut or have been so stupid as to wander blatantly over the property line in broad daylight.

"The name's McEnroe."

"Like the tennis player?"

He snorted at the inference, as if he'd heard it a million times. He probably had. "No relation. I'm Chase McEnroe."

"And you work for Caleb Johnson," she said, leaning over the saddle horn and pinning him with her wide gray-green eyes. Her braid of sun-streaked hair fell forward over one shoulder to settle over the swell of her breast and she forced a cold smile. "Well, let me tell you, Mr. Chase not-related-to-the-tennis-star McEnroe, this is my land and I don't like anyone, especially one of Caleb Johnson's hands, snooping around. So you can take a message to your boss and tell him the next time he sends one of his flunkies around here, I'll call the sheriff."

McEnroe's blue eyes sparked and his square jaw slid to the side as he stared at her. "I think the line you're looking for is: 'Tell your double-crossing boss that the next time one of his low-life ranch hands steps one foot on my property, I'll shoot first and ask questions later.'"

Dani fought the urge to smile and arched an elegant dark brow at the man. "You're an arrogant S.O.B., aren't you?" *Not like the usual scum Caleb Johnson hired. Too smart. McEnroe wouldn't last long with Johnson.* Oddly, Dani felt relieved.

His brilliant blue eyes narrowed and his lips twisted cynically as he glanced again at the rifle. "Look, I'd like to sit around and trade insults with you, but I've got work to do."

"Work? Like trespassing?"

"I was just looking at the stream."

"On *my* side of the fence."

"I know."

"*That's* your job?" With a disbelieving sigh, she sat back in the saddle, balanced the rifle on her thighs and crossed her arms under her chest. "Surely you can come up with a better excuse than that."

Lifting a shoulder as if he didn't really care what she thought, he stuffed the tail of his shirt beneath the waistband of his jeans and tightened his belt buckle.

"So why are you here? I've already told Johnson that I'm not going to sell my land to him. *Ever.* He can build his resort right up to the property line if he wants to, but the only way he'll get this land from me is over my dead body."

"Look, lady," McEnroe said, his face relaxing slightly as he yanked off his hip waders, poured the water out of them and stepped into his scruffy boots. "I don't really give a damn one way or the other what you do. Johnson just asked me to check out the stream, and I did. Since it runs through your property, I climbed through the fence and took a look."

"Why?"

"I don't really know if it's any of your business."

"You're on my land aren't you?"

"A mistake I intend to rectify immediately," he said, grabbing his waders and creel before walking toward the sagging fence. He slipped through the slack barbed wires while keeping his eyes focused on the Winchester.

"You can tell Johnson one more thing," she said as he turned toward the Jeep parked in the middle of the field next to hers.

Chase faced her again, impatience evident on his angular features. "What's that?"

"Tell Johnson that I've hired a lawyer and if he tries any of his underhanded stunts again, I'll sue him."

"Tell him yourself," McEnroe replied furiously. "I'm out of this mess—whatever the hell it is."

With his final remark, he shook his head angrily, strode to the Jeep, climbed in and forced the vehicle into gear before starting it. The Jeep roared through the parched field, leaving a plume of dust in its wake as it disappeared through a stand of pine.

"I will," Dani decided, once she was sure Chase McEnroe, whoever the devil he was, had left and wasn't returning. "And that's not all I'll tell Johnson!" With the reins curled through the fingers of one hand, she turned the gelding toward the house and leaned forward in the saddle while gripping the unloaded rifle in her other hand.

Traitor got the message and eagerly sprinted up the slight incline toward the house. The wind whipped over

Dani's face, cooling her hot skin as the quarter horse sped toward the barn, moving effortlessly over the cracked earth.

"I won't let them beat us," Dani said, as if Traitor could understand her. "Not while there's an ounce of life in my body. Caleb Johnson can hire all the new hands he wants, I won't sell! This land belongs to me and some day it's gonna be Cody's!"

She thought back to the man wading in the stream. He was different from the rest of Johnson's crew, less rough around the edges. "Just give him time," Dani muttered, reining Traitor to a stop near the weathered barn before dismounting.

After just two weeks of working for Caleb Johnson, Chase McEnroe would forget to shave, learn to spit tobacco juice in a stream between his teeth and drink himself into a drunken stupor every Friday night at the local bar in Martinville.

"What a waste," Dani said, shaking her head sadly as she thought about the furious man. She tied the reins of the gelding's bridle around a fence post near the barn, removed the saddle and started brushing Traitor's tawny coat, but thoughts of Chase kept nagging at her. She remembered his cool, blue eyes, his hard, tanned muscles, the thick thatch of dark blond hair that glinted like gold in the late summer sun and the leashed fury in his rigid stance.

"It just doesn't make any sense," she thought aloud, removing the bridle and giving Traitor a quick slap on the rump. With a snort, the horse took off to join the rest of the herd. Why would a man like Chase McEnroe hook up with the likes of Caleb Johnson?

CHASE GROUND THE Jeep to a halt in front of the two-storied farmhouse. Swearing loudly, he stormed into the building without bothering to knock. The sharp thud of his boots echoing on the polished hardwood floor announced to the entire household that he was back…and he was furious.

"Okay, Johnson," Chase said, every nerve ending screaming with outrage as he pushed open the door of Johnson's office and forced his way into the room. "Just what the hell have you gotten me into?"

Caleb Johnson had the audacity to smile. He didn't look much different than he had the day that Chase had met him two and a half years ago. Johnson was still a robust man who had grown up in Montana, been prominent in local politics and acquired land around Butte for less than fifty dollars an acre. At seventy, his eyes were still an intense shade of blue, his tanned skin was nearly wrinkle-free and only the slight paunch around his middle gave any indication of his age.

"What do you mean?" Caleb was already pouring bourbon into a shot glass. He set the drink on the corner of the desk, silently offering it to Chase, and then poured another stiff shot for himself.

Chase ignored the drink and crossed his arms over his chest, pulling the fabric of his shirt tight across his rigid shoulders. "That *woman! Danielle* Summers. She's got one helluva bone to pick with you and I'm not about to get into the middle of it!"

Caleb seemed almost pleased. He fingered his string tie and settled into the oxblood cushions of the leather couch. "You met her, did you?"

Chase's eyes darkened. "Met her? She almost used my butt for target practice, for crying out loud. Look, Johnson, getting myself shot was not part of the deal!"

"She wouldn't shoot you."

"Easy for you to say!"

"She doesn't like violence." Caleb sipped his drink and smiled.

"Like hell!"

"Dani Summers wouldn't harm a flea."

"Then what the hell is she doin' out riding her property like some goddamned sentry!" Chase shook his head and pushed his sweaty hair out of his face. He saw the untouched drink on the desk, decided he needed something to calm him down, reached for the glass of bourbon and drank a long swallow. "I don't like being threatened, Caleb."

"Don't worry about Dani."

"Don't worry about her!" Chase was flabbergasted by the older man's calm. He took another swallow of bourbon. "Okay, you're right. I won't worry about her, because I won't deal with her or anyone else who points a rifle in my gut! Let's just forget the whole deal, okay?"

"No dice," Caleb said, "this is important."

"So is my life."

"I told you; the woman detests violence. She just wants to be left alone."

"So why was I walking on her property today?" Chase demanded, his jaw tight.

"Because it won't be hers for long."

Chase circled the scarred oak desk and leaned one hip against the windowsill. Rubbing his chin, he surveyed his partner and the place Caleb Johnson called home with new eyes. Braided rugs covered hardwood floors, pine walls were little more than a display case for weapons and tools of the Old West, a stone fireplace filled one wall and the furniture within the room was heavy, masculine and slightly worn. "She gave me a message for you. Words to the effect that you'd better leave her alone or she'd call a lawyer."

"She can't."

"Why not?"

"Hasn't got the money." Caleb downed his drink casually and lifted his feet to place them on the magazine strewn coffee table.

Chase's gut twisted and he experienced the same feeling he had felt on the day when he'd reluctantly accepted two hundred thousand dollars from Johnson; the feeling that he was just a marionette and that Johnson was pulling the strings. "How do you know how much money she's got?"

"Common knowledge." Caleb smiled smugly and balanced his drink between his hands. "Her husband left her and her kid about six or seven years ago. The guy just vanished. Word has it that he took off with a hotel clerk from Missoula, but that's just gossip. Anyway, all Dani Summers had left is a nine-year-old kid and a dust bowl of a piece of property that she tries to scratch a living from."

"So why doesn't she irrigate and make the land more productive?"

"Irrigation costs money."

"Which she doesn't have."

"Right."

"But surely a bank would loan her the money, unless she's mortgaged to the hilt."

"Who knows?" Caleb took a swallow and lifted his shoulders. "Maybe she's a bad credit risk."

"You wouldn't happen to be on the board of the local bank?" Chase asked, suddenly sick with premonition.

Caleb's smile widened.

"You are a miserable son of a bitch!"

"Just a practical businessman."

"And you want her land," Chase said with a renewed

feeling of disgust. "Dani Summers is the same neighbor that wouldn't sell to you two years ago, isn't she?"

Caleb grinned and a satisfied gleam lighted his eyes. "Her two hundred and forty acres sit right smack in the middle of my property. I can't very well develop the entire piece into a resort without it."

"If the land is so useless, why doesn't she sell?"

Frowning into his drink, Caleb shrugged. "Who knows? Just some damned fool notion. You know women."

Not women like Dani Summers, Chase thought with a sarcastic frown. She was the kind of woman who spelled trouble, and Chase prided himself in avoiding any woman with problems. The way he figured it, he had enough of his own. Now it looked like he was right in the middle of the proverbial hornet's nest.

"Can't you build Summer Ridge without her property?"

Caleb's scowl deepened. "No."

"Why not?"

Caleb hesitated and studied Chase's intense features. The kid had so much to learn about business. It was about time he started. Caleb gambled with the truth. "Her place, the Hawthorne place, goes up to the foothills. And the hot springs are right there, at the base of the mountains."

Chase eyed his partner with new respect. "The Hawthorne place?"

Caleb swatted in the air as if at a bothersome insect. "Yeah, the Hawthorne homestead. She was a Hawthorne before she married Summers."

"So Dani Hawthorne Summers's land isn't as worthless as you'd like her to believe."

"Don't get me wrong," the older man said testily. "I've offered her…a reasonable price for that pathetic farm."

"But she won't sell and you've come up against the first person you've ever met who wouldn't bend."

"I wouldn't get so lofty, if I were you. Remember, I bought you a couple of years ago."

Chase didn't bother to hide his cynicism. "I remember."

"Good. Then as long as we understand each other, why don't you find a way to get Dani Summers to sell her land to me?"

"That wasn't part of the bargain. I said I'd check out the streams and do the work to make sure that the trout will run again, but I'm not dealing with *that* woman. No way." Chase finished his drink and placed his empty glass on the windowsill.

"What if I said that I'm willing to sell you back my part of your company if you can get her to sign on the dotted line?"

Chase tensed. He'd wanted to get rid of the yoke of Caleb Johnson's partnership for nearly as long as he'd agreed to it in the first place. Coming to Caleb's ranch had been the first step, and now Caleb was dangling the final carrot in front of Chase's nose; the remaining twenty-five percent of the company would be his again, *if* he could convince Dani to sell her land. In all conscience, Chase could hardly afford to turn the offer down, yet he regretfully answered, "Can't do it."

"Why not?"

"The lady doesn't want to sell. She does have that right."

"Persuade her."

"Ha!" His gaze centered on Caleb's calm face. "She doesn't look like the type who's easily convinced."

Caleb smiled again. "Well, it's up to you, McEnroe. Either you want your company back, or you don't."

"I just don't like all the strings attached."

"Think of it this way, without Dani Summers's land, you won't be able to make Grizzly Creek viable for re-stocking of the trout, will you? The stream cuts right across her property. One way or the other, you've got to convince Dani Summers she has to sell her land to me."

Chase felt his back stiffen. "And how do you expect me to do that?"

"That's your problem." Caleb winked wickedly. "Use your imagination. She's been without a husband for over six years. Almost alone all that time." He took a long, satisfied swallow of his bourbon. "Women have needs, y'know."

Chase laughed aloud at the arrogance of the man. "You expect me to try to seduce her?"

"Why not? Pleasant enough business, I'd say. Good lookin' woman."

"You've got to be out of your mind! That lady wanted to kill me today!"

"What can I say? She's passionate. I bet she'd be a regular she-cat in bed."

"And you're a ruthless bastard, you know that, don't you? I can't believe we're having this conversation!" Chase moved off of the sill and looked through the window at the well-maintained buildings comprising the center of the Johnson property. He tried to ignore the unwelcome sensation stirring inside him at the thought of making love to Dani Summers. In his mind's eye he could envision her supple, tanned body, her rich, honey-brown hair streaked by the sun, her small firm breasts... God, it had been a long time since he'd been with a woman....

Caleb smiled to himself at Chase's reaction. "I didn't get where I am today by letting opportunities slip by me."

"And I'll wager that you've made a few of your own."

The older man smiled. "When I had to."

Chase stood and shook his head. "This time you're completely on your own. I don't bed women for business."

"Your mistake."

"Look, I've already told you that I'm out of this problem between you and Dani Summers." Chase walked to the door, placed his hand on the knob and jerked open the door. When he turned to face Caleb again, the fire in his eyes had died. "Why don't you just leave her alone? From what you've said tonight, I think the lady needs a friend rather than another enemy."

"Precisely my point," Caleb agreed with a crooked smile as Chase walked out of the room. "Precisely my point."

"Did we get any mail today?" Cody asked as Dani came into the house. The boy was sitting at the kitchen table, drinking a glass of milk. Sweat was curling and darkening his hair and dripping from his flushed face. A dusty basketball was tucked under one of his arms and Runt, a small Border collie, was lying on the floor beneath the table.

Silently cursing her ex-husband, Dani shook her head and offered her son an encouraging smile. "I don't know. I haven't been to the box."

"I'll get it." Cody finished his glass of milk, dropped the basketball and ran out of the room with the dog on his heels.

"Damn you, Blake Summers," Dani said. "Damn you for getting Cody's hopes up." She stood at the kitchen window, leaned against the counter and watched her son run the quarter mile down the dusty, rutted lane to the mailbox. In cut-off jeans and a faded T-shirt, the black dog at his heels, Cody sprinted along the fence.

Dani's heart bled for her son each time the boy brought up the subject of his father. Maybe she should have told him all of the painful truth—that Blake had never wanted the boy, that he'd had one affair after another, that he'd only married Dani because she'd inherited this piece of land, the Hawthorne property, from her folks, that the property Blake had owned, the Summers's place, he'd sold to Caleb Johnson and then gambled the money away....

She squinted against the late afternoon sun and watched as Cody, his slim shoulders slumped, his tanned legs slowing, walked back to the house. Maybe it was time she talked to him about his father. At nine, Cody was nearly five feet and was just starting to show signs of pre-adolescence. Perhaps he was mature enough to know the truth.

She met her son on the porch.

"Nothin' much," Cody said, handing her a stack of bills and shrugging as if the missing letter didn't mean a thing to him.

"You got your fishing magazine," she said, trying to hand him back a small piece of the mail. He didn't lift his eyes as he pushed open the screen door.

"Cody—"

The boy turned to face her. "Yeah?"

"I know you were expecting something from your father."

Her son went rigid. His brown eyes looked into hers and Dani knew in that moment that she couldn't talk against Blake—not yet. "What about it?"

"He didn't say when he'd visit or write again," Dani pointed out.

"But it's already been three months."

"I know. Maybe he's been busy."

"And maybe he just doesn't care. Not about me. Not

about you!" Cody's lower lip trembled but he managed not to cry.

"Don't think about it," Dani said, trying to comfort him.

"Don't think about my dad?" he repeated angrily. His small fist balled against the worn screen. "Don't *you* think about him?"

"Sometimes," she admitted. *Like now, when I know you're hurting.*

"You should be waitin' for him to come home!"

Dani pushed the hair that had escaped from her ponytail off her face. "I waited a long time, Cody."

"And then you divorced him," the boy accused.

Dani forced a sad but patient smile. "I know it's hard for you to understand but I can't…*we* can't live in the past."

"But he wrote me!" Cody said, his voice cracking. "He wrote me a letter and said he was comin' home!"

Dani leaned a shoulder against the side of the house. "I know he did, sweetheart—"

"Don't call me that! It's for babies."

"And you're not a baby anymore, are you?" She reached forward to push his hair out of his eyes, but he jerked away.

"Aw, Mom. Give me a break!" Cody walked into the kitchen and the screen door groaned before slamming shut with a bang.

Dani looked down at the crisp white envelopes in her hand; no letter from Blake. She didn't know whether it was a blessing or a curse. Cody was getting harder to handle each day.

With a sigh Dani walked through the house to the back porch and sat for a minute on the rail to stare at the property her great-great-grandfather had homesteaded nearly a hundred years before. The sprawling acres of the farm stretched before her. A few stands of oak, pine and cottonwood spotted the acreage that descended to Grizzly Creek before slowly rising to the foothills of the hazy Rocky Mountains. Waves of intense heat distorted the image of the cattle trying to graze in the dry pastures.

Thank God the creek was still running! And the snowpack on the mountains was still visible. So this year, at least, she wouldn't run out of water.

So what was Chase McEnroe doing in the stream? A new fear paralyzed her as she thought about the rugged-looking stranger and the fact that he worked for Caleb Johnson. Surely Caleb wouldn't stoop to sabotaging her only source of water for the cattle, would he? He'd tried a lot of underhanded methods to force her to move, but he wouldn't...*couldn't* cut off her water!

"I think it's about time to pay my neighbor a visit," she muttered to herself as she straightened. *Maybe tomorrow.* Right now she had to deal with Cody, so Caleb Johnson and Chase McEnroe would have to wait.

JUST BEING ON Caleb Johnson's land made Dani's skin crawl. The man was poison and she could feel it as she parked the pickup and walked up the brick path to the imposing two-storied farmhouse. Built of sturdy white clapboard with black shutters at the windows and a broad front porch running its width, the house was as imposing and cold as Johnson himself.

Dani pounded on the front door and waited impatiently for someone to answer.

Someone did, but not Caleb Johnson. Instead of being able to vent her wrath on Johnson as she had hoped, Dani was standing face to face with Chase McEnroe for the second time in two days.

At the sight of her, Chase's eyes narrowed and his jaw tightened. "If it isn't Calamity Jane," he drawled, moving out of the doorway as if to let her pass. "What can I do for you?"

"Nothing," she replied stiffly. A nervous sweat dampened her palms. It was one thing to come across this man when she had the advantage of being on her own property, astride a large gelding and holding a rifle. Standing toe to toe with him on Caleb Johnson's front porch was another matter entirely. Bracing her slim shoulders, she stated her business. "I'm looking for Caleb."

He lifted a skeptical eyebrow. "He's not here right now."

"Where is he?"

"In town."

"When will he be back?"

"I don't know." Chase offered her a humbling grin. "I'm just the help." His smile became hard. "You remember—the arrogant S.O.B. and flunky you caught on your land."

"I remember," she replied, returning his stare without flinching. Pride lifted her chin and kept her gaze cool. "I just hope you gave Johnson my message."

"Loud and clear."

"Then I guess we won't have a problem anymore, will we?"

"Not as long as you keep that rifle locked in a gun closet and throw away the key."

"I don't think so, Mr. McEnroe. Not until I'm sure you'll stay off my property." She saw the tightening of his jaw and decided to make herself crystal clear. "And that includes staying away from any water running through my land. I have water rights and I intend to protect them."

"With a shotgun."

"Rifle," she corrected, realizing he was baiting her. "And whatever else it takes to get the message through your boss's thick skull: My property is not for sale or lease. He can build a city the size of New York around my land and I won't change my mind."

Chase leaned against the doorjamb and crossed his arms over his chest. Some of the harshness left his features. "Tell me, Mrs. Summers," he suggested, noting that Dani bristled when he mentioned her marital status. "Are you always so tough?"

"Always," she lied. "Especially when I'm dealing with Caleb Johnson *or* his hands."

Chase's lips curved into an amused smile and his brilliant blue eyes softened to the point that Dani noticed how handsome his angular features could be. "I'll tell him you dropped by."

"And you'll let him know it wasn't a social call?"

"My guess is that you haven't dropped over here with an apple pie or for a leisurely chat in years," he mocked.

"Just give him the message."

"Are you expecting a response?"

"No." She placed her hands on her slim, jean-clad hips. "As long as you and the rest of Johnson's employees stay on this side of the fence, I'm satisfied. If not, I'll contact my attorney."

"And what's the attorney's name?"

Dani forced a smile though her stomach was churning. The man had just called her bluff. "Let's try and keep him out of it," she replied. "I don't think Caleb wants to get into a legal battle any more than I do."

"He claims you don't have an attorney; that you're bringing up this potential lawsuit as an empty threat."

"Try me," Dani said, hoping that she wasn't provoking McEnroe into following her suggestion. "I just hope it doesn't come to a costly legal battle. Neither Caleb nor I want the adverse publicity or the expense."

"I don't know," Chase thought aloud, walking to the post supporting the porch roof and leaning against the painted wood. "Caleb seems to have his mind set. He's already spent a fortune on architects, engineers, surveyors, lawyers and politicians. I don't think one more stumbling block is gonna deter him."

"We'll see," she said grimly, anger coloring her face.

"I'm afraid we will, lady," he agreed, seeing for the first time the trace of fear in her large gray-green eyes.

"Just tell him why I came by."

Dani turned on her heel and tried to ignore the dread stealing into her heart. So Johnson was going to play hardball. She walked down the brick path and ignored the urge to run. She could feel McEnroe's eyes on her back as she climbed into the pickup and shoved it into gear. As she cranked the wheel and turned the ancient rig around, she slid a glance through the window toward McEnroe. He was still where she'd left him, on the porch, leaning casually against the post and watching her intently. She could feel the burn of his eyes against her skin.

Oh, God, she thought desperately. *Johnson won't be satisfied until he takes it all.* Then, forcing her fatalistic thought aside, she muttered, "Pull yourself together, Dani. Dammit, Johnson can try to take your land, but if he does he'll find that he and McEnroe and anyone else who's involved with him will be in for the fight of their worthless lives!"

CHAPTER TWO

FOR THREE DAYS Dani watched Chase.

From her vantage point at the house, she had a view of the surrounding property from all angles. To the east toward the county road, there were only two small fields that were filled with livestock. Hereford cattle and a few horses mingled and grazed in the dry fields. To the west, behind the cabin, the larger acreage dipped down before slowly rising at the base of the mountains. Grizzly Creek, running south from Caleb Johnson's land, cut through the westerly side of her property in a clear blue ribbon and offered the only respite, save her hand-dug well, for the parched land.

Dani gave credit where credit was due, and Chase McEnroe was the most persistent man she'd ever met. Though he'd stuck to his part of the bargain and stayed on Caleb Johnson's property, he'd pushed the boundaries to the limit, often walking along beside the fence posts and surveying the water rushing through her land.

She observed him wading in the creek, sometimes with another man, but usually alone. Though she never really understood why, she watched him from a distance.

One day, while she had been bucking hay, Dani had seen Chase fly fishing in the stream. Later, after she and Cody had stacked the bales in the barn, she'd observed Chase digging in the streambed. Dani had never caught him on her side of the fence, although he strayed near the property line, staring over the barbed wire to her land and the life-giving water slicing through the dry fields.

"I wonder what Johnson's got up his sleeve," she muttered to herself as she hoed a row of potatoes in the small garden near the backyard. An uneasy sensation had been with her ever since she'd spoken with Chase at the Johnson farmhouse. There had been something in his eyes, something close to pity, that had made her back stiffen in pride and had caused a stab of dread to pierce her heart. "That man knows something," she decided, straightening and leaning on her hoe to ease the tight muscles of her lower back. "And if I were smart, I'd try to find out what it is."

It was nearly dusk and McEnroe was still near the creek, shading his eyes against a lowering sun as he studied the rippling water. It crossed Dani's mind that he might wait until it was dark and then trespass on her land. By why? And what would he find in the darkness?

"And who cares?" she said aloud, grabbing her hoe and walking angrily back to the house. Sweat was dripping down her dust-smudged face as she shoved the hoe into the shed near the back porch and went inside.

Cody was propped on the worn sofa in front of the television and Runt was parked on the floor in front of him. At her entrance, Runt lifted his black head and thumped his tail on the floor; Cody hadn't noticed that his mother had come into the house.

Dani looked around the room and frowned. The dinner dishes were still on the table and Runt's dish was empty. "Cody?"

He slid a glance in her direction but didn't move. "Yeah?"

"I thought you were going to clear the table."

"I will...I will."

Dani sat on the arm of the overstuffed couch and smiled at her son. "I was hoping it would be sometime this century."

"Aw, Mom," Cody grumbled, his face crumpling into a frown as he tried to concentrate on the television.

"I mean it."

"I said I'd do it, didn't I?"

Sighing, Dani leaned against the back of the couch. "Look, we had a deal. You feed Runt, do the afternoon chores and clear the table, right?"

"Right."

"I think it's only fair that you do them the minute they need to be done."

He looked at her blankly. "Why?"

"Because the cattle, horses and dog need to be fed on time. As for the dishes, I'd like to clean them up and put them away before midnight, okay?"

Cody, wearing his most put-upon expression, sighed loudly. "Things wouldn't be like this if Dad was home," the boy said, glancing out of the corner of his eyes for her reaction.

"You don't know that."

"You wouldn't have to work so hard and…and…neither would I!"

Dani tried to hold onto her patience. "Cody, you have to understand that things never would have worked out between your father and me even if he had stayed on the farm."

Cody remained silent, staring at the television. As Dani rose from the couch, he muttered, "You never gave him a chance." And then, seeing his mother stiffen, he said a little louder, "The kids at school say he ran off with another woman. Is that true?"

"Where did you hear that?" she asked. "School's been out for a couple of months."

"Is it true?"

Dani's shoulders slumped and she rubbed her temples. She was too tired to start this kind of conversation with Cody, but saw no way to avoid it. "I think so," she admitted.

"Why?" Cody turned his accusing brown eyes on her.

"I don't know."

"I heard the kids talkin' at school on the day that I got the letter from Dad."

"You took it to school?"

"Yeah." He chewed on his lower lip. "Maybe it wasn't such a good idea, huh?"

"What do you think?"

"Isabelle Reece told me that her pa says Dad left because you weren't woman enough to hold him."

Dani felt her throat tighten but managed a smile. "That's the way Isabelle's father *would* say it. I wouldn't put much stock in Bill Reece's opinion..." She took hold of Cody's hand and squeezed his fingers before letting go. "Things aren't always quite that simple."

"Dad hurt you, didn't he?" Cody deduced.

"A little."

"Do you still love him?"

Dani paused. It was a question she'd asked herself often in the past six and a half years. "No." She saw her son cringe. "Oh, I did love him. Once. A long time ago."

"But what happened?"

"A lot of things, I guess," she admitted. Dani felt the sting of tears behind her eyes but refused to give in to the urge to cry over Blake Summers. What they had shared was long over. "We got older, grew in different directions. Your dad wanted to sell the farm and move to Duluth."

"Minnesota?"

"Yep."

"Why didn't you?"

Dani hesitated. "It was hard for me to leave the farm."

"Why?"

She lifted a shoulder. "The same reason it would be hard to leave now. This place means a lot to me and I'm not talking about money. It's been in the family for so many years."

"So?"

"So I love it."

"More than you loved Dad."

Dani smiled sadly. "I don't like to think so. I know it's hard for you to understand but when your dad left me, my mother—your grandmother—was still alive. She lived here, with us. The farm was really hers, you know. I couldn't ask her to sell it. Her great-grandfather had homesteaded this piece."

"Big deal!"

"It was a big deal. Still is. Anyway, I told your dad I would move with him, but he claimed that he needed the extra cash from the sale of the property to get settled in Duluth.

"When he finally left, Grandma was sick and you were very young. It was the middle of winter and he said he'd send me some money in the spring so that I…we—you and I—could join him."

"But he never sent the money."

"Right."

"And he found another…woman?"

"I guess so," Dani said quietly, seeing no reason to bring up the fact that Blake's interest in other women had started long before he'd left Montana.

Cody sat still for a minute before turning large, hope-filled eyes toward his mother. "So maybe he's changed his mind and wants to come back. Maybe now he'll come home."

"He didn't say that in his letter, did he?"

"He kind'a did. Remember. He said, 'See ya soon. Love, Dad.'"

And it had been nearly three months since the damned letter had arrived.

"And he said that he'd write again," Cody added. "So maybe he is coming home. Maybe he's on his way back here right now! Wouldn't that be great!"

Hating to dampen Cody's spirits, she offered him a small smile. "I don't think he'll be back. At least not for a while."

"But when he gets here?" Cody asked hopefully.

"*If* he gets here," she said with a sad smile, "we'll just have to cross that bridge when we come to it, won't we?" She cocked her head in the direction of the kitchen. "Now, I'm going upstairs to shower. Why don't you tackle the dishes?" She slapped him fondly on the knee. "Deal?"

"Deal," he replied, rolling off the couch and nearly falling on top of Runt, who growled at having to move from his favorite position near the fireplace.

Dani climbed the stairs and heard the sound of plates rattling as Cody cleared the table. *He's a good boy,* she thought to herself. *You've just got to take the time to talk with him and quit avoiding the truth about his father.*

Forty-five minutes and a relaxing shower later Dani came down the stairs to find Cody back in front of the television, a huge bowl of popcorn in his lap. The table had been cleared and the dishes had been placed in the dishwasher. The mess from making the popcorn still littered the kitchen, but Dani decided not to mention it.

"You've been busy, haven't you?" she asked.

"Yeah. I decided you were right about the chores."

"Aren't I always?" she teased.

"Oh, Mom, give me a break!" But Cody laughed and offered Runt a piece of popped corn, which the anxious dog swallowed as if he had been starved for days.

One glance at the dog's bowl near the back door indicated to Dani that Runt had been fed recently. As she straightened the kitchen, cleaning the counters that Cody had missed, Dani called over her shoulder, "I think it's about time you went to bed, don't you?"

"It's still light out!"

Dani glanced out the window over the sink. The only illumination over the land was from the silvery half moon. "It's not light and it's nearly ten," she pointed out as she finished wiping the counters.

"Just a little longer," the boy begged.

"All right. When the show's over, then you can read in bed for a while, but I think you'd better hit the hay soon, my friend. Big day tomorrow."

"Doing what?"

"Guess."

Cody groaned. "Hauling hay again."

"You got it."

"So why are you all dressed up? Is someone coming over?" the boy asked with a frown as he stared at his mother.

"Hardly. It's too late for company." Dani laughed and shook her head. The damp strands of her long hair brushed the back of her blouse. "And, for your information, I'm not dressed up. You're just used to seeing me in my work clothes."

Cody eyed her clean jeans and crisp cotton blouse. "So why didn't you put on your pajamas?"

"Too hot and I thought I'd drink some lemonade on

the back porch." She turned to face her son, an affectionate grin spreading across her tanned face when she recognized the concern in his eyes. "Hey, just because I changed from dirty work clothes doesn't mean you have to give me the third degree. But thanks for the compliment."

A few minutes later, Runt pricked up his black ears and growled just as the sound of an approaching engine caught Dani's attention.

"Hey, Mom. I think somebody's here," Cody said, looking over his shoulder and silently accusing her of lying. "You said you weren't expecting anyone!"

"I wasn't…I mean, I'm not." Dani was drying her hands on a dishtowel just as there was a knock on the door. She glanced through the window and recognized Chase McEnroe, who was standing on the porch. *Now what,* she wondered, inwardly bracing herself for another confrontation with Caleb Johnson's most recent acquisition.

Opening the door, she pursed her lips and stared into his eyes. "Obviously you don't know how to take a hint, Mr. McEnroe."

"I was in the neighborhood," he commented dryly.

"Hey, Mom. Who is it?" Cody asked, dragging himself off the couch and sauntering to the door.

"This is Mr. McEnroe—"

"Chase," he corrected, smiling at the boy and offering his hand.

"And this is my son, Cody," Dani said, introducing the boy as Cody took Chase's hand and looked at the man suspiciously.

"Chase works for Caleb Johnson," Dani continued, and Cody immediately withdrew his hand. "I think maybe you should go upstairs to bed," Dani said. "Obviously Mr. McEnroe has business to discuss with me."

"You sure?" Cody asked.

"Positive." Dani's eyes left her son's to stare into Chase's enigmatic blue gaze.

"Okay." Cody went to the bottom of the stairs, looked over his shoulder, whistled to Runt, and then ran up the stairs, the black dog following eagerly. A few seconds later Dani heard the door to Cody's room close.

Crossing her arms under her breasts, she leaned a hip against an antique sideboard near the door. "What do you want?"

"To talk with you."

"So talk."

"This may take a while."

Sighing, Dani gestured toward the living room. "Okay. Come in."

Chase sauntered into the room, eyeing the contents of the cabin. Rustic pieces of furniture, well worn but comfortable, were placed between family antiques and heirlooms. A hand-knit afghan was draped over the back of the couch and pieces of embroidery and appliqué adorned the wooden walls. It was small, but homey and comfortable. *The house fits her,* Chase thought as he took a seat on the hearth of the stone fireplace and leaned forward, hands over his knees, *just as Caleb's meticulous but cold farmhouse fits him.*

Deciding that beating around the bush wouldn't accomplish anything, Dani walked into the living room, snapped off the TV, sat on the arm of the couch and faced him. "So, what do you want? Why are you here?"

Chase smiled. A brilliant, white-toothed grin slashed his tanned face and made his blue eyes sparkle. "You can drop the tough lady act with me."

"It's not an act."

"That's not what Caleb says."

Dani's lips tightened and a challenge flashed in her

eyes. "Caleb doesn't know me very well. Otherwise he wouldn't keep trying to force me into selling my place to him."

"By offering you a reasonable price for it?"

Dani wasn't about to confide in one of Johnson's men; whether he was interesting or not. "Reasonable?" she repeated, rolling her eyes. "Look, Mr. McEnroe, obviously you came here for a reason, so why don't you get to the point and tell me what it is?"

"All business, right?"

"Right. Shoot," she encouraged and Chase laughed out loud. It was a deep rumbling sound that bounced off the rafters and dared to touch a secret part of Dani's heart.

"Bad choice of words," he said.

"Okay." She smiled in spite of herself. "So why are you here?"

"I want answers."

"From me?"

"To start with." He stood up and stretched before reaching upward to the rifle mounted over the mantel.

Dani bristled. "What do you think you're doing?" she demanded, leaping up and stepping forward.

He ignored her outcry and opened the chamber of the weapon. It was empty. "Just checking," he said, almost to himself.

"On what?"

"To see which one of you is lying. You or Caleb Johnson." He replaced the Winchester and looked over his shoulder at her. "So far the score is zero/zero for the truth."

"I think you'd better leave," she said, angry with herself for allowing him to enter her house in the first place.

"Not yet."

"If you don't—"

"Yeah. I know, I know." He walked around the room, staring at the woven baskets, brass pots, worn furniture and scratched wooden floor. "If I don't leave, you'll call the sheriff or that fictitious attorney of yours."

Shaking with anger, Dani stifled an urge to scream at him, and planted her hands firmly on her hips. "Just what is it you want, Mr. McEnroe?"

"How many times do I have to tell you to call me Chase?"

"And how many times do I have to tell you to get off my property?"

"I'll go, I'll go," he agreed amiably, though his jaw was hard. "I just want some answers."

Her temper snapped. "Well, so do I! Just who are you and why are you here?"

"I told you who I was, the other day, when you so graciously pointed the barrel of your rifle at me. As to what I do, I own a small business, the headquarters of which are located in Boise," he said, focusing his sky-blue eyes on her. "I rehabilitate streams, like Grizzly Creek, to make them viable for trout."

"Come again?"

He smiled slightly. "A lot of streams and rivers have become too dirty for the fish to spawn."

Dani shook her head and held up her palm to quiet him. "I don't believe you."

"Why would I make it up?"

"Heaven only knows. Probably because Caleb Johnson asked you to."

Pushing his hands into the pockets of his jeans, he leaned against the fireplace, his broad shoulders resting on the mantel. "Contrary to your opinion, I don't do everything Johnson asks me to."

"Then you'll be fired soon," she said flatly.

"I don't think so. Caleb Johnson and I are partners."

"Partners!" Dani repeated, the word strangling her throat. *Good Lord, that was worse!* "In what?"

"A few years ago, I needed capital. For my business." He looked at the pictures on the mantel and fingered one of Dani and Cody sitting astride the buckskin. In the snapshot Dani was laughing, her arms securely around a grinning four-year-old Cody. Chase stared at the picture a long time, taking it from its resting place on the mantel.

"You were saying," she prodded, feeling his presence filling the small cabin. Just the fact that he was in her home made her uneasy; more aware of him as a man, and less threatened. She had to remind herself that he was the enemy.

He returned the photograph to its spot. "I was telling you that just when my business needed funds for advertising and expansion, Caleb Johnson walked into my life."

"Convenient," she said dryly.

He frowned at the distasteful memory, remembering the unlikely events and odd set of circumstances that led Caleb Johnson to his door. "Maybe too convenient," he agreed, bothered again by Caleb's association with his mother. Stepping away from the fireplace, Chase looked out the back window, toward Grizzly Creek. "Anyway, Caleb offered me two hundred thousand dollars to become partners with me, and I took his money because I thought Relive needed a shot in the arm."

"Relive?"

"My company."

"Oh. And so Johnson provided it."

"Right."

"Money." Dani sank onto the couch. "Of course. That's all a man like Johnson can understand." She looked at Chase thoughtfully.

Chase was mesmerized by her stare. Her gray-green eyes seemed to look past the surface and search for the inner man.

"Let me guess," Dani said. "There's a catch to this 'partnership.'"

His dark brows rose appreciatively. "A small one. Johnson has agreed to sell a quarter of the company back to me if I can rehabilitate Grizzly Creek. But I can't do that without your cooperation."

Here it comes, she thought. "What kind of cooperation?"

"If you won't sell or lease your land to Caleb—"

"I won't. You know that."

"Why not?"

Because Caleb wants it all and this farm is all I have; this land and my son. "Johnson's a snake. I don't like him and I don't trust him."

"What's the difference? His money is green."

Her eyes flashed. "Money isn't the issue."

"What is?"

"My right to live here, on this land, without *having* to sell. It's not that I'm really against the resort; I'm just against the resort on *my* land."

"Isn't that a little proprietary?"

"Damn right. The way I look at it, I am the proprietor. And maybe I would have changed my mind if Johnson would have played by the rules."

"He didn't?"

"What do you think?"

"I don't know."

Dani's muscles ached with tension. "Believe me, he's tried everything he could to get rid of me and it sticks in my throat."

"So you try to thwart him."

"I see it as exercising my rights," she pointed out, her voice rising.

Chase thought for a moment. He really didn't blame Dani. Didn't he have some of the same reservations about Caleb himself? Some of the things Caleb had told him just didn't quite seem to hold water. He tried a new tack. "Then I want your permission to work in the water on your land."

"Forget it." She shook her head, and the glow from the dim lights in the room caught in her hair. "I told you: I don't trust that man and I don't trust you."

"So what has Caleb Johnson done to make you so suspicious?"

Dani laughed bitterly and looked at her hands. "Everything short of planting explosives in my house," she said, and then, realizing that Chase might have come for the express purpose of prying information from her to take to his "partner," she became quiet.

She heard him approach, but didn't expect the touch of his fingers to warm her shoulder. Surprised, she raised her head, her startled gaze meeting his.

"You can trust me," he said, his voice deep and slightly husky. "I'll be straight with you."

Dani stared at the sincerity of his features, the honest lines of his rugged face, the depths of his deep blue eyes. If there were any one she could trust, she felt that Chase McEnroe might just be the man.

He started to bend over her, and for a moment Dani had the absurd impression that he might kiss her, but he drew away and she shook her head at her own stupidity. If men like Blake and Caleb Johnson had taught her anything, it was never to trust a man who had an ulterior motive.

"I think you'd better go," she whispered, shifting so

that his fingers no longer touched her. "And don't come back."

"You think I'm your enemy."

"You are."

"Me and the rest of the world?" he asked. "Or just men in general?"

Stung and seething, Dani stood and faced him. "You, Caleb Johnson and anyone else, man or woman, who tries to steal my land from me."

"Steal?" His eyes narrowed thoughtfully. "Caleb Johnson tried to *rob* you of this land?" He seemed genuinely surprised and more than a little dubious.

Dani's lips twisted at the irony of it all. "Go ask Johnson about it," she said. *As if you don't know already.* For all Dani knew about him, Chase could be a consummate actor playing a well-rehearsed role or a simple con man lying through his beautiful Colgate-white teeth.

"I will," he promised, heading for the door.

"Good!"

When he got to the door, he hesitated, and his broad shoulders slumped as he turned around. "Dani?"

She didn't answer, but inclined her head.

"For what it's worth. Whatever this…problem is between you and Johnson, I'm not part of it. I told Johnson as much."

"But you *are* his partner."

Chase ground his back teeth together. "That's right," he admitted.

"And you did come here to get me to either sell, lease, rent or let you use my land."

He looked at her silently and the tension in the air seemed to crackle with the fire in her eyes.

"Then you have to understand, Mr. McEnroe, you can

stand in front of that door until hell freezes over and I won't believe a word you say."

A muscle worked in the corner of his jaw and his blue eyes blazed angrily. "Okay, lady, have it your way. I just thought I could help you. Sorry if I wasted your time!"

Chase strode angrily out of the room, letting the door slam shut behind him. The hot night air did little to cool his seething temper as he strode to his Jeep, climbed inside and roared down the long lane leading back to the country road and eventually to Caleb Johnson's property.

Just a couple of months, he thought with an inward groan, *and then I'll be out of it. I'll be able to leave Dani Summers, her suspicious kid, and Caleb Johnson. Then they can all go for each other's throats, for all I care!*

He slowed as the Jeep reached the main road. When the vehicle had come to a complete stop, Chase cranked the wheel of the Jeep hard to the right. Right now he couldn't face Caleb Johnson's smug face or the smell of the old man's money. Seeing the way Dani Summers lived soured Chase's stomach.

In the distance, the lights of Martinville brightened the night sky. The town wasn't much more than a grocery store, post office, gas station and a couple of churches, but it did have a bar. Chase decided that the smoky atmosphere of Yukon Jack's had to be more comforting than the cold interior of Caleb Johnson's house. Anything did.

Unreasonably he thought about Dani again, and he experienced a tightening in his gut. She was beautiful, no doubt about it. With wavy sun-streaked hair that fell almost to her waist, high, flushed cheekbones and wide sensual lips, she was the most attractive woman he'd met in a long while.

The fact that her eyes could look right through him only added to her appeal and innate sexuality. She was trim and lean, probably strong and obviously intelligent; attributes Chase didn't normally look for in a woman. However, he sensed that Dani was different than the women he'd seen over the past few years and it worried him. It worried him a lot.

"Don't forget the chip she's got on her shoulder," he warned himself, trying to discourage his fantasies of the spitfire of a woman. "And the rifle—loaded or unloaded. A dangerous lady any way you cut it."

So why then did he think about the photograph on the mantel? A snapshot of a laughing woman and happy child astride a rangy horse in the bright Montana sun. The image lingered in his mind even as he parked the truck, stepped across the concrete sidewalk and strode into the noisy, smoke-filled interior of Yukon Jack's.

CHAPTER THREE

"THAT'S THE LAST of it," Dani said, wiping the sweat from her eyes.

"Thank God," Jake responded with a groan. The lanky boy was one of the two brothers Dani had hired to help her haul the baled hay into her barn.

It was late in the season for cutting hay, but with the unexpected breakdown of her equipment earlier in the summer, she'd been forced to rent a baler from a neighboring rancher after he'd finished with his own fields. Though she couldn't prove it, she suspected that her machinery had been tampered with—by someone from Caleb Johnson's place—just as she suspected other problems at the farm had been instigated by Johnson or one of his hands. The stolen gasoline, sick cattle and broken hay baler were just a few of the worries she'd faced in the past year. Maybe they were coincidence. But the fact that the problems had increased since she'd refused to sell all of her farm to Johnson made her uneasy. Very uneasy.

She slid an angry glance toward the neighboring acres and frowned. "You're imagining things," she muttered as she put the tractor into gear. "Just because you couldn't get a part to fix the old baler." With a roar the tractor started moving again.

Cody, Jake and Jonathon climbed onto the top of the bales stacked carefully on the trailer as Dani drove slowly toward the barn through the straw stubble in the field.

It was nearly twilight, but she had opted to work late

rather than face another day painstakingly driving the tractor through the fields and lifting hundred-pound bales of dry hay onto the flatbed trailer. Dani hadn't wanted to gamble that her cut hay might get ruined in the rain. She looked at the purple sky and noticed the clouds silently gathering overhead. If the weather forecast were to be believed, there was a good chance of thundershowers later.

The old tractor chugged up the slight incline to the barn and Dani carefully backed the trailer into the open door. The boys, though tired and dusty, put on their gloves and began placing the bales on the elevator and stacking them in the loft.

Dani cut the engine of the tractor and hopped to the ground. Climbing into the hayloft, she began to help Cody and Jake stack the bales while Jonathon loaded the elevator. The interior of the weathered barn was dark and musty, but the scent of freshly mown hay mingled with the dust.

"That about does it," Dani said with a tired grin as Jake shouldered the last bale into place. After climbing down the ladder, she tossed her gloves onto an old barrel and pushed the hair from her face. "Now, who wants a Coke?"

"Make mine a double," Jake teased, offering Dani a cocky sixteen-year-old grin as he jumped down from the loft.

"Mine, too," his younger brother agreed.

"Cody?"

"Yep," her son said with a smile.

"You got it," she laughed. "And Cody, you're off duty tonight; I'll do the chores and clear the table. You've worked hard enough for one day."

Cody beamed, scratched Runt behind the ears and walked with the other boys to the back porch. Dani went inside the house, pulled the Cokes out of the refrigerator

and opened the chilled bottles before returning to the back
porch and passing them around. Jake held the cold bottle
to his hot forehead before tossing back his sweaty head,
placing the bottle to his lips and swallowing the contents
of the bottle in one long drink.

"I get the message," Dani said, returning to the house
and grabbing three more Cokes. She took them to the
back porch and was relieved that the boys' thirst had apparently slackened. Cody, Jake and Jonathon were content to sip from their bottles.

"I'm gonna get the mail," Cody said, while the two
older boys sat on the rail finishing their drinks.

Dani felt her heart twist in pain. Cody never gave up
thinking that his dad would write him again. "All right."

Cody whistled to Runt and ran around the corner of the
house. Dani's shoulders slumped in defeat and she took
a long swallow of the cold cola. Every day this summer
Cody had run to the mailbox expecting a letter from his
father and it had never come. Dani didn't think this day
would be any different. Nor would the days that followed.
If only Blake hadn't written the one friendly letter and
buoyed Cody's spirits.

If I ever get my hands on him, I'll strangle him, she
thought angrily, her fingers tightening around her bottle.

While the two brothers talked, Dani leaned against a
post supporting the roof of the porch and stared across
the fence to Caleb Johnson's property and Grizzly Creek.
Things had changed in the past week.

The day after Chase had come to her house, heavy
equipment had rolled over Johnson's land. Not only had
there been dredging in the creek, but several loads of
gravel had been carefully spread in the water, and a few
fallen fir trees had been strategically placed along the
banks of the stream.

While Dani had been bucking hay, she'd observed Chase, stripped to his jeans, as he supervised the operation. He was always at the creek at sunrise, carefully studying and working in the clear water. He supervised the placement of the gravel and boulders as well as the digging of deeper pools in the channel of the stream.

She couldn't help but notice the rippling strength of his muscles as he'd helped pull a log into position, or the way his shoulders would bunch when things weren't going just as he'd planned. The bright sun had begun to bleach his blond hair and his skin had darkened with each day. From her position driving the tractor, Dani had been able to observe him covertly and she'd begun to recognize his gestures; the way he would rake his fingers through his hair in disgust, his habit of chewing on his thumbnail when he was tense or the manner in which he would set his palms on his hips when he was angry.

Several times she'd found him looking her way, and each time that he'd caught her eye, he'd offered a lazy, mocking grin. One time he'd even had the nerve to wave to her, and Dani, her cheeks burning unexpectedly, had responded by quickly stepping on the throttle of the tractor and turning her full attention to the task of getting the hay into the barn.

"What's goin' on over there?" Jake asked when he noticed Dani staring at the heavy machinery on the adjoining property.

"I think Johnson's hired someone to clean up the creek—make it more livable for trout." Actually she knew it for a fact. Just to make sure that Chase had been straight with her, she'd called the Better Business Bureau in Boise and found out that Relive Incorporated was, indeed, a business owned by Chase McEnroe and Caleb Johnson.

"So he's cleaning up Grizzly Creek for that resort, Summer Ridge or whatever it's called, right?"

"Right." Dani's back stiffened slightly.

"Is it named after you?"

Dani smiled at the irony of the question and shook her head. "No. I'm really a Hawthorne," she explained. "This land is Hawthorne land and the piece next to it, the land where the equipment is parked, used to belong to the Summers family."

"But not you?"

"No…it was owned by my husband's family," she said, feeling rankled again when she thought about Blake and how he had sold his family's homestead only to gamble away the money.

"My pa can't wait for the resort," Jake said. "He says it will put Martinville on the map."

"No doubt about it," Dani replied with a frown.

"Pa says that his business is bound to double over the next year or two, with all the workers Johnson will have to hire. And then, once the resort is open, Pa expects to make a bundle!"

"Nobody's *ever* made a bundle selling groceries," Jake's younger brother, Jonathon, commented with all the knowledge of a fifteen-year-old.

"Just you wait!"

"Mom! Hey, Mom!" Cody screamed at the top of his lungs as he raced around the corner of the house. His boyish face was flushed with excitement and he was nearly out of breath.

Dani's heart constricted.

"He wrote again! Look! There's a letter from Dad!" Cody was jumping up and down with his exhilaration and Runt was barking wildly at the boy's heels.

Dani nearly fell through the weathered boards of the

porch. *Damn you, Blake!* She managed to force a tender smile for her son. "What did he say?"

"That he's comin' home!" Cody looked from one of the Anders brothers to the other. "You hear that, *my* pa is comin' home!"

"Home? Here?" Dani asked.

"Yep! To see us and Uncle Bob!" Cody was holding the letter triumphantly and Dani guessed from the way that Cody was acting that Jake and Jonathon were two of the kids who had given him trouble about his absentee father. The brothers had the decency to look sheepish and Dani had to bite her tongue in order to refrain from giving the boys a lecture on the cruelty of gossip. At nine years of age, Cody would have to fight most of his own battles. And this time, at least for the moment, he'd won.

"I think we'd better be goin'," Jake said, handing Dani his empty bottle.

"Just a minute and I'll pay you." She took the bottles, placed them in the case by the back door and went into the house to the old desk in a corner of the kitchen. Once there she withdrew the checkbook from the top drawer, sighed when she saw the balance, and paid the Anders brothers their wages.

"Here you go," she said, giving each boy a check when she returned to the porch. "And thanks a lot."

"You're welcome, and you'll give us a call if you have any more work to do?" Jake asked.

"Sure thing," Dani said.

Jake sighed in relief. "Hey, Cody, good news about your dad," the cocky sixteen-year-old said.

"Yeah," Jonathon added, following his brother around the corner of the house. A few seconds later the rumbling sound of Jake's pickup could be heard as they drove off.

"I told you he'd come back!" Cody said, his brown eyes bright with pleasure.

"You sure did," Dani replied, feeling the corners of her mouth pinch. "Why don't you let me read what he said?"

"Sure." Cody handed the letter to her, and Dani skimmed the hastily scrawled note. It was less than a page but there was the promise that Blake would return to Martinville "sometime this fall." She looked at the postmark. It read Molalla, Oregon; a town Dani had never heard of.

The letter was vague enough not to pin Blake down but with enough promise to keep Cody's hopes up. Dani felt all the rage of seven long years sear through her heart.

"When do you think he'll get here?" Cody asked.

"I don't know," Dani replied honestly.

"Before school starts?"

"I...I wouldn't count on it...."

Cody flinched. "Yeah, I know *you* wouldn't. But *I* do! Dad says he's comin' home and he is!" He started to walk into the kitchen but stopped, a sudden uncomfortable thought crossing his mind. "When Dad gets here, he will stay with us, won't he?"

"No, Cody," Dani said, taking a firm stand.

"Why not?"

"Because your father and I aren't married. He can't stay here. It wouldn't be right."

"But he's my dad and he lived here before!"

"I know, but Blake will probably want to be in town with his brother, Bob. He won't want to stay here."

"You don't know that! He's coming back for me and *you*! So you'd better let him stay here because if he has to live with Uncle Bob, then I'm going to live with him!" Cody said, taking the letter from her hand and marching through the door.

Why now? Dani wondered, fighting the tears behind

her eyes. *Why did Blake have to come back—or promise to—right now, when Cody was the most trouble he'd ever been and Caleb Johnson was hell-bent to take her land from her?*

"Don't borrow trouble," she whispered staunchly to herself. Blake hadn't returned in seven years; there was little chance he'd show up at all. *Either way, Cody would be brokenhearted all over again.*

"Just stay in Oregon, Blake," she muttered, looking past the equipment on the Johnson property. It was nearly dark and the field was empty of the workers that had been there during the day. Even Chase seemed to have disappeared. *Probably plotting with his partner,* she thought bitterly, but couldn't really make herself believe that Chase was quite that treacherous. "And neither is a rattlesnake," she muttered as she looked at the troublesome sky.

Thunderclouds, heavy with the promise of rain, roiled over the peaks of the Rockies to darken the evening sky.

A cool summer shower. That was what she needed, Dani thought sadly. The summer had been unbearably hot this year and all of the tension with Cody as well as Caleb Johnson and Chase McEnroe was getting to her. The thought of rain pelting against the windowpanes and settling the dust was comforting. Maybe the rain would wash away some of the strain…but not if Blake were really coming back.

With a sigh Dani walked into the house and deduced from the muted sound of rock hits coming from a radio that Cody was in his room. She wanted to go to her son, try to reason with him about his father, but decided it would be better to wait until they had both cooled off.

Wearily climbing the stairs, she stopped suddenly as the thought struck her that Blake might be returning to

Martinville with the express purpose of taking Cody away from her. "Not in a million years!" she thought aloud, her fingers clenching the banister. As quickly as the horrible thought came, it disappeared. Blake hadn't wanted Cody in the first place; he'd even gone so far as to suggest that Dani have an abortion in the early months of her pregnancy. So why would he want a nine-year-old boy now?

Refusing to be trapped in the bitter memories of her stormy marriage to Blake, Dani stripped out of her dirty, sweat-soaked clothes, brushed the dust from her hair and twisted it to the top of her head before settling gratefully into a hot bath.

The warm water eased the tension from her stiff muscles and lulled her into a sense of security. If Blake had the audacity to try and claim Cody now, he'd have the surprise of his life. Long ago Dani had shed her mousy personality in favor of that of a new independent woman. No one, not even Blake Summers, would take her son away from her; just as she wouldn't allow anyone to steal her land. And whether Chase McEnroe knew it or not, that's exactly what Caleb Johnson had tried to do over the past few years. He'd offered to buy her out far below the market value and then he'd tried to say that *she'd* swindled him on the sale of the Summers' place. Yep, Caleb Johnson was as crooked as a dog's hind leg, and he wanted her land; the land her grandparents had worked to save in the Depression, the land her ancestors had cleared and farmed with the strength of their backs and the sweat of their brow.

And maybe you're being a fool, she thought as she squeezed the rag over her shoulders and let the hot water drip down her back. *Maybe you should just sell the place and live comfortably for the rest of your life.*

"Never," she whispered to herself. "At least not to Johnson."

She smiled to herself with renewed determination and settled lower in the tub.

CHASE STARED AT the lights in the cabin windows long after he'd seen Dani go inside. The first heavy drops of rain had begun to fall and he was still deciding whether or not to confront her again. It had been nearly a week since she'd thrown him out of her home. For six days he'd respected her wishes and kept away from her, but watching her work in the fields, her lithe body handling machinery and heavy bales of hay that would have strained the muscles of a man twice her size, gave him second thoughts.

"You're a fool," he chastised, but ignored his own warning and slipped through the barbed wires before climbing the short hill toward the cluster of buildings on the small rise.

The rain had begun in earnest. Large drops slid down his face as thunder rumbled in the mountains. He picked up his pace and ran the last hundred yards to the shelter of the barn before shaking the water from his hair and striding to the back porch.

Dani was already there, sitting in an old rocker near the door and wearing only her bathrobe.

"Dani?" Chase called, hoping not to startle her.

She nearly jumped out of her skin at the sight of him. "What're you doing here?" she asked, recognizing his voice before being able to discern his craggy features.

"Escaping the storm."

Leaning back in the rocker, she narrowed her eyes as she studied him. "So why didn't you escape to Caleb Johnson's house?"

"Too far away." He walked up the two steps to the

porch and rested one hip against the rail as he looked at her. "Besides, I wanted to talk to you again."

"I thought we settled everything last time."

"Not really." He leaned against the post supporting the roof of the porch, folded his arms over his chest and stared down at her with shaded eyes. The rain had turned his blond hair brown and dampened the shoulders and back of his shirt. "I've been doing a lot of thinking lately. The last time I was here you insinuated that Caleb tried to steal your land."

"It wasn't an insinuation."

"Fact?"

Dani hedged. "Not exactly…"

"Then what happened?"

A simple question. And one of public record. Then why did she hesitate to tell him? "Why don't you ask Johnson?"

"He put me off, just like you. Right now he's out of town."

"For how long?"

"A few more days."

Dani's teeth clamped together. She still hadn't had it out with Caleb.

"Look, I'd just like to know what's going on between the two of you because, whether I like it or not, I've been put right smack dab in the middle of your…disagreement."

"Disagreement?" she repeated, smiling at the understatement.

"For lack of a better word."

Drumming her fingers on the edge of the rocker, she looked across the sloping land and listened to the heavy raindrops pound against the roof and run in the gutters. "It's no secret really," she said, turning to face him again. "About two years ago, Caleb Johnson tried to take me to court. He insisted that the land my great-great-grandfather had homesteaded—this place—wasn't staked out properly, and according to his survey, I was actually living on what is now his property."

"That should have been easy enough to prove."

"You'd have thought so," she whispered.

"So?"

"Well, Johnson's land is more than just his. Part of it used to belong to my ex-husband, Blake. He sold it to Caleb Johnson years ago, when we were first married. My property, which is known as the Hawthorne place, bordered Blake's family's acreage. Once Blake sold out to Johnson, Caleb became my neighbor."

"And the Summers' place doesn't exist any longer."

"Right. It's all part of Johnson's spread, although he made one minor concession to Blake's family and decided to name his resort Summer Ridge."

"What does that have to do with property lines?"

"Johnson claimed that when Blake sold him the land, he'd meant to include the strip of my property on the ridge of the mountains." She pointed westerly, toward the Rockies. "I don't farm the entire acreage; part of the land rises into the foothills."

"And has hot springs on it."

Surprised, she stiffened in the chair. "That's why Johnson wants the land so badly, I suppose."

Chase shifted and rubbed his hand around the back of his neck. "I suppose. So what happened?"

"Nothing."

"Nothing?"

"The judge threw the case out of court. It cost me several thousand dollars in legal fees, but the land is mine."

"How did Caleb take the news?"

"Not particularly well. It's common knowledge that he owns several of the judges in this part of the state. I'm willing to bet that some have even invested in Summer Ridge. Fortunately I ended up with a judge who didn't happen to be in Johnson's back pocket."

"What do you mean?"

"Just that Johnson has powerful friends." Her small jaw was thrust forward and her eyes were guarded. "And I don't trust any of them, including you."

"I didn't say I was his friend."

"Partner. That's good enough." Standing, she cinched the belt of her robe more tightly around her waist. "Though Caleb Johnson didn't end up with my land, he still put a noose around my neck. I had to go into debt to pay off my lawyer and mortgage this land. I got behind on my taxes and it took me two years to get back to even again." Her blood boiled at the injustice of it all and her voice trembled slightly. "I offered to sell him part of the farm once. It wasn't enough for him. He tried to wheel and deal and swindle me on that piece as well as the rest of the farm! So I'm through dealing with him. As far as I'm concerned, I wouldn't give him the satisfaction of buying one square inch of this property!"

"No matter what?"

"No matter what! So, if you're entertaining any ideas of persuading me to sell, you'd better forget them."

"That's not why I'm here."

She lifted a delicate dark brow and cocked her head to the side. "What then?"

He shrugged. "I don't know. I guess I just wanted to see you again."

Brace yourself, Dani, don't fall for his line. You don't know a thing about this McEnroe character, she told herself. She took a step backward, toward the door. "Why?"

"I only wish I knew," he said, shaking his head. "You're a very beautiful woman. Intriguing."

"A challenge, Mr. McEnroe?"

A crooked smile slid over his face. "Maybe—"

"Then forget it. I don't like dealing with anyone associated with Caleb Johnson. I don't know why you got roped into being his business partner…oh, yeah, it was something about giving your business a shot in the arm financially, wasn't it? Well that doesn't wash with me. There are lots of ways to raise capital. You don't have to go crawling to the likes of Johnson!"

"He came to me."

"Why?"

"A good question," Chase remarked thoughtfully. How many times had he asked himself why Caleb had traveled all the way to Boise? It just didn't make a whole lot of sense. And the answers Caleb had given him were vague, as if he were hiding something from Chase. The situation made Chase uneasy and restless.

"You were right about one thing," Chase said, straightening from the rail and advancing upon her.

Dani stood her ground. "Just one?"

"Everything has a price," he whispered. "And believe me, I'm paying for my partnership."

As Chase slowly walked the few steps separating them, Dani felt her pulse begin to race. "I feel sorry for anyone who gets involved with Johnson," she said.

"I don't want your pity." Chase stood inches from her and Dani was wedged between the screen door and the wall of Chase's body. He sent her a sizzling look that seared through all facades to cut into the woman within.

"Then what is it that you want?" she asked, wincing at the breathless quality in her voice.

He placed one hand against the wood frame of the door near her head. "I just want to get to know you better," he whispered, his head lowering and his lips brushing across hers.

Dani's heart began to hammer in her chest. The feel of his warm lips against hers was enticing. Little sparks of excitement tingled beneath her skin. *This is madness,* her conscience screamed as the kiss deepened, but she didn't draw away from him.

He placed his free hand on the other side of her head, trapping her, but he didn't touch her except for the fragile link of his lips against hers. She smelled the rain in his hair, tasted the hint of salt on his lips....

Dani should have felt trapped and she knew it, but she didn't. Instead she felt the wondrous joy of being wanted and desired—more a woman than she'd felt in years.

"I—I think you should go," she said, clearing her throat when he finally lifted his head to gaze into her eyes.

"Why?"

"It's late."

"Not that late."

"Chase—" Her voice caught on his name. "Look, I think it would be better if we weren't involved."

"Too late."

The man was maddening! "I...look, I just can't. I don't have time—"

"Sure you do." His lips captured hers again and this time he wrapped the strength of his arms around her body. She felt small and weak and helpless, emotions she usually loathed but now loved.

"Chase— Please—" she whispered, but her words sounded more like a plea than a denial.

His tongue slid easily through her parted lips and her hands, pressed against his chest, were little resistance to his strength. She felt the corded power of bunched muscles beneath his wet shirt and the exhilaration of his tongue tasting hers.

Moaning as his hands pulled her closer still, she didn't realize that her robe had gaped open and that the swell of her breasts and the pulse at her throat were visible in the darkness. She was conscious only of the strong fingers holding her tight, the muscular thighs pressed against hers and the pounding of her heart as it pumped blood furiously through her veins.

When he lifted her head to gaze at her, his gaze had become slumberous, smoldering with a passion so violent he could barely keep his head.

Dani felt the rapid rise and fall of her breasts in tempo with her labored breathing.

Gently he kissed her cheeks and her neck before his mouth settled on the ripe swell of her breast. Dani gasped. His lips and tongue felt hot and wanton.

"Dani," he choked out, his voice rough, his breath warm against the cleft between her breasts.

She tried to think, tried to push him away, but couldn't find the strength or desire to let him go. Crazy as it was, she wanted to be with him, to get to know him, to lie with him. He was like no man she had ever met and he sparked something in her that she had thought was long dead.

"Oh, God," he whispered when he gently tugged on her robe, baring her breast. The dark tip pointed proudly into the night.

"Please, don't," she whispered, summoning all of her strength and pulling on her robe.

All of his muscles slackened and he leaned against her. "I can't apologize for what's happening, Dani," he said, his breath ruffling her hair. "I've tried to fight my attraction to you and I've failed." He sighed loudly before staring into her eyes and softly tracing her jaw with a long, rough finger. "I didn't want any of this to happen, y'know."

Swallowing, she placed her arms over her chest and stepped away from him. "Neither did I."

"But it's there."

"Not if we don't let it be," she said, her head clearing a little. "Look, I really can't get involved with anyone now. Especially not you."

"Why not?"

"You're Caleb Johnson's partner, for God's sake!"

"So you can't trust me?"

"Would you?" she demanded, her eyes bright.

Tortured by the bewitching gleam in Dani's gaze, the thick strands of her vibrant hair, the proud lift of her chin, Chase had to look away. "Maybe not."

"Then we understand each other."

"Not quite." He turned to face her again and this time frustration contorted the shadowed contours of his rugged face. He balled a fist and slowly uncurled it, as if in so doing he could release the sizzling tension that twisted his insides and made him burn with lust. "What I don't understand is why I can't keep away from you, why I can't quit thinking about you, why I lie awake in bed with thoughts of you. I don't want any of this, lady, and God knows I didn't ask for it, but it's there. I can't get you out of my mind and, unless I miss my guess, you feel the same way about me."

He reached for her and when she tried to pull away, he jerked her roughly to him. "You can't deny that you want me just as much as I want you."

"I don't want you!"

"Liar!"

"Chase, don't!" Dani felt like slapping him but when his lips came crashing back to hers, she kissed him hungrily and the fire in her blood raged wildly in her veins. An ache, deep and primal, awakened within her body and her fingers caught in the rain-dampened strands of his hair.

"Don't what?" he rasped, once his plundering kiss was over.

"Don't make me fall for you," she whispered, surprised at her own honesty.

He let out a sigh and tried to control his ragged breathing, his thudding heart. He noticed the worry in her eyes and attempted a smile that failed miserably. "All right," he finally agreed, wiping an unsteady hand over his brow. "I'll leave you alone, if that's what you want."

"It's what I want," she lied.

"Because you don't trust me," he said flatly.

"Because I *can't*, dammit!"

Chase looked up at the pouring rain before glancing back at Dani. "Just remember that you're the one who set down the rules," he said. "I can't promise that I'll stick to them, but I'll try." He gave her a scorching glare that touched the forbidden corners of her heart before he slowly walked away from the porch and into the pelting rain.

Dani clutched at the lapels of her robe, feeling more alone and desolate than she had in years as she watched Chase disappear into the darkness.

CHAPTER FOUR

ALL THROUGH THE night, Dani listened to the sound of the rain running through the gutters and wondered what had happened to Chase. More to the point, she wondered what she was going to do about him. No matter which way she thought about it, Chase McEnroe was Caleb Johnson's partner. Even though he was attractive, her reaction to him was all wrong and much too powerful to ignore.

"Of all the men in the world, why him?" she asked herself as she tossed on the bed and flung off the covers in disgust. Sitting upright, her hair tangled and messed, she stared out the rain-streaked window and thought about the way she'd melted inside when he'd kissed her.

Even in the darkness she could feel her cheeks burn in embarrassment as she remembered how her heart and breasts had responded to the warmth and tenderness of his touch. "Oh, Dani," she sighed, flopping back on the pillows and trying to slow her racing pulse, "what have you gotten yourself into?"

CODY, HAIR STILL dripping from a quick shower, bounded down the stairs and took a seat at the kitchen table.

Hoping that the strain of the night didn't show on her face, Dani looked up and smiled at her son. "Good morning," she said as she placed a platter of pancakes in front of him.

"Mornin'." He poured syrup on his pancakes before

lifting his eyes to stare at his mother. "What was that guy doin' here last night?"

Dani felt her back stiffen, but managed to pour a cup of coffee with steady hands, blow across the hot liquid, and meet her son's curious gaze. "Chase?"

"If he's that new guy who works for Caleb Johnson."

"One and the same," Dani admitted pensively. Thinking back to her intimate conversation with Chase on the back porch, Dani blushed and took a sip from her mug. "I didn't know you were awake."

"I couldn't sleep. My window was open and I heard him talkin' to you. What'd he want?"

Dani lifted her brows. "Didn't you hear that, too?"

"I couldn't hear what you said. Too much noise because of the rain. I just heard voices."

Thank God.

"But I knew he was here." He looked away from Dani and concentrated on the thick stack of pancakes and a bowl of peaches Dani had set on the ancient table.

"How?"

"Recognized his voice."

Her feelings in an emotional tangle, Dani sat across from her son and toyed with her breakfast. She knew that she couldn't trust Chase, but there was something about the man, something earthy and seductive, that she couldn't forget. She glanced out the window toward the creek where Chase and at least one other man were working, and wondered again why he'd come up to her house in the middle of the rainshower.

"Mom?"

"What?" Dani turned her attention back to her son and realized he was waiting for an explanation. His dark eyes were round with concern. "Don't worry about Chase," she said, hoping to put Cody's worries to rest. "He stopped by last night because he wants my permission to work on the creek where it cuts through our property."

"Why?"

Dani lifted a shoulder. "Beats me…Caleb probably asked him to, I suppose."

Cody made a sound of disgust and finished his pancakes. He took a long swallow of his milk, watched his mother over his glass and wiped his mouth with the back of his hand.

"More?"

"Naw."

"Next time, use your napkin," she said automatically. She studied her son as Cody scraped his chair back from the table and carried his dishes to the sink.

How like his father Cody looked; the same curly dark-brown hair and deep brown eyes. Except for the lack of cynicism twisting the corners of his mouth and the honest warmth of his smile, Cody was growing up to be the spitting image of Blake.

"Why're you hanging out with one of Caleb Johnson's men?"

"Hanging out with him?" Dani repeated with a laugh. "I'm not."

Hopping up on the counter and swinging his legs, Cody looked at his mother and frowned. "But you don't hate him—not the way you hate the rest of Johnson's men."

"I don't *hate* anyone. Not even Caleb Johnson. As for Chase, I don't even know him."

"Doesn't matter. You like him."

Dani smiled and finished her coffee.

"You do like him, don't you?"

"It's not a question of liking him; I just don't know him."

"You didn't throw him off the place last night or the

other night, either," Cody pointed out. He picked up a fork from the counter and began twirling it nervously between his fingers.

"That's not as easy as it sounds."

"It's your land."

"Well, yes, it is. And it means a great deal to me. Maybe more than it should."

"Why?"

She hesitated a moment. Could Cody possibly understand her love and obligation to the family farm? Probably not. "I'm attached to this place for sentimental reasons. Lots of them. For quite a few generations someone from my family—your family, too, y'know, has lived here and worked hard to keep the land in the family. Even when times were hard; a lot harder than they are now. It just seems a shame to give it all up so that Caleb Johnson can build his resort."

Still sitting on the counter, Cody dropped the fork into the sink. "Would a resort be all that bad?"

"I don't know." She stood and placed her cup and saucer in the sink. Bracing herself against the edge of the counter and looking up at her son, she tried to think calmly about the resort she found so threatening. But it wasn't the resort itself; it was Johnson and his methods that made her blood boil. "Not really, I guess. A resort would benefit a lot of people and change the complexion of the town."

"That would be good."

"Maybe. Maybe not. I'm not really sure. It certainly would mean more money and economic development for the town. But with that would come people, tourists, new zoning, new roads and construction. Sleepy little Martinville would grow up. Fast."

"Good!"

Dani smiled sadly and bit into her lower lip. "Maybe it's selfish of me to want to keep the land." She looked through the open window to the dry fields, across the silvery creek, past the few scrubby oak trees to the gently rising land near the mountains. In the distance the proud Rockies cut through the blue morning sky to be rimmed by a few scattered clouds.

"So why don't you sell?"

"I was going to once," she admitted, thinking back to how foolish she'd been to trust Caleb Johnson. "Right after Grandma died; you weren't even in school yet. Johnson and I'd agreed on the price for the back fifty acres. However, when it got down to signing on the dotted line, Caleb pulled a fast one and said he'd decided he needed all my land. All or nothing. I just couldn't sign away *all* of Grandma and Grandpa's land. So it was nothing. Caleb's been fuming ever since."

"And causing trouble?"

"Which I can't prove."

"I think he's behind everything that's gone wrong around here," Cody proclaimed.

"Not everything," Dani replied. "Sometimes it was just fate or mistakes that I made."

Cody shook his head firmly. "I think he poisoned the cows when they got sick and I'll bet he stole our gas!"

"We don't know that."

"Who else?"

Dani's brows drew together in concentration. How many times had she asked herself the same question? How many nights had she lost sleep wondering if Caleb were really as bad as she thought he was? "Good question."

"What I don't get," Cody said with a look far wiser than his years, "is why he wants *all* of this land?"

"Another good question." She rumpled his dark hair affectionately. "I wish I had the answers."

Cody looked up at the ceiling and shifted uneasily, avoiding Dani's gaze. "Isabelle Reece said her pa thinks you're a fool."

Dani laughed. *A fool!* Well, maybe she was. Judging from her reaction to Chase, she certainly felt the part. "So when did Isabelle Reece's dad become an authority?" Dani teased.

Cody looked down at her and grinned. "On being a fool?" he repeated. "Oh, I get it: it takes one to know one?"

"Something like that." Dani laughed and tapped him on the knee. "Now, if I've answered all of your questions, Detective Summers, why don't you hop down and feed the livestock while I tackle the dishes?"

"But I wanted to go fishin'."

"Later, sport. I'll be out in a minute to help."

Cody swung his legs and jumped down from the counter. "Mom?"

She turned on the water. "Yeah?"

"So where does this Chase guy fit in?"

"I wish I knew," she admitted, squirting liquid dish soap into the sink. She'd wondered the same thing all night long. Her feelings for Chase were hard to define but the tangled web of her emotions was frightening, very frightening. For seven years she'd known exactly what she wanted from life and in just two weeks, he'd upset everything she'd been so sure of.

"Well, I wouldn't trust him," Cody said with authority. "Anyone working for Caleb Johnson is trouble."

"Is that what Isabelle Reece's pa says?" she asked, looking over her shoulder at her son.

Cody grinned at his mother. "I guess I'll have to ask."

"Don't bother," Dani said, slinging her arm around the boy and giving him a hug. "Somehow I have the feeling that once school starts, Isabelle will let you know."

"Yeah. She probably will."

Cody was laughing as he walked out the back door and called to Runt. The black dog stretched his legs and then followed Cody outside.

Once she was done with the dishes and the kitchen was straightened, Dani took off her apron and grabbed her gloves as she shouldered open the back door. As she walked toward the barn, she glanced across the fence to the spot where Chase and his men were working. Chase was easy to pick out. Taller than the other two men, he was shirtless and bare headed, his blond hair shining with sweat in the summer sun. He was leaning against the side of a dirty dump truck, ignoring the work going on around him and watching her every move.

Dani's heart leaped unexpectedly and vivid memories of the night before flashed in her mind. She could still smell the rain, taste Chase's lips, feel his hands sliding between the lapels of her robe....

"Mom?"

Dani nearly jumped out of her skin. She hadn't realized that she'd stopped walking toward the barn. "Oh, what?"

Cody was sitting on the fence post. He cocked his head in the direction of the barn. "If ya don't mind?" Hopping to the ground, he reminded her, "You're the one who wants the animals fed early."

"So what have you been doing?"

"Waiting for you."

"Cody—"

"It's hard for me alone," he said, looking suddenly contrite.

The boy was only nine. "Sorry," she apologized

quickly. The she jerked on her gloves and walked into the darkened interior of the barn.

The cattle were already inside, lowing loudly and shuffling for position at the manger.

"Why were you staring at Johnson's land?" Cody asked.

"I was just thinking."

"I know that much." Cody frowned as he climbed the ladder to the loft and began dropping some of last year's hay bales to the main floor below. "I saw." He looked down at her from the loft above and his brows were drawn together in frustration. "You were looking at that guy again."

She cut the strings on the bales with her pocketknife and began breaking up the hay before tossing it into the manger. "I just can't figure him out."

"If I were you, I wouldn't try." Cody leaped down from the loft, his boots crunching on some spilled grain as he landed on the dusty floorboards.

Dani shook her head. "Next time, use the ladder—"

"Aw, Mom."

"I just don't want you to break your neck. Especially in front of me," she added, trying to lighten the mood.

"I'm not a little kid anymore," Cody said firmly.

Dani's smile was bittersweet. "That's what worries me." She watched her son as he rationed out the grain for the cattle. His body was changing; he was growing up faster than she wanted him to. "I'll check the water and you can sweep the floor, okay?"

"Okay," Cody grumbled.

Dani walked from the barn and into the bright morning sunlight. Stuffing her gloves into the back pocket of her jeans, she began filling each of the troughs near the barn with fresh water. As she waited for the troughs to fill, listening to the cool sound of rushing water pounding against the old metal tubs, she chanced looking at Chase again.

He wasn't leaning on the dump truck any longer. Instead he was shoveling mud from the bottom of the creek and supervising the planting of several trees near the deep hole he was creating. The morning sun caught in his blond hair and gleamed on the sweat of his back. His back and shoulder muscles, tanned and glistening in the sun, stretched fluidly as he worked.

"Hey, Mom, watch what you're doing!" Cody yelled as he walked out of the barn.

Shocked out of her wandering thoughts, Dani noticed that the trough was overflowing; precious water was swirling in the tub before running down the hillside in a wild stream.

"For crying out loud," she chastised herself as she turned off the water and looked over her shoulder to the other trough, where Cody was furiously twisting the handle of the spigot.

Frowning, he wiped his hands on his jeans as he approached. "You've got the hots for that guy, don't you?"

"Cody!"

He shrugged and pouted. "Well, don't say I didn't warn you about him."

"I wouldn't dream of it," Dani remarked. "Hey...wait a minute. *You're* warning *me*? What do you know about 'the hots'?"

Knowing he'd managed to goad his mother, Cody looked slyly over his shoulder before saying, "Isabelle Reece says her pa—"

"I'm not sure I'm ready to hear this—"

"Just kidding, Mom," he said, a grin growing from

one side of his boyish face to the other before he sobered again. "But…"

"But what?"

"You haven't forgotten about Dad, have you? He *is* coming home."

Not wanting to cause her son any further pain or confusion, Dani had trouble finding the courage to tell him the truth and burst his bubble of hope. "When your dad gets here, we'll talk. All of us."

Cody visibly brightened.

"But you have to understand that we don't love each other anymore; not the way a man and wife love each other."

Doubts filled his eyes. "But you were married!"

"Unfortunately people change."

"Or give up," he accused, his small jaw tight, his dark brows pulled together and his eyes bright with challenge.

"Or give up," she agreed. "I'm not saying I was right—"

"You weren't! You should have stayed married to him!"

"Believe me, I tried."

"Not hard enough!"

"Cody—"

Tears filled his eyes and he tried to swallow them back. "Can I go fishin'?"

"Now?"

"Yeah."

"I think we should talk about this."

"What good will that do?" he threw back at her. "Nothin's gonna change. I still don't have a pa. Just like the kids say!"

"That's not true!"

His defiance eased a bit. "I just want to go fishin', okay?"

Pain twisting her heart, guilt washing over her in hot waves, Dani nodded tightly. "The sooner, the better," she said before her anger subsided. "Just be back by noon, okay?"

"Sure."

He started to turn, but she stopped him by touching his arm. He jerked it away. "Where are you going fishing?"

"Probably the hole near the south fork."

"Okay. Do you want to take something to eat?"

Forcing a smile, he fished in his pocket and pulled out three candy bars. "I'm all set."

"For nutritional suicide."

Cody swiped at his tears and Dani pretended not to notice. Turning his back to her, he went to the back porch, grabbed his fishing pole and stained vest and whistled for Runt. Then he was off, running through the fields toward the foothills with the dog racing ahead, frightening grasshoppers, birds and rabbits in the stubble of the pasture.

With a tired sigh, Dani walked up to the porch, reached for her hoe and leaned on it while watching her son until Cody was out of sight. What had she done to the boy? Should she have stayed married to a man she didn't love, a man who had done everything in his power to hurt and embarrass her for the sake of her son?

Without any answers to her questions, she looked across the fence to the Johnson field. Chase was there, standing with his muscled back to her and staring at Cody's retreating figure as the boy crawled under the fence separating one of her fields from another before disappearing through the brush at the far end of the pasture.

CHASE WATCHED THE boy and dog sprint through the dry fields and, for a moment, he remembered his own youth and the warm Idaho summers.

The boy ducked under the fence and disappeared into a thicket of blackberries and brush, the lop-eared dog on his heels. Chase couldn't help but smile. Cody and his beautiful mother made him feel dangerously younger than his thirty-four years.

For the first time in what seemed forever, a woman had gotten under Chase McEnroe's skin. It had been only hours since he'd left Dani but, despite his promise to the contrary, he was already restless to be with her again. The fact that she was near enough to see only made it worse.

He jabbed his shovel into the soft ground near the bank and cursed quietly to himself. The memory of touching her had made the rest of the night excruciating. He'd lain awake for hours, twisting and turning on sweat-dampened sheets and feeling a gentle but insistent throb in his loins. A throb that reminded him of her willing, warm body, softly parted lips and perfectly rounded breasts. Hell, he'd felt like a horny kid all over again. Just because of one damned woman!

Dissatisfied with life in general, Chase continued to dig, throwing the power from his tense shoulders and arms into each jab. The ground around the creekbed gave way under the thrust of his shovel. Swirling muddy water filled the hole.

Still he couldn't get Dani out of his mind and it sure wasn't for lack of trying. Telling himself that he had to avoid her at all possible costs, he plunged into his work with a vengeance, thrusting his shoulders and mind into the task of working the creek and getting the hell out of Montana as soon as he could.

All morning he'd made impossible demands on the men and himself, trying to exorcise Dani's image from his mind.

But each time he looked up from his work, she was

there. Whether she was standing at the kitchen window, working with the cattle, or as she was now, hoeing that miserable patch of ground she considered her garden, she was there; only several hundred yards away.

The effect was devastating for Chase. *Torture,* he thought angrily to himself, working so close to her was sheer torture. "She's just a woman," he grumbled to himself, "just one woman!"

"Hey, Chase! Over here!" Ben Marx, one of his employees, shouted, dragging him out of his fantasies about Dani.

"What?"

"I don't know," Ben said. He was a young, bearded man who had been with Chase for nearly two years, ever since Eric Conway had walked out on Relive to start a rival company. Ben's hat was pushed back on his head, sweaty strands of sandy hair were protruding under the brim and the man himself was staring at a large ten-gallon metal drum that he'd pulled from the creek. Rotating the drum on the ground, he gave out a long, low whistle just as Chase approached.

"Looks like an old barrel of some kind of herbicide," Ben said.

"Herbicide?" Chase repeated, bending to examine the can.

"Wait a minute. There it is. Dioxin."

"And you found it in the creek?"

Ben glanced up at Chase. "Buried in the creekbed."

"How deep?"

Ben shrugged his shoulders. "Hard to tell. We've been working here for quite a while, so I can't be sure, but probably four, maybe six inches. And look here," he pointed to what would have been the lid of the barrel. "It's been punctured."

"Intentionally?"

"I don't think a woodpecker made those holes, do you?"

"Son of a bitch!" Chase jerked his gloves from his back pocket and rotated the metal drum again. The label was scratched and muddy, but some of the letters were still visible. The lid of the drum had a few barely visible holes in it. "No wonder there's no fish in the creek…" His eyes narrowed on the empty can.

"You reckon it wasn't empty when it was buried?" Ben asked, reaching into his breast pocket and pulling out a crumpled pack of cigarettes.

"Hard to tell."

"Who would bury a drum so close to the creek?" He lit the cigarette and inhaled deeply.

Chase's mouth pinched. "I can't hazard a guess," he said sarcastically. "Show me exactly where you found this."

After wrapping the drum in oilcloth and placing it in the back of his Jeep, he followed Ben back into the water and stared at the hole Ben had been digging when he'd unearthed the barrel of poisonous herbicide, if that's what it was.

"I was just smoothing the bottom of the creek out, makin' it ready for more gravel when I decided to deepen it near the bank. My shovel struck metal, so I worked to find out what it was."

"Don't touch anything," Chase commanded. "I want to take some samples of the water and the soil." He returned to his Jeep for his hip waders and sterile vials and set about collecting the samples, careful to label each specimen. Then, muttering under his breath, he crawled through the rusted wires of the barbed fence and began taking soil and water samples a few feet inside Dani's boundaries.

"Tell the men to take the rest of the day off," Chase said. "And I don't want any of them in the creek without waders."

Ben nodded.

"As for drinking from the creek—"

"No one does."

"Let's keep it that way. And don't say anything about this," Chase warned, looking at the man on Johnson's side of the fence.

Ben took a final drag on his cigarette before flipping it onto the muddy bank of the creek, where it smoldered and died. "You can count on me. I've heard tales about that one," he said, nodding in the direction of Dani's house. "If she finds out you've been on her land again, there'll be hell to pay."

Despite the cold dread stealing through him, Chase forced a sly smile. "No reason to disturb the lady, right?"

"Right." Ben chuckled, took off his gloves and grinned lazily. "Leastwise, not by steppin' on her land." He looked at Dani's house again and his gaze grew distant. "But there are other ways I'd like to bother her."

A muscle tightened in Chase's jaw and his blue eyes turned stone cold. "Not a good idea, friend," Chase said.

"No?"

Chase was spoiling for a fight and he knew it. But having it out with Ben Marx was just plain stupid. He ground his back teeth together and said, "Considering how she feels about Caleb, I think it'd be best if you left her alone. Don't you?"

Ben read the message in Chase's glare. His lazy smile dissolved under the intensity of Chase's cold eyes and he reached for another cigarette. "Whatever you say; you're the boss."

"Then it's understood that Dani Summers is off-limits to anyone working for me." Chase could hardly believe what he was doing; acting like some fool male dog staking out his territory. With his own men, no less! And yet he couldn't stop himself or the feeling of possession that ripped through him any time another man said Dani's name.

"Sure, sure," Ben said hastily. He'd been on the receiving end of Chase's wrath enough times to know that he didn't want to cross McEnroe. Especially about a woman. Chase was a fair employer but if pushed hard enough, he had a temper that wouldn't quit. In Ben's opinion it didn't make much sense to get him mad.

"Good. Make sure the rest of the men get the word. And don't tell anyone about the drum of dioxin or whatever the hell it is. I want to check it out first." *And then there'll be trouble. Big trouble.*

Ben lit his cigarette, shoved his hat over his brow and nodded mutely.

Chase glanced uneasily up the hill to where Dani was working in the garden, but, as usual, she seemed disinterested, as if she weren't paying any attention to what was happening on the property adjoining hers. He hoped to God that it wasn't an act and waded farther downstream to the middle of Dani's land before taking more samples.

DANI PURSED HER lips in frustration as she watched Chase slip through the fence. Seeing him out of the corner of her eye, she leaned on her hoe, wiped the sweat from her forehead and wondered if she really wanted to make a scene in front of his crew. Not that she wanted to, but damn the man, he was forcing the issue! She watched him walk backward, downstream, farther onto her property.

And just last night he'd promised to stay away. Now he was breaking his word, pushing her to the limit in full view of his workers. After her argument with Cody, she was in no mood to get into another fight. But she really didn't have much of a choice.

With a sigh she put the hoe on the porch, wiped her palms on her jeans and started through the gate and down the sloping field to the creek.

Chase was there, just as he had been the first time she'd come across him, except for the fact that he was about a hundred yards away from Caleb's land and right in the middle of hers. He was digging on the bank and taking samples of the water. *Her water.*

She felt her pulse begin to race but assured herself that it was because she was furious with him as well as Caleb Johnson.

"I thought you understood that I didn't want you here," she said as she approached the bank.

"I did." He looked up, smiled, and then went about his business.

Infuriated, Dani planted her hands on her hips. "I wasn't kidding about calling the sheriff."

"Go ahead—call him."

"Chase—"

He looked up again, his piercing sky-blue eyes causing her stupid heart to flutter. "At least this time you didn't bring that damned rifle."

"I hoped that I didn't need it."

"You don't." He offered her a brilliant smile that was meant to dazzle away her worries. It softened her heart, but didn't quite convince her head that he was on the up-and-up.

"What're you doing?"

"Taking samples."

"I can see that, but *why*?"

"I just want to check the creek. Remember, I did ask for permission."

"And I didn't grant it."

"Right."

"So you just barged right over here anyway." She crossed her arms under her breasts and didn't bother to hide her exasperation.

He grinned again and muttered, "Actually I tried to sneak."

"In broad daylight? When I was up in the garden?" She smiled despite the headache beginning to pound at the base of her skull. "I'll admit that I don't know you very well, but I doubt that you were trying to sneak. You did a much better impersonation of a cat burglar last night."

The corners of his lips were drawn down and deep furrows lined his tanned brow. "Maybe we'd better not talk about last night."

Dani couldn't agree more. "I don't want to talk about anything. I just want to know why you're defying me."

"I don't like edicts."

"But this is my land—"

"So I've heard. About a hundred times. From you." He sighed and placed another small vial into his fishing creel before wading downstream deeper into her property.

"I know why you're here."

"Sure you do. I told you, I'm taking samples."

"That's not the only reason. You're proving to those men—" she made a sweeping gesture to Johnson's land where Ben Marx was pretending not to see the ensuing argument "—that I can't tell you what to do."

"They have nothing to do with this."

"Like hell!"

His face went taut, his chin tight with determination. "For once, just trust me."

"Chase—"

But he was backing up again, watching the water as it rushed into a thicket of brush and trees at the corner of the field. The stand of cottonwood and pine offered the only seclusion and shade in the entire field. Beneath the leafy trees, hidden in the brush, Chase was out of view.

Dani had to walk into the thicket to carry on the conversation. She had to bend to avoid the low branches that caught on her blouse. Chase had stopped between the scraggly cottonwoods clinging to the banks of the stream. Ignoring her, he began once again to take samples of the water.

Furious, Dani stood on a large boulder near the water's edge. "I thought you understood." She glanced upstream, but couldn't see if Chase's men were watching. The branches offered both shade and privacy as a slight breeze whispered through the canopy of leaves above the creek.

"I do. But this was something I had to do, okay?"

"And leave it at that?"

"For now."

"No, Chase. No, it's not okay. Look, I thought you were different from the rest of Caleb's hands. I thought you would keep to your part of the bargain."

His muscles tensed and he replied flatly. "My bargain's with Johnson."

"I see," Dani said, her stomach tightening with disappointment. Despite his arguments otherwise, Chase was solidly in Caleb Johnson's corner. He was the enemy. "Then I think you'd better move it and get out of here because I really am going to call Tim Bennett."

Chase raised a skeptical brow but continued to work.

"He's the sheriff," Dani clarified.

"I *know* who he is. I just don't give a damn."

"You've certainly got a lot of nerve! More nerve than brains."

His shoulders slumping slightly, Chase dropped the final vial into his creel and stared up at her. Even enraged, she was beautiful.

Standing on the bank, with the warm morning sunlight drifting through the shimmering leaves of the cottonwood, her arms crossed angrily under her breasts, her chin held high, Dani looked almost regal. She hadn't bothered to tie her long hair back and it billowed away from her flushed face in the heavy-scented summer breeze. "And you're gorgeous," Chase replied, studying the pucker of her lips and the fire in her hazel eyes.

"I don't want to hear it."

"Sure you do."

"Calling attention to my looks right now in the middle of this argument is a typical male trick to change the subject!"

"It's no trick," he said calmly, wiping his wet hands on his jeans while he stared at her.

Dani's eyes followed the movement and she had to tear them away from his flat abdomen and the tight faded jeans that rested on his hips.

She licked her dry lips and he smiled; that same lazy, seductive grin that made her heart flutter expectantly. "Just get out of here," she said, hating the breathless tone of her voice.

"Dani—"

"What?"

"Why don't you ask me to stay?" He stuffed his gloves

in his back pocket and began slowly walking through the knee-deep water and toward the shore.

Her defenses melted and she leaned against the white bark of a cottonwood for support. "Are you always going to fight me?" she asked.

"Only when I have to." He waded out of the stream and stood next to her, kicking off his boots.

She tried not to notice the way the sweat ran down his throat, or the way his hair curled at his neck, or the fluid movement of his shoulder muscles when he leaned back against one of the lower branches of a scrub oak. "And when is that?" she asked, her throat suddenly tight. "When Caleb tells you to?"

His jaw hardened and he stretched out an arm along the branch to break off a small twig and rotate it between his fingers. "Contrary to what you think, I don't do everything Caleb suggests."

"You could have fooled me."

His eyes stared deep into hers and her chest seemed suddenly tight. Breathing was nearly impossible. "Why do you hate him so much?"

She smiled despite the tension charging the summer air. "Hate's too strong a word," she said, remembering that Cody had accused her of hating her neighbor earlier in the morning.

"What would you call it?"

"I don't trust him."

"So I gathered." He cocked his head to the side. "But you never really said why."

"He's done a few things that, though I can't prove… I'm convinced— Wait a minute. Why should I tell you?"

"Because I asked. Look, Dani, I'm not against you."

"That's hard to believe."

"Is it?"

She stared into the honesty of his clear blue eyes and wanted to trust him with all of her heart. Instead she shrugged. "I thought I already explained all that."

"Not really. Why are you so dead-set against Summer Ridge?"

"I'm not against the resort, not really. I'm against the fact that come hell or high water, Caleb Johnson thinks he can manipulate me into selling my property. It might sound corny, but this land means a lot to me."

"Meaning that you want a higher price."

She ran her fingers through her hair and sat near the edge of the stream. Linking her arms around her knees, she stared at the rushing water. "You'd better watch out, McEnroe. You're starting to sound like him."

Picking a blade of dry grass and chewing on it, he sat next to her with his bare feet sticking out in front of him, his thighs nearly brushing hers. "So if it's not money, what's the problem?"

Dani glanced into his concerned eyes. "Did Caleb tell you I was willing to sell some of the acreage to him?"

"No."

"About two years ago, I think," she said remembering the meeting at Caleb's house. "He'd even agreed to the sale. But then he changed his mind, he wasn't satisfied; he wanted the whole farm."

"And you didn't want to sell."

"Not all of it. My great-great-grandparents homesteaded here and I wanted to keep it in the family." She picked up a handful of dirt and let it slip between her fingers. "This land is all my folks ever had and they worked until they dropped to keep it."

"So you've been preserving the heritage—for what, your son?"

"If he wants it."

"And what if he doesn't?"

Dani frowned and clasped her hands together. "I've thought about that, and I suppose if Cody inherits it and wants to sell, he has that right." She pushed the hair out of her eyes and smiled. "It certainly won't matter to me then."

"So you don't trust Caleb because he tried to buy all of your farm."

She avoided his eyes. "There were other reasons."

"Name one."

"I can't," she admitted. "It's just a feeling that I have; nothing I can prove."

"Prove?" When she didn't respond, he reached over and touched her cheek with his index finger. "Prove what?"

"Nothing," she said quickly.

"Dani," he whispered, pulling her chin so that she was forced to stare into his eyes, "you can trust me."

"Aren't you the man who just said he had a bargain with Johnson—not with me?"

His gaze slid to her mouth. "What do you think Caleb has done to you?"

Gambling, she said, "I think he's done everything he could think of to discredit me, make me sell my land to him and ruin me financially."

Chase dropped his finger and whistled softly. "Heavy charges."

"Like I said, there's nothing I can prove." She tossed a rock into the creek. "At least not yet. So, how come you're involved with him?"

"Good question."

"You went to him when you needed financing."

"Actually, I'd never laid eyes on him before. But he knew all about me and my company."

"Isn't that odd since your company is located in Boise?"

"I don't know," Chase admitted, his blue eyes clouding as he pondered the question that had been nagging at him for over two years. "There wasn't much competition in the business at the time. Relive Inc. had a corner on the stream-rebuilding market and Johnson claimed to have known my mother, before she was married."

"She's never mentioned him?"

Chase shook his head. "She's dead."

"Oh...I'm sorry."

Shrugging off the uncomfortable feeling that settled on him each time he thought about his mother knowing Caleb, Chase placed his hands behind his head and leaned against the trunk of a cottonwood. "So why don't you tell me what, specifically, Caleb's done to make you so damned mad?"

"I don't think that would be wise."

"Why?"

"Probably for the same reason you won't tell me why you decided to ignore my edict, as you called it, and cross the fence."

A slow smile spread across his rugged features and his eyes warmed as he looked at her. "Maybe I just wanted to see you again."

"So you waded in a frigid creek with all those bottles of yours? No way."

Seductive blue eyes delved into hers. "It worked, didn't it?" he asked, brushing a golden strand of hair from her cheek and letting his fingers linger at her nape.

Dani's breath caught somewhere in her throat. "Don't you have work to do?"

"Probably." He inched his head closer to hers until the warmth of his breath fanned her face and his arms surrounded her shoulders. With eyes fixed on hers, he leaned closer still, and his lips brushed slowly over hers in an agonizing, bittersweet promise that destroyed all her defenses.

I can't let this happen again, Dani thought, but didn't stop him. His fingers caressed her arms as he drew her closer, tighter against his chest and she could hear her thundering heartbeat echoing his. When he pressed his mouth over hers and kissed her, she felt the raging passion that had been destroying his nights and driving him insane during the day. Its fire ignited her own blood and it coursed in wild, hot tandem through her trembling body.

His tongue sought and danced with hers and she didn't protest, but linked her arms around his neck, moaning his name as he unbuttoned her blouse and caressed her breast in slow, sensuous circles that awakened dangerous fires deep within her soul. His hands were warm and comforting against her skin and a fine tremor in his touch told her just how easily his control could slip.

He kissed the top of her breast, letting his tongue wet the lacy edge of her bra and the warm skin peeking through the sheer fabric.

"Please, Chase," she whispered brokenly, knowing she should break off the embrace but unable to find the strength to do anything but surrender to his lovemaking.

Looking up, he saw the doubt in her eyes. He groaned and rolled away, closing his eyes and mind to the thundering desire.

Dani felt suddenly cold and very much alone.

"Oh, Dani," he whispered hoarsely, lying on his stomach and willing the swelling in his jeans to subside. "If you only knew what you do to me." Though his eyes were still closed, he rubbed them with his thumb and finger and massaged the bridge of his nose. "I don't know how much more of this I can take."

She swallowed the lump in her throat along with her

pride. "Why are you trying to confuse me?" she asked, her voice raspy as she buttoned her blouse.

"I'm not."

"Then why don't you make up your mind?"

"I don't understand."

"Neither do I, Chase. But it sure looks like you're playing both ends against the middle."

"Meaning?"

"That one minute you're telling me that your only allegiance is to Caleb Johnson, a man who's tried everything he can think of to ruin me, and the next minute you're... you're...*acting* like you care for me!"

"It's not an act," he admitted. "I do care for you. Too much, I think."

She smiled sadly. "I wish I could believe you."

"Just trust me—"

The same old words! Trust me! Sadness sizzled into anger. Anger at her twisted emotions and anger at him for confusing her. "*Trust you?* How can I? I don't believe in blind trust, Chase." *Not since Blake left me.* "You promised that you'd stay off my land and leave me alone. The minute my back was turned you were here again, digging in the mud and taking water from the creek."

"Dani—"

"I'm not through!"

"Just wait a minute! Listen to you! Why do you care if I'm on your land? I'm not hurting a damned thing!"

She was trembling with passion and rage, confusing the two, wishing that she'd never laid eyes on the enigma that was Chase McEnroe. "Not hurting anything?" she repeated. "Well, maybe not yet! But you're working for Johnson, and God only knows what he's got up his sleeve!"

She started to get up but he grabbed her wrist, pulling her close to him. "You know, you act like you've got something to hide."

"Me!" She laughed at the absurdity of the situation but couldn't help being mesmerized by his gaze. "Why don't you go track down your boss? Ask him about my dead cattle. Ask him about the time I was going to sell off part of the property to him. Ask him about my hay baler! And ask him about the time he tried to siphon off all the water in Grizzly Creek for his private lake!"

She wrenched her arm free and stood staring down at him. She was shaking with rage. "For all I know, you're just part of one of Caleb's schemes. I wouldn't put it past him. He probably asked you to come over here and try to work your way into my confidence by any means possible!"

Chase's square jaw tightened and his clear eyes clouded when he remembered Caleb's suggestion that he bed Dani. He tried not to let his thoughts show, but his very silence was incriminating.

"Oh, my God, Caleb is behind this, isn't he?" she guessed, feeling suddenly sick. She could read the evidence in Chase's eyes. Bitterly she turned away in disgust, and self-loathing overwhelmed her. "And it's laughable what easy prey I am!"

"What happened between us has nothing to do with Johnson," Chase said, rising to his feet.

"Like hell!" She backed into a tree and stood looking at him. Her face was pale, her expression stricken. "Just get off my property and don't ever come back!"

"Dani—"

"You're a bastard," she said. "A first-class A-1 bastard, and I never...*never* want you to set foot on this place again!"

"You're making a mistake," he said slowly. A muscle worked in his jaw and the skin over his forearms tightened.

"Not nearly as bad as the one I almost made."

He pushed his hands into the back pockets of his jeans and looked upstream through the leafy overhanging branches of the trees to the fence and beyond, where his men and machinery were still in position on Johnson's property. When he turned to her again, he was able to control some of his rage. "I didn't want any of this to happen."

"Good. Then we can both forget that it did."

"I want to help you," he admitted, and the torture in his voice almost convinced her. But not quite.

"I don't want to hear any more of your lies. Now just get the hell off my property!" Reaching down, she scooped up his fishing creel. "And take all of this with you!" She threw it at him, but the toss went wild. Chase scrambled to catch it, but the creel fell on the rocks near the bank. The glass within the wicker basket tinkled and shattered. Mud and water started trickling through the woven bottom of the creel.

"No!" Chase was horrified. He picked up the creel and opened the lid, eyeing the shattered vials, oblivious to the water running through the wicker and down his jeans. "Do you realize what you've done?" he accused, fire returning to his eyes as he looked up at her. "Every vial is ruined!"

"I don't really give a damn!"

He let the creel fall to the ground and advanced upon her. "What was in those jars might just have been the evidence you need!"

"Evidence?"

"That Caleb isn't on the up-and-up!"

"What? How can water samples—" Shaking her head as if to clear it, she focused sharp hazel eyes on him. "If you expect me to believe that you were trying to prove that Caleb Johnson is a crook, you've got another guess coming! You're his partner," she reminded him, her voice rising. "You owe him a ton of money as well as your entire business!"

Chase was standing over her, looking down at her with judicious blue eyes. His nostrils were flared, his chiseled mouth tight. "Go ahead and believe what you want to, lady, but I'm going to get to the bottom of this feud between you and Johnson with or without your help."

"Be my guest," she threw back at him, "as long as it's not on *my* property!"

He looked like he wanted to kill her. The frustration and anger in his look bore deep into her soul. Dani's heart froze and her lips parted in surprise when he grabbed her, jerked her body against his and forced his head downward so that his lips crushed hers and stole the breath from her lungs.

Struggling, she managed to pull one of her hands free and she swung it upward, intending to land it full force on his cheek. But he was faster than she would have guessed and he grabbed her wrist, pinned her hand behind her and continued kissing her, forcing his tongue through her teeth, moving his body sensually against hers until, to her mortification, she felt her body responding. Her breasts peaked, her heartbeat accelerated and she felt like dying a thousand deaths.

When he lifted his head from hers, he slowly released her, dropping her hands. How he was coming to loathe himself. "Oh, God, Dani," he whispered, pushing the hair out of his eyes with shaking fingers. "I'm sorry."

She swallowed and let out a shuddering sigh. "So am I."

"You are, without exception, the most beautiful, intriguing and frustrating woman I've ever met."

"And you're the most arrogant, self-serving bastard I know," she said, holding the back of her hand against her swollen lips.

He stepped toward her, but she held up a trembling palm. "Just leave," she whispered. "Go away. Get away from me! Why don't you find the next train to Boise and jump on it! I can handle Caleb Johnson by myself!"

"Can you?"

"Yes!"

His jaw thrust forward, his eyes glinting a silver-blue, Chase reached down, jerked on his waders, picked up his creel and strode along the bank.

Dani watched him leave, positioning herself outside of the thicket so that she could follow his movements as he walked through the trees and into the sunshine, across the field and through the parted strands of barbed wire. Tears stood in her large eyes and she wondered why she couldn't find the strength to hate him.

CHAPTER FIVE

EARLY IN THE afternoon, wearing a proud smile and water-logged jeans, Cody returned with two small trout in his possession. Runt scampered up the two steps of the porch and flopped in the shade to pant near Dani's chair.

She was sitting in her favorite rocker, mending some of his clothes and hoping that a few pairs of the pants would still fit him for the coming school year.

"Congratulations," she said when Cody proudly displayed his catch. "Looks like we have fish for dinner."

Cody made a face. "I *hate* fish."

"Then you should have thrown them back," she said, smothering a laugh.

Sitting down on the top step, he glanced up at her. "What were you doin' at the creek with that guy?" he asked.

Taken by surprise, Dani looked up from her mending and then slowly set the torn shirt aside. "You were there?"

"Yeah. Well, no, not really. I was just comin' back and I'd planned on fishin' in the hole below the fork in the creek. You know, by the cottonwood trees."

Dani nodded, hoping that her cheeks weren't as warm as they felt. She'd never thought about Cody surprising her and Chase. But then, she hadn't expected to find Chase in the creek…on her side of the fence.

"I saw that Chase What's-his-face—"

"McEnroe," Dani supplied, meeting her son's curious stare.

"Yeah. I saw him walking back to Johnson's property. He looked madder than a wet hen. You were standing down there." He gestured toward the cottonwood stand. "And you were watching him leave and looking real sad."

Dani folded her hands on her laps. "So you saw that, did ya?"

Cody nodded. "Was he bothering you?"

"A little," she hedged. "I caught him trying to take water samples," she explained. "We had a rather un-friendly...discussion."

"You mean a fight."

"I mean a battle royal."

"What does he want with our water?"

"Beats me," Dani admitted, wondering the thousandth time exactly why Chase was so anxious to get water from her side of the fence. And what did it have to do with "evidence"? Damn Chase McEnroe; he held all the cards. And he knew it. "I suppose he wants the water because Caleb probably told him to get it."

"And he got mad when you told him to leave."

The understatement of the century. "Very."

"I thought you told him not to come back here." Cody began playing in the dust with a stick and avoided Dani's eyes.

"I did."

"Well?"

"I don't know why he keeps comin' back," she admitted, gazing across the dry fields. "I guess maybe it's just part of his job."

"Or maybe he likes you." Cody glanced over his shoulder again, pinning his mother with his dark brown eyes.

"Why would you say that?" Dani asked, worried that she and Cody were about to argue again.

"Because you always do. When some girl gives

me trouble at school, you always say it's because she likes me."

Dani laughed and wiped the sweat from her forehead. "I do, don't I? And you never believe me."

"Maybe you're right."

"That's a big concession coming from you."

Cody's solemn face split with a smile. "I figure you've got to be right part of the time—"

"Get out of here," she teased, her eyes sparkling.

Standing, he winked at his mom. "How about a Coke?"

She eyed him and nodded. "You go get cleaned up and I'll get us each one. Then I think you'd better brush up on your schoolwork."

"Why?"

She stood, wrapped both arms around the post supporting the roof and stared across the creek. "Summer's almost over, Cody," she said reluctantly, her fingers scratching the peeling paint from the post. Soon Chase and all the problems he brought into her life would be gone. And those problems would be replaced with new ones from Caleb Johnson. "Go on. Scoot," she said to her son.

"Aw, Mom—" He let out an exaggerated sigh. "I'll start tomorrow night. Okay?"

"Is that a promise?"

Cody nodded but bit at his lower lip.

"I'm going to hold you to it."

"I know, I know," he mumbled as he slipped through the creaking screen door and hurried up the stairs.

A few minutes later Dani heard the sound of water running in the pipes. She folded her mending and glanced down the hill to Johnson's side of the fence. All the equipment was still in position, but no one was in sight. They'd probably all gone up to the house for lunch.

"And good riddance," she murmured, but the ache in her heart wouldn't subside.

WATER WAS STILL dripping from Cody's dark hair when he bounded down the stairs half an hour later. He grinned at his mother when he saw the two glasses of Coke on the table.

"I saved you from a fate worse than death," Dani remarked, shooting him an indulgent look. She was standing at the stove and frying Cody's trout. Both small fish sizzled as they browned in the pan.

"How's that?" he asked.

"We're eating the fish you caught for lunch."

"Wait a minute—"

Careful not to spill the grease, Dani scooped the fish from the pan and set them on a platter lined with paper towels. "That way you don't have to have them for dinner tonight."

"Mom—" he began to protest, but she placed the platter on the table between her plate and his.

"Eat, son, and I promise not to give you any lectures on starving children in the rest of the world," Dani said as she sat at the table, took a fish and wedge of lemon and began squeezing lemon juice on the tender white meat.

With a grimace, Cody speared the remaining fish and placed it onto his place as he sat down. Drinking plenty of Coke between each bite, he mumbled and grumbled to himself.

"Great trout," Dani teased, her eyes sparkling.

"Don't rub it in." But Cody returned her smile. "Have you got the mail today?"

Dani nodded.

"Was there, uh, anything for me?" he asked, staring down at his plate.

Dani forced a smile she didn't feel and the piece of trout she was chewing stuck in her throat. "Not today."

"Oh." Her son slowly speared another piece of fish and Dani's heart twisted.

The phone rang and Cody raced to get it. After a short conversation, he hung up and returned to the table. "That was Shane. He wants me to spend the night."

"Tonight?"

"Uh-huh. I told him it was okay. It is, isn't it?"

Dani shrugged. "Sure. But next time maybe you'd better ask first, don't ya think?"

"I guess so. He said I could come over about four."

"Good. I've got to run into town for some groceries anyway. I'll drop you off then. Okay?"

"Great!" With that, Cody was up the stairs, packing a change of clothes and his treasures into his bag. Dani watched him take off with a trace of sadness. He was growing up so fast and slipping away from her.

With a philosophical frown, she got up and cleared the table. Little boys grow up, and if their mothers are smart, they let them, she told herself. Wondering why it had to hurt so much, she set the pans on the counter and turned on the hot water. As the sink filled, Dani glanced through the steam and out the window. Work had picked up on the Johnson place again. Men were digging and heavy machinery was placing logs and boulders in strategic positions along the creek.

Two men she didn't recognize were planting saplings along the bank, but nowhere did she see Chase. *No big loss,* she told herself, but felt that same dull pain in her heart. "You're a fool," she muttered. "A first-class fool." Then she attacked the dishes as if her life depended upon it.

CHASE DIDN'T STOP fuming all the way to Johnson's house. He'd spent the last four hours with the manager of an independent chemical laboratory, and his blood was boiling. As he'd suspected, the drum that Ben had found in the creek had held dioxin. There were still traces of the herbicide in the empty can. Although more tests were to be run and eventually the county agriculture agent would have to be notified, Chase was convinced that someone had intentionally put the drum of dioxin in the creek to poison the water. But why? To kill the fish? Ruin the plant life? Get rid of the illegal toxin? Not likely.

No doubt, Caleb Johnson would know.

Though he ached to have it out with Caleb, for the time being Chase had to sit tight. Or as tight as his temper would let him.

Parking his Jeep near the barn, he cut the engine and hopped out of the cab. Trying to control his anger, he strode through the front door of Caleb's home. Aside from Caleb's housekeeper, who was humming and rattling around in the kitchen, the house seemed to be deserted.

Chase hesitated only a second before walking into Caleb's study, pulling out the files and finding the documents he wanted. His jaw working in agitation, he read the appraisal reports, geographic studies, mortgage information and every other scrap of paper dealing with Dani's farm. When he'd finished with the file he replaced it, and the anger in his blood had heated all over again.

"You miserable son of a bitch," he muttered as he slammed the file drawer shut and walked down the short hallway to the back of the house and the kitchen, where Jenna was working and humming to herself.

"Hasn't Johnson shown up?" Chase asked the elderly woman as he grabbed a bottle of beer from the refrigerator.

"He came in 'bout twelve-thirty," Jenna replied as she continued rolling out pie dough.

Chase could barely control himself. "He didn't bother showing up at the creek."

"Oh, no, he's too busy working with some new quarter horses."

"At the stables?"

Jenna shook her gray head and wiped her hands on her flour-dusted apron. "I'm not sure. He took off for the stables but he said something about taking the horses over to the track."

Chase started for the door but paused and took a long swallow of his beer. "You've known him for a long time, haven't you?"

"Since we were kids," Jenna replied.

Leaning against the door, Chase looked directly at the plump woman with the unlined face and pink cheeks. Jenna Peterson was the only person on the whole damned Johnson spread that Chase felt he could trust. "And would you say he's trustworthy?"

She seemed surprised and turned quickly from the marble counter. "Oh, yes," she said. "When he was younger, while we were in school, he was straight as an arrow, don't you know?" She smiled as she stared out the kitchen window. "But that was years ago."

"What about now?"

"Still the same man...but—"

"But?"

"Oh, well, nothin' really. He's different, of course. But we all grew up. After school, I lost track of him, got married myself and had the kids. I didn't think much about Caleb, only what I heard from the town gossip mill. It wasn't much. But several years later, after his folks had passed away, I heard that he was marrying some girl from another town."

Chase's eyes grew sharp. "I didn't know he had a wife."

"Oh, he didn't. Seems this woman wouldn't marry him for some reason or another; no one really knows for sure. He came back here and threw himself into this farm, hell-bent on expanding it and making it the best in the state. Worked at it for years."

"So why the resort? Why is it so important to him?"

Jenna glanced at him with kind blue eyes. "You have to remember that Caleb hasn't got a family. No sons or grandsons to carry on his name. He needs something to be remembered by."

"So that's the purpose—immortality?"

"Maybe a little. Besides, a man has to do something to keep busy. Just 'cause you reach a certain age is no reason to curl up and die."

"I suppose not," Chase thought aloud, taking a long swallow of beer. "But, tell me, do you think that he would do anything…underhanded to get the resort going?"

"Illegal, you mean?"

Chase didn't answer.

"I doubt it."

"Not even bend a few rules?"

Jenna's countenance became stern. "You don't like him much, do you?"

Chase's brows drew together thoughtfully. "I don't think it's so much a question of liking the man; I'm just not sure I can trust him."

Jenna sighed and shook her head as she placed the top crust over the sugared apples in the pie pan. "All I know is that he's been a fair employer. And—" she paused in her work to look Chase straight in the eye "—you're special to him."

"I don't think so—"

Jenna waved off his thoughts. "I've seen him with a lot of men. He treats you different."

"Different? How?"

Jenna thought for a moment, trying to find just the right words. "Like you was kin," she finally said, nodding as if in agreement with her thoughts. "That's it. He treats you like he would a son, if he had one."

Chase experienced a strange tightening in his gut and he forced a smile. "Fortunately, I already had a father. He died a few years back, but I certainly don't need Johnson to fill his shoes."

"I don't think Caleb would want to try."

"And I don't think Caleb thinks of me as anything but a business partner," Chase said, taking another swallow of his beer and sauntering out the back door.

Flies and wasps were trapped in the hot back porch. They buzzed in frustration against the old screens as Chase passed through. He stopped to adjust the brim of his Stetson and walked out into the late afternoon sun.

Caleb was leaning over the top rail of a fence, staring out at the dry pasture where his herd of horses was grazing on the sun-parched grass.

Chase felt the anger ticking inside him like a time bomb. How much of Dani's story was true—that Caleb had done everything he could to run her off her land? And how much was just her imagination running wild? Did Caleb know about the drum of dioxin poisoning the water? Just how far would the old man go to achieve his ends? Stomach tight from reining in his anger, his jaw clenching rigidly, Chase approached the older man.

"We sure could use some more of that rain we got the other night," Caleb observed, spotting Chase.

Rain. The other night. Dani. "Weather service predicts another shower in the next couple of days."

"Good."

"How was the trip?"

"'Bout what I expected."

Chase put his foot on the bottom rail of the fence and tried to appear congenial. An actor he wasn't, but he could remain calm if he had to. And right now, he had to. Dani's future was on the line. *If he believed her.* Things just weren't black and white anymore, and gray never had been Chase's favorite color. "Sounds good," he remarked.

"Could've been better."

"Or worse."

"I s'pose." Caleb swatted at a fly and swore under his breath. "Damn things. Used to be able to get rid of them."

"But not anymore?"

Caleb grimaced. "It's a helluva lot tougher now."

"So what do you use to keep the insects and the foliage in control around here?" Chase asked, his eyes skimming the fields to watch the scampering foals kicking up their heels around their sedate dams. The mares stood in pairs, head to buttocks, flicking at flies with their tails and ears.

"Whatever is available." Caleb leaned back and eyed the younger man. "And whatever the government allows us to use. They're getting stickier all the time."

"No doubt about it. Used to be a time when you could use DDT or dioxin and no one cared," Chase said evenly, his gaze flicking from the grazing mares to Caleb and back again.

"Made ranchin' a helluva lot easier," Caleb agreed with a lazy smile.

"Ever use the stuff?" Chase asked.

"Sure. A lot. When it was legal. But that was a long time ago. Had to get rid of all of it."

"How'd you do that? Bury it?" Chase felt the tension in his muscles, but forced a calm expression, as if he were just making idle conversation.

Caleb's watery eyes narrowed but he shook his head. "Hell, no. Couldn't. Afraid it might seep out into the ground; get into the grass and then the food chain. Nope. I turned all mine in to the agriculture department. And let me tell you, it's been hell to keep the blackberries and tansy under control ever since." He slapped the rail and straightened, changing the course of the conversation. "So, tell me, how's it been goin' around here? Everything on schedule?"

"We're a little behind," Chase admitted, "but not much. Another couple of weeks and it'll be over."

"So you got through to Dani Summers?"

Chase grimaced. "No. I doubt if anyone can."

Laughing lewdly, Caleb agreed. "A regular spitfire, that woman." His eyes gleamed. "Come on, boy, don't tell me you haven't noticed."

"I noticed. She was the lady with the gun aimed at my gut, remember."

"Just a little scare tactic."

"Well, it worked. She scared the hell right out of me!" Chase took a swallow of his beer and tried to appear anything but involved with Dani Summers. It was hard not to think of her sparkling green-gray eyes and her tawny, sun-streaked hair falling to her waist.

"Bah! You wouldn't be a man if you weren't interested in a piece like that."

Rage flooded Chase's veins, and his blue eyes, when he turned them on Caleb, became ice cold. "Not my type."

"Not her husband's, either, I'd guess," Caleb drawled, noticing the muscle jump in Chase's jaw. The kid was a cool one, Caleb thought as he watched Chase standing in front of him, leaning over the fence, nursing a bottle of beer, looking as if he couldn't give one good god-damn about the conversation and yet listening to every detail. Caleb smiled to himself. Things were beginning to look up.

"Why don't you tell me about her old man," Chase suggested.

"Not much to tell. A bastard, the way I hear it. He sold his land to me and took off with the money and another woman, leaving Dani with a little kid and a sick mother." Caleb ran his rough fingers along the top rail. "Like I said, that woman's a helluva scrapper." He paused. "Reminds me of your ma, when she was a girl."

Chase ignored the remark. He didn't want to think about his mother and Caleb. Not now. "So you tried to get Dani Summers's husband to talk her into selling her farm to you."

Caleb shrugged his wide shoulders. "Business is business. And she would've been better off selling. She could've bought a little house in town, put some money in the bank and been able to take care of her kid proper-like."

"She's doing a good job with the kid."

"You met him?"

Chase's jaw thrust forward. "Once."

"A good kid?"

"Yeah. I'd say so."

"Hard for a single woman to handle a boy that age."

"Like I said, she seems to be doin' fine." Chase finished his beer and straightened. "She also told me that she was ready to sell off a parcel to you once, but you reneged."

"Wasn't enough land."

"But you'd agreed to it," Chase pointed out.

"Changed my mind," Caleb said defensively. "Just like I intend to change hers."

"By any means possible?"

"Within the law, boy," Caleb said. "Any means within the law." He eyed the empty brown bottle in Chase's hand. "Now, how about you comin' into the study and we'll have ourselves a real drink while you tell me how Grizzly Creek is comin' along? I plan to start building just as soon as all of the permits are approved, and I want that creek stocked and proved viable by the time the brochures go into print next summer."

"I said I'd be done within the month."

Caleb slapped him on the shoulder. "I know, I know. But I want to be sure that the trout survive and spawn, y'see. *And* we're not done until Dani Summers comes around. You'll have to work on her side of the fence, as well."

"It won't happen," Chase said.

"Sure it will. It just takes a little time." Caleb had begun walking to the house. He was a big, lumbering figure who strode with the authority of one who knew that his commands would be obeyed without question.

Chase gritted his teeth and followed, remembering the information he'd found in Caleb's study. He hesitated but then took off after the old man. For the time being, at least, he'd have to listen to all of Caleb's demands and pretend to follow them to a T. But just until he found out what made Caleb Johnson and Dani Summers tick.

DANI SHOVED THE pickup into gear and waved at Cody, but he didn't even notice. He and Shane were already playing catch with a basketball as they walked to the park to meet a few other friends for an impromptu game.

"You'll roast in this heat," Dani had warned, but Cody had smiled and waved off her fears.

"Better than playing in the snow and ice," he'd said, laughing as he'd tossed the ball to Shane.

"Okay. I'll pick you up in the morning," she'd said, but Shane's mother had insisted that she would bring Cody home the following day.

"So it looks like it's just me and you, right?" Dani scratched Runt behind his ears as she drove away from the Donahue's house.

Runt whined and stuck his head out the window.

"Benedict Arnold," Dani said with a laugh as she scratched the dog's back and drove through town to pick up groceries and supplies.

Once the pickup was loaded, she drove out of town, intending to return home. But at the corner of her property she hesitated, and rather than turning toward her house, she stopped and let Runt out. Once the dog had run up the lane, she drove north to the next tree-lined road, the long gravel drive leading to Caleb Johnson's farmhouse. She had business to settle with Johnson, and there was no time like the present to take care of it.

Her heart hammering nervously in her chest, she drove through the stately oaks and pines and parked her pickup between the barn and the house. With more determination than courage, she hopped out of the cab and strode around the house to pound on the front door.

Within minutes the door swung inward and Jenna Peterson, Caleb's cook and housekeeper, was standing in the expansive entry. She smiled at the sight of Dani.

"Dani! This *is* a surprise."

"Hi, Jenna," Dani greeted, trying to calm herself and be polite. "How've you been?"

"Can't complain. And yourself?"

"Good," Dani said automatically.

"And that boy of yours," Jenna said, stepping away from the door. "He's growin' like a weed. The spittin' image of his dad."

"You've seen Cody?"

"School pictures, last year. My youngest grandson is in the same class. Come in, come in. Can I get you something? Iced tea?"

Dani smiled at the older woman's hospitality and felt a little foolish. "No, thanks. I'd just like to see Caleb for a couple of minutes. Is he in?"

"You lucked out," Jenna said with a grin. Dani doubted it. "Caleb's in the study with Mr. McEnroe."

Dani's stomach tightened, but she managed to hide her case of nerves. "Good. I may as well kill two birds with one stone."

"Pardon?"

"It's nothing," Dani said with a smile. "I'd just like to talk to Mr. McEnroe as well."

"Wonderful!" Jenna walked to the double doors off the foyer and knocked softly before entering and telling the men that Dani had arrived.

"Always ready to have a neighborly chat," Caleb said loudly. Dani inwardly cringed. "Send her in."

As Jenna opened the door, Dani walked through. She looked around the room and saw Chase standing near the window, a drink in his hand, his shoulder leaned against the frame. "Afternoon," he drawled.

"Chase," she said. Her heart leaped at the sight of him, but her face was set with determination. Gritting her teeth but managing a slight nod in his direction, she finally turned her attention to Caleb.

The older man was seated behind the desk, his glasses perched on the end of his nose, his eyes assessing her every move. He'd half stood when she'd entered the room but now was sitting again.

"Well, Mrs. Summers," he said, leaning back in his chair and observing her over the rim of his glasses. "Can I get you a drink?"

"No, thanks."

Caleb grinned. "I see. Business as usual. That's what I admire about you, Dani, the way you always come straight to the point. Now, to what do we owe the honor?"

Dani stood directly before Caleb's desk. She couldn't see Chase, but she could feel his eyes boring into her back. Without flinching, she held the older man's gaze. "I just came to tell you that I don't want any of your hands on my land. And that includes Mr. McEnroe."

"Has there been a problem?" Caleb asked, feigning concern.

"On more than one occasion."

Caleb turned to Chase. "Nothing I heard about."

"You can cut the bull, Caleb. You know I was on Dani's land," Chase said before finishing his drink and setting it on the windowsill.

"I hadn't heard that she objected."

"Sure you did," Chase said calmly.

Dani took an uncertain step toward the desk, glanced at Chase who seemed to be watching her with amusement, and poked a finger onto the polished wood. "Then let me make myself perfectly clear. I don't want *any* of your associates near my land. As I told Mr. McEnroe, I'm willing to call the police, the FBI or the President—anyone I can to keep you off my place!" She was shaking with rage, but her eyes remained calm and fixed on Caleb Johnson.

Caleb spread his hands over the desk and lifted his shoulders. "Don't you think you're being a little melodramatic, Dani? After all, we are neighbors. Just calm down and I'll pour you a drink or a cup of tea. Jenna's baked a fresh apple pie and if I do say so myself, it's the best in the county."

"No, thanks." She turned on her heel, caught Chase's eye and strode toward the door.

"Dani—" Caleb's voice accosted her.

She turned slowly to face him.

"Let's not act like enemies, all right? You never know when you might need my help."

"Is that a threat?" she asked.

"Of course not. Just some neighborly advice. And, as for your land, it might be simpler for all of us if you just sold out to me."

Chase straightened. "For how much, Caleb?" he asked cynically, eyeing the older man.

"That's between Dani and me."

"Is it?" Chase walked over to a filing cabinet, withdrew a file and tossed an appraisal of Dani's land onto the desk. "Is that the figure you're talking about?"

Caleb's countenance changed. His face whitened. "Not quite that much—"

"I didn't think so," Chase muttered.

"Just who the hell do you think you are, going through my files?"

"Your partner," Chase said flatly as he walked out of the room, taking hold of Dani's arm and pulling her with him.

"What was that all about?" she asked.

"I did some digging today," he said. "And I'm not talking about the creek. Seems that Caleb might just be interested in your land for more than the resort."

"What do you mean?"

"I'll tell you later," Chase said, looking over his shoulder to see Caleb, still red-faced, sitting at his desk. "Now

I think you've made your point; you'd better leave before all hell breaks loose."

"I'm not afraid of Johnson," she said.

"Then maybe you'd better be." With a look of cold determination, Chase let go of her arm and inclined his head to her pickup. "Leave Johnson to me," he suggested.

"This isn't your fight—"

"Oh, but it is," Chase disagreed with a cynical smile. "More than you can guess."

CHASE'S ENIGMATIC WORDS were still echoing in Dani's ears when she finally got home. What was he doing, putting himself between Caleb and her? A thousand questions flitted through her mind as she put the groceries away and managed stacking the sack of grain in a corner of the barn. By the time she was done, she still had no answers but felt hot and gritty and in desperate need of a shower. She wiped the sweat from her forehead with her hand and felt the dirt streak her skin.

"This is certainly no life for a prima donna," she said to Runt as she headed inside.

The sun seemed hotter than it had been before the other night's rainshower. Though it was late in the afternoon, shimmering waves of heat distorted Dani's view of her acreage. She shaded her eyes and looked northwest, over the fence, to the banks of the creek on Caleb's side. There was no activity. All of the men seemed to have taken off early.

So what was Chase doing? she thought idly and then frowned when she remembered the confrontation with Caleb. She went inside and stayed under the cool shower longer than she needed. After washing her hair and wrapping it in a threadbare towel, she slipped into a cool summer sundress and went downstairs to make a pitcher of lemonade.

"It's too bad Cody isn't here to share this with me," she said to the dog, who perked up his ears, cocked his head and resumed whining at the door. "For Pete's sake, Runt, stop moping will ya? You're giving me a case of the blues."

After making the lemonade and watching the slices of lemon swirl in the glass pitcher, Dani poured herself a tall glass, pressed it against her forehead and closed her eyes. Already she was beginning to sweat.

She combed her hair and sat on the back porch sipping the cool liquid and thinking of Chase. She couldn't forget nearly making love to him at the creek, or the way he'd come to her defense at Caleb's house. But he'd said he was Johnson's partner, not hers. His loyalty was with Caleb Johnson—or was it? And what had he hoped to accomplish by taking soil and water samples from her land? *Evidence,* he'd said. But evidence against whom?

"Stop it," she said when the questions got too confusing. With a sigh, she tried to concentrate on a mystery novel she'd been reading long before Chase had stormed into her life, but the pages didn't hold her interest and it was hard to see in the gathering twilight.

Disgusted with herself, she tossed the book aside, continued rocking in the chair and watched a vibrant sunset as the sun settled behind the Rocky Mountains and the sky turned from vivid magenta to dark purple.

She wiped the perspiration from her neck and throat with a handkerchief and turned, gazing over the darkened fields to the north, to Caleb Johnson's property, to Chase…

CHAPTER SIX

CHASE WALKED BRISKLY around the stable yard, as if with each stride he could shake the rage that burned in his gut. He felt as if he were on a tightwire and that no matter which way he turned, he was going to fall off into the black abyss of the future.

With an explicit oath, he headed back to the house—to face his partner. *Partner.* The word stuck in his throat. He'd been a fool to accept Caleb's money in the first place and now he wondered just what his partner's intentions were.

Walking through the open door and into Caleb's study, he wasn't surprised to find the old man still sitting behind his desk, his face ruddy with alcohol, his blue eyes small and hard. A near empty bottle of Scotch sat on the corner of his desk and the glass he sipped from was full.

"Looks like I can't trust anything you say," Caleb growled in disgust. He took a long swallow of Scotch. Some of his anger had cooled, but his fertile mind was working fast. His fingers twitched nervously around his glass. "Just what the hell right do you have to snoop in my files?"

"As much right as you have to try and swindle Dani out of her land."

"Swindle?" Caleb sneered. "I just wanted a fair price."

"Do you call a hundred thousand under market fair?"

"That land's worthless."

"Not to you—or her." Chase's eyes cut through Caleb's anger. "She seems to think you've tried to sabotage her."

Caleb had the audacity to grin, as if Chase's anger amused him. "Sabotage? Don't tell me you believe her."

"I don't know what to believe."

"Sabotage," Caleb snorted again, his lips twisting sarcastically. "Sounds like somethin' she'd say. I know she's had a run of bad luck, but I don't see how she can blame me."

Chase ran his fingers through his hair, stretched his tense shoulders and sighed. "I'd just like to know where you get off trying to buy off everyone who gets in your way!"

"Business is business," Caleb retorted, refilling his glass. "Maybe someday you'll learn." He pointed a condemning finger at the younger man. "And you'd better hope it's soon, before a traitor like Eric Conway tries to steal all of your business again. He almost did it once before and I might not be around to bail you out again."

Chase didn't flinch even though the thought of Eric Conway's betrayal still bothered him. "I didn't ask for your help."

"But you certainly took it, didn't you? And now you've got to help me get the Hawthorne place."

"I don't see how that's possible."

"Convince Dani. There must be a way to get to her."

"Forget it." Chase reached onto the windowsill and grabbed his hat. With a grimace, he forced the old felt Stetson onto his head.

Caleb snorted when he saw the determined set of Chase's jaw. "Going somewhere?" he mocked.

"Out." Chase reached for the door but the old man's voice stopped him.

"To find Dani Summers?"

Chase hesitated. "Weren't you the one who suggested I get to know her better—use my imagination?"

Caleb's eyes became slits. "She really got to you, didn't she? So much in fact that you're willing to hack off your nose to spite your face."

Chase lifted his chin a fraction and regarded Caleb with cold eyes. "Don't wait up."

Taking a sip from the drink he was cradling in his hands, Caleb said, "I wasn't planning on it. I was waiting to hear just how you think you can handle Dani Summers."

"Handle her?" Chase repeated, his back stiffening. "Look, not that it's your business, but as far as I'm concerned I'm not dealing with Dani about her land. Not anymore. Face it, Johnson, the lady doesn't want to sell. Not you, or me, or anyone else on God's green earth can get her to change her mind!"

With the intention of letting Caleb stew in his own juices, Chase stormed to the door of the study.

Instead of ranting and raving as Chase had expected, Caleb just smiled smugly to himself and said in a voice loud enough so that Chase would hear, "Well, we'll just have to see about that, won't we?"

Chase walked out of the house and slammed the door behind him. God, he'd had enough of Caleb Johnson to last him a lifetime, he thought as he jumped into his Jeep.

Through the open window, Caleb watched as Chase ground the gears of his sorry-looking vehicle and roared down the tree-lined lane. Then Caleb put on his reading glasses and searched for a telephone number he'd written on a scrap of paper only two days before. Finding the hastily scratched note, he reached for the phone and dialed, looking distractedly at the cloud of dust Chase was leaving behind him.

Angry with Chase, but knowing he still held the trump card, Caleb balanced the receiver between his ear and shoulder, poured himself another stiff shot and waited impatiently as the long-distance call connected.

CALEB'S OMINOUS THREAT hung in the hot summer air and nagged Chase as he drove away from Johnson's spread. What had the old man meant? His mouth compressed tightly and he squinted through the dust and grime on the windshield and wondered what the devil Caleb was up to. The sun had already set and lavender shadows had begun to stretch over the farmland, but Chase was oblivious to the beauty of the surrounding countryside. His fingers were coiled tightly around the steering wheel and his shoulder muscles were bunched, as if he were spoiling for a fight.

"Relax," he told himself as he switched on the lights and radio and tried to think of anything but Johnson's greed or Dani's precarious position. "Caleb couldn't have anything to hold over Dani." But he couldn't forget the glint of satisfaction in Caleb's pale eyes or the older man's knowing smile. "Don't let him get to you," he told himself.

He drove recklessly toward Martinville and the noisy raucous anonymity of Yukon Jack's. All he needed was a couple of beers, some loud music and the smoky oblivion that the bar offered so that he could forget about Caleb Johnson, Summer Ridge and Dani Summers.

However, forgetting about Dani wasn't all that easy. As some of his anger dissipated and he eased up on the throttle, his thoughts swirled back to her. Now that Chase knew that Caleb had tried to buy the Hawthorne place for much less than it was worth, he was furious.

And so was Caleb. Chase knew that the old man had wanted to tear him apart after the confrontation with Dani in Johnson's study. Caleb had been just sly enough to rein in his temper and that worried Chase—a lot. Because whether he liked the fact or not, his concern wasn't for himself, or his company. Not any longer. Right now, he was worried sick about Dani.

Dani.

Just at the thought of her, unwelcome emotions surfaced and the image of making love to her burned in his brain. In his mind's eye he saw her skein of honey-brown hair, loose and wild in carefree sun-kissed curls, her face flushed with desire, her green-gray eyes warm with excitement and longing.

"Get a hold of yourself," he said, stepping on the gas again and heading into town. "Forget her."

He drove straight to the bar, parked the Jeep, stuffed his keys into his pocket and walked into the dimly lit room, where he took a table in the corner and ordered a beer. He sat alone, ignoring speculative glances from some of the women patrons, and nursed his beer while pretending interest in a dull game of pool.

The conversation around him didn't spark his interest until he overheard one brawny, bearded man—one of the two men shooting pool—trying to convince his friend that Caleb Johnson's Summer Ridge was the best thing that had happened to Martinville in years.

Chase heard only snatches of the conversation over the clink of bottles, click of billiard balls and spurts of laughter.

"Yep. Think of the value of your old man's farm," the bearded man was saying. "…double in price within the year. Same with the price of mine. A few years ago, I couldn't give that rock pile away. Now, thanks to Johnson, it's worth a fortune!" He grinned, showing off a gap in his teeth, while he chalked his cue. "No more cleaning barns and fixin' fence for me, no-siree-boy. I plan on spendin' my time in the Bahamas countin' my money!"

His friend laughed and offered a quiet reply that Chase couldn't hear.

"Oh, she'll sell, all right," the brawny man insisted, signaling to the barkeep for another beer and finally getting off his shot. "Six ball in the corner pocket." He waited until the ball had rolled across the green felt into the appropriate hole. "The way I see it, Dani hasn't got much of a choice..."

Chase's every muscle tensed, but he continued to lean back in his chair and eye the two men from beneath the brim of his hat.

"...no one's yet managed to stop Johnson. Remember Red Haines? He fought Johnson, too, and look what happened. One minute Red's all set to fight the zoning commission and what-have-you, insisting that Johnson's a crook, and the next thing ya know, he's changed his tune. If ya ask me, Red was just holdin' out for more money— same as Dani Summers...nine ball in the side—"

Chase scraped his chair back just as the ball banked away from the pocket.

"Damn!"

"So you think Dani's just waitin' for a better price," the skinny friend prodded as he eyed his shot.

"'Course she will. She always was a smart one, y'know. She'll come around to Johnson's way of thinking, you wait and see. And then watch out!"

His teeth clenched, Chase left some change on the bar and walked outside, taking in the clear night air. As he walked back to his Jeep he uncurled his fists and relaxed the muscles that had tightened while he had listened to the conversation at Yukon Jack's.

"You're losing your grip, old boy," he told himself as

he drove out of town. When he reached the rutted lane leading to Dani's house, he slowed the Jeep and, with a curse at himself, yanked on the wheel at the last minute. The wheels slid a little on the sparse gravel, but Chase held the Jeep steady up the rutted lane to Dani's house.

DANI WAS STILL sitting on the back porch when the sound of an engine cut through the night, disturbing the gentle drone of insects. Her heart started to pound expectantly when she realized the engine probably belonged to Chase's rig and that he was driving up the lane toward the house. She took the final swallow from her glass just as she heard the engine die.

Please, Chase, go away, she prayed, though her pulse raced with excitement. She heard him knock loudly on the front door of the cabin. Steadying herself, she stood and walked around to the front of the house.

He was standing under the porch light. His face was taut, his lean features harsh under the soft glow from the solitary lamp. His shirt sleeves were rolled up his arms and he held his hat in one hand.

"You don't have to wake the neighbors," she said, climbing the two steps to the porch.

"Neighbors?" His gaze cut across the ghostly fields. In the distance, lights winked from houses positioned along the main highway. Somewhat closer, the lights from Caleb Johnson's large house burned in the darkness. Chase's lips drew together in a thin, determined line. "Impossible."

"Maybe," she agreed, leaning one shoulder against the house.

"And if you're talking about Caleb, I don't really give a damn if I wake him or not. Besides, he'll probably drink himself to death before the night is over."

"I don't suppose he's too happy with what happened this afternoon," Dani observed.

"I'd say he'd like to kill me," Chase said. "He seems to think I owe him my life."

"Maybe you do," she said gently. "Two hundred thousand dollars is nothing to sniff at."

One corner of his mouth lifted sardonically. "I know you probably won't believe this, but I can't be bought."

"Does Caleb know it?"

"Not yet."

Dani sighed and ran her fingers through her long hair. "Don't let him know it. Otherwise, you'll find yourself in a world of hurt."

"Like you?"

"I do okay."

He chuckled and as he gazed into her eyes he felt as if he'd finally come home after a long hard-fought battle. "Yep," he agreed. "I suppose you do."

"And you?"

"I can handle myself."

"Even with Caleb?"

"Especially with Caleb."

"I hope so," she said, glancing anxiously away.

He offered her a lazy smile. "Do you?"

Dani lifted a shoulder and the strap of her sundress slipped. "I don't want anyone to get caught in Caleb Johnson's trap."

"Including me?"

"Yes. Including you," she admitted honestly.

"Then we're friends?"

"Of a sort, I suppose. I don't really know...but..."

"But what?"

"But sometimes I'd like to think so," she admitted, adjusting the wayward piece of fabric.

Chase reached forward and helped her place the strap back on her shoulder. His fingers lingered against her neck and Dani shivered unexpectedly.

"What about now?" he asked. His expression became less cynical and his eyes darkened as he stared at her. "Are we friends now?"

Nervously she lifted a brow and then swallowed. "You mean, because of this afternoon, when you came rushing to my defense against Caleb?" She paused and bit her lower lip pensively. "Well, yes, I guess I'd have to say that *tonight* we're definitely friends."

His gaze softened and he offered her his most engaging smile. "Then why aren't you inviting me inside?"

"Good question. And one that I don't have a good answer for," she admitted, taking a step backward. "Probably because I'm not sure it would be such a good idea to be alone with you."

"Why not?"

"I thought we settled 'why not' at the creek...and again, in Caleb's house."

Chase let out a sigh and rolled his eyes heavenward. "And just two hours ago, I thought I'd never darken your doorstep again. But here I am."

"Why?"

"Maybe to apologize," he said thoughtfully, his voice as low and seductive as the cool breeze blowing from the west.

"And maybe to try and wear me down so that I'll sell my land to Caleb."

"Do you really believe that? After this afternoon in Johnson's study? If you don't remember who was on that white charger—"

She shook her head and laughed. The lamplight caught in the long, silken strands of her hair, turning the soft brown to gold. "Like I said, I really don't know what to believe. Not anymore. But I've got to hand it to you, McEnroe, you don't give up easily."

"Not when something is important." He lifted his hand to touch the bottom of her chin, forcing her gaze to meet his.

She swallowed against the dryness settling in her throat. "And this is?" she asked. "Is it that important to get your company back?"

His finger slid sensually down her neck to rest on her shoulder, near the strap of her sundress. "It was," he admitted, his eyes following the path of his finger. "But I'm afraid it's gone further than that."

"Oh?"

"Much further."

"What's that supposed to mean?"

His eyes centered on her lips. "This whole mess is driving me out of my mind. And it isn't just my business anymore. Hell, I'm not sure I really even give a damn about it, not after all the trouble I've had with Johnson. But you. You're something else again. What was important to me is all confused and the damnedest thing is that all I can think about is you. And me. Together."

She licked her lips and waited, her heart hammering so loudly it drowned the other sounds of the night.

"*You're* what's important to me. *You*, Dani."

Hating herself for asking, she took a step backward to break the intimacy of the moment and whispered, "Why, Chase?" Her voice was raspy with emotion. "*Why* am I important? So that you can get your company back? So that you can get your job with Caleb completed and go back to Idaho?" She inched backward until she felt the rough siding of the house.

"If only things were so simple." He ran one hand over

his face and leaned his back against the screen door as he stared into the night. Shoving his hands into the front pockets of his jeans, he rotated his head between tense shoulders. "Everything was so cut and dried a few weeks ago. Black and white. No gray. Now everything's a mess." He looked at her and saw the skepticism in her gaze. "I just know that nothing's been the same since I met you."

"Better or worse?"

His smile was easy, lazily stretching over his tanned skin. "A little of both maybe."

"It couldn't be all that bad because you're still here, when I told Caleb I didn't want any of his men on my land."

Chase ran a tired hand over his chin. "I'm not one of 'his men.' If I were, I wouldn't have saved your neck today."

Dani's chin jutted forward a bit. "Saved my neck?" she repeated. "I was doing fine—"

"You were losing control." Chase moved and sat on the railing of the porch, while his gaze cut across the fields to the hill on which the Johnson house stood. "Caleb had you just where he wanted you and—"

"And?" she asked, defiance sparking in her eyes.

He glanced back at her. "—and you've got a gorgeous neck."

"You're changing the subject."

"No, I'm not."

"Then you're being an arrogant, chauvinistic male." But she couldn't help but grin, exposing the hint of a dimple.

"I'm being honest. And that kind of insult went out in the seventies."

"You are, without exception, the most frustrating man I've ever met."

"I hope so, lady," he whispered, his eyes lingering on her mouth. Reaching forward, he placed his hands on either side of her waist and drew her nearer so that she stood facing him, close enough to feel the heat from his body, smell the liquor on his breath, see the shadows in his eyes.

She had to swallow and lick her suddenly dry lips. "So, why are you here?"

He shrugged, but his gaze never left her face. "I thought maybe I'd take you and Cody to dinner. You know, as sort of a peace offering for trespassing on your land earlier in the day."

"Cody's at a friend's for the night."

"Too bad." But his grin widened.

"I can see you're heartbroken," she mocked.

"Don't get me wrong, I like your son…but I can't knock the chance to be alone with you. Since Cody's already gone, how about just you and me?" He reached up and brushed a wayward strand of hair from her cheek. "Maybe it's time we got to know a little more about each other."

"I thought you said that you were partners with Caleb."

Chase frowned. "I still am. Whether I want to be or not. Does that brand me?"

She wanted to smile but couldn't. "In more ways than one, I'm afraid."

"How about what happened at Caleb's house this afternoon?"

She tried to pull away from him, but his fingers closed tightly over her waist. "I'm not sure I understand what happened."

"I found out that Caleb tried to cheat you."

"Is that the evidence you were talking about at the creek," she said and then stopped. "No, it was the water samples. What do they have to do with Caleb trying to buy out my property?"

"I wish I knew," he admitted, trying to put together the pieces of the strange puzzle. "Maybe Caleb is just playing games."

"With my water?"

Chase's eyes grew cold. "Believe me, what's happening with your water isn't a game," he said. The lines around his mouth deepened into sharp grooves. *Unless it was a deadly game, and if it was, Caleb would have more than Summer Ridge to worry about.....*

"Chase..." Dani's brow was puckered, her eyes concerned. "What is it? There's something you're not telling me..."

Deciding that worrying her needlessly would cause more harm than good, Chase tried to forget his suspicions, at least for the night. He offered Dani a lopsided grin and touched his nose to hers. "There's a lot I haven't told you," he said. "And a lot you haven't told me. Let's discuss everything over dinner."

"I don't know—"

"Afraid to fraternize with the enemy?"

She lifted a shoulder and grinned. "Something like that."

"Just once," he said slowly, his eyes delving into hers, "I want you to let all your defenses down. Okay? Forget that I have anything to do with Caleb Johnson or that Johnson even exists."

"That's a pretty tall order."

"Come on, Dani. Just take me at face value."

She looked at the lines of honesty creasing his skin near the corners of his eyes and mouth. She studied the hard but clean angles of his face. And she stared into his eyes. Dear God, those vivid blue eyes would be her downfall; they seemed to cut clear to her soul. On looks alone, she couldn't doubt him, and for the first time since she'd met him, she didn't try.

"All right," she whispered. "I'll give it a shot."

He laughed, a warm sound that echoed through the still night.

"Bad choice of words," she admitted, her eyes crinkling at the corners and her lips lifting into a graceful smile that Chase found irresistible.

"I'll forgive you," he said, brushing his lips against hers with a tenderness that made her heart ache. She felt his fingers grip her waist, warming her skin through the light fabric of her dress, leaving soft impressions on her flesh.

"You'll forgive me," she retorted, trying to sound and feel offended when all she could concentrate on was the warmth of his lips against hers, the feel of his hands as they circled her and pressed against her naked back, the sound of her heart thundering in her chest.

"If you beg me—"

"Chase McEnroe!" she said, lifting her head. But any further arguments were quickly stilled by the sweet pressure of his mouth on hers and the wet feel of his tongue touching hers, darting into and stroking the inside of her mouth and destroying any thoughts of breaking the embrace. It had been so long since she'd been wanted by a man, so long since she'd wanted to be with one. And this man, damn him, was so very special.

She felt the strap of her dress fall again and then the heat of Chase's lips as he touched her neck and shoulders, kissing her exposed skin and the top of her breast. Legs trembling, she leaned back against the post, lost in his seductive power.

One of his hands splayed against the firm muscles of her back and the other came forward, reaching up to claim one breast and touch the smooth skin rounding softly over the top of her dress.

Groaning, he slid lower. His tongue was rough and warm, leaving dewy impressions on her dress as he knelt and kissed her cotton-draped torso, burying his face in the smell and feel of her. Caught in the folds of her skirt, he captured the rounded swell of her buttocks and pulled her urgently forward.

His breath was warm and it fanned the wanton fires of desire in her blood. He held her close, her abdomen positioned near his face. Her hair fell down to her hips, brushing against the back of his hand. She struggled, but not to break away from him, only from her own heated fantasies of making love to him all night long.

"I want you," he whispered into the dress, his breath permeating the soft cloth and burning against her flesh, turning her insides liquid. "And you want me—you can't deny it."

"Wanting isn't enough," she whispered.

Standing, but still holding her close, he shifted against her, pressing her against the post, letting her feel the hard need rising within him while the weathered wood cooled her back. His eyes were dark and glazed, his fingers twining in the golden strands of her hair.

"I wish I'd never met you," he admitted, hating himself for his need to bare his soul. "Because you've been driving me out of my mind. I've never wanted a woman, any woman, the way I want you. I know this is crazy, but I can't fight it any longer."

She tried to reply, but couldn't find her voice. The thick night air grew tense.

"Tell me no," he whispered, kissing her lips and letting his hand tug on the strap of her dress, pulling the ribbon of fabric still lower until her breast was free and the soft white mound with the dark nipple protruded forward, eager for his touch.

She reached up, covering herself with one hand, and he placed his larger hand over hers, gently kneading the soft, warm flesh. A warm glow started burning deep within her as he clasped her wrist and forced the hand away, baring her skin to the moonlit night. "You can't hide from me," he said, tracing the point of her nipple with the finger of his free hand. "And you don't want to."

"It's just that I...I don't know what I want." Deep within her, an ache had begun to throb, destroying her rational thought.

"Let me love you."

"Oh, Chase— Oh, God," she whispered as he bent forward and kissed the point of her breast, teasing it lightly with his lips, wetting it and letting it cool in the still night air.

Dani was dizzy with desire, her knees threatened to collapse beneath her, but she managed to claim one last doubt. "I...I just can't forget about Caleb."

Chase stiffened, his eyes sparkling as they delved into hers. "Caleb has nothing to do with this."

"But...but today, by the creek. I saw your reaction. I know that Caleb suggested that you..."

"The hell with Caleb Johnson," he swore, his eyes blazing. "If you believe anything on this earth, Dani, you've got to believe that what's happening between you and me had nothing, *nothing* to do with Johnson or his damned resort. I didn't want to fall in love with you, God knows I hate myself for it, but I can't deny it either."

Before she could protest, he captured her parted lips with his mouth, his arms surrounding her possessively, his tongue searching her mouth for its mate. Without thinking, she molded herself against him, felt the heat of his body surround her and knew that tonight she was his and his alone!

He picked her up and carried her inside the dark house, letting the screen door slam shut behind him.

Dani couldn't stop returning the fever of his kisses. Even when he laid her on the worn rug near the fireplace, she clung to him, almost desperate for the comfort and warmth of his body next to hers. She didn't cry out when he found the zipper of her sundress and slowly slid the dress off her body, easing the soft cotton fabric over her breasts, hips and down her legs.

Pale light from a crescent moon and a few winking stars filtered through the open windows. It was just enough illumination to allow her to see the shadowed contours of his face, to read the passion in his slumberous eyes.

She was cool for a moment, the sultry summer air drying the perspiration clinging to her skin. But as Chase slipped the dress past her ankles and began kissing her bare legs, moving upward with his lips, caressing the smooth skin of her hips and abdomen as he gently pulled her tighter against him, the yearning within her ignited to sparks of desire, long dead but now white hot.

When she was lying beside him, pressed hard against his body, he struggled out of his shirt and cast it aside and then kicked off his jeans. He began rubbing the length of his sinewy body over hers, letting her feel the strength of his corded muscles, the power of his raw masculinity, the smooth texture of his flesh against hers.

She touched him hesitantly at first, but when he moaned against her hair, she couldn't stop herself from tracing the firm line of his muscles with her fingers, and she felt him suck in his breath when she circled his flat, hardened nipple.

"You have no idea what you do to me," he groaned as he rolled atop of her, holding her face between his hands as he slowly parted her legs and moved gently, watching as he embraced her, dipping his head to touch his mouth to hers as he found her.

She felt the softness of his lips on hers, the gentle warmth of his fingers molding her breasts and the heart-stopping ecstasy of union when he entered her. Her heart was hammering expectantly, her breath shallow and tight as he moved, slowly at first and then more quickly when she responded, holding him close, her fingers digging into the hard muscles of his back, her voice whispering his name over and over as her blood ran in hot rivulets through her veins.

She felt warm and loved and whole and the joy in her heart increased with the tempo of his lovemaking until she felt she couldn't breathe, couldn't speak, couldn't do anything but quiver in the warmth and desire controlling her mind and body.

She closed her eyes in that final moment when both their bodies released the tension that had built between them for weeks. She cried his name and quaked with an inner, rocking explosion that caused a thousand shooting stars to burst inside her head. Tears of joy and relief filled her eyes when the weight of his body fell against her, his flat chest crushing her breasts, his belabored breathing whispering against her ears and the pounding of his heart echoing the rapid thunder of hers.

"Oh, God, Dani," he murmured at length, gazing into her eyes and cradling her small face in his large, rough hands. "What are we going to do?"

"I don't know." She brushed his golden hair off his brow, smoothing the deep furrow lining his forehead.

Slowly, through the haze of afterglow, her mind began to clear. "We'll have to go on as we have, I suppose."

"I can't." He saw the tears standing in her eyes and kissed them as he rolled onto the shabby carpet and wrapped his arms lovingly around her.

"We don't have a choice."

"There are always choices," he whispered.

"Chase—"

"Shh." He placed a finger to her lips. "For just this once, don't argue with me."

His gaze slid down her body, and he noted the sheen of perspiration on her skin, the soft bend of her waist, her rounded hips and slim legs. "You're an incredibly beautiful woman."

Balancing on one elbow, she laughed, brushing aside her remaining tears and tossing her hair away from her face. Even in the darkness, the silken strands shimmered gold. Chase reached forward and touched a wayward curl that fell across Dani's shoulder and brushed across the tip of her nipple.

"Lady Godiva," he whispered, and Dani laughed again.

"I don't think so. Besides, she was more than a little notorious."

"So are you."

"Me?" She shook her head and Chase was mesmerized by the tousled honey-gold curls sweeping over her breasts. "You've got the wrong lady."

"Do I?" His teeth flashed in the darkness and he traced the round edge of her nipple with his finger, watching as the dark peak stiffened. "I hope not. I hope to God not."

Then he bent forward and circled her nipple with his tongue and Dani felt shivers of delight dart up her spine. "Chase…please…I don't think—"

"Don't think." He kissed her again; gently at first and

then harder and with a hungry, burning passion that surprised even him. It was as if he couldn't get enough of her, as if he had to claim her as his own, brand her with his mark.

Deftly he lifted her to her feet and then into the air, carrying her up the stairs, holding her body against his and pausing only slightly at Cody's room before walking down the hall to her bedroom and placing her on the old four-poster. The springs squeaked, the mattress sagged and the old hand-pieced quilt her grandmother had made for her slid off the bed. But Dani didn't notice. She was concerned only with Chase and giving and receiving the warm comfort he offered.

He rolled over her and parted her legs with his and she welcomed him again, offering herself eagerly and never once thinking that their lovemaking was for only one night.

DANI WOKE WITH the dawn. Sunlight was streaming through the open window, birds were chirping merrily and the cattle were already bawling for breakfast.

Chase was still asleep. Sprawled over three-quarters of the bed, with one tanned arm draped possessively across Dani's breasts, he snored against the pillow.

She watched him quietly, noticing the way his blond hair fell across his forehead, how his dark lashes rested over his angular cheeks, and how his relaxed back and shoulder muscles rose and fell with his steady breathing.

Her heart swelled at the sight of him and she had to tell herself that what had happened only hours before could never be repeated. No matter how right making love to Chase had felt, she still couldn't trust him. One foolish night could be forgiven, another would be suicidal because the closer she got to Chase, the closer she wanted to get.

"It would be so easy to love you," she whispered, kissing him on the forehead before lifting his arm and slowly sliding out of the bed. "Too easy. Too convenient." *And Caleb Johnson was probably banking on the fact that Dani would fall for Chase.*

Determination clenching her jaw, she pulled clean clothes from her bureau, glanced in the mirror to assure herself that Chase was still sleeping soundly, and after tying her hair back, slipped into jeans and a T-shirt.

Then, before her wayward mind could convince her to crawl back into bed with Chase, she hurried out of the room and down the stairs. She'd just about made it to the kitchen when she saw the pile of discarded clothes lying on the floor. Her sundress and Chase's jeans were wrinkled and piled negligently together.

"Oh, Dani, how could you have been such a fool?" she wondered aloud, rolling her eyes to the ceiling and the room overhead where Chase was sleeping peacefully. "You can't fall in love with him, you just can't!" She picked up the clothes and folded them, frowning at the wrinkles in her sundress and remembering all too vividly how the soft material had been crushed.

She hurried outside. It was early. The air was still crisp and cool and she went through her morning chores by rote, her thoughts not on feeding the cattle and horses or watering the garden, or even on petting Runt, though she managed to do all those things and more. Her mind was with the man in her room, the man she'd spent the night with: Caleb Johnson's partner.

Daylight made things so much clearer. "You're doing everything imaginable to get hurt," she chastised herself once she was inside the barn and the scent of dust and hay filled her nostrils. Her eyes adjusted to the dim interior and she looked around it lovingly. Old bridles, saddles and blankets were hung on the wall or sat on sawhorses in the corner. Huge bins of wheat and corn were still nearly overflowing, and the cattle and horses were shifting restlessly on the other side of the manger, chewing noisily, or indignantly stomping their feet or flicking their ears at the ever-present flies.

"God, I love this place," Dani whispered. "How can I ever give it up?" Slumping onto a broken bale of hay, she took off her gloves and set them on an old barrel where she kept her oats.

"Regrets?" Chase's voice was clear and loud.

Dani nearly jumped out of her skin. Heart pounding, she looked up and saw Chase lounging against the barn door, his arms folded over his chest, the bright morning sunlight at his back. His blue eyes looked deep into hers.

"A few, I guess," she admitted, standing nervously and dusting her hands together.

"I thought we got over that hurdle last night."

"Last night…" To her embarrassment she blushed. "Look, Chase, I—I'm not a prude, not really. But neither am I the type of woman who sleeps with men I barely know."

"You know me."

"That's the problem; I don't. I don't know a damned thing about you! Oh, sure, I know that you own a company and you're Caleb Johnson's partner and you owe him a bundle of money, and he knew your mother way-back-when, but that's about it." All her insecurities came right to the surface. "I don't know anything else. You could be married with a wife and six kids."

"I'm not married and I don't have any children." He pushed his hair out of his eyes and shook his head. "But you knew that, didn't you? Certainly you know enough about me to realize that I wouldn't be here if I had a family."

"What I know is that you're here and you're Caleb's partner."

He let out a long, tired sigh.

"Actually," she said, leaning over the top of the manger and scratching a two-year-old heifer between the eyes. The cow jerked her head upward and Dani took her hand away, leaning on it instead. "You're here *because* you're in business with Caleb."

Anger pinched the corners of his mouth. "I'm in Martinville because of Caleb, yes. And I want to work the creek because of him." He started advancing upon her. "But being here, with you, has nothing to do with Johnson. I'm here because I want to be with you; because for a reason I don't understand, I'm compelled to be here."

He didn't stop until he'd reached her and once there he placed his arms around her waist. Dani knew that she had to break free or she'd be lost to him, but when she tried to struggle, his arms tightened and he had the audacity to smile. "Tell me you didn't want last night to happen."

"I didn't."

He kissed her slowly, lazily. "Tell me you regret it."

Warmth began to spread throughout her body. "I—I regret it," she whispered.

Chase's eyes centered on her racing pulse, visible in the hollow of her throat. "Tell me it will never happen again."

"It won't…oh, Chase…please, don't," she said, but couldn't help sighing against him when his hands slid under her T-shirt and splayed familiarly against the muscles of her back. She trembled at his touch and her mouth parted expectantly as he kissed her.

"Tell me you don't love me," he prodded.

"I don't even know you."

The hands tightened. "Say it then."

"I don't...I don't love you."

"And you're a liar." His fingers began to move sensually against her skin and he lifted his head to stare into the uncertainty in her eyes.

"Chase—" She tried to push against his chest but his next words stopped her cold.

"I love you, Dani. It's as simple as that. I love you and I don't know what the hell to do about it. My instincts tell me I should run, just like yours tell you to, but I can't."

She swallowed and tried to stop the thundering of her heart and her rapidly racing pulse.

"Dani, I want you to marry me."

CHAPTER SEVEN

DANI BIT BACK the easy answer because she knew that marrying Chase would be a mistake, possibly the biggest mistake of her life.

"This isn't the eighteen hundreds, you know," she said quietly. "You don't have to make an honest woman of me just because of last night."

His lips thinned as he stepped nearer and touched her shoulders. "I want you to marry me," he repeated, stroking her cheek. "I don't have any ulterior motives and this has nothing to do with Caleb, your creek or guilt about last night." His sky-blue gaze caressed her face. "I'm thirty-four years old and I want you for my wife. Is that so hard to believe?"

"In light of the circumstances—"

"The hell with the circumstances! Marry me, Dani."

Her heart was beating rapidly in her chest and all of her irrational female emotions were screaming inside her head, *Yes, yes, I'll marry you.* "I—I'd like to," she whispered. "But there's so much to consider."

"Such as?"

"Oh, Chase—"

"Such as?"

Her lips compressing, she pushed her hair out of her eyes. "Such as Cody, for one thing."

"I'll adopt him."

"Just like that?"

Chase muttered to himself and then shook his head.

"Of course not. It will take time. He doesn't much trust me yet."

"I wonder why," she taunted. "It couldn't be because you're Johnson's partner, or that you keep trespassing on my land, or that you always seem to be getting into fights with me, could it?"

Chase pinched the bridge of his nose. "I'll work things out with Cody. Now, give me another reason."

Her hazel eyes narrowed. "Okay. What about the fact that you live in Idaho and my life is here, on this farm?"

"For as long as you own it, you mean."

"Okay, there's another point. And a big one. *Caleb. And Summer Ridge.* The creek. It's the whole damned mess, the reason you're here in the first place. You're Caleb's partner. You can't get out of that, not until you convince me to sell my property to him, right?"

He lifted a shoulder. "Essentially."

"Then I'd say we have some pretty hard bridges to cross before we even talk about marriage."

He didn't seem convinced, but rammed his fists into his pockets. His thick brows pulled into an angry scowl. "Okay, Dani, we'll play it your way for now. But just answer one question."

"If I can," she agreed.

"Do you love me?"

The question hung in the air. She swallowed back the thick knot in her throat. "I don't know," she whispered, thinking back to the love she'd shared with Blake and how fragile it had been. Her feelings were strong for Chase, very strong, but to label them love? "I—I think it would be very easy to love you…"

"But you won't let yourself," he said flatly.

"I can't. Not yet." She cleared her throat and held up her hand, as if she could make him understand. "If things were different; if Caleb weren't trying to manipulate me, if you weren't his partner and if Cody…were more secure in his relationship with his father, I think I would fall in love with you very easily."

"A lot of ifs and none of them can be changed." He kicked at a bale of hay and then dropped onto it as he reached for a piece of straw and twirled it between his fingers. "You know what I think?"

"I'm not sure I want to."

"I think you're afraid, Dani. Afraid to fall in love, afraid to trust, afraid to feel." He studied the dry piece of straw before looking up at her. "I think your husband hurt you deeper than you want to admit and so you avoid any relationship with strings attached."

Her eyes clouded. "Then I would never have let you into my house last night," she whispered. "'Cause I've never met a man with more strings tied around him than you've got!"

Chase's head snapped upward but before he could reply, she marched out of the barn and up the short rise to the house. Kicking off her boots, she strode into the kitchen and poured herself a strong cup of coffee. Sitting at the table, she was angrily looking through the window and across the fields when she heard Chase enter.

"There's coffee in the pot," she said, glancing at him before looking out the window again.

"Thanks." He poured a cup, took a long swallow, turned a chair around and straddled it while his eyes were focused on Dani. "I'm sorry," he said gently.

"Don't be."

"I said some things I shouldn't have."

"No…it's all right," she said, thinking how close he'd come to the truth. She had been running from men, avoiding them, afraid of being hurt again. Blake's betrayal had cut deep. In some ways both she and Cody were still bleeding.

"You want to talk about it?"

She lifted her shoulder and blew across the hot coffee. "I don't think so."

"Maybe I can help." He reached across the table and took her hand in his. The tears she'd fought all morning formed in her eyes. "I do care about you," he whispered. "More than I want to. Dani, just believe me: I love you."

"If only it were that simple," she said, her voice catching. Brushing aside her tears, she slowly withdrew her hand from his. "How about some breakfast?" she asked, hoping to lighten the thickening atmosphere in the room. "Ham and eggs?"

"Sounds great." He leaned across the back of the chair and smiled at her, a warm, lazy grin that stretched across his face and stole into her heart. "And I still owe you dinner. How about tonight?"

"Tonight? Cody will be home."

"He's welcome, too."

"I'll think about it," Dani said. Finishing her coffee, she got up from the table, took a few things from the refrigerator and pulled a cast-iron skillet from the cupboards. She cut thick slices of ham and slipped them into the fry pan. As she made breakfast, she was aware that Chase was silently sipping his coffee and watching her.

"The newspaper's in the box," she offered.

"Later. Right now I'm enjoying the view."

"That sounds like a line, cowboy," she remarked, looking over her shoulder but laughing nonetheless.

"It was."

"At least you're honest—" she said and dropped the egg she was cracking onto the floor. "Damn!"

"I've got it." Chase got out of his chair, grabbed a

wet dishrag and began mopping up the mess. Dani bent down to swipe at the floor with a couple of paper towels. "I try to be, y'know," Chase said, when most of the broken egg had been placed in Runt's bowl and the floor was clean again.

"Try to be?"

"Honest."

"Oh." Dani avoided his eyes and concentrated on the hash browns and ham and eggs that were still cooking on the stove. How desperately she wanted to believe him. Feeling his arms wrap around her waist and the warmth of his breath brush against her hair, she closed her eyes for a blissful second before opening them again and concentrating on the sizzling eggs.

"Careful," she admonished gently. "I'd hate to spill this hot grease—"

"Dani…"

"What?" She turned in his arms and his lips caught hers, kissing her with a hunger that stole the breath from her lungs and left her weak with longing.

"You can't deny what we feel for each other."

"I haven't. I'm just not sure I want to label passion as love."

His thick brows lifted. "How much passion have you felt for other men?"

"I haven't…not since Blake."

"Then why do you have so much trouble admitting that you love me—because of him?"

"Maybe a little," she conceded, turning again and busying herself with the meal.

"You can trust me, y'know," he whispered, kissing the back of her neck gently. "I won't hurt you."

Please don't, she thought but said nothing as she slipped the fried eggs, ham and hash browns onto a platter. Chase let go of her and was seated at the table by the time she'd finished buttering the toast and had placed silverware, plates and jam on the red-and-white-checkered cloth.

"Looks great," he mumbled.

"Especially when you're starved," she teased.

He took a bite and winked at her. "Especially when you're on the other side of the table."

"Don't—"

"Don't what?" His amused eyes sparkled a crystal blue as he continued eating and watching her.

"Don't be charming. Okay? I just can't handle it this morning."

"Why not?"

She spread raspberry jam on her toast and avoided his gaze. "You wouldn't understand."

"Try me."

After several seconds of trying to eat breakfast and avoiding the subject, she pushed her plate aside in disgust. "It's just that I've got too much to think about right now. Cody's trying to grow up too fast, he's waiting on pins and needles for a father who won't show up, the farm's barely surviving, half the equipment is broken down, Caleb's trying everything he can to convince me to sell and—"

"And some guy you barely know who works with your worst enemy has just asked you to marry him."

"Yes! Yes!" she said, nodding. "It's just too much right now. Understand?"

"Nope. You were right. I don't understand. Because you could make your life so much simpler if you just learned to trust a little."

She glared at him across the table, picked up her plate and carried it to the sink. "So you have all the answers, don't you?"

"Not all of them," he admitted, finishing breakfast and bringing his plate to her.

"Name one question you don't have an answer for," she baited.

He poured himself another cup of coffee and lounged against the doorframe as he thought. "I don't know what happened to your cattle last year. Didn't you say something about them getting sick?"

"My cattle?" She looked up sharply and then shrugged. "It was a mix-up, I guess. They got into some old pesticide we had around here. A couple died. Two cows and a calf had to be killed, but the rest survived."

"A pesticide?" Chase's countenance grew hard.

"No, that's wrong. It was really a herbicide—an old can of dioxin got spilled in the barn, though it beats me how it happened. I didn't even know we still had any of the stuff around."

"You said you blamed Caleb."

"I said I'd like to blame him."

"But you can't?"

"I didn't catch him snooping around my barn, if that's what you mean. He's been careful to stay on his side of the fence—until you came along."

"And broke all the rules."

She grinned at the pile of suds in the sink. "Maybe not all of them, but more than your share."

He finished his coffee and set his empty cup on the counter. "I've got to run," he said. "Can't keep Caleb waiting too long."

Dani grimaced but didn't argue. She needed time to think. Alone. Before Cody returned. Chase had upset her life more than she would have ever thought possible.

She watched from the porch as he drove away, his Jeep leaving a plume of dust in its wake. Wrapping her arms around the post supporting the porch roof and leaning against it wearily, she closed her eyes to the obvious fact that she loved him with all of her heart.

"Loving Chase is crazy," she told herself. "He'll only cause you heartache because no matter what he says, he still works for Caleb Johnson."

The Jeep turned left at the end of the drive and Dani watched sadly as it climbed the hill leading to Caleb Johnson's rolling acres of Montana farmland.

She felt like crying but instead clenched her teeth with renewed determination. No matter how much it hurt, she would never let Chase know how she felt about him. Their lovemaking of the night before would never be repeated!

CODY RETURNED FROM Shane's five dollars richer.

"Let me get this straight," Dani said, trying to remain calm and watching her son smooth the crumpled dollar bills on the kitchen table. "You were gambling for baskets?"

"Yeah, and Shane and I beat these two other guys."

"Who were they?"

Cody shrugged. "Beats me, just a couple of kids that Shane knew. Don and Mark, I think."

"Slow down, will you?" she begged. "How could you bet? I didn't think you had any money on you."

"Fifty cents."

"And you bet it and came out with five dollars?" Dani asked, astounded.

Cody opened the refrigerator and pulled out the pitcher of lemonade. "Don't you understand about betting, Mom? Shane and I were ahead and the other guys kept pressing their bets."

"What does that mean?"

"Double or nothing." He poured himself a tall glass of lemonade and polished it off in three long swallows.

"What if you would have lost?"

He shrugged and poured another glass. "I would have owed the other guys."

The headache Dani had been fighting all morning began to throb. "How would you have paid them back?"

"From my allowance for the chores."

"But that's for college."

"Not all of it." Cody scowled at his mother.

"I just don't like you gambling."

"Aw, Mom, lighten up. Okay? It was just a bet on a ball game, not the end of the world!" He walked into the living room, switched on the television, kicked off his shoes and flopped onto the couch.

"I think we need to talk about attitude."

"Again?"

She walked into the room and sat on the arm of the couch. "Cody—"

"Geez, Mom, lay off, will ya? I'm sorry I brought up the lousy game. I thought you would be thrilled." He turned his attention toward the TV, drank his lemonade and effectively ignored his mother.

After counting to ten, Dani said, "I'm glad you had a good time with Shane. I'm also happy that you enjoyed your game and that you won, *but* I'm just not that crazy about the gambling."

"Why not?"

"Usually, when people gamble, somebody loses money they can't afford."

"Then they shouldn't bet," Cody said philosophically.

"Precisely."

Cody slid her a knowing glance. "You're just mad because of Dad, aren't you?"

"What do you mean?"

"I heard you say that Dad gambled all of his money away. Somethin' about the cash he got from Caleb Johnson for his land. He went to Las Vegas or somethin'. Right?"

"Reno," she replied woodenly. "But how did you know—"

"I heard you say a couple of things and then some of the kids at school...." He shrugged one shoulder as if the subject were of total disinterest to him.

"Let me guess: Isabelle Reece."

Cody grinned and finished his drink. "Yeah. Not too hard to figure, huh?"

Dani pursed her lips together. "Seems that Isabelle's father knows more about our family than he does his own."

"Maybe his own family is boring."

"I'd be glad to take a little of that boredom right about now," she whispered, slapping Cody's knee affectionately. "Listen, Diamond Jim, just try not to get into any high-stakes poker games, okay?"

Cody laughed and nodded as he handed his mother his empty glass. "Okay, Mom. It's a deal."

It had better be, she told herself as she walked back to the kitchen and tried not to compare her son with his father.

THE MOONLIGHT CREATED a silvery ribbon that danced and fluttered on the rippling water. Chase waded carefully under the fence while darting glances up the hill toward Dani's house. Nervous sweat ran down his neck and between his shoulder blades. If Dani caught him now....

Silently cursing himself for his duplicity, he carefully took the water and soil samples he needed, quickly labeling each one with the aid of a flashlight and water-proof pen.

"Damn you, Johnson," he muttered, moving downstream and working as quietly as possible. His waders slid on the rocky bottom of the creek, but he managed to stay on his feet and slip the vials into his creel.

The sound of the rushing water filled his ears, but still he strained to listen for any noise disturbing the night and hoped against hope that Dani was safely tucked in bed and sleeping soundly. He heard the distant sound of a dog barking and Runt's sharp answer.

Go back to sleep, Chase thought. *Whatever you do, dog, don't wake the house!* But Dani's cabin remained dark, no lights flickered on.

By this time Chase had made his way to the cottonwood stand and he had to bend to avoid the overhanging branches of the scrub oaks and cottonwood trees. It was darker in the thicket, more private, but he couldn't help feeling that he was betraying Dani even as he tried to help her.

You're just trying to get to the bottom of this, he told himself for the thousandth time. *And you can't tell her what you've found until you're sure.*

Runt barked again and this time the sound was much closer. Chase froze. *Damn!* He squinted through the branches but could see nothing but the dark shapes of the cattle slowly moving in the adjoining fields.

Letting out a relieved breath, he placed the final sample in his creel and decided to get out while the getting was good.

"What're you doin' here?" a boy's voice demanded.

Chase turned and found Cody standing on the bank of the creek.

Great. Just what I need. "I wanted some soil and water samples."

"From our land?" Cody asked. The boy's dark hair was askew and he was wearing only hastily donned cutoffs.

"Yes." Chase waded to the edge of the creek.

"I don't think you should be here, Mr. McEnroe—"

"Chase."

Cody crossed his arms over his bare chest and his jaw jutted out angrily. "Does Mom know about this?"

"Not yet."

"She won't like it."

Chase looked at the sky and then shook his head. "Maybe not at first, but I'll explain why I needed them."

"Then why don't you do it right now," Dani suggested as she approached. Unable to sleep herself, she'd heard Runt bark, Cody go downstairs and out the back door. After flinging on her robe, she'd followed her son and hadn't caught up with him until now, when he was confronting Chase, who was standing, predictably, she supposed, in the creek. "I thought I told you to stay off my property," Dani said and then ran her fingers through her tangled tresses. "But then I forgot, you don't pay any attention to what I say."

"Mom?" Cody asked.

"You go back to the house," she said. "You know better than to get up in the middle of the night."

"But I heard Runt—"

"Take him with you."

Cody looked at his mother and then back to Chase. "Maybe I should stay."

"I can handle this," Dani said angrily. "Go back to the house. If I don't come up in half an hour, call the sheriff and tell him that one of Caleb Johnson's men is trespassing!"

Cody's eyes rounded in the darkness, but he did as his mother had commanded. With a short, sharp whistle at the dog, he was gone.

"You don't have to get melodramatic," Chase said angrily, wading out of the creek. "I get the message."

"About time."

"Dani, look. I only want these samples to prove that Caleb's trying to force you off your land."

"How?"

"I'm not sure yet. But I will be soon. Can you trust me for a few more days?"

"You're pushing it, Chase. Why didn't you tell me you needed some more samples?"

"I thought that was pretty obvious since you ruined the last ones. And I thought you knew I needed these—"

"So you had to come trooping out here in the middle of the night?" she mocked, pursing her lips together. "You could have told me—last night or this morning. Or didn't it occur to you?"

"I wanted to wait until I was sure."

"Sure?" she repeated, her fury causing her to shake. "Of what? That I'd fall for you?"

Chase swore angrily. "Didn't I stand up for you yesterday?"

"Yes," she said tightly, trying to hang on to her rage. But seeing Chase in the moonlight, his shirt fluttering open, his straw-blond hair mussed in the night breeze, did strange things to her.

"Didn't last night mean anything?" he asked softly.

She had to remind herself that she was outraged. "I don't know. You tell me."

"Nothing's changed."

"Except that you snuck over here again, without my knowledge, and started digging in my creek. It's not that

I really care if you're on my land anymore," she admitted, "it's all this sneaking around and mystery that I don't understand. From the first time I saw you, you haven't been straight with me."

"I have."

"Then what the hell are you doing here?"

"Looking for proof."

"Of what?"

He stared straight into her eyes. "That Caleb knowingly contaminated your water."

"What!"

"Look, Dani. Just go home and go to bed. I'll contact you when I know more," he promised, as he climbed the short rise of the bank to stand next to her.

"But…wait a minute. What are you saying? Caleb contaminated my water."

"The creek."

"With what?"

"Dioxin."

"Dioxin?" she repeated, incredulous. "Is…is that why you were asking me about herbicides earlier today?"

"Yes."

"You thought I'd done it?"

"No, I just wanted to be sure."

The weight of what he'd said to her made her lean against the trunk of a tree. "But…how?"

"The other day—the day you destroyed my first samples—I found an old five-gallon drum of something buried in the creekbed, just on the other side of the fence. I had it checked. It was dioxin, but what I don't know yet is why the drum was buried, who buried it, and whether it was done for malicious intent."

"But you think so," she whispered, shivering with dread.

"Didn't you say some of your cattle died last year?"

"Yes, but—"

"Did they drink from the creek?"

"Of course."

"And the rest of the herd?"

"Wasn't affected. A few got sick, but they recovered. You know, I had this...feeling, I guess you'd call it, that Johnson was behind the poisoning, but I wasn't sure. Oh, God," she whispered, not really wanting to believe that Caleb Johnson was so desperate he would stoop to killing her livestock.

"I'm still not sure that Caleb was involved. But I'm working on it."

She stared up at him and noticed his blue eyes had darkened to the color of midnight as he walked over to her. "You know, I really want to believe you, to trust that you're on my side."

"But you don't?"

"I didn't say that," she whispered. He jerked off his gloves and touched the underside of her jaw. In the moonlight her hazel eyes looked silver. "It's...it's just that I don't really know what to think. Ever since you've come here, nothing has made a lot of sense."

"Just trust me."

"Oh, God, Chase, I want to!" she said, her throat tight as his cool lips touched hers. Willingly, she wound her arms around his neck and sighed when he parted her robe to touch her breast. Her thick hair streamed down her back in soft waves of brown and gold.

"I love you, Dani," Chase admitted against her neck. "Just remember that I love you—"

"Mom!" Cody's voice, distant but worried, cut through the night.

"Oh, Lord, I told him to call the sheriff, didn't I?"

Pushing Chase aside, she clutched the lapels of her robe in one hand. "I'm coming," she called before turning back to Chase. "Just don't lie to me," she whispered. "For God's sake, Chase, don't lie to me."

And then she was off, running through the rough field and up to the house. She glanced back once. Chase had walked out of the trees and was standing, feet wide apart, shirt billowing in the breeze, and watching her. Her heart squeezed painfully at the sight of him and though she stumbled once, she continued to the house.

By the time she reached the back porch, she was out of breath and shaken.

"Are you okay?" Cody asked, his eyes round with worry.

"Of course I am, sport," she said, hugging the boy. "I can take care of myself."

"But that guy works for Johnson."

"I know, but I think he's different than most of Johnson's men—hey, you didn't call the sheriff, did you?"

"Not yet."

"Good." She sighed and hugged her son, but Cody's expression was puzzled.

"How can you be sure? That he's different, I mean?"

"I don't know. Maybe intuition." She planted a kiss on the top of Cody's head. "Now you go upstairs and go to bed, okay?"

"Okay," Cody said begrudgingly as they walked through the screen door.

Dani lingered at the door for a minute, staring down toward the creek and squinting into the darkness as a cloud passed over the moon.

Chase was gone, or at least she couldn't see him. Involuntarily she placed her fingers to her still-swollen lips and wondered if trusting Chase would only cause her heartache.

SHE DIDN'T HEAR from him for the rest of the week. Deciding that he'd probably come to his senses and had just given her some cock-and-bull story about the drum of dioxin, she tried to ignore the pain in her heart and told herself that it was all for the best that she hadn't seen him again.

"So why have you thought about him day in and day out for the past week?" she grumbled, driving back from Martinville with a load of seed grain for the October planting of winter wheat.

The pickup bounced as she tried to avoid the most severe potholes in the rutted lane. Before the weather changed, she'd have to buy several yards of gravel and spread it over the rough road.

"Just one more expense," she told herself. *One of a hundred that she couldn't afford.*

Chase's Jeep was parked near the house. Dani's pulse jumped at the sight of the dusty vehicle. Why was he here? Did he know that she'd be gone?

She got out of the pickup warily and heard the sound of voices near the barn. Following the noise, she rounded the corner of the house and saw Chase and Cody playing one-on-one basketball on the far side of the barn where Cody had hung a hoop two years earlier. The netting had all but rotted off the metal rim, but Cody still used the basket for practice.

Both Chase and Cody were into the game, to the point that neither one had heard or seen her arrive. In the shade of an ancient apple tree that stood near the back porch,

Dani watched as Chase played with Cody, gave the boy pointers, and in the end, let him win.

"Good match," he said, his low voice drifting up to the house as he clapped Cody on the boy's bare back.

"Aw, you let me win."

"You think so?"

"Didn't ya?" Cody asked, his brown eyes crinkling at the corners, his sweaty, heat-reddened face beaming up at the tall man.

Chase was wiping the sweat from his face with his T-shirt and his taut muscles rippled in the hot summer sun. His blond hair hung limply over his forehead in dark, wet strands. "How about a drink?" he asked the boy.

"Sure, Mom's got some lemonade and maybe a couple bottles of Coke." Cody started sprinting toward the house before he noticed his mother. "Hey...when did you get here?"

"Just a couple of minutes ago." Dani cocked her head in Chase's direction. "What about him?"

"Oh, I don't know. A while."

"I'm surprised you let him stay."

"Why not? You do," Cody said, before dashing to the house.

Dani was still watching Cody's vanishing act and wondering what to do about it when Chase approached. He saw the vexed expression clouding her clear eyes. "Don't worry about him," Chase suggested, cocking his head in the direction of the house as Cody sprinted up the steps and ran inside. "He's a good kid." Sweat was still trickling down his neck.

"But he's growing up."

"They all have a habit of doing that."

"I know," she whispered. "But sometimes it just seems to come too fast."

Chase draped a familiar arm around her shoulders. "I don't know a parent who would disagree with you."

"How did you convince him to let you stay?"

"That wasn't so easy," Chase drawled, offering her a lazy smile. "He wasn't too keen on me showing up."

"I'll bet not."

"But I told him I was a friend of yours."

"Oh, great."

"Yeah, that wasn't the smartest thing I'd done. But I noticed he was packing around a basketball and I offered to show him how the game was played."

"And?"

"He didn't think he needed a teacher."

Dani laughed. How many times had she seen Cody's stubborn streak surface?

"But I wasn't about to take no for an answer. I wanted to wait for you. So I offered to play him one-on-one for the privilege of staying."

"And he agreed?" Dani was surprised.

"Not exactly."

"Well?"

Chase's grin broadened. "He wanted to play for a dollar a game."

"Oh, God," she groaned.

Chase squeezed her shoulders and wrapped his T-shirt around his neck. "Don't worry. He didn't take the shirt off my back. See, I've still got it." He grinned and his eyes sparkled with the afternoon sunlight. "And don't bother with a lecture, I gather he already had one."

"Apparently it didn't work." She pursed her lips and started for the house.

Chase's fingers tightened around her arm. "Don't say anything to him."

"Why not?"

"'Cause part of the deal was that I wasn't supposed to let you know anything about it. And," he smiled to himself, "I think he learned his lesson."

"Oh, no," Dani whispered. "How much does he owe you?"

"You don't want to know."

"Yes, I do! He's my son and—"

"And I think his gambling days are over. Let it lie."

Dani let out a sigh of frustration. "All right. This time. But if he ever so much as—"

"He won't."

"You sound so sure of yourself."

"I am. It's a lesson my pa taught me when I was just a little older than Cody. We were playing cards with a neighbor and Dad let me bet against him. I kept pressing my bets and I lost to the point that I owed the guy over two hundred dollars. I spent that whole summer working off my debt doing yard work for the neighbor."

"And regretting every minute of the card game."

"You got it."

"So how is Cody going to pay you back?"

"He doesn't have to. I let him off the hook this time. But I doubt if you'll ever have trouble with him gambling over his head again."

"I hope you're right."

Cody returned with three glasses of lemonade, downed his and, after asking permission, took off on his bike to visit the Anders brothers.

"Don't bother them if they're working," Dani said as the boy hopped on his ten-speed.

"I won't! I already called. Jonathon wants me to go fishin' with him." Then he pedaled out of sight with Runt galloping behind the back wheel.

Chase leaned against the fence under the shade of the

apple tree. "He's a good boy," he observed, finishing his drink. "You worry about him too much."

Dani swirled her ice cubes in her glass and stared across the fields to the creek. "Something I just can't help."

She felt Chase's hand on her shoulder, his fingers gentle as they forced her to turn and face him.

"Have you wondered why I stayed away this past week?" he asked.

"I thought you'd changed your mind."

"Nope. First, I didn't want Caleb to get too suspicious. If he gets wind of the fact that I found that drum of dioxin, he'll cover his tracks."

"So that wasn't just a story."

"What? The herbicide?"

She nodded.

"No. But I'm still doing some checking with the agriculture department and the extension office. I want to make sure I know where I stand before I confront Caleb."

"I see."

He studied the doubts in her eyes and then let out a long breath of air. "Besides, I had to stay away because I wanted to give you some time to think things through, to realize that I was sincere. I thought you'd come to the same conclusion that I have; that we love each other and should be together."

"Like some fairy-tale romance," she countered.

He grimaced and leaned over the fence. "Like two sensible people would. You can't tell me you haven't thought about it."

"To tell you the truth, I haven't thought about much else," she admitted.

"And?"

She sighed and lifted a shoulder. "I think we should

just give it a little time, that's all. I—I want to be sure this time."

"I thought you realized that I'm not like your ex-husband," he said softly.

She flinched and bit her lower lip.

"And I won't hurt you or Cody."

She forced a trembling smile and looked into his eyes. They were a clear ocean-blue that seemed to see into the shadowed corners of her soul. "I'd like to marry you," she admitted huskily. "But I can't. Not yet. I just need a little time to think things through."

"I'll be here about two more weeks," he said.

"And then?"

He raked his fingers through his hair. "Then it will be near the first of September. I have another job to go to."

"In Idaho?"

Shaking his head, he stared across the fields and watched the grazing cattle. "Central Oregon. Then I'm back in Boise."

She ran her fingers along the top rail of the fence and shivered despite the heat. "And what about Caleb Johnson?"

"I don't know."

"You told me part of your deal with him was to get me to sell off my land."

"He'd like that. For the final twenty-five percent."

"And…and do you think that by marrying me you could convince me to sell my land and move to Boise with you?"

His brow creased and impatiently he ran a hand over his tight jaw. "You still don't trust me, do you?"

"I want to."

"But it's impossible?" he said, his temper flaring.

"I'm just trying to be cautious."

Closing his eyes, he tried to count to ten. He got lost at three. "Son of a bitch!" he whispered through clenched teeth and began pacing along the fence line. "You don't trust Caleb and with good reason, and I'm convinced that he'd do just about anything to get you to move off this land, but for crying out loud, Dani, I am not asking you to marry me because of Caleb Johnson! Or my company! As far as I'm concerned, he can keep the final twenty-five percent of the company. He's in a minority position and will have no authority! I can do as I goddamn please!"

He walked up to her and with his face twisted in anger, took hold of her shoulders. "And what I want, lady, is you! I've waited and been patient and asked you nicely to marry me, and you've pussy-footed around the issue, as if I've got some dark ulterior motive. Now I realize that you have your reasons to doubt me, but dammit, I love you!"

His lips came down on hers hungrily and his strong arms wrapped around her so tightly and possessively that she was barely able to breathe. He moaned into her mouth and his broad hands covered her back, pulling her close to him, against the hard wall of his chest and between the muscular lengths of his legs.

"Dear God, Dani," he whispered into her hair, his breath ragged and torn, his heart thundering in his chest. "Just say yes."

She swallowed hard, looking into his deep blue eyes and, with a trembling smile, nodded. "Yes, Chase," she said irrationally. "I'll…I'll marry you."

"Thank God." A weary grin stretched from one side of his face to the other and he kissed her again, softly this time. "I've spent the last week lying awake at night and wondering what I'd do if you turned me down."

"And what did you decide?"

His smile turned wicked. "It was simple. I was going

to ask Jenna Peterson to watch Cody and then I was going to kidnap you and take you to a mountain cabin and hold you hostage until you agreed to become my wife."

Dani laughed and winked at him. "Maybe I should have held out," she said. "Sounds like I missed out on a lot of fun."

Chase pulled her close and traced the angle of her jaw with his finger. "I'll make it up to you, I promise." His lips captured hers in a bittersweet kiss filled with the promise of the future.

"And what will Caleb say about this?" she asked.

"Let's not worry about Caleb," he said. "We've got better things to do."

"Such as?"

He released her slightly and let his arms rest on her shoulders. "Well, I can think of a lot of things…" His eyes slid suggestively down her neck to the fluttering pulse at the base of her throat. "But they can wait…for a little while. How about a picnic?"

"A picnic—now?" She was surprised.

"Sure. Sort of a celebration. You could show me around this place." He straightened. "I'll shower and you can throw some things into a basket."

Dani laughed. "You're starting to sound like a husband already."

He arched a thick brow. "On second thought, you could shower with me…"

"Then we'd never leave."

"That would be okay."

He leaned closer, but she pushed against his shoulders with her flat hands. "Later, cowboy. Right now, you hit the showers, and I'll pack and leave a note for Cody."

They walked into the house, arms linked, and Dani felt as if she were on top of the world.

The only trouble with being on the top, she told herself cynically when she heard the sound of the shower running and had begun making sandwiches, was that there was only one way to go.

CHAPTER EIGHT

THE EASIEST WAY to get to the site of the original homestead house was on horseback, so while Dani fixed a lunch that could be carried in saddlebags, Chase saddled and bridled the horses. The ride across the creek, through a series of fields and finally into the wooded area surrounding the old buildings, took about twenty minutes.

Dani pulled Traitor up short, and the rangy buckskin, his ears flicking backward, responded with a toss of his head. Chase rode Whistlestop, a heavy-boned bay mare. At the top of a small knoll he held his restless horse in check beside Dani.

"So this is where it all started," he said.

"At least for the Hawthornes," she replied. Indicating the surrounding hills with a sweeping gesture, Dani looked lovingly over the sprawling acres of farmland and pockets of timber. "This—" she pointed to what had once been a large two-story farm house "—was the spot my great-great-grandparents chose to homestead." Dropping the reins over Traitor's head, Dani heard the bridle jingle as the horse grazed on the dry grass and weeds.

Chase still sat astride Whistlestop, leaned forward and squinted into the late afternoon sun. With a backdrop of virgin-growth timber and the craggy Rocky Mountains reaching up to the Montana sky, the ancient house looked pitifully neglected; a skeleton of what had once been a grand old farm house now surrounded by thistles and brush.

The main timbers sagged, all of the windowpanes had long been broken, and the roof had collapsed on the second story, exposing the interior to the rugged elements of the harsh Montana winters. Blackberry vines, now laden with heavy fruit, had crawled over what had been a broad front porch and clung tenaciously around the doorway.

Some of the wallpaper, bleached and stained, was still visible where part of the second story walls had been torn away by the wind.

"It was beautiful once," Dani said, eyeing the sad, dilapidated structure.

"I can see that." Chase got off the mare and let the horse graze. Pushing his hands into the back pockets of his jeans, he continued to study the old house while he walked toward Dani. He placed an arm around her shoulders and some of the poignant desolation that had crept over her disappeared.

"The hot springs are over there." She pointed to the stream seeping through the earth near the back of the house. "And since there wasn't hot and cold running water when the house was built, the spring was a real luxury. Hot water could be carried into the house."

"So what happened?" he asked. "Why wasn't the house kept up?"

"Money," Dani said with a frown. "When my grandparents were young, sometime in the thirties or forties, I think, they built the cabin that Cody and I live in because it was so much closer to the road. It was cheaper to build and make modern with gas and electricity and running water than to rebuild this place. And they always thought that if they got enough money together, they'd restore the old house."

"But it didn't work out."

"No." She walked up to the porch, touched one of the

rotting timbers at the corner of the house and sighed. "It's a shame, though. I've seen old pictures of it. This front porch ran the whole length. It really was very grand…"

"Let's look inside."

"I don't think it's safe."

"I'll make sure it is before we step on any rotted out boards."

"But the berry vines; the door is nearly blocked off—"

"Come on. Where's your sense of adventure?" He took her hand in his and gently pulled her forward. With his free hand he managed to push the undergrowth aside and break a path to the front door. Bees buzzed in the berry vines overhead and the thorns caught in Dani's hair and blouse, but Chase, bending over slightly to protect himself, was finally able to lead her through the open doorway.

It had been a long time since she'd been inside the house and the years and weather had taken their toll on the place. The wooden floors were scarred and dulled by a thick covering of dirt. Though the stairs were still intact, the banister had long since fallen away and lay in scattered pieces in the entry hall. Cobwebs hung in dark corners and broken glass littered the floor.

Chase reached down and picked up one of the hand-carved balusters, cleaning off the dust to stare at the once beautiful spoke that had helped support the railing. "How old is this house?" he asked, looking around. On either side of the main hall were two large rooms, each with a blackened fireplace on the outside walls.

"I don't know exactly. Over a hundred years."

"At least." Walking into what must have been a dining room, Chase stopped at the fireplace. "It looks like the mason knew what he was doing." He placed a hand on the ancient bricks and noted the few places where the mortar had begun to crumble. With a frown, he went through an open archway.

Following, Dani walked through the big dining room and down one step into the kitchen. It was a lean-to room, only one story, with a fireplace all its own. There was a huge black pot still hanging from a hook over the hearth. The hinge groaned when Chase tried to wipe the cobwebs from the ancient kettle.

"I'd love to rebuild this house," Dani thought aloud.

Chase looked up at the sagging ceilings and broken walls. "You'd have to start from the ground up."

"I know. It's just a pipe dream, I suppose."

Chase took hold of her hand. "Don't ever give up your dreams, Dani."

She laughed and shook her head. "But I'd never be able to afford to restore this place."

"If you think that way, you've lost the battle before it's even begun." He kissed her on the forehead and wrapped his arm protectively around her shoulders. She leaned her head against his chest as they walked through the splintered back door and into the bright afternoon sunlight.

"You do see why I love this land, don't you?" she asked suddenly, biting her lip and staring at the stark mountains jutting up against the brilliant blue sky. "My family has been here for generations... I just can't stand the thought of these beautiful hills covered with asphalt, burger stands, condominiums and hotels. Is that selfish?"

"I don't know," Chase admitted. "Seems like there should be a way to compromise."

She nodded and walked over to Traitor to get the lunch from the saddlebags. Chase grabbed the rolled blanket from his horse and spread it on the ground under a rough-barked pear tree.

After sitting down, Dani placed the sandwiches, ap-

ples and oatmeal cookies on the old quilt and then poured
Chase a cup of iced tea. "Maybe I should just sell out to
Caleb Johnson," she said distantly, but then shook her
head. "Maybe if it were anyone else—but it's just Caleb's
damned take-it-all attitude that drives me out of my skull.
The man is poison."

"I'd like to disagree with you," Chase said as he took
the cup Dani offered. He leaned on one elbow, unwrapped
a sandwich and started to eat as Dani poured another cup
of tea for herself.

"But you can't argue the point, can you?"

"Not unless he had nothing to do with the drum of
dioxin."

"Have you asked him about it?"

"Not yet. But I'll have to soon," he answered, finishing his sandwich.

"What are you waiting for?"

"The right time, I suppose. When I've got all the information I need to back me up."

"Such as?"

He shrugged and reached for an apple, polishing it
on the tail of his shirt. "Such as knowing for sure that
the dioxin belonged to him and that he had it placed in
the creek himself; that it wasn't the accident of a care-
less hand who worked for him. There's still a chance that
Caleb told one of his hands to get rid of the herbicide and
the guy thought the best place to store it would be to bury
it in the creekbed."

"You don't believe that."

"Nope. I think it's pretty obvious Johnson isn't on the
up-and-up. I just don't know why he dragged me into it."

They ate in silence and slowly the black cloud that had
settled over Dani disappeared. The late afternoon sun was
warm as it filtered through the branches of the pear tree

to dapple the ground in bright splotches of light. The late summer air was fresh and clean and a few leaves had already turned yellow with the promise of autumn.

Finished with his lunch, Chase stretched out on his back and clasped his hands under his head to stare through the leafy branches to the sky. "Come here," he suggested.

"I am here."

"No, over here," he said, patting the blanket beside him. "I want you right here."

"Any particular reason?"

"Quite a few, actually. But the most important is that I'm going to be gone for a few days."

"Gone?" she repeated, her head jerking up. The thought that he wouldn't be near hit her full force.

"I'll be back. Promise. There's just a couple of loose ends I have to tie up back in Boise."

"No one else can handle them?"

He sighed and shook his head. "Apparently not."

"Don't you have a supervisor or vice-president or something."

"Nope. I tried that once. A man by the name of Eric Conway worked with me." Chase scowled at the thought of Eric's betrayal. Personally and professionally Eric had managed to cut him to the bone. "We were best friends until he decided to form his own company, take all my staff and techniques and hightail it."

"Oh."

"Since then I haven't trusted anyone to do some of the work. So, I've got to go home for a couple of days."

"Just as long as you come back," she whispered, hiding the disappointment that tugged at her heart. She put the remains of the lunch into the saddlebags and sat next to him, her hands folded over her knees, her eyes mere slits as she squinted west toward the mountains. Tendrils of hair escaped unnoticed from the braid she wore down her back.

Chase reached upward and brushed one of the locks of honey-brown hair away from her face. The caress of his fingers against her cheek made her tremble.

"Until I met you, I'd never wanted a woman to spend the rest of my life with me."

"Have you changed your mind?" She looked down at him, saw the twinkle in his eye and felt his fingers against her back as he tried to unwrap the band that held the single plait of hair in place.

"Nope."

"How can you be so sure of yourself?" she asked.

"Maybe because I haven't experienced a bad marriage." He pulled the band from her hair and watched in fascination as the tight braid loosened.

"Toss your head," he said.

"Oh, Chase, honestly—"

"Come on."

She laughed and shook her hair free. In glinting, sun-brightened highlights, it fell past her shoulders to her waist in soft tangled waves.

"That's better," he said with a crooked, charming grin, his hand sliding down her back.

"I think you're just trying to change the subject."

"Wouldn't dream of it. What do you want to know?"

Smiling sadly, she pushed the hair from his eyes. "You said you haven't been married."

"That's right."

"But surely there have been other women…"

"A few."

"And no bad memories?" she asked skeptically.

"None that I care to remember," he said, thinking for a minute about the one woman he'd trusted; his secretary and lover, Tracy Monteith, the woman who'd run off with Eric Conway when Eric had started a rival company. Later Chase had learned that Tracy had only used him to gain information for Eric. Tracy and Eric had been married just about as long as Eric's company had been in operation.

"What is it?" Dani asked, seeing the painful play of emotions on Chase's rugged face.

"Nothing important," he said, pushing himself up on one elbow and wrapping his other arm securely around her waist.

"So you can just forget any of the bad relationships you've had?"

"I try to. No reason to dwell on them."

She couldn't find fault with his logic.

"But then I don't have a kid who reminds me of what happened."

Dani forced her sad thoughts out of her mind and smiled at Chase. "I wouldn't trade Cody for the world," she said. "Sure, sometimes he reminds me of Blake, but that's okay. I mean, Blake is Cody's father and no matter how painful the marriage eventually became, I did end up with my son and managed to hold on to the farm. Some women aren't so lucky."

"Do you still love him?" Chase asked, his eyes delving into hers.

"Cody asked me the same thing," she whispered.

"Well?"

"No. I did once. When I was very young, before Cody was born and when my folks were still alive. But that was a long time ago..." She avoided Chase's eyes and slid away from him. "I don't know why I'm feeling so melancholy. It's silly really. Probably because of the old house. It looks so sad and lonely up here, falling apart and—"

Chase had taken hold of her arm and pulled her against

him with such force that she was left breathless as she half lay across his chest, her golden hair streaming over them both. "All I want to do is make you happy," he said slowly. "And I promise that I'll never hurt you."

She swallowed against the thick lump forming in her throat as he placed a hand behind her head and drew her face to his. "I love you, Dani," he said slowly as he kissed her. "And I don't want you to ever forget it."

"I won't." She breathed softly into his mouth and he groaned, pulling her on top of him and kissing her face, her neck, her hair.

She felt the buttons of her blouse give way and her breasts spilled forward against his chest.

Groaning, Chase tugged at their clothes until they were both naked on the blanket, her white skin touching his tanned muscles, her beautiful dark-tipped breasts supple and ready for the feel of his fingers and mouth, her long hair streaming down to brush and tickle his skin erotically.

Taking her nipple between his lips, he felt her quiver and moan his name while her fingers worked their magic on his skin. He held her as close as he could, pressing urgently against her, feeling the need to protect her. For even as he began making love to her, he felt a quiet desperation deep in his soul, as if forces outside his control would drive her away.

Closing his eyes against the ugly thought, he moved against her until he was spent and then, cradling her head against his chest, whispered words of love in the shade of the tree, oblivious to the humming insects or the sweet scent of the honeysuckle and lilacs that filled the air around them.

THE FIRST WARNING that things weren't going smoothly came just two days later. Dani hadn't heard from Chase, but wasn't particularly worried as she knew that he was back in Boise. She was still thinking about his proposal and the consequences of marrying him when she drove into Martinville for a week's worth of groceries on Friday morning.

Cody was with her and not particularly pleased about it. Pouting, he'd propped himself against the passenger side of the pickup. Runt was standing on top of Cody, his black nose poked through the partially open window that allowed some fresh air inside the stuffy cab of the truck.

"I don't want to go shopping," Cody grumbled as Dani pulled into the parking lot.

"But you need some new school clothes and shoes," she pointed out.

"Not today! School's still a few days off."

"And all the sales have just started."

"Aw, Mom," he grumbled, getting out of the pickup when Dani had parked between the faded lines on the dusty asphalt. "Give me a break, will ya?" Angrily, he slammed the door of the pickup, nearly clipping Runt's nose in the bargain.

"Be careful," Dani reprimanded.

"Oh, sure."

The dog paced and whined, sticking his head out the open window.

"We'll only be a couple of minutes," Dani said, patting Runt's head and glancing pointedly at her son. Then, thinking the dog would be too hot inside the cab, she let Runt out and had him sit in the back of the truck. "Just don't bark your fool head off, okay?"

The temperature seemed to soar as Dani walked across the hot parking lot to the store. Things were no better inside Anders' Super Market. The air conditioning had gone out and one of the coolers had broken down.

"Land o' mercy," Marcella Anders said to Dani as she carefully repacked the meats into the remaining, still-cold display case. "And every repairman in town working overtime. I hope to heaven this meat doesn't spoil." She was a large woman, big boned and heavyset. She wore her graying hair piled high on her head and a starched white apron over her clothes. For nearly as long as Dani could remember, Marcella had worked in the meat department of her husband's store.

"It's been incredibly hot this year."

"Don't I know it?" Marcella grumbled. "Brings out the worst in people, ya know. Just yesterday, Jenna Peterson came in here fit to be tied."

"That doesn't sound like her," Dani remarked, thinking of Caleb Johnson's kindly housekeeper as she eyed the packages of frozen fish.

"No, indeed, it don't. But she was in a regular tizzy, let me tell you. Something about one of Caleb's men…a new man he'd hired. Jenna seemed to think that this man was no good, just on Caleb's payroll to cause trouble."

Dani felt her face go pale. "Did…did she tell you the man's name?" she asked, looking Marcella square in the eyes.

"Nope. I think she wanted to tell me more, but she thought better of it, ya know. Jenna needs her job; she practically supports her daughter and grandson and she never was one to gossip much."

"Loose lips sink ships," Dani said to herself, thinking about Chase and finding him in the creek in the middle of the night. And now he was gone…

"Pardon?"

"Nothing," Dani said, and forced a smile. "You were right, it was probably just the weather."

Marcella's face pulled together in a thoughtful frown.

"I hope so," she said aloud. "I wouldn't want to think that any of Caleb's men are dishonest. The people of this town, we're all countin' on that resort of his. My husband thinks it'll triple business in the next year. He's already had the plans drawn up to expand, put in a delicatessen and a garden department." Marcella chuckled to herself as she placed the last package of meat into the full display case. "This is his big chance, he thinks. Just like most of the rest of the folks in this town."

"Except Mom," Cody said.

Marcella nodded curtly. "Well, we're all entitled to our own opinion, aren't we?" she said, still smiling as she wiped her hands on her apron. "It's a free country."

"Yes," Dani said, pushing her cart forward.

"See ya around," Marcella said, and moved down the meat counter to help another customer.

Dani pushed her cart down the crowded aisles and tried to concentrate on shopping, but found it nearly impossible. She came out of the store with only half the items she'd planned to pick up.

"You think Mrs. Anders was talking about Chase, don't you?" Cody said once they'd climbed back into the pickup with Runt.

"I don't know."

"I can tell it's what you think."

She eased the truck into the sparse traffic of the main street of the small town and pushed the hair from her eyes at the one stoplight near the gas station. "I didn't say that."

"You didn't have to."

Dani sighed and looked at her son. "How about getting those school clothes now? We can drop Runt and the groceries off and run into Butte, maybe eat dinner in the park."

"If you really want to," Cody replied.

"I really want to."

"Okay," Cody said without much enthusiasm.

Later, once they'd managed to finish the necessities, Dani and Cody sat on the grass in the park and watched as children ran and played on the various pieces of equipment.

The bustle of the city was in sharp contrast to the sleepy little town of Martinville. In Dani's estimation, Butte was a major metropolis. She laughed to herself when she thought what people from New York or Los Angeles would think of her perception.

"Somethin' funny?" Cody picked a blade of grass and tore it into small pieces.

"Not really," Dani said with a smile for her son. "But what about you? Is something bothering you?" Dani asked. "Looks like you've got something on your mind."

The boy shrugged. "I guess," he said, looking away from her.

"What is it?"

"Chase McEnroe."

Dani let out a long sigh. *Here it comes,* she thought. "What about him?"

"You're serious about him aren't you?"

Dani thought for a moment and decided her son was entitled to the truth. "Yes, I am."

Cody hesitated a minute. "You gonna marry him?"

"I don't know. Maybe."

"And what about Dad?"

Dani leaned back on her elbows, watching as the late afternoon shadows darkened the grass. "I don't really know, I guess. I haven't thought it all through yet."

"He's comin' home, ya know."

"Oh, Cody," she said on a long, wistful sigh. "Just because you got a couple of letters—"

"It's more than that, Mom," Cody cut in angrily, confusion clouding his brown eyes.

"Cody—"

"He called."

"What!" Dani's world seemed to stop spinning. For a minute she couldn't speak. *"When?"*

"When I got back from the Anders' house the other day. You and Chase were on that picnic at the homestead house…"

Catching her breath, she nodded to her son. "Go on."

"I'd only been home a little while. The phone rang and it was Dad. He said he was on his way."

Dani was stupefied. "He can't come home, not now," she whispered.

"Why not? He is my dad."

Sitting upright, she let her head fall into her open palms and tried, for Cody's sake, to pull herself together. "But why…why now?" she wondered. "And why didn't you tell me when I got home?"

"Chase was there. I didn't think it would be a good idea."

"But that was two days ago!"

Cody looked away. "I know. But I didn't want you to get mad at me."

"I'm not mad at you, honey. I just wish you would have told me about this sooner." And then seeing the wounded look in his eyes, she touched his hand and offered him an apologetic smile. "Look, honey, I'm sorry I overreacted. Okay? It's just such a shock."

"But he wrote. Twice. I told you he'd come back."

"That you did," she said with a sigh.

"You didn't believe it, did you?"

"No, not really. Not after this long," she admitted, bracing herself and managing a worried grin. "But it looks like I was wrong. When will he get to Martinville?"

"He didn't know."

"So what's he going to do when he gets into town?"

Cody bit at his lower lip and dropped the shredded blade of grass. "He said he'd call."

"Good."

"You will let me see him, won't you?"

Dani let out a long breath and fought the worry in her heart. "Of course I will," she said, trying to keep all of her worst fears at bay. "He's your father."

Cody's face split into a wide grin and impulsively he hugged his mother. "It's gonna work out," he said, his brown eyes sparkling. "And we'll be a family again. Just you wait and see!"

THREE DAYS LATER, Dani was up to her elbows in blackberry juice.

She finished cleaning the spatters of juice from the kitchen counters and then tossed the stained rag into the sink and glanced out the window at the freshly turned earth stretching from the house to the road in a dark swath. Rubbing her tired muscles, she wondered what had possessed her to plow the front field because now she was faced with the prospect of harrowing it and getting it ready for the October planting of wheat. The ground had been nearly rock hard and it had taken hours to turn the sod.

Her back and shoulders ached and the tip of her nose was sunburned. "This is no life for a princess," she scolded herself, and laughed as she finished sealing the small jars of blackberry jelly she'd made earlier in the morning.

After washing her hands, she walked onto the back

porch and noticed that there was no activity on Caleb's side of the fence. Some of the heavy equipment was still parked near the stream, but it was much farther upstream and Dani couldn't see any men working in the creek.

"Chase is probably just about done," she murmured. And then what was she going to do? Marry him? Sell the farm to Caleb? Pull Cody out of school and move to Idaho or stay where she was? And what about the rumor in the grocery store that Caleb's new man was trouble?

Shaking her head as if she could dislodge the doubts from her mind, she frowned to herself and wondered when Chase would return and if he'd been able to confront Caleb about the herbicide.

"Stop it," she told herself, jerking off her apron and tossing it over the back of a chair. She walked down the two steps of the porch and leaned over the top rail of the fence, watching the horses trying to graze or find a shady spot in the open fields.

"We sure need rain," she murmured to herself, looking upward at the clear blue sky.

Her thoughts were disturbed by the sound of a truck rolling up the drive.

Thinking Chase might have returned, Dani, her brow furrowed, walked around the outside of the house and frowned when she didn't recognize the battered pickup slowing in the front yard.

But by the time the driver had cut the engine and stepped from the cab, Dani realized that her life had just changed forever and the meeting she had been dreading for the better part of seven years was about to take place. She was staring face to face with Cody's father!

He didn't look much different than the day he'd left all those years ago. Tall and rangy, with dark hair turning silver at the temples, Blake Summers was still a handsome, rugged-looking man. With flashing dark eyes, a gaunt, weather-toughened face softened by a sheepish grin, he sauntered toward the house.

"Dani." He stopped a few feet from her.

Knowing the blood had drained from her face, she managed to meet his wary gaze. "What are you doing here, Blake?" she demanded.

"'Bout time I came back, don't ya think?"

"I think it's probably too late."

"Still an optimist I see," he said, with a knowing smile.

"Don't bait me," she snapped, as the years seemed to slip away. She could still remember the day he had slammed the door in her face, leaving her crying for him to return to her and her young son. Shaking, she swallowed hard. "Why now—why'd you come back?"

Ignoring her question, he took a seat on the top step of the porch and mopped his sweaty brow with a handkerchief. "God, this heat is miserable," he said, and then chuckled as he gestured toward his old pickup. "The air conditionin' is out." Fishing a cigarette from his shirt pocket, he lit up and blew a long stream of smoke into the clear air. Squinting against the smoke, he looked around the place. "Been plowin' I see."

"I asked you a question, Blake," she said calmly, although her insides were churning with emotions she'd hoped were long dead.

"Didn't Cody get my letters?"

"Yes—"

"I said I was comin' to see him." Blake settled against the porch column and smiled engagingly. "And he told you I called?"

"Just the other day." She leaned against the hot fender of his truck for support, oblivious to the dirt and oil brushing against her jeans.

"Well, like I said, I think it's about time I got to know the boy, don't you?"

"I'm not sure it's such a good idea," she said honestly, fear squeezing her heart at the thought that Blake would take Cody away from her.

Blake didn't even blink. "Geez, you're a suspicious thing."

Cocking a golden brow, she explained, "It's been a long time—nearly seven years. Cody doesn't remember you, not really. Now, all of a sudden, you're interested in becoming a father. I'd just like to know what made you change your mind."

"Nothin' special," he said. "Maybe I just got tired of driftin'." He took another drag from his cigarette.

"So you drifted back here." Dani's eyes narrowed a bit. "I don't know if I can believe that."

Blake shrugged. "Can't blame you, I guess. But, in time, everyone grows up. Includin' yours truly. God, Dani, I'm thirty-five years old."

"So you came all the way from…wherever you were in Oregon just to see your son?"

"That's about the size of it." He tossed his cigarette into the dirt, grinding it out with the heel of his boot. "That and the fact that the job in Molalla gave out. I thought maybe I'd try my luck here, in Martinville."

Dani's heart sank. Blake. *Here*. Wanting to be with Cody.

"The talk is that there will be a lot of work soon as Caleb gets goin' on Summer Ridge."

"So I've heard," she said wryly, trying to disguise her fear. She refused to show any weakness to the man who had stripped her soul bare and left her to fend for herself.

Blake pressed his lips together and looked over the

hazy fields. Standing and stretching, he came up to Dani
and grinned. "So where is he?"

"Cody?"

"Yep."

"At a friend's," Dani replied, an uncomfortable tightening in her stomach warning her not to trust Blake.

"When will he be back?"

"I'm supposed to pick him up before supper."

"I'll do it," Blake decided, with a sharp nod of his head.
"May as well jump in with both feet."

Dani's heart dropped through the floor. Whatever
Blake's game was, he intended to play out his hand to
the end. "It's hard for me to believe that you really want
to see him," she said furiously, "since you wanted me
to have an abortion when I turned up pregnant and then
walked out on us barely three years later!"

"I know. I know," he cajoled, lifting his hands in the
same patronizing manner he'd used when she'd been his
wife. "But can't you believe that I've had a change of
heart?"

"It's hard."

"Let me go get my boy, Dani," he begged.

Dani wavered, but only for a minute. "I...I think it
would be better if I picked him up," she said cautiously.
"You can see him here when he gets home."

Blake ran a hand over his chin and smiled lazily, his
dark eyes regarding Dani with practiced seduction. "Is
that an invitation to dinner?"

Clenching her teeth against her impulsive response,
Dani studied the man who had once been her husband.
He'd aged in the past seven years. Features that had once
been boyishly charming were now gaunt and grizzled.
"I think it would be okay if you ate here tonight. Cody's
been anxious for you to return."

"What about you, Dani?" he asked, stepping closer to her.

"I think it probably would have been better if you'd stayed away."

He reached up to touch her hair, but Dani, still holding her ground pushed his hand aside. "Haven't you missed me?"

"Not for a long time," she stated.

"Ya know, there's still a chance that we could work things out," he suggested, his brown eyes saddening a little. "I could make it up to you."

"Never."

"You're sure of that?"

"More sure than I've been of anything in a long while," she said, her hazel eyes focusing on his face, her jaw jutting with renewed determination. "And since you're Cody's father and he wants to see you, I won't get in the way. But I'm telling you this straight out, Blake: Don't try to make trouble. Not for me. Or Cody. We're happy here and we don't need you."

"A boy needs a father," he contradicted.

Dani bit back the fury on her tongue. "Maybe that's true. But he needs a father he can depend on, a man who will stick by him no matter what, not someone who abandoned him when he was barely two years old then plans to waltz back into his life when he's half grown. Think about it, Blake. And before you entertain any thoughts of ruining what Cody and I have together, think how it will affect your son!"

"I never said I wanted to make trouble."

"Good. Then I'll try to remember that."

"You'd do that much for me?"

"No. For Cody." Her lips tightened. "I'm not giving you back your son; you threw away that right a long time ago when you took off without a backward glance. But I won't deny Cody the right to know his father *unless* you do something I don't approve of."

Blake's smile twisted appreciatively. "That almost sounds like a threat, Dani."

"It is."

He shook his head as if in utter amazement. "You sure have changed."

"You made me change. I learned to depend on myself."

"And I respect ya for it."

"Don't try to flatter me, Blake. It won't work. If you want to see Cody, come back here at six-thirty. Otherwise get out of my life."

He took one step closer, looked deep into her eyes and saw the sparks of ready-fire in their depths. "I'm stayin' at Bob's place, but I'll be back," he said softly, touching her on the underside of her chin.

She jerked away from him. "Fine," she retorted and watched as he climbed back into his pickup and drove away.

CHAPTER NINE

"HEY, MOM, SOMETHIN' wrong?" Cody asked on the way home from his friend's house.

"Not really," Dani lied, her fingers sweaty around the steering wheel, her teeth sinking into her lip as she drove the pickup out of Martinville.

Cody shrugged and stuck out his lower lip thoughtfully. "You looked kind'a worried."

"Don't I always?" she teased, but the joke fell flat. She tried to lighten the mood by ruffling his hair, but Cody moved his head to avoid contact.

"Come on. Somethin's buggin' you. I can tell." He slid down in the seat and propped his knees against the dash of the pickup while glancing at his mother. "Caleb Johnson did something again didn't he?"

"Not that I know of," she said with a sigh. "Okay, Cody, I guess I'll have to level with you."

"'Bout time."

Bracing herself for an emotional reaction from her son, she said, "I was going to wait until we were home, but you may as well hear it now: Your dad is back in town."

Cody didn't move a muscle, just stared at her with round brown eyes. "You saw him? When?"

"Earlier. He stopped by the house…looking for you. He'll be back for dinner."

"Tonight?"

"Tonight."

Letting out a piercing whoop that any coyote would

envy, Cody pounded his fist against the seat of the truck and grinned from ear to ear. "I told ya, didn't I? I told ya that he was comin' home."

"That you did," Dani admitted, turning the old truck into the drive. The pickup bounced its way up the lane. "You never lost faith."

"This is great!" Cody said, beaming and hardly able to sit still.

When Dani parked the old truck near the side of the house, Cody reached for the door handle and climbed down, but Dani took hold of his arm. "Cody—"

"Yeah?" He swiveled his head around, his bright teeth and dark eyes flashing eagerly.

She had trouble finding the right words, but her face was lined with concern. "Look, I don't want to burst your bubble, but I just don't want you to be disappointed. Don't expect too much of your father."

Cody jerked his arm away from her and gestured dismissively. "He's back, Mom. That's all that matters. And if you weren't so hung up on Chase McEnroe, you'd be happy, too."

"Chase has nothing to do with this."

"Like hell!"

"Cody!" But the boy was off, dashing across the gravel and beating a path to the back door.

Dani lifted the two sacks of groceries she'd bought before she'd picked up Cody and walked inside the house. Setting the bags on the counter, she listened to the sound of the shower running and Cody's off-tune singing.

"I hope I'm up to this," she thought aloud, placing the meat and vegetables in the refrigerator. Feeling that the dinner with Blake was sure to be a disaster, she put the rest of the groceries away and started preparing the meal. The first step was lighting the barbecue on the back porch. After seeing that the charcoal was burning, she came back inside, noted that the shower had quit running and started cutting greens for a salad.

Cody, wet hair gleaming, was back downstairs in fifteen minutes. He was wearing some of the new clothes they'd purchased in Butte and a smile as wide as his face. "What can I do to help?" he asked.

"Here, why don't you slice the loaf of French bread?" She took a deep breath and added, "Look, I wasn't too crazy about what you said to me earlier."

"What?"

"You know what. Just try to control your temper, okay?"

"Okay," the boy agreed sullenly, looking out the window before grabbing a knife and slicing the loaf.

Dani pursed her lips and gazed fondly at her son. "Don't you like Chase?"

Cody shrugged. "He's okay."

"I thought you were getting along—"

"I said he's okay, didn't I? It's just that he's not Dad, if ya know what I mean."

"I guess I do," she said, feeling a dull pain deep in her heart. Cody would never accept Chase as a father or even a stepfather while Blake was around. And, regretfully, Cody had that right, she supposed.

"When did he say he'd be here?"

"Six-thirty."

"It's almost that time already." Cody looked out the window and his brows drew together in vexation. "You're sure you said six-thirty?"

"I'm sure. Now, don't worry; he said he'd come," she replied, slicing a ripe tomato from the garden and trying to ignore her own doubts about the evening.

"Aren't you going to change clothes or something?"

Cody asked as he fidgeted between the front door and the kitchen.

"No." She started buttering the bread.

"But you could put on one of those dresses—you know the ones you always wear when Chase comes over."

Dani whirled to face her son. She saw the expectation in his eyes and had to bite her tongue to keep from telling Cody exactly how she felt about his father. Instead she put her hands behind her and gripped the counter tightly. "Look, Cody, I don't 'dress' for Chase or anyone, for that matter. I realize this is probably hard for you to understand and I don't really know what you think is going to happen tonight, but you may as well know that there's no chance your dad and I will get back together."

"You don't know that—"

"I do," Dani said firmly.

"But maybe he's staying!"

Dani couldn't stand the pain written all over Cody's eager face. Looking out the window, she saw Blake's pickup turning into the drive. With a sinking feeling, she said, "Your father said something about staying at Uncle Bob's, looking for a job around town, but that doesn't mean it will work out. It also doesn't mean that he and I will ever get back together again. And I already told you that Blake couldn't stay here in the house with us." She turned to Cody, her eyes honest and kind. "You have to face the fact that it's over between your dad and me."

"But you won't even give him a chance—" Cody heard the sound of Blake's pickup and froze. He went to the window and watched as his father slid out of the truck, stretched, and with hat in hand, sauntered up to the front porch.

As soon as Blake knocked, Cody opened the door. Blake Summers and his son stared at each other for a minute before Blake opened his arms and the boy ran to him and hugged his father fiercely. "Dad," Cody choked out and Dani's heart nearly broke.

"Well, look at you," Blake said, clapping Cody on the back and then holding him at arm's length. "Ain't you grown up?"

"Not quite," Cody muttered.

"Oh, I don't know 'bout that." He walked into the kitchen and watched as Dani, balancing a platter of raw steaks, stepped outside to broil the meat.

Through the screen door, she could hear Blake and Cody talking, slowly at first and then more rapidly. *Like long lost buddies,* she thought, trying not to worry. Cody had the right to know his father; she couldn't deny him.

"How about gettin' your old man a beer?" Blake asked, and soon the sound of a can popping open reached Dani's ears.

Oh, God, Blake, please don't drink. From firsthand experience, Dani knew that Blake Summers and alcohol didn't mix. Never one able to hold his alcohol, Blake became at first friendly, then belligerent, and eventually violent when he drank. It was only one beer, she reminded herself, and maybe he'd changed.

Nonetheless, she couldn't get the steaks turned and broiled fast enough.

When she returned to the kitchen she found that Blake and Cody were in the living room involved in a heavy discussion about the NBA draft. Safe enough, Dani thought with relief and tossed the salad.

"Time to eat," she called over her shoulder, and Blake got up and stretched. He took the spot that used to be his at the table.

"That's where Cody usually eats," she said.

"It's okay," the boy insisted. "Dad can sit wherever he wants to."

"Thanks, son. And how about another beer?"

"Sure." Cody nearly tripped over himself to get to the refrigerator to serve his father.

Inwardly cringing, Dani served the meal, and smiled politely at Blake's compliments.

It took some effort, but she slowly began to relax as the conversation flowed easily and stayed clear of sensitive subjects. Blake seemed to take a genuine interest in Cody, and though Dani still didn't trust the man's motives, she was pleased to see how Cody responded to his father. Soon the meal was finished and Dani served dessert.

"Apple crisp," Cody said appreciatively as she set the pie plate on the table. "My favorite."

"Mine, too," Blake agreed with a slow grin.

News to Dani; Blake had never been one for sweets.

"You know," Blake said, his near-black eyes moving from his son to his ex-wife. "Your mom is one of the best cooks I've ever met. That was a fine meal, Dani. Fine." He leaned back and patted his belly to show his appreciation.

Dani felt her jaw tightening, but forced a thin smile. "Thanks."

"Always did say you were a helluva cook."

She let that one slip by; no reason to get into an argument in front of Cody. Her son wasn't old enough to understand that Dani wanted to be more to her husband than a cook and a maid. "How about coffee?" she asked, her nerves raw. Soon, she hoped, Blake would tire of their company and leave.

Blake shook his head. "Too early for me." He reached for his beer and realized the can was empty. "I could stand another one of these, though."

"I think we're about out—"

"No, Mom. There's one more can in the fridge and an-other six-pack on the back porch."

"But it's warm," she protested.

Blake held up his hand and waved in the air before smiling at Cody. "No matter. Why don't you get me the last cold one and put the rest in the cooler, boy?" Then, ignoring the challenge in Dani's eyes, he settled back in his chair and lit a cigarette.

Cody got up to do as he was asked, but Blake put a hand around the boy's wrist and winked at him. "After that, you can go out in the pickup and reach under the seat. I got you a surprise."

"I don't think—" Dani started to say, but held her tongue.

"Great!" Cody's eyes lit up. As quickly as possible he served Blake the beer and hurried out the front door.

Once the boy had gone outside, Blake smiled to himself and nodded in satisfaction. Popping the tab on the alumi-num can and watching the frothy beer roll down the side, Blake squinted thoughtfully through the smoke from his cigarette and offered Dani a seductive grin. "You've done a helluva job with him, Dani. He's a good kid."

"Can't argue with that." She began to clear the table and put the dishes in the sink.

"Thank God for small favors," Blake said.

"What's that supposed to mean?"

"Just that you've been on my case since I got here, spoiling for a fight."

"I just don't think I'm ready to have you back in town," she admitted. "Cody and I were getting along just fine without you."

Blake leaned back in the chair, propping his boots on Cody's vacated chair, his eyes becoming slits as he watched her work. "I can see that. It couldn't have been easy doing it all by yourself."

She lifted a shoulder. "It wasn't so bad. We've made out all right. Like you said, he's a good boy."

Stroking his chin and rocking the chair back on its two hind legs, he said, "I can see that. But then, he's had a good mother." Blake's voice was soft and warm, almost tender, but it didn't touch Dani the way it once had. In fact, Blake's attempts to close the gap between them only increased the distance. He stubbed his cigarette out in the ashtray.

"You don't need to compliment me, Blake, but what I would like to know is why you want anything to do with Cody." She stacked the dishes near the sink and turned to face him and all the old anger that she'd tried to repress for her son's sake rushed to the surface. "It's been seven years, for crying out loud. *Seven years!*"

"Maybe it's not just Cody I want," he said.

That did it! What little patience she'd held on to was instantly replaced by anger and resentment. "I don't want to hear any of this, Blake. You had plenty of chances to come home, way back when we both wanted and needed you, but we don't; not anymore—"

He stood and walked over to her and wrapped one big hand around her waist. "Just relax, Dani, and remember how good it was between us."

"I remember, all right. I remember that I was never enough woman for you—wasn't that how you phrased it?—that you never slept at home, that you didn't want Cody, that you tried to get me to sell my land, when my mother was ill, to pay your damned gambling debts! If you think for one minute that you can con me into believing that you've changed, you've got another think coming!"

She stepped away from him and though he reached

for her, the ice in her eyes and proud lift of her chin convinced him that she meant every word she said.

"I'm only putting up with you because I think Cody has the right to know his father!"

An excited scream came from outside and Cody ran into the house carrying a brand new .22. "Hey, Mom, look. Dad bought me a gun!"

"What!" she said, horrified.

"It's just a little .22," Blake said.

The anger she'd felt earlier was nothing in comparison with the rage that consumed her now. "You can't keep a .22," she said, shaking as she looked first to Cody and then past her son to Blake. "What's the matter with you?" she demanded. "You can't give a nine-year-old boy a rifle!"

"It's not a rifle; just a .22. I had one when I was his age."

Cody's grin fell and to his embarrassment, tears started to form in his eyes. Hastily he swiped them away. "Come on, Mom, lots of kids have 'em."

"And you're not 'lots of kids.' You know how I feel about guns. They're a big responsibility."

"He can handle it," Blake said.

"How would you know? You've been gone most of his life! How can you tell after just an hour that he can handle a .22, for God's sake!"

"Dani—"

But she couldn't think straight. All she knew was that Blake, whether intentional or not, was ruining her relationship with her son. "I think you'd better leave, Blake. It's late."

"Mom, no!" Cody wailed, looking frantically from one parent to the other. "It's barely eight o'clock. Dad, please, stay—" Eyes red-rimmed, Cody stared at his mother, silently pleading with her to change her mind.

Dani felt like dying on the spot, but though her insides were shaking, she ignored the desperation in Cody's eyes and said softly, "And when you go, take this damned thing with you." She took the gun from Cody and shoved it into Blake's hands.

"You can't—" Cody said, tears now streaming down his face.

"Maybe when you're older," she said, touching her son's shoulder. He recoiled as if she'd bitten him.

Blake's face turned granite hard. "Maybe I judged you too quickly, Dani," he said furiously. "Looks like you're not such a perfect mother after all."

"Just leave, Blake," she said through clenched teeth. "Before we say something we'll both regret and our son can't possibly be able to understand."

"I think you've already taken care of that!" he replied, his dark eyes blazing as he took the gun, offered a few words of comfort to his boy and walked out into the night. Cody stood at the screen door, crying and sobbing bitterly.

"Cody, I'm sorry that—"

"No, you're not!" the boy said, turning and screaming at her. "You're glad he's gone! You chased him away! *Again!* You didn't want him here, didn't think he'd come back and now that he did, you sent him away!" Sniffing and wiping his hand under his nose, Cody glared at his mother. "I hate you!" he said angrily. "I wish I lived with Dad!" He stomped up the stairs and slammed his door so hard that the windowpanes rattled.

"Oh, dear God," Dani whispered, supporting herself by holding on to the railing of the stairs. Cody's shot had hit its mark and Dani felt her heart crumble into a thousand pieces. The one thing in the world she'd hoped to avoid, she'd managed to do. Inadvertently she'd pushed Cody away from her.

Walking up the stairs, she stopped at Cody's room and quietly tapped on his door.

"Go 'way."

"I think we need to talk."

"No!"

She cracked open the door. Cody was lying on the bed in the semidarkness. His back was turned to her. "Son—"

"Leave·me alone!"

"Okay, I will," she said, fighting her own tears. "But we'll talk in the morning and I want you to know one thing."

No response. He didn't move except for the rise and fall of his shoulders and back as he breathed.

"I love you, Cody, and everything I do is because I want to protect you and help you grow up to be a responsible person. Believe me, not letting you have something is really harder than giving in."

"Sure. You just didn't want me to have something my dad, *my dad*, gave me!"

"No, Cody—"

He sat up suddenly and turned his red face to her. "You said you'd leave me alone!"

Quietly she closed his door and walked down the stairs to the living room. She saw the empty beer cans on the hearth, noticed the still dirty pots and pans in the sink and realized that her life would never be the same. Blake was back in Martinville and for some reason known only to him, he wanted to make amends with his son. Maybe she was too suspicious; maybe she should take Blake at face value, believe that he'd finally grown up and wanted to share the responsibilities of a son....

Cold dread settled between her shoulder blades. It was

already starting, she realized in wild desperation. Blake was back and was trying his damnedest to increase the rift between Cody and her.

"I can't let it happen," she told herself as she picked up the beer cans and tossed them into the plastic sack on the back porch. "No one is going to stand between me and my child!"

She tried to clear her mind and found it impossible. Her thoughts were swimming, her entire world off balance. "If only they'd leave us alone," she thought, thinking about Blake and Caleb.

Walking down the two steps to the backyard, she looked up the hill to the Johnson farm and her thoughts turned to Chase. Where was he and when would he be back? If he were here, things would be better...so much better.

THE NEXT MORNING Dani had already watered the garden, fed the cattle and horses, showered, dressed in clean clothes and started breakfast before she finally heard Cody rustling around upstairs. He came down the stairs a few minutes later. Barefoot, tucking his shirt into his pants and eyeing his mother cautiously, he walked into the kitchen.

"Feeling any better?" Dani asked.

Cody didn't respond. Taking a chair at the table, he didn't even bother to look up when Dani placed a stack of waffles and two strips of bacon on a plate and set the hot breakfast in front of him.

"I think we should talk," she said.

"Don't want to," he grumbled, spreading jam on his waffles before attacking them hungrily.

Her stomach in nervous knots, Dani sat down at the table across from her son and cradled a hot cup of coffee in her hands. She studied the anxious lines of his young face and wished she could make growing up easier on him. "Just because I don't let you have everything you want doesn't mean that I don't love you," she said. When Cody didn't respond, she sat back in her chair and blew across her coffee. "You hurt me very badly with the things you said last night."

He ignored her and kept eating in sullen silence.

"I had trouble sleeping."

"That makes two of us," he admitted.

"Believe it or not, I don't want to stand between you and your father—"

"Then why wouldn't you let me keep the .22?" Cody demanded, dropping his fork and piercing her with furious dark eyes. "You just didn't want Dad to give me something."

"No…I didn't want your dad to give you something you weren't ready for. A .22 is still a gun, Cody. A weapon. It's dangerous."

"I'd only use it on rabbits and birds—"

"Is that what you want to do? Go hunting?"

"Why not?"

"You've never shown any interest in it before."

Cody's lips pressed together. "Maybe that's because you've always treated me like a baby."

"And having a .22 makes you a man?"

"I just don't like being treated like a little kid."

"You're not. You have responsibilities around here, and you get paid for them. I think you're a very grown-up nine-year-old."

"Then—"

"But guns are for adults. Period."

Cody's chin stuck out and he crossed his arms over his chest. "Don't you think my father has any say in it?"

"Not when he's been gone for seven years." Dani forced a sad smile at her son. "I'm not trying to stop you from growing up, you know, I just want to make sure that you do it one step at a time."

When Cody realized she wasn't about to change her mind, he bravely fought off another round of embarrassing tears.

"I know you've missed your dad, and I hope that the two of you can make up for lost time," she said, wondering if she really believed her own words. "But you're my responsibility and I have to do what I think is best for you."

"Even if Dad disagrees."

"Yes."

He studied his remaining waffles and pushed them aside. "Would you let me live with Dad?" he asked suddenly.

Dani's stomach dropped, but she tried not to show it. Though she couldn't imagine her life without Cody, she managed to meet his inquiring gaze with steady eyes. "I don't think so," she said honestly. "Oh, I suppose if you were really unhappy with me and I thought Blake would do a better job of being a parent, then maybe I'd agree that you should live with him. But I think it's a little too early to make that kind of decision, don't you?"

"I don't know." He couldn't keep the anger out of his voice.

"Well, there's one thing you'd better think about."

"What's that?"

"I won't be threatened. And I won't let you play me against your father."

"What do you mean?"

"Exactly what I said. As long as you're with me, which I hope is for a very long time, we do things my way."

"And I don't have any say in it."

She shook her head and laughed. "You know that I always listen to you, don't you?"

He shrugged his shoulders.

"Sure you do. And neither of us wants to argue anymore. So, let's put it aside for now. I fed and watered the animals for you this morning. I figured you might want this last day off to do whatever you want. Tomorrow's a school day."

"Don't remind me," he groaned, but picked up his plate and carried it to the sink.

"If you want, you can have Shane over or maybe one of your other friends."

"Thanks, Mom," he said, as if understanding she was trying to mend fences. "But I don't think so. Dad said he'd come by. Maybe we can go fishin' or somethin'."

"Maybe," Dani agreed, silently telling herself it was the boy's right to be with his father.

"You won't get mad?"

"Not unless he tries to give you the gun again."

"Good." Cody went outside and Dani finished her coffee.

A few minutes later, she was hanging clothes on the line when she heard the sound of an engine coming down the drive. Bracing herself for another confrontation with Blake, she hurriedly snapped a clothespin on the last corner of the sheet just as there was a knock on the front door. She glanced out the window and recognized Chase's Jeep.

Thank God!

Heart beating wildly at the sight of him, she threw open the screen door and fell into his arms. "Thank God you're back," she whispered, clinging to him, drinking in the smell and feel of him as his arms surrounded her.

A lazy grin slid easily over Chase's face. "I sure didn't expect this kind of reception, lady." But his arms closed securely around her waist and he rested his head on the top of hers. "It's been a helluva week and I'm glad I'm back." He placed an index finger under her chin and tilted her face so that he could look into her troubled eyes. "What's wrong?"

"Wrong?" she repeated.

"Yes—something happened." His jaw hardened and his eyes narrowed suspiciously. "What's Caleb done now?"

"Nothing…it's nothing to do with him," she said, breaking out of his embrace and rubbing her arms as if suddenly chilled.

"That's hard to believe."

"Cody's father came back yesterday."

"What!"

"My reaction, too," she whispered.

Chase went stock-still. "And?" he prodded.

Dani let out a long, worried sigh. "And he had dinner with us last night."

Chase's face became hard, his eyes slits as he walked over to the fireplace, leaned against the mantel and watched her. "Just like that—all of a sudden?"

"No. There were some letters and then Cody got a call from him…I just can't believe he's here."

"Neither can I," Chase muttered. "Strange, don't you think?"

"What do you mean?"

"He's been gone for—what, six years?"

"Seven."

"And now, just when things are coming to a boil with Johnson, when I'm out of town, he shows up." Chase paced in front of the fireplace, rubbing the back of his neck, and his suspicions gelled. "Son of a bitch," he muttered under his breath, his fists balling.

"He said something about a job giving out; that he wanted to get to know Cody—"

Chase cranked his head to stare at her. "You believe him?"

Dani sighed and dropped onto an arm of the couch. "I don't know what to believe. All I know is that I don't want him here and Cody does. So—I let him come over, just last night. Things were going along just fine until after dinner when Blake tried to give Cody a gun—a .22— and I objected. We argued and I ended up asking Blake to leave with the gun."

"And Cody didn't like it."

"No." She shuddered. "He screamed and yelled at me, told me he hated me, said he wanted to live with his father..." Her voice cracked and she had to take a deep breath to control herself. "I...I stood my ground, but—"

"You're afraid you're losing him," Chase guessed, coming up behind her and placing his hands on her shoulders. She was turned away from him, but the tender warmth of his fingers soothed some of her fears. He nuzzled the back of her neck and the strength flowing from his body to hers helped ease her fears.

"I just wish Blake had never come back," she said bitterly, balling her fist and pressing it to her lips.

"Maybe it's better that he did," Chase said, trying to stamp down his own insane feelings of jealousy. "Cody needed to meet him; see what kind of a man his father is."

"If I just hadn't gotten so...angry."

"Shh. Don't blame yourself for doing what you think was right." Chase rotated her and folded her body neatly to his. "He's not going to come between you and Cody or us."

She heard the beating of his heart, felt the security of his hard, strong body against hers. Her arms wrapped around Chase's neck and she sighed in contentment when he kissed the top of her head. "I'm just glad you're back," she whispered.

"Mom?" Cody stepped through the screen door and stopped dead in his tracks when he saw his mother and Chase. "Oh, no," he whispered, starting to back out of the room and staring at Dani with accusing eyes.

Dani extracted herself from Chase's embrace and followed her son to the porch. "What did you want?"

"Never mind," he grumbled.

"Cody—"

"He's the reason you don't want Dad around, isn't he?" he said, jerking his head in the direction of the house just as Chase came outside.

"Of course not—"

"Why don't you just go away, mister," Cody said, squinting up at Chase. "Instead of trying to be friends with me and coming on to my mom, why don't you just go back to Caleb Johnson's place, where you belong? Or better yet, go to Idaho or wherever it is you come from!"

"Cody!"

But Cody didn't bother listening. Instead he jumped on his ten-speed and rode the bike around the corner of the house and down the lane as fast as he could.

Dani started after him and got as far as the side of the house where her pickup was parked before Chase grabbed her arm and restrained her from running after the boy. "Let him go."

"I can't!"

"He needs to blow off some steam, work things out in his own mind," he said. "Let him cool off. He'll be back."

Knowing in her heart that Chase was right, Dani looked despairingly down the drive to the rapidly disappearing image of her son. "It's just so damned hard to let go."

"I know." Chase tugged at her arm. "Come on. Let's go inside. I'll buy you a cup of coffee."

"I don't think I could eat or drink anything," she said.

"Try. For me."

Once in the kitchen, Chase poured them each a cup of coffee and then, as Dani carried the cups outside, he followed with the red enamel pot.

They sat together in the quiet shade of the apple tree and watched the sheets billowing in the slight morning breeze.

"Feeling better?" Chase asked.

"A little," she said, and then amended the statement. "Make that a lot."

"I thought so. At least I hoped."

The crown of her head was warm from the morning sun. A slight breeze cooled her skin and Chase's presence gave Dani a sense of peace and contentment she'd been lacking in the past few days. If only Cody were here to share this blissful serenity, life would be perfect.

"He'll be back," Chase whispered.

"You're sure?" Her smooth brow puckered with worry.

"I promise." He touched the side of her face, caressed her cheek, and let his fingers tangle in the soft honey-colored strands of her hair.

"I could almost believe anything you told me," she said with a dimpled smile.

"That's encouraging. Listen." Over the hum of insects and the whisper of the wind in the leaves overhead, the sound of a pickup as it turned into the drive caught Chase's attention. "I'll bet Cody ran into a friend who gave him a lift home."

"I hope you're right," Dani said, standing and running

to the front of the house only to have her soaring expectations dashed to the ground.

Blake.

"Oh, God," she whispered, her throat tight. Cody's bike was in the back of the pickup and Cody was sitting in the cab of his father's truck as Blake maneuvered the pickup up the twin ruts of the lane.

"I take it Cody's with his father." Chase grabbed his hat and put it on.

"You take it right."

"Do you want me to leave?" Chase asked, though he had no intention of doing anything of the kind.

"No...it's all right."

"Good." Chase's chiseled mouth was set firmly and his arms were folded over his broad chest as he crossed his ankles and leaned against one of the fence posts.

"Mornin'," Blake said as he got out of the cab of his truck.

Chase touched the brim of his Stetson in reply. The hat shaded his eyes and gave him an opportunity to watch Blake Summers. He felt immediate dislike for the man but didn't say anything because of the boy. Instead he held his tongue for a later time, when Cody wasn't present. The effort made his muscles ache with tension.

"I—I didn't expect you back so soon," Dani said, looking nervously from Blake to Chase and back again.

"Found my son hightailin' it into town. Thought I'd better find out why."

A muscle jumped in Chase's jaw, but still he leaned on the fence post, as if content to stay out of a family argument.

"We had a little misunderstanding."

"A big one, the way I hear it."

"It was just a disagreement, Blake." She turned concerned eyes on her son. "Cody, are you okay?"

The boy lifted a shoulder and stared at her with total disrespect. "I guess so."

"You know I don't like to fight with you."

"Then why's he still here?" Cody asked, pointing at Chase.

Chase shifted, pushed up the brim of his hat and straightened. Walking over to Dani and standing near her, he introduced himself to Blake and was offered a tight-lipped nod in return.

"Chase is here because I want him here," Dani said, feeling color burn her cheeks.

"Just like Dad's here 'cause I want him here," Cody retorted. He took a step closer to Blake and continued to glare at Chase.

"The boy and I plan to go fishin'," Blake said. "He claims he's got himself a right good hole above the south fork." Blake glanced at Chase and his lips twisted downward before he looked back at Dani. "So if ya don't mind—"

"I don't mind, as long as you stay on the place."

Cody took hold of Blake's arm and eagerly started leading him to the back of the property. "Come on, Dad, you're gonna love it!"

"I'm sure I will," Blake said as they passed Dani and he darted her a quick, assessing glance. He was wearing a smile that didn't seem quite natural and his skin was taut over the angles of his face. He hadn't shaved and there were bags below his reddened eyes.

Dani's stomach curled. She'd seen Blake in the same shape before; hungover and surly after a long night's binge.

"Why did he come back here?" she asked herself once Blake and Cody were out of earshot.

"Your guess is as good as mine," Chase said, rubbing his jaw thoughtfully as he watched Cody and Blake walk past the barn. "Maybe he's feeling mortal; needs the security of knowing his son."

"And maybe he's up to no good," Dani thought aloud.

"Time will tell."

"That's what I'm afraid of," Dani said. "I just hope that he doesn't hurt Cody."

"So you honestly don't think that Blake is just here because he loves his son?"

"I don't think Blake Summers is capable of love," she said firmly, as Blake, Cody and Runt waded across the creek and walked through the final field before disappearing into the thicket of brush and pine trees in the foothills.

CHAPTER TEN

CHASE NOTICED THE lines of worry etching across Dani's forehead and the way she chewed on her lower lip long after Cody and Blake had left. "Maybe you'd better tell me if you want me to stick around," he suggested.

"What's that supposed to mean?" she asked, turning her attention to him.

He was standing in the shade of the apple tree. Reaching upward, he picked an apple that was beginning to stripe red over green and tossed it in the air, catching it deftly. "Just that I don't want to interfere—cause any more problems between you and Cody."

"You aren't."

"I heard what he said."

"I know, but he was angry with me, not you. He can't seem to understand that what Blake and I shared is over. He thinks we should be able to resurrect it somehow."

Chase shoved his hands deep into his pockets. "And what do you think?"

"Honestly?"

He nodded, his firm mouth turning down at the corners. "Honestly."

"I wish he'd never come back. That he'd just leave us alone."

Chase's thick brows arched. "Well, once the newness of having his dad around wears off, maybe Cody won't be so quick to champion Blake's cause. Right now Blake's come back for the boy and that makes him a hero in Cody's eyes. But you've always been here for him. Cody's a smart boy. He'll come around."

"I doubt it," she said with a sigh as she walked back toward the house. "But I don't suppose there's any point in brooding. Blake's back and that's that. I'll just have to learn how to deal with him."

Chase grinned. "That's the spirit." He tossed the apple to her and she caught it. Smiling, she took a bite of the tart Gravenstein and then made a face. "I think you rushed this one," she said, opening the screen door and waiting until Chase had walked inside.

"Meaning the apple?" he asked.

"I don't know; I get a feeling you rush everything. Jump in feet first."

"Sometimes."

She straightened the afghan on the back of the couch before going into the kitchen. "Can I get you something? Coffee? Tea? Or—" she opened the refrigerator and peeked inside "—uh, we still have some orange juice, half a pitcher of lemonade and a few cans of beer that Blake hasn't found."

"Coffee's fine." He walked to the kitchen and leaned one shoulder against the arch separating the rooms as he watched her nervously pour the hot liquid into heavy ceramic mugs. "Try to relax."

"Easier said than done," she admitted.

"Great. Then I don't suppose you want to hear what I found out while I was gone."

Looking over her shoulder and seeing his grim countenance, she braced herself for the worst. "More bad news?"

"I'm afraid so."

"I may as well hear it," she said with a sigh and then forced a feeble grin. "Give it to me straight." Handing him a cup of coffee, she took a sip from her mug and sat at the table.

"It looks as if Caleb put the drum of dioxin in the creek on purpose."

"He admitted it?" she asked dubiously.

"No, but I managed to talk to the hand that actually did the dirty work, a guy by the name of Larry Cross. Shortly after Johnson asked Cross to puncture the lid and bury the drum in the creekbed, Caleb gave the guy his walking papers…along with quite a substantial amount of money to keep quiet."

"So why did he talk to you?"

"Johnson's money didn't last long. And the man wasn't opposed to making a few extra dollars on the deal."

"So you bribed him?"

"Paid him for information."

"Same thing." She dropped her chin into her hand and fought off the waves of depression that threatened to wash over her. "When it rains, it pours," she said, drinking thoughtfully from her cup. "And they say trouble comes in threes."

"They might be wrong."

"I don't know. First Blake wanting to be with Cody, then proof that Caleb would stoop to just about any lengths to get me to sell my farm and then—" She stopped mid-sentence, as if in not speaking the thought would make it go away.

"Then what?" Chase asked, crossing the room, turning a chair around and straddling the seat.

"Well, it's nothing really," she said, her hands beginning to sweat.

"Something's wrong."

"Maybe—"

"Why don't you tell me about it?"

Why not? No time like the present to get things out in the open. "Cody and I were in the grocery store the other day and I heard a rumor about one of Caleb's hands."

"That doesn't surprise me," Chase said, noticing the band of freckles across her nose. "What about him?"

"I'm not really sure. But Jenna Peterson is pretty upset with him. The way I heard it she doesn't trust him."

"What's his name?"

"I…don't know. She didn't say. But it's some new guy who works with Caleb."

"Maybe he hired someone when I was gone," Chase said thoughtfully. "But even if he did, that doesn't sound like Jenna. She's usually a rock. The only person on the whole damned spread I can trust."

"That's what makes it so worrisome," Dani admitted, her hazel eyes staring at Chase's rugged face. It was a handsome face, hard around the edges, but softened by a sensual dimple when he smiled. The self-effacing glint in his clear blue eyes balanced the determination in the set of his jaw and the pride in his bearing. Chase was a contradictory man of so many emotions and passions, and Dani loved him so much it hurt.

"Wait a minute!" he said, holding his cup, his blue eyes becoming hard. "You heard a rumor and you thought it had something to do with me, didn't you?"

"I don't know who it was about—I just want to know if there's any truth in it. It would take a lot to upset Jenna Peterson. She's worked with and trusted Caleb Johnson for years."

"Dani," Chase said, his lips whitening at the corners as he tried to stay calm, "I've done everything I can to be straight with you!" Scraping his chair back, he stood, rammed his hands, palms out, in the back pockets of his jeans and began pacing. "I don't know what more I can do or say to let you know I'm on your side." His boots clicked on the cracked linoleum with each of his long, impatient strides. "I've found evidence you need against Caleb, I stood up for you when you came ranting and raving into his house, and I've done everything short of throwing my contract into his face." Spinning on his heel, he impaled her with his furious gaze. "Lord, woman," he said through clenched teeth, "I've even asked you to marry me and you still can't trust me! What the devil do you want from me?"

"Just honest answers, that's all," Dani said, feeling a little contrite but still angry. All the frustrations of the past weeks burned inside her. "I feel manipulated by the whole lot of you—Caleb, Blake and you!"

Chase came over to the table and placed his hands flat on the polished maple. Pushing his face to within inches of hers, he stared straight into her eyes. She could see his rage in the flare of his nostrils, the way his skin tightened over his tense jaw and the flecks of blue anger in his eyes. He was trying to hold his temper in check, but failing miserably. Rapping the table with his index finger, he growled, "I don't like being put in the same corral as Caleb and Blake, lady. All I've ever done is try to help you—whether you believe it or not. Now, if you don't want my help, fine. All you have to do is say the word and I'm outta here."

Her throat was dry, her emotions raw, but she tossed her head back and glared at him. "I trust *you*, Chase. As a person."

"What the hell is that supposed to mean?"

"It's just that this whole damned situation has gotten to me. Not only is Blake back, maybe with the intention of taking my son from me, but now we know for sure that Caleb will do anything, *anything* to get me off my land.

If that isn't bad enough, you're partners with the man, for God's sake!"

"So we're back to that, are we?"

"I don't think we ever got past it."

"And *I* don't know why I have to keep proving myself to you." His eyes narrowed and his hand reached forward to clasp her wrist. "I think we'd better settle this right now! Come on!"

"Wait a minute—"

He jerked her out of the chair, grabbed his hat and shoved it onto his head as he walked out of the door with Dani, still in tow, continuing to protest loudly.

The day had turned hazy and dark clouds had begun to surround the mountain peaks. "Where do you think you're taking me?"

"Away."

She looked back at her house in confusion. "But I just can't leave. Cody—"

"Cody's with his dad!" Chase snapped. "Do you think Blake will hurt him?"

"No, but—"

"Then come on! We'll be back by the time that Cody gets home!"

"But I should leave him a note!"

"Yeah, maybe you should. But you don't have time." Chase jerked open the door on the passenger side of the Jeep and waited for her to climb in.

"It will just take a minute to scribble a note," she said, the wind picking up and whipping her hair around her face. "Be sensible, Chase."

"I have been! Now it's time we did things my way!"

Dani stood her ground and didn't get into the Jeep. "Where are we going?"

"To Johnson's."

"What the devil—"

"I'll explain later," he said, eyeing the darkening sky and releasing her. "Go on, write your damned note. But be quick about it."

Anger radiating from her body, she marched back to the house, wrote a quick message to her son and strode outside. Chase was where she'd left him, leaning insolently against the side of the dusty Jeep, the door of his vehicle still swung open and waiting.

"Has anyone ever told you you're an arrogant bastard?" she asked as she climbed into the Jeep.

"You! Several times." He slammed the door shut, ran around the front of the vehicle, climbed in the driver's side and then did a quick U-turn in the driveway, spinning gravel from under the tires as the Jeep bounced down the long lane leading to the main highway.

Dani sat with her arms crossed over her chest, staring straight ahead. "Do you mind telling me what you've got up your sleeve?"

"You'll see," Chase said grimly, shifting down and barely slowing as he turned off the highway and into Caleb's tree-lined lane. The Jeep roared up the gravel drive and Dani's stomach twisted nervously at the thought of confronting Caleb again on his property. After all, she'd never caught Caleb himself on her land and none of what he'd done to her could be proven—until now.

"Get out," Chase ordered once he'd parked the Jeep.

"Wait a minute—"

"You wait a minute! You're the one who's been itching to have it out with Johnson. Okay, here's your big chance. Let's go."

"But what if Larry Cross lied? It's just his word against Johnson's."

"Except that I've got the evidence, remember?"

"Which is?"

"The drum of dioxin—the drum that Caleb purchased."

Without any further words, he jumped out of his side of the Jeep, slammed the door shut and waited, his jaw set in anger, as Dani climbed out of the rig and fought the urge to run away. She was seeing a side of Chase she hadn't seen since the first day she'd watched him wading in the creek. But then she'd had the advantage; she'd been on her property and in the right. Now she wasn't sure whose side he was on and even where the battle lines were drawn.

Trust him, she told herself as she stood next to him.

Chase scanned the stable yard, his eyes going over every inch of the clean white buildings and fence surrounding the parking lot behind the large farmhouse. Then, seeing the object of his wrath, he took Dani's hand in his and started walking quickly to the track where Caleb was watching his latest acquisition sprint at breakneck speed for a quarter of a mile.

"Here we go," Dani muttered under her breath as they approached Caleb and the old man turned toward them.

Frowning slightly at the sight of Dani, Caleb leaned one elbow over the top rail of the fence and straightened the string tie at his neck.

"Mrs. Summers," he said congenially. "How're you?"

"Well as can be expected," she replied, glancing nervously at Chase and wishing she'd refused to come with him. Beneath the facade of neighborliness, she could see Caleb's hostility, feel his hatred.

Caleb glanced at the threatening sky. "Looks like we'll be gettin' that rain we need tonight. Weather service says that we'll have a few storms in the next few days…" Pleasantries aside, Caleb got down to business. "Now, what brings you here this afternoon?" he asked, looking pointedly at Chase. "I don't s'pose it's to see my new colt run, now, is it?"

"No," Chase said, leaning his back on the fence and eyeing the horse as the stocky colt, done with his sprint, was being walked around the track. The horse's dark muscles gleamed with sweat and he was blowing hard. Chase eyed Caleb.

Dani watched Caleb's reaction.

The older man's mouth twitched nervously and his blue eyes were filled with impatience and subdued anger.

"Actually Dani didn't want to come up here. It was my idea."

"Oh?" Caleb's jaw slid to the side but he refused to be baited. Chase would get to the point. Eventually. And if given enough rope, the younger man would hang himself. Caleb made a mental note to give him all the rope he needed.

"Yep. Y'see, while I was in Idaho, I did some checkin' around."

"On that job in Spokane?"

"That, too," Chase said slowly. "But I was looking into something else; something that happened here last year. I managed to locate a man who used to work for you. A man by the name of Larry Cross. You remember him?"

Caleb nodded slowly and waved at the boy who'd ridden the colt during the workout. "Keep cooling him off and then put him back in his stall. Jim'll clean him up," he called to the hand before turning back to Chase. "Larry Cross? Sure, I remember him."

Dani felt the sweat run down her back, though the breeze whispering through the pine trees near the track was cool.

"I had to let him go," Caleb admitted. "Turned out he was stealing me blind, selling part of my feed to friends of his. I couldn't prove it, of course, but I think he was into cattle rustlin' as well. I'm surprised you bothered to look him up."

"Seems he had a few other tricks up his sleeve."

Caleb frowned. "Wouldn't surprise me."

"He placed a drum of dioxin in the creekbed last year. The poison got into the water and killed several of Dani's cattle."

"You're sure of that?" Caleb asked, rubbing his chin and glancing sideways at Dani.

Her heart beginning to pound, she nodded.

"I've got the empty drum," Chase remarked.

Caleb's bushy eyebrows raised and he drew his mouth into an exaggerated frown. "Sounds like something Cross would do."

"He claims you were behind it."

"'Course he does."

"He says you did it to give Dani a bad time; ruin her herd, force her to sell her property to you."

Caleb snorted, but beads of sweat had broken out over his brow. He mopped his forehead with a handkerchief he found in his pocket. "Well, what did you expect him to say—that he was behind it himself?"

"No. Because it doesn't make any sense that way. Why would he want to hurt Dani?"

Caleb stared at Dani with cold, cruel eyes. "Who knows? Maybe he was involved with her. She's been alone a long time till you came along—"

Chase took a step closer and curled his fingers over Caleb's arm. "Don't even suggest—"

"I never met anyone named Larry Cross!" Dani said angrily, color flushing her face. She tried to step forward but felt Chase's hand grip her forearm and restrain her as he backed a few steps away from Caleb.

Caleb shrugged. "I can only guess at his motives, but the man was bad news. I got rid of him as soon as I found out about him, but I didn't know about any drum of dioxin."

"What about the time you tried to siphon off all the water from Grizzly Creek for your own private lake?" Dani demanded, her fury getting the better of her tongue.

"Well," Caleb said, spreading his hands, "I'd like to blame Cross for that one, but I'll have to own up to it. I thought I'd be able to deter a little water for the lake without interrupting the flow too badly. Looks like I misjudged."

"Looks like," Dani agreed, her eyes narrowing to slits.

"But I admitted it and as soon as I realized that you weren't getting enough water, I scrapped my idea for a lake."

"But you didn't know anything about a drum of dioxin?"

"Nope," Caleb said, shaking his head slowly. "First I've heard of it."

"Cross says different," Chase said.

"Cross would."

"He claims you paid him to keep quiet. To the tune of five thousand dollars."

Caleb laughed outright. "I'm not the kind of man who likes to throw money away," he said. "You know that. I gave Cross the boot and an extra week's pay and, as far as I'm concerned, he was lucky to get that." He smiled smugly. "Check the books if you don't believe me."

"I have."

"Well?"

"Nothing."

Caleb lifted his shoulders.

"Cross is willing to testify."

"It's just his word against mine, McEnroe. Who do you think the judge would believe?" Smiling, he slapped the top rail of the fence. "Now, how about a drink—or some lunch?"

"No, thanks," Dani said. "Cody's expecting me back."

"But I would like a chance to talk to Jenna," Chase said, propelling Dani toward the house.

"I don't think that's possible," the older man replied.

"Why not?"

"Didn't you know? Jenna left me high and dry. Yes, sir! Just two days ago. Took off and swore she wasn't comin' back."

Chase, his countenance grim, whirled on his boot heel to face the old man. "Why?"

Dread, cold as winter night, skittered down Dani's spine.

"She claimed she was moving…somewhere in Wyoming, I think. Has a sister near Laramie or Cheyenne or somewhere. Couldn't even give me a couple weeks notice, if ya can believe that."

"I believe it," Chase said through clenched teeth. "But I think you put her up to it."

"Now why would I do that? Best cook in the county. Jenna's been with me for nearly twenty years and just the other day, quick as a cat climbing a tree, she up and quits."

"So who's taking care of the house?" Chase asked.

Caleb seemed more relaxed. "Maria. Wife of one of the hands. She's got lunch on the table, I reckon. Sure you can't stay?"

"Positive," Dani cut in before Chase could say anything. They had been walking toward the house through the parking lot and Dani stopped at Chase's Jeep.

The wind caught on one of the shutters and it banged

against the barn. "Looks like we're in for a nasty one," Caleb said.

Chase glanced up at the threatening sky. "I'll be back later."

"Good." Caleb clapped Chase on the back and then walked slowly toward his farmhouse.

"So what do you suppose prompted Jenna to quit?" Chase asked once they were back in the Jeep and heading toward Dani's farm. Big drops of rain began to pelt from the sky, hitting the windshield and running down the glass in grimy streaks. Chase snapped on the wipers and squinted as he turned off the main road.

"You don't believe him," she said flatly.

"Not for one minute. Do you?"

"No."

"I didn't think so," Chase muttered, parking the Jeep by the house. "Maybe we'd better do some checking around."

"Now?"

"Before Jenna has a chance to leave town."

"I can't go," Dani said, eyeing Blake's pickup. "Not until I've touched base with Cody. They shouldn't be out in this storm...." She hoped that Blake and Cody had enough sense to come back to the house.

Chase looked as if he were about to argue, but kept quiet. Instead he jumped down from the Jeep and held his jacket over Dani's head as they ran to the house. Once they were on the porch, Chase wiped the raindrops from his hair. "Caleb certainly is a cool one, isn't he?"

"As ice." Dani held the screen door open with her body to allow Chase to pass. "It's spooky."

"Spooky?" he repeated with a laugh.

"Laugh if you want, but that man gives me the creeps. I've never met anyone who can talk out of both sides of his mouth the way that Caleb can," she said while rubbing her arms before shaking her head at the impossibility of the situation. "I hate to admit it, you know, but I suppose I owe you an apology."

"Probably," Chase agreed. "But let's call it even."

"Fair enough." Dani flashed a quick smile and then walked to the window near the fireplace and stared across the fields and past the creek. "I wish I knew what Caleb was up to," she said, idly brushing the dust from the windowsill with her finger. "But then, I wish I knew what Blake wanted, too."

"And me?" Chase asked, standing beside her.

"Yes," she admitted with a thoughtful frown. "I'd like to know what you really want."

"It's simple," he said. "I just want out of the yoke of this mockery of a partnership with Caleb and I want you to come to Boise and marry me."

"You make it sound so easy." Sighing, she leaned against him, grateful for his strength.

"It could be, if you'd let it." He reached into his pocket and withdrew a small black jeweler's box. "Open it," he instructed as he wrapped her small hand around the velvet case.

Dani felt tears in her eyes as she snapped open the case and viewed the dainty gold ring with a large pear-shaped diamond. Her throat was so swollen, she couldn't speak.

"I was going to wait until tonight, when we were alone and Cody was in bed...but I hadn't counted on Blake showing up or all your suspicions about my being involved with Caleb."

"I don't know what to say," she whispered, eyes brimming with unshed tears.

"Just say yes."

Pausing only a moment, she extracted the ring from

its case and slid it onto her finger. "Yes," she murmured, closing her eyes and letting the tears drizzle down her cheeks.

Chase took her face in his hands and kissed the salty tracks on her skin. "I love you, Dani. And no matter what happens, we'll pull through this together." Kissing her gently on the lips, he silently promised her a future of togetherness and joy.

Dani slid her arms around his neck and listened to the comforting beat of his heart. Desperate for the security and love he offered, she returned his kiss and managed to forget, for a little while, all the problems still plaguing her.

CODY AND BLAKE hadn't returned. Dani was worried, but Chase insisted that she calm down. "Every good fisherman knows that the best time to catch fish is just as the sun sets," he said.

"But it's after nine! And it's been raining off and on all afternoon. And the wind—" As if to add emphasis to her words, the wind picked up and banged a branch of the apple tree against the back porch. "Oh, God," she whispered, still pacing back and forth. "Something's wrong. I can feel it."

"Do you want me to go looking for them?"

"No— Yes— No, I don't know what to do," she moaned, running her fingers through her hair. "Damn!" Perching on the edge of a chair, she rested her chin on her hands and tried to ignore the worries nagging at her. "You know, before this all started, I used to be a competent woman—"

"I remember," he said, smiling and glancing at the empty rifle hanging over the fireplace. "Look, Cody knows the way home. He'll be back soon—"

Just then, they heard Runt's familiar bark. Dani leaped

out of the chair and opened the door to allow a drenched dog into the house. He ran into the kitchen, shook his coat and checked his bowl for dinner scraps.

Dani walked out to the back porch and though it was dark, she saw Cody running up to the house. Blake was several yards behind the boy.

"Thank God," Dani whispered.

"Hey, Mom," Cody cried jubilantly, "we caught a million fish!"

"A million?" she repeated.

"Well, maybe twelve or thirteen," Cody corrected, pushing his hair out of his eyes and streaking his forehead with mud. Then he clomped onto the back porch and tried to knock the mud from his shoes. He set his pole and creel against the rail.

"I was worried about you," Dani said softly.

"Aw, Mom—"

"Why?" Blake asked, finally catching up to the boy.

"It's late and the storm—"

"Just a little rainshower, Dani. And it's not that late— only a little after nine—"

"Nearly ten," Dani corrected. "And Cody has school tomorrow."

"He'll make it, won't ya, boy?" Blake asked, kicking off his boots as if he intended to stay, and then seeing Chase in the doorway, changed his mind. Swearing to himself, he put the boots back on his feet. "So ya still got company, huh?"

"That's right."

Blake ran a hand over his beard-roughened chin. "I thought maybe you'd let me stay the night—" Then, seeing the fury blazing in Chase's eyes and the way the man's shoulders bunched, as if he'd like nothing better than to whip the tar out of one Blake Summers, Blake added, "On the couch of course."

"No."

"Other plans?" Blake asked, eyeing Chase as he walked through the door and stood beside Dani.

"That's enough, Summers," Chase warned, his lips thinning menacingly.

Blake shivered and stood.

"Cody, I think you'd better go upstairs and get cleaned up and ready for bed," Dani suggested, smelling the fight that was brewing between the two men.

The boy stood his ground, though he chewed anxiously on his lip. "But, Mom—"

"Now."

Swallowing hard, Cody looked to his father, but Blake just slowly shook his head. "Listen to your ma, boy. It's time I was shovin' off anyway." He stood and scowled darkly at Chase as he brushed his hands on his jeans.

"You can stay," Cody blurted out, his boyish, confused eyes darting from one adult to another. "I have an extra bed in my room and—"

"Not tonight, son," Blake said after reading the warning in Dani's eyes and the set of determination in her jaw. "Another time, maybe."

"And maybe not," Dani said.

Smiling briefly at his son and then sending Dani a threatening glance, Blake walked off the back porch and around to the front of the house. A few seconds later Blake's pickup roared to life.

Cody, who'd stood stock-still throughout the argument, ran through the house to the front porch, where he waved frantically at his father as the taillights of the pickup faded into the night.

Without another word, the boy dashed up the stairs

and into his room. A few seconds later he stomped to the bathroom and took a shower.

"Do you want me to talk to him?" Chase asked.

Dani shook her head. "No. I think this one is between Cody and his mother."

"Then maybe I should go." He took her into his arms and kissed her gently on the mouth.

Warmth invaded Dani's body, coloring her face. "You can stay," she whispered.

Groaning and hazarding a glance at the stairs, Chase shook his head. "You need time to sort things out with Cody, and besides, I still need to check on Jenna Peterson. I don't buy Caleb's story. My guess is that he fired her. Now the only question is why?"

"Not the only question," Dani said with a sigh.

"First things first," Chase said, releasing her. "You deal with Cody and I'll be back as soon as I can."

She watched him leave and slowly closed the door when his Jeep was out of sight. Then, ignoring the loneliness settling over her, and with renewed determination, she mounted the stairs to tell her son that she was going to marry Chase McEnroe.

CHAPTER ELEVEN

THE NEXT MORNING Dani still hadn't talked to her son. After Chase had left the night before, Dani had tried to talk to Cody, but he'd refused to speak to her. Now, nothing had changed, she thought ruefully as she swept the kitchen floor and waited for him to get up.

He waited until the last minute before dashing down the stairs and pausing at the table for breakfast. While she put the jug of milk on the table, he sat, avoiding her eyes, his fingers nervously drumming on the polished wood.

"Slow down a minute," Dani said with a warm smile. "I think we've got a few things we should discuss before you take off for school."

"But I'm already late—"

"I know. But I can drive you. I want to talk."

"'Bout what?" He poured milk on his cereal and started eating.

"Last night, for starters," she replied, leaning on the broom. "And then maybe just about us—you and me— and how we're going to handle dealing with your dad now that he's back in town."

Cody's eyes flashed. "*I* can handle dealing with him just fine."

"You think so?" she said gently, trying with difficulty not to sound like a dictator.

"You're the one with the problem, Mom."

"Believe it or not, Cody, I'm trying to be very open-minded about this and work it out so that we're all happy."

After putting the broom back in the closet, she poured a cup of coffee and took a chair opposite him.

"Humph," Cody said stubbornly. "I suppose you think you're gonna try to tell me when I can be with him."

"No, but—"

"Sure you are!"

Dani held up her hands to ward off the battle, and Cody stared straight at her left hand, his mouth dropping open and his eyes reflecting an inner pain at the sight of her engagement ring. "Where'd you get that—from Chase? You're gonna marry that guy, aren't you?" he said, balling a fist and pounding it on the table, his face flushing red and contorting in a battle against tears of outrage. "Dammit!"

"Cody!"

"Well, are you?" His brown eyes pierced hers and though she ached to soften the blow, she had to tell him the truth.

"Okay. Yes, Chase asked me to marry him and I agreed, but I was going to talk it over with you before we made any definite plans."

"It looks pretty definite to me!" he shouted, pointing at the ring angrily before pleading with her. "Mom, don't do this! Not now." And then a look of new horror spread over his face and his tears began in earnest. "Oh, I get it. You're doing this *because* of Dad, aren't you?"

"Your father has nothing to do with the fact that I want to marry Chase—"

"But Dad loves you! He told me so, just yesterday!" Cody cut in.

"He doesn't love me, Cody—"

"He does! I asked him and he told me he never stopped loving you or me! He wants to come back and you...you're marrying a man who works for Caleb Johnson just to keep Dad and me apart!" Livid, he pushed his chair back, grabbed his backpack from under the table and flung open the front door.

"Oh, Cody, I would never—"

"You would! You have!" he screamed. "You couldn't even give Dad a chance, could you?"

With that, he ran outside and raced down the hill to the bus stop.

"That does it!" Dani said, thinking about chasing him down and even following the bus to school if she had to. She'd reached for her keys and purse and taken a step toward the door before she thought better of her plan and sagged against the wall. Following Cody would only end up in another bitter argument that would probably embarrass them both in front of his friends and teachers. He would never forgive her.

Knowing that she had to give him time to cool off and think rationally, she hung her keys back on the hook in the kitchen and watched him anxiously through the window. The bus stopped at the end of the lane, honked and waited as Cody ran the final few yards and climbed aboard.

"When he gets home, we're having it out—all of it!" she promised herself angrily. "I've got to make him understand that I'm marrying Chase for both of us." *And no matter how much it hurts, I'll get used to the fact that Blake is back and Cody needs to spend time with him,* she added silently to herself.

WHEN CODY DIDN'T get off the bus after school, Dani tried not to panic. Several times in the past, Cody had gone to a friend's house without telling her. Though she'd made him promise never to go anywhere without calling her, she rationalized that he'd left in a huff in the morning and was probably childishly attempting to punish her by staying away from home.

And it was working. She glanced at the clock every two minutes and listened for his step on the back porch while folding clothes in the kitchen.

Where was he? She thought about calling Chase, but didn't. "Stop it, Dani," she told herself. "Don't depend on him too much. This is your problem. You can handle it." But deep down she yearned to pour her troubles out to him. Absently, she toyed with her new ring. "It'll all work out," she told herself and looked out the window, wondering where the devil Cody was.

After a half an hour of waiting, she couldn't stand the suspense and dread beginning to settle on her shoulders. She started calling all of Cody's friends, beginning with Shane Donahue. Twenty minutes later, she replaced the receiver slowly and felt her insides begin to quiver in fear. No one had seen her son.

"Blast it, Cody," she whispered. "Where are you?"

Her heart beating double time, she called the school and was connected with Cody's teacher, who explained that Cody hadn't been in school all day.

Panic swept over her as she listened to Amanda Ross's apologies and worries. Hanging up the phone with shaking fingers, Dani closed her eyes against the very real fear that Blake had taken Cody away from her.

She could imagine the scene: Cody, still brooding from the fight with Dani had gone to Blake's brother's house, had found Blake and told him that his mother intended to marry another man and move far away, taking Cody away from his father. Blake's natural response would have been to comfort the child and take him away from the intolerable situation.

"Oh, no," she whispered. "Please, God, no." Images of

Blake and Cody rambling across the country in Blake's battered old pickup filled her mind before other, more terrifying thoughts struck her. Maybe Cody wasn't with his father. Maybe he'd taken off on his own, or started hitchhiking to God-only-knew-where.

Trying to think clearly, Dani called Blake's brother, who lived in Martinville, but no one answered. She slammed the receiver down and held it in place before scrounging in the desk for the phone book and looking up the number of the company where Blake's brother worked. No good. She was told politely by the receptionist that Bob Summers was out of town on a sales trip.

"What now?" she wondered. Then, trying to keep a level head, she hastily scrawled a note to Cody, hung it on the refrigerator and ran out the back door. "Come on," she said to Runt, who took his cue and followed her outside. When she opened the pickup door, the dog leaped into the cab. "Let's hope we can find him," she confided as she started the truck and put it in gear.

Dark clouds swept over the sky, shadowing the land. The wind, hot and dry, blew leaves and dust across the road. "Looks like we're in for a good one," Dani said to Runt while eyeing the purple, roiling sky and praying that Cody was safe. "Oh, son, use your head and come home!"

She tore out of the driveway like a madwoman, and though she tried to calm herself, she could feel her heart in her throat, beating at twice its normal rate. Sweat dampened her arms and back and her fingers were clenched around the steering wheel as she drove into the quiet school parking lot.

"You're sure he was never here, today?" Dani asked Cody's teacher once she'd dashed through the hallways to his room in the elementary school.

Amanda Ross was visibly distraught. "Yes, but I

thought he was probably just ill. I had no idea—" Then, catching herself, she touched Dani on the arm. "I asked all the teachers; no one saw Cody—not even the duty teacher who supervises the playground in the morning before the final bell when the kids go into their classrooms."

"But I saw him get on the bus—"

"I know. I called over to the bus barns and talked to the driver of the bus Cody rides. The driver remembers picking up Cody and bringing him to the school. So we know he got here, but from that point, no one's sure what happened. From what I can tell, Cody never came into the building or even stopped at the playground. With all of the students arriving by bus and car, he could very easily have walked off the grounds unnoticed."

Sick with worry, Dani sat on a corner of Cody's desk and swallowed back her tears as she looked at the empty chair. "So no one knows where he is?"

"I'm sorry," Amanda said. "Is there anything I can do?"

"I don't know."

The young teacher thought for a moment before broaching what she knew would be a sensitive subject for Cody's mother. "I heard that his father was back in town," she said gently.

"Yes, but not with me. And no one answers at his place."

"Do you think Cody's with him?"

"I don't know," Dani admitted, pressing a finger to her temple. "I hope this is just one of Cody's pranks to get back at me; we had an argument this morning." She pursed her lips together and stood. "I hope to God that Blake hasn't taken off with him."

"So Cody was pretty upset when he left the house?"

"Beside himself." Her heart twisting, she looked at

Cody's teacher. "I—I was going to run after him, but I thought maybe we should both cool off before we got into another disagreement."

"I see." Amanda rubbed her arms and nodded. "He does have a stubborn streak."

"Like me."

"Have you gone to the police?"

"Not yet. I thought I'd get my facts straight first. Look, can I talk to the bus driver?"

"Sure. You can use the phone in the office to call over to the bus barns."

The phone conversation was short. Unfortunately the bus driver wasn't able to tell her anything other than the fact that Cody had definitely gotten to school. Dani hung up the receiver and felt her shoulders slump under the weight of not knowing what had happened to her son.

"Any luck?" Amanda said hopefully.

"None."

"Listen, why don't you call me in the morning?" Amanda suggested. "If Cody hasn't shown up, all of the teachers will ask their classes about him. Maybe one of the children will know where he is. And I'll call all the students in my class tonight, if that will help."

"Thank you," Dani murmured as she walked out of the building.

"Good luck."

Without much hope, Dani drove away from the school and after stopping at Blake's brother's house and finding no one home, she steered her pickup to the police station, where she reported Cody missing, talked to the sergeant, filled out a missing person's report and gave the police one of the pictures of Cody she kept in her wallet. She repeated the procedure at the sheriff's office

and, finally, drained and exhausted, she returned to her
dark, empty house.

Runt barked excitedly and whined at the door as Dani
opened it, but she walked into the shadowed house with a
heavy heart. Nothing had changed. Cody hadn't returned.
The note she'd written him was still on the refrigerator,
the ice box hadn't been raided, there was no loud music
filtering down from his room, nor any dirty tennis shoes
or books scattered in the living room.

The pain in her heart wouldn't go away. Nor would her
wild imagination, filled with horrible scenarios of what
had happened to her son, be still.

Once she'd had a steadying cup of coffee, she called
everyone she could think of, including the Anders brothers and, much as it rankled, Caleb Johnson.

"Well, I'm sorry to hear that your boy's missin'," Caleb
said, his insincerity drifting over the wires. "Anything
I can do?"

"Just let me know if you see him," Dani replied.

"Will do. And I'll tell the hands."

"I appreciate it."

"Good."

"Caleb—" she said, hating herself for having to ask
anything of the old man, but desperate to find her son.

"What?"

"Is Chase there?"

"Not now. Seems he had some business in town and
then he went right down to the creek. But I'll tell him
you called," Caleb said coldly. "Soon as I see him again."

"Thanks."

She managed to get through the evening chores alone,
all the while listening and praying for the phone to ring. It
took twice as long to feed the cattle and horses and by the
time she was done, she was sweaty, dirty and despondent.

Rain peppered the tin roof of the barn and gurgled in the gutters, and the wind, blowing with gale force, shrieked around the buildings.

"Let him be safe," she prayed quietly over the restless shifting of the cattle and the whistle of the wind. The facade she'd held in place all day began to slide away and tears slid down her cheeks.

Too tired to wipe them aside, she sat on a bale of hay and sobbed quietly to herself. "Oh, Cody," she whispered to the dark interior of the barn while listening to the rain, "where are you?"

THROUGH THE SHEETS of rain, Chase looked at the stream and silently congratulated himself on a job well done. The clear water swirled over deep pools and rippled over strategically placed rocks and logs as it ran its course through Johnson's land. Now, if Caleb kept to his word and didn't disturb the banks while constructing his resort, there was no reason Grizzly Creek wouldn't become one of the best trout fishing streams in western Montana.

He glanced at the sky and hunched his shoulders against the thick rain that was pouring from the heavens. Water ran past the collar of his jean jacket and slid down his back. *Miserable weather,* he thought in agitation, *and unusual. Hot and dry one minute, a downpour the next.*

"That about wraps it up," Ben Marx said with a satisfied smile as he lit a cigarette and pushed his shaggy wet hair out of his eyes.

"All that's left is to stock it."

"And then we're outta here, right?"

Chase nodded and wiped his hands on his jeans. "Right. You and the rest of the crew can leave tonight if you want; I'll finish up with some of Johnson's hands."

"Whatever you say!" Ben drew on his cigarette and let

it dangle from the corner of his mouth. "Right now I'm going to get the hell out of this rain and head into town. Check the action at Yukon Jack's. I could use a beer and a change of scenery."

"Take Frank and Brent with you," Chase suggested, and watched as the bearded young man shouted to the rest of the men. They all climbed into a pickup, waved to Chase, and drove across the field to the gate in the corner and the dirt road leading to the center of Johnson's farm.

Chase waited until they were out of sight and then slipped through the fence and ran up the slight incline toward the back of Dani's house. He hadn't seen her all day. Throughout the afternoon, he'd experienced an uncanny sensation that something was wrong; he attributed his discomfiture to the trouble with Cody the night before and the fact that the boy obviously preferred his father's company to Chase's.

"Can't blame the kid," Chase told himself, wiping the rain from his face and hair before sauntering up the back steps. He rapped on the screen door with a knuckle and wondered why none of the interior lights had been turned on.

"Cody?" Dani called, jumping to her feet. She'd been sitting in a corner of the couch, her feet tucked beneath her, her fingers absently scratching Runt's ears.

"Nope. Sorry to—" Chase walked into the room and met her halfway. Immediately he saw the pain in her eyes. "—disappoint you. Dani?"

She couldn't help the small cry that caught in her throat as she ran to him and threw her arms around his neck. "Oh, God, I'm glad you're here," she whispered into his wet shirt. "Just hold me. Please."

He did just that. Resting his head on her crown, he

tightened his grip and said softly, "Believe me, I have no intention of ever letting you go."

"Why didn't you come sooner?"

"I was working…" He held his head back and studied her tear-filled eyes. "Hey, wait a minute. Something is wrong. Really wrong. Maybe you'd better sit down." Guiding her to the couch, he scrutinized her while she slipped back onto the worn cushions and sniffed back her tears. "What's going on?"

"Didn't Caleb tell you?"

"I haven't seen him all day," Chase replied, every muscle in his body tensing. "What's he done?" He pulled a clean, slightly damp handkerchief from the pocket of his jeans and wiped the back of his neck.

"It's not Caleb," she said, shaking her head and sighing.

His jaw clenched. "That bastard of a husband of yours has something to do with this, doesn't he?"

"It's my fault," she breathed, gathering her courage. "All my fault."

"What is?"

"Cody," she choked out, pressing the back of her hand to her lips and looking up at Chase. "He's missing."

"Missing? What do you mean?"

"Just that. He got on the bus around seven-thirty this morning and no one's seen him since."

"You're sure?" Sitting on the arm of the sofa, his blue eyes scanning her white, pinched face, he placed his large hand on her shoulder and her fear infected him. Dani wasn't a woman who panicked easily. Usually strong, now she was scared to death.

"I've called everyone, looked everywhere," she said, standing, pacing and wringing her hands.

"Wait a minute. Slow down and back up," he insisted, taking hold of her and sitting her back on the couch. "Now why don't you start at the beginning. Cody got on the bus to go to school—then what happened?"

Slowly, in a slightly broken voice, she told him every last detail of the search for her son.

"You should have come to me."

"I—I couldn't. I didn't know where you were and… well, you know how it is with Caleb. I did call him and he said he'd get word to you."

"He didn't bother."

"Figures." Dani sniffed.

"You haven't heard from Blake?"

Dani shook her head and sighed. "Nothing."

Pacing the length of the house, Chase tried to unscramble his jumbled thoughts while his suspicion increased. Chase didn't trust coincidence and there were just too many coincidences in Dani's life right now. "I wonder if this has anything to do with Jenna Peterson taking off?"

"I don't see how. Jenna had an argument with Caleb and Cody…Cody's probably run off with his father. They could be in North Dakota by now, or Idaho…or Canada. I wouldn't put it past Blake to take him out of the country."

"But why, Dani?" Chase asked, his thick brows pulled over his eyes as he strode purposefully into the kitchen, rummaged in Dani's cupboards, found a dusty old bottle of Scotch and poured them each a stiff drink. He carried the glasses in one hand and the bottle in the other as he came back into the living room and snapped on one of the table lamps.

"Why did Blake take Cody?" she repeated. "To be with his son, of course."

"I don't think so." Chase handed Dani a glass. "Drink it." When she started to protest, he set the bottle on the table and wrapped her fingers around the glass. "Just this once, Dani, don't argue."

"But Cody's got to be with Blake—they're both missing."

"You think." Chase downed his drink in one swallow and poured himself another. His knuckles whitened around the glass as he frowned into the amber liquid. "Y'know...there are just too damned many twists of fate around here to suit me."

"I don't understand."

"Don't you think it's odd that Jenna Peterson, a woman who's worked for Caleb for years, took off about the same time that Blake blew into town?"

"But Blake's been writing Cody for months—"

"And don't you think it's just a damned sight too convenient that both Blake and the boy are missing—right after we confronted Caleb Johnson with the fact that we know he's done everything from poison your water to low-ball you on the land to get you to sell out to him."

Dani sipped from her drink and a chill ran down her spine. "You're trying to tell me that Caleb's behind Cody's disappearance."

"I'm saying that I don't trust him and that things are happening too fast to be just a matter of fate." He glanced out the window to the gathering storm. "You're the one who put the idea into my head, y'know. You said it yourself: You were tired of being manipulated. I think it's about time to set a few things straight with my 'partner.'" He finished his drink and set the glass on the table with a thud. "Get your coat. This time when we talk to Johnson, we're going to get some answers—straight answers!"

"YOU CAN'T BE SERIOUS!" Caleb said, shaking his great head and even managing a nervous laugh. "I don't know anything about your son's disappearance other than what you told me on the phone this afternoon."

He was standing near the fireplace in his living room and looking at Dani and Chase as if they were out of their minds.

"Why did Jenna leave?" Chase demanded.

"I told you, I have no idea."

"I talked to her daughter. She said that when Jenna left the woman was beside herself. Jenna apparently had an argument with you and something happened to make her leave. It had something to do with someone you've hired recently..."

Caleb's eyes grew cold. "We had words," Caleb admitted.

"About?"

The old man stepped forward, close enough that he could reach forward and touch Chase. Instead he rubbed the back of a leather couch and concentrated on the hard angles of Chase's face. The younger man was regarding him warily, silently accusing him with those damned indifferent eyes—eyes so much like his own.

Dani, her arms wrapped around her torso, felt suddenly cold; a premonition of what was to come. "I just want to find my son," she interjected, looking from the face of one angry man to the other. Tension radiated between them.

"Just as I wanted to find mine all those years ago," Caleb said evenly.

"Pardon?" Dani said. "*Your* son? But I didn't think—" She broke off midsentence and saw the unspoken message pass from Caleb to Chase.

Beneath his tan, Chase blanched, all of his muscles tightening in revulsion, his back teeth clamping together in denial. "What are you trying to say, Johnson?"

"It took me a long time to find you. Ella hid her tracks well," Caleb said.

"You're out of your mind!" Chase said angrily.

"Face it, boy: I'm your father!"

"What the hell is this, Johnson?" Chase demanded, getting hold of himself and eyeing the older man with a deadly calm that belied the raging torrent of emotions roiling deep inside. "This is just another ploy to avoid the subject—"

"It's something I've been meaning to bring up for some time."

"Like hell!" Chase's anger boiled to the surface. "I'm sick of your lies. Come on, Dani!"

He turned to go, but Caleb's words stopped him. "This is no lie, boy. Jenna guessed the truth and knew how you felt about me. Seems you'd had a discussion earlier. When I told her that I was going to spring the news on you, she had one helluva fit. Told me to leave well enough alone."

Chase's eyes narrowed to hard, glinting slits. His back and shoulder muscles bunched and it took all of his control to keep his hands off Caleb's throat. "You're wrong!"

"Why do you think I went to the trouble of finding you? There were a dozen other companies I could have contacted. Eric Conway underbid you by thirty-five-hundred dollars. You can check it yourself, in the study. It's all in the files. But I wasn't interested in the lowest bidder," he said with chilling clarity. "I wanted you, and don't flatter yourself thinking it was because you were the best!" Laughing at his own weakness, he said, "I had this stupid, mortal desire before I died to meet the only son that I'd sired."

Hatred and fury radiated from the younger man. Chase grabbed hold of Caleb's shirt, the clean, starched fabric wrinkling in his angry fists. "You're lying. This is just one more of your cheap tricks to blow smoke in my face!" His nose was pressed up to Caleb's, and his furious blue eyes burned into those of the older man. "Now why don't you tell us the real reason Jenna left. While you're at it, you can tell Dani how you're involved with her ex-husband and where the hell her son is."

"I don't know."

"You're pushing it," Chase warned through clenched teeth.

Caleb glanced nervously at Dani and then fixed on Chase. "Let go of me and I'll prove it."

Chase hesitated and his nostrils flared. "Go ahead." He unclenched his fist and Caleb smoothed his shirt.

Without a word Caleb walked out of the living room, crossed the foyer and walked into his study. He was gone several minutes. When he returned he carried a faded photograph in one hand and a stack of letters banded together in the other.

He dropped everything on the glass-covered table near the fireplace. Dani stared at the picture in disbelief. It was a grainy photo of a man and woman, their arms linked, a cocker spaniel pup at their feet. She didn't recognize the short, blond woman in the picture, but the man was Chase—or someone who looked enough like him to be his brother. *Or his father!* Shock waves rippled through her as she accepted what Chase couldn't.

"Isn't that your mother?" Caleb demanded, pointing at the woman.

"Looks like her," Chase admitted slowly. Stunned, Chase fought the truth that stared him straight in the face.

"And the dog—didn't you grow up with a black cocker pup?"

"It's not the same dog."

"Named Charlie."

Chase didn't move. His guts wrenched painfully as he stared at the picture.

"And what about the man?" Caleb asked. "Is that your pa?"

"No!"

Caleb snorted and shook his white head. "Give it up, son. That's me!" He tapped his finger on the slick picture. "And the first time I saw you, it was like lookin' into a mirror thirty years ago!"

Chase flinched and tried to hold on to his temper. "I don't believe you. I don't know how you manage to—"

"Then look at the letters. They're all addressed to me, in your ma's handwriting. Read what's inside," the old man demanded, pushing the stack of letters from the table and letting them scatter on the floor. "They're from your ma all right. And they even told me about you. But of course, that was when she'd already made plans to marry another man. She never told me his name and it took me nearly thirty years to track you down. By then she and her husband were both gone."

Chase picked up a letter, scanned the handwriting and then crumpled it in his fist. Anger and disbelief mingled into an ungodly rage that contorted his features and made his insides knot. "Go to hell!"

Dani took hold of his arm. "Let's go— Come on, we've got to find Cody. It's obvious he can't help us."

"And all this time you thought another man was your pa," Caleb taunted.

Chase coiled like a rattler ready to strike and his eyes sparked, but there was a trace of wariness in his voice. "If you knew all this when you first came to me, why didn't you tell me?"

"Would you have believed me?"

"I still don't."

Caleb shrugged his big shoulders. "Then it didn't really matter none, did it?"

Dani watched the argument with growing horror. Whether Chase believed it or not, it was evident to her that he was Caleb's son. Sick with the thought, she backed to the window, watching as the two men glared and argued with each other, their voices climbing with the fever pitch of emotion. Chase, ready to strike, ready to lash out at the cause of his pain, and Caleb, smug in his knowledge of the truth.

"You miserable son of a bitch," Chase said, his anger finally exploding as he crashed a fist into the wall. A painting slid to the floor with a thud, the expensive frame splintering apart. "Why did you drag me into all this? Why didn't you leave me the hell alone?"

"Because I didn't want to die without seeing you. Some day you might have children of your own. Then you'll understand," Caleb predicted.

"But all this plotting and sneaking around." Chase rubbed the bridge of his nose and tried to stave off another wave of fury. He wanted to crash his fist into Caleb's smirking face but realized that injuring a seventy-year-old man would prove nothing. He was shaking with rage, his voice low and firm as he pierced Caleb with eyes so like the old man's.

Dani shuddered and backed out of the room.

"Listen to me, Johnson, I don't want to talk about this....I don't want to *think* about it! I just want to find Dani's boy!"

"I have no idea where that kid is—"

"Let's go!" Chase said, grabbing Dani's arm and propelling her to the door.

Dani glanced at the letters on the floor, the photograph on the table and Caleb's ruddy face. "No," Dani said, holding up her hands and backing toward the door. "I think you should stay here and work this out. He's your father, Chase. Your own flesh and blood!"

Stunned and bewildered, she tried to make some sense of it all—deal with the emotional onslaught that twisted her into a thousand little pieces. Chase—Caleb's son? She was numb with shock and didn't think she could stand another. "I'll go home and wait for Cody—"

She raced for the door and ran outside, grateful for the cool air as it pushed her hair from her face. The wind was lashing furiously at the house and rain was peppering the ground in thick drops, settling the dust and splattering on the flagstone walk.

"Dani—" Chase called after her and followed her into the stormy night. He caught up with her at the pickup, his hands jerking on her shoulders and forcing her to face him. "Where are you going?"

"To look for my son!"

"I'll drive—"

"Don't you think you'd better stay here and work things out with your *father*?" she said sarcastically. "How long have you known about this, Chase?" she demanded, knowing she was being irrational, but losing all control of her emotions. "First I thought you worked for Caleb, then I found out that you were his partner, but it's more than that, isn't it? *You're his son, Chase. His son!*"

He looked at her as if stricken, his blue eyes filled with shock and rage. "You think this was some kind of plot? That I was involved?"

"Oh, Chase," she moaned, rain drenching her hair and shoulders, drops streaming down her face. "I don't know what to think," she admitted, "but I can't worry about it. Not now. Not until I find Cody—"

The sound of an explosion ripped across the land, and

Chase reached for Dani, pushing her hard against the pickup, protecting her body with the strength of his.

"Oh, God, what was that?" she whispered, clinging to the rough fabric of his denim jacket.

"No!" Chase let go of her suddenly and ran to the fence on the south end of the parking lot.

Her heart slamming in her chest, disbelief and horror wrenching her face, Dani followed him and looked down the hill to her property and saw a blaze of fireworks reaching up to the black heaven. Orange flames stretched upward like a hand from hell and scraped at the black, smoke-filled sky.

"Oh, God…"

"It's the storage shed…where you keep the tractor," Chase said, pulling her away from the terrifying spectacle. "Come on."

Caleb had come out and was standing on the back porch. "Call the fire department! Send them to the Hawthorne place," Chase commanded, yelling over the storm. "And find someone to take care of Dani!"

"You're not leaving me!" she shouted, her eyes round with horror. "I've got to go home."

"There's nothing you can do—"

"Let go of me!" she hissed, running to the pickup and wrenching open the driver's door. "Cody might be down there!" She jumped into the pickup and reached into her pocket for her keys.

His jaw tight with determination, Chase climbed in after her, ignoring her protests while he started the truck and drove down the rain-slickened drive toward Dani's house.

She stared at it with dull eyes, her heart filled with dread as she tried to cling to the hope that Cody was far away from the inferno.

The house was illuminated by the orange and red flames that licked up to the sky.

"We can't get any closer," Chase said, maneuvering the truck through the first open gate to a field several hundred yards from the house and keeping the lane free for the fire trucks.

"I'm going up there!"

"No way—"

"Cody might be there!"

"I'll go look for him! You stay here."

"Not on your life!" She shoved open the passenger door and Chase jerked her back into the cab, her hair flying into her face, her eyes wide with fear and anger. "Let me go! Chase, I have to—"

"Dammit all anyway!" With a curse, Chase drove up the rest of the driveway. The pickup bounced up her lane and before Chase stopped the vehicle, Dani jumped from the cab. Heavy black smoke filled the air while the rain still poured from the sky.

"Cody!" she screamed, swallowing back her fear and desperation. "Runt!" *God, where was the dog?* Shimmering heat radiated from the buildings behind the house; even the driving rain couldn't contain the blaze.

Chase was on her heels as she sprinted up the two steps and raced into the house. Shouting Cody's name at the top of her lungs, she ran through the rooms. She bounded up the stairs and flung open the door to Cody's room.

"Runt's missing," she screamed at Chase. "Cody must've come home— Oh God!" On the bed was the note she'd left on the refrigerator. Beside the note was his backpack, the same backpack he'd taken to school, and through the window ugly flames brightened the sky, coloring the room with flickering orange shadows and filling the air with acrid smoke.

"No!" Dani screamed. "Oh, God... Oh...God!" And then she fell, feeling Chase's strong arms surround her before she hit the floor.

CHAPTER TWELVE

WHEN DANI OPENED her eyes, she had trouble focusing. She felt a sensation of movement…and noise, lots of noise, sirens shrieking, men shouting, and stench…something burning….

Blinking twice, she found herself in Chase's arms. He was carrying her down the driveway, away from the house. "No," she whispered, her throat dry. "Chase…let me down!"

"This time we're doing it my way, lady," he said through clenched teeth. His hair was slicked down with rainwater and his face was streaked with mud and soot.

"But Cody—"

"I'll find him." Trucks were rushing past them, and one paramedic stopped to talk to Chase.

"Is she all right?"

"I think so—"

"I'm fine," Dani insisted. "Please, put me down!" Once on her feet she stared in amazement at the scene in front of her. Fire trucks were pumping water from the creek and hosing it over the storage shed, and men, neighbors she supposed, were letting the animals out of the barn, into the farthest fields from the house. The cattle lowed and the horses raced.

"Where did everyone come from?" she asked.

"Caleb called the fire department and the neighbors heard the blast—you've been out of it for a little while."

Placing a hand on her head, she tried to think past

the headache and her burning eyes. Finally her thoughts began to clear and crystallize with fear. "Wait a minute. Where is Cody? His backpack was on the bed, I saw his shoes and the note I'd written. He was home, Chase! In that house—" She pointed to the wet, dark home she'd shared with her son. "Dear God, where could he be?" Attempting to jerk free and climb back up the hill, she fought the strong arm around her.

"You can't do anything more," Chase said. "Let the fire department handle the fire."

At that moment the Anders' truck pulled into the lane. Marcella, her face a mask of horror, was at the wheel. "What the devil's goin' on?" she asked. "I was just on my way home from the store when I saw all the commotion—"

"The storage shed caught fire and the gas tank blew," Chase filled her in.

"Good Lord!" Marcella looked at all the frantic activity and her face became grim.

"Oh, no," Dani whispered, understanding the explosion. "But how…"

"Fortunately Dani didn't have much gas in the tank," Chase continued.

"Thank God," Dani murmured.

"You still lookin' for your boy?" Marcella asked.

"Yes." Dani's clouded eyes brightened. "Have you seen him?"

"'Fraid not. And the boys, they've been lookin'. Neither one of them has seen him anywhere in town."

"I only hope he's safe," Dani said, thinking about Cody's things in the house. "Let go of me," she said, starting for the house again.

"If you'll look after Dani, I'll check the barn," Chase

said. "I want to talk to the fire chief and use his phone, if I can."

"I don't need to be taken care of! I'm coming with you."

"Whoa," Marcella said kindly. "The way I hear it, you've had yourself enough shocks for one day. Sit with me here in the truck till he gets back. I've got coffee and doughnuts I was bringing home."

"I couldn't eat a thing," Dani said, while Marcella opened the door of the truck and helped a protesting Dani inside.

"Well, the least you can do is share a cup of coffee and keep me company. Chase, he'll find your boy."

"God, I hope so," Dani whispered, cradling the top of the thermos in her fingers and staring through the rain-streaked windshield toward her house and the scarlet flames beyond.

THREE HOURS LATER the fire was contained. Blackened pieces of the shed were still smoldering, but all in all, the fire had run its course, taking with it the tractor, plow, harrow, baler and trailer and leaving charred skeletons of what had once been Dani's equipment.

Dani had suffered through what seemed a thousand questions from the fire chief and the police, because the fire department suspected that the fire had been set intentionally.

"I was up at Caleb Johnson's when I heard the explosion," Dani said for the fifth time to yet another deputy from the sheriff's department. Bone weary and worried sick, she was tired of the questions and unspoken accusations. "You can ask him or Chase McEnroe. He was with me at the time."

"Where's he?"

"Looking for my boy."

"The boy you reported missing?"

"Yes." She'd gone over it a hundred times. "I could tell that Cody had been home; his shoes and backpack that he'd taken to school, along with a note I'd left him, were in his room."

"Do you mind if I take a look?"

"Please do," she agreed, closing her eyes and twisting her neck to relieve the strain of her shoulder muscles. "Just, please, find my son."

"You haven't seen him since the fire?"

"I haven't seen him since this morning!" Dani followed the young deputy into the house. It had been saved, but reeked of drenched soot. The walls were water stained from the efforts of the firemen to save the house and several windows had been broken from the water pressure of the gigantic hoses.

Fortunately, the Anders brothers and several of the neighbors had tended to the animals for the night, and once the young deputy left, promising to return in the morning, Dani was left alone with Marcella to wait for news of Cody and Chase.

"Where do you think Chase is?" she asked, running her fingers through her hair.

"Like I said before, he's lookin' for the boy."

Restless, Dani paced the living room, ignoring the fact that the floor was still wet. "Why don't you go home now?" Dani asked, offering Marcella a smile as she looked around the rooms. "There's nothing anyone can do tonight and I'm fine. Really."

"Not until Chase gets back," Marcella said, plopping herself onto the sofa and picking up a magazine.

"It's nearly ten—"

"And everyone in my family is old enough to take care

of himself! The boys know where I am if they need me."
She read one headline in Cody's fishing magazine and
then tossed the slick-covered periodical on the table. "How
about if I make you a sandwich or a hot bowl of soup?"

"I don't think so; but if you're hungry—"

"Nonsense! You look like you haven't eaten for days.
No wonder you fainted upstairs what with all the excitement around here!" Against Dani's wishes, Marcella made
herself right at home in Dani's kitchen, donned an apron
and rummaged around in Dani's cupboards until she finally found a pan and a can of soup. In less than ten minutes, she had Dani at the table, drinking warm broth, and
was listening attentively while Dani explained everything
that had happened over the last few weeks.

"My Lord!" Marcella exclaimed. "No wonder you're
upset with Caleb. And now he turns out to be Chase's father!" She tapped her fingers on the rim of her coffee cup.
"You know, if you would have told a few people around
town, maybe we all wouldn't have been so gung-ho on
this Summer Ridge project."

"I couldn't say anything," Dani said. "I really didn't
have any proof until Chase found the drum of dioxin and
located Larry Cross. Besides, it all would have sounded
like sour grapes." She looked at the clock again. Eleven-
thirty. Still no sign of Chase or Cody.

"Why don't you go upstairs and get cleaned up?" Marcella suggested. "I'll tidy up the kitchen—"

"Please, don't bother."

"Go on. I can wait for Chase just as well as you can.
And if the phone rings, I'll catch it. Now, go on, scoot!"

Dani was too tired to argue. She settled into the hot
tub and listened to the sound of Marcella cleaning the
dishes. Smiling sadly to herself she remembered years
ago, when she'd been a teenager, how she'd liked to lis-

ten to the comforting sound of her mother rattling around in the kitchen… But that was long before Cody had been born. Now he was missing.

She washed her hair and scrubbed the grime from her body before wrapping her hair in a bath towel and slipping into her robe. Still rubbing her hair with the towel, she walked down the stairs and stopped midway when she heard Runt's familiar bark at the back door. Dani's heart leaped to her throat. "Cody!" she shouted.

Racing down the remaining stairs and to the back door, she let the dog inside and saw Cody and Chase trudging up the backyard. Without another thought, Dani flew down the steps, her long wet hair streaming behind her, tears of relief flowing from her eyes.

Cody threw himself into her arms and clung for dear life. "Mom," he choked out. "Please don't be mad at me!"

"Mad? For what?"

"For takin' off from school and hiding," he said.

"It's all right. Everything's all right now that you're safe," she choked out, clutching her boy in a death grip and turning tear-filled eyes up to Chase. "God, I was worried sick about you." Still clinging to her son, she noticed the tired lines of worry on Chase's face. She'd never been so glad to see anyone in her life! "Where did you find him?"

"At the homestead house."

"Thank you," she whispered, straightening and throwing her arms around his neck to kiss him full on the lips. "I was afraid I'd lost you both."

"Never, lady. You can't get rid of me that easy."

She sniffed back her tears.

"I think we'd better go inside," Chase said. "This boy here is starving and dead tired and there's a lot you need to know about what happened."

Marcella was standing in the doorway and tears filled

her eyes. She dabbed at the corners of her eyes with the hem of Dani's apron. "Don't you worry about anything," she said. "I'll get Cody a good, hot meal while he goes upstairs and cleans up." With that she bustled into the house.

It was nearly two hours later when Marcella had gone home and Cody, exhausted from a long, harrowing day, fell asleep in Dani's arms. Finally, weary but content, Dani came down the stairs just as Chase hung up the phone.

"Okay, out with it," she said, leaning against the wall while Chase dropped onto the couch. "I know something's up, so you may as well level with me. Did Cody set the fire in the shed?"

"No," Chase said, rubbing his neck with his hands.

"Let me do that," she insisted, standing behind the couch and rubbing his tight shoulder muscles. "So who did?"

"Blake."

"Blake!" Dani was thunderstruck and angry. Her fingers worked furiously on his muscles. "But why? And how do you know?"

"Whoa, slow down, take it easy, will ya?" he said, jerking away from her strong fingers.

"Oh, sorry."

"Cody saw his dad light the fire."

Dani didn't move. "Wait a minute. Back up. Cody was here when the fire started?"

"Right. Apparently, Cody walked home early in the night and intended to make up with you. But we were up at Caleb's place. Cody went upstairs and looked out the window and saw Blake in the shed, so he walked outside just as the shed caught fire and blew sky high."

"Oh, my God," Dani whispered.

"Cody was scared out of his wits. He didn't know where you were and he was afraid that his father was hurt or killed. After doing a quick search for Blake, he ran to the old house to sort things out. When I got there, he was ready to come home."

"But why didn't he just stay here—on the property, or go to a neighbor's?"

"Because he was confused! You have to understand that he'd just suffered a major disappointment. The father he wanted so badly had shown his true colors and turned out to be a criminal. That's not easy for Cody, or any of us to understand."

"So where is Blake?"

"Who knows?"

"But why would he want to blow up my farm?"

"I don't think he wanted to— I think he was paid to," Chase said grimly.

"Oh, no. You're not back to that again, are you? You really think Caleb was behind it?"

"Positive."

"But how?"

"Come here."

She walked around the couch and he took hold of her wrist, pulling on it gently so that she fell on top of him. "You're getting me dirty," she protested with a smile.

"That's not the half of it." He drew her head to his, wound his fingers in her still damp hair and breathed deeply of the scent of her. "God, I've missed you." Kissing her softly, he groaned when her body molded easily to the hard contours of his.

He started kissing her face and pushing the robe off her shoulders, when she stopped him. "Wait a minute, hero," she said. "First things first. Tell me what else you know."

"Anyone ever tell you that you've got your priorities mixed up?"

She laughed. "Come on, out with it."

"Okay. I talked to Jenna Peterson earlier on the phone."

"When?"

"Just a few minutes ago, when you were upstairs with Cody."

"At this hour?"

"I decided that the sooner we figured this out, the better. Her sister had told me that she was due back tonight, so I gambled and called. It worked out."

"So what did she say?"

"Jenna left Caleb, not because of me, but because she knew that Caleb had put Blake Summers on his payroll."

"What!"

"That's right. When I couldn't convince you to sell, Caleb got hold of Blake."

"But why?"

"Because he knew that Cody had received a letter from him. The way I see it, Caleb figured Blake was his ace in the hole. If Blake showed up, either one of two things would happen: Blake would work his way back into your heart and convince you to sell—"

"No way!"

"—or scare you into wanting out of this town and away from him. What Johnson didn't count on was the fact that you weren't going to let Blake boss you around. Apparently Blake figured it out, too. My guess is that he has some sort of deal with Caleb—a deal like Larry Cross had and if he convinced you one way or the other to move, that he'd get a bundle of cash. Why else would he come back now, try to make amends with his son and then set fire to your shed?"

"If he did it."

"You don't think he did?"

She smiled into his eyes. "I don't know what to think. I just know that I'm glad you're here with me, that Cody's safe and that we can be together tonight. Tomorrow morning we'll deal with everything."

"Such as fire inspectors, insurance investigators, nosy neighbors—"

"Wet hay, frightened animals, Caleb, Blake and the rest of the world," she murmured, placing her head against his neck. "But it really doesn't matter," she whispered, shuddering. "A few hours ago, when I thought Cody might be dead and I didn't know where you were, I realized that nothing, not even this land, is worth all this trouble—"

"Shh," he said, pulling the afghan over them both. "Sleep. Don't think about giving up the land tonight. If you do, Caleb's already won."

"I'm just tired of fighting..." she murmured, snuggling against him.

"So am I, Dani," he agreed, kissing her hair. "So am I. But I won't let Johnson win...even if it does turn out that he's my father."

With his arms wrapped around the woman he loved, Chase McEnroe stared at the ceiling long into the night and silently vowed that no matter what happened, he would never give up Dani or her son. With every ounce of strength he could find, he'd fight Caleb Johnson for Dani's right to own this land she loved with all of her heart.

Dani woke up with a crick in her neck. She moved her head from side to side and found herself staring into the most brilliant blue eyes she'd ever seen.

"Morning," Chase drawled, smiling down at her.

"Lord, what time is it?"

"After seven."

"Ooh," she groaned. "I've got to get up and feed the animals. And Cody'll miss the bus—"

"Let him."

"What?" Rubbing her eyes, she tried to clear the cobwebs from her mind.

"Give the kid a break—"

"But school barely started."

"I know, but this is a special day."

"Oh?" She pressed closer to him. "Tell me more—"

"We're going to talk to the minister of your choice and plan a wedding for next week."

"Oh, Chase, how can you even think about getting married so soon?" she said, laughing at the absurdity of the situation.

"I've had all night," he replied, dead serious. "And there's no way around it, lady. We're getting married next Saturday come hell or high water."

"Such a wonderful proposal," she mocked. "How could any woman refuse?" She stretched and pulled herself upright, ignoring the slumberous look of passion lurking in Chase's stare. "But I think I'd better talk to Cody."

"I did."

She'd started to stand and walk to the kitchen, but she whipped her head around, her long golden hair streaming behind her. "When?"

"Yesterday. When I found him at the homestead house. I told him how I felt about you and him and I told him I wouldn't get in the way of his relationship with his natural father even though I wanted to adopt him."

"And?"

"And he seemed to accept the idea. But then, he was pretty disappointed with his father."

"I can imagine…" She looked longingly up the stairs.

"You go on up," Chase suggested. "See what he has to say. I've got a few calls to make anyway."

Dani walked up the stairs and knocked softly on Cody's door.

"Huh?" she heard from within the room and then an excited yip from Runt.

"Can I come in?"

"Sure." Cody was lying in the bed with half the covers spread upon the floor. When Dani opened the door to his room, Runt ran out like a shot.

"How're ya feelin'?" she asked.

He frowned. "Okay, I guess. Mom, I'm real sorry I took off. It's probably my fault that Dad came back to the shed and...and...well, you know."

"Don't blame yourself," Dani said, sitting on the edge of the bed and pushing Cody's tousled hair out of his eyes. "I'm just glad that you're home and safe."

"But the equipment—"

"Can be replaced. You can't."

Cody swallowed hard and then sat up and hugged her with all the strength of his nine years. "I love ya, Mom," he said to his own embarrassment.

"Oh, honey, nothing could be better," she said, her eyes filling with tears.

"'Cept maybe marryin' Chase?" he asked.

"What do you think about it—would you be willing to give me away?"

"Huh?"

Dani laughed at his perplexed expression and then explained about a simple wedding ceremony. Though not jumping for joy, Cody seemed to accept the fact that she would marry Chase.

"Okay, I'll give you away," he said blushing. "As long as it's not for good."

"Silly!"

"Where would we live?"

"Good question," she said. "Why don't you ask Chase? He thinks you deserve a day off from school."

"Great!"

"I'm not so sure about it—"

"Maybe having Chase as a stepdad wouldn't be so bad after all!" Cody said, leaping out of bed.

"I don't think so—but, look, you can't get out of doing your chores, okay?"

"Okay," he grumbled, reaching for his favorite pair of jeans.

Still smiling to herself, Dani went into her bedroom, combed the tangles from her hair, put on a little makeup and changed into a summer dress. By the time she was back downstairs, Cody had already talked to Chase and was in the barn feeding the animals.

Chase was seated at the kitchen table, his feet up on a free chair while he sipped coffee. He looked very proud of himself.

"You look like the cat who caught the canary," she observed as she poured a cup for herself.

"Not a canary, but the prettiest woman east of the Rockies."

"Give me a break." But she laughed despite his outlandish compliment. "What have you been up to?"

"More than you want to know."

"Try me."

"Okay." He held up one finger. "I called the police, they already have Blake in custody."

Shaking, she sat down and let her head fall into her hand. "No," she whispered.

"Yep. He turned himself in because he was scared to death that he'd hurt or even killed Cody. Apparently, Blake hadn't thought anyone was home; then he saw Cody just before the gas tank blew and then he couldn't find the boy. He admitted to being in league with Caleb, and the police are up at Johnson's house now. I told them about the dioxin and they're trying to get in contact with Larry Cross. You'll probably hear from the D.A. He'll want to know if you want to press charges."

"I see," she whispered. "So how does that affect you?"

"It doesn't. Blood or no blood, Caleb Johnson was never my father. But, I did call him; told him everything we knew, and believe it or not he's agreed to lay off you."

"I'll believe that when I see it."

"Oh, it won't be that hard since he'll probably be in the penitentiary for the rest of his life."

"And you don't care?" she asked gently.

"He's never been a father to me. What happened between him and my mother was something that occurred before I was born." He took a long sip from his coffee. "But, I made another agreement with him."

"Now what?" she groaned.

"I'm moving my company to Martinville."

"That, I like."

He stood and came over to her chair, taking her hand and drawing her to her feet. "I thought you might. The next part is even better, I hope. I told Caleb that since he's bound and determined to build Summer Ridge, that we would deed over the rights to the hot springs to him."

"You what!"

"Just listen, okay? He'll have to divert the water down the hill, of course, through the trees, to the back of his resort."

"I don't know about this—"

"In return, he'll grant us the right to control the water flow. With the money we get from the sale of those water rights, we're going to restore the old homestead house and maybe add on a couple of extra rooms," he said.

"Oh, Chase," she said, happiness swelling in her chest. "That's wonderful, but it's a big house. Why more rooms?"

"Modern ones—such as bathrooms with plumbing and a nursery—"

"A nursery?" she said, laughing.

"At least one." He stood and took her into his arms. "Now, what do you say?"

"What took you so long to come into my life?" She looked up at him with bright hazel eyes, all the love in her heart reflected in her gaze.

"Then next Saturday is a good day for a wedding?"

"If we can't do it tomorrow—"

He swept her off her feet and grinned. "You know, I've just had a change of heart."

"Oh?"

"Yep. Maybe we should send Cody to school after all. Then we'd have the rest of the day together."

She smiled seductively. "Sounds like heaven, but you already made a promise that he could stay home."

"My mistake," he groaned and kissed her neck. "But just you wait, lady. Once Cody goes to sleep tonight…"

"Promises, promises," she quipped.

"That's right," he said. "Promises for the rest of your life." Then he kissed her gently, his mouth softly moving over hers, causing her heart to pound and her pulse to flutter.

"Forever?" she asked.

"Forever."

* * * * *

New York Times bestselling author

LINDA GOODNIGHT

**welcomes you to Honey Ridge, Tennessee,
and a house that's rich with secrets and brimming
with sweet possibilities.**

THE
MEMORY
HOUSE

A HONEY RIDGE NOVEL

NEW YORK TIMES BESTSELLING AUTHOR

LINDA GOODNIGHT

Memories of motherhood and marriage are fresh for Julia Presley—though tragedy took away both years ago. Finding comfort in the routine of running the Peach Orchard Inn, she lets the historic, mysterious place fill the voids of love and family. Life is calm, unchanging…until a stranger with a young boy and soul-deep secrets shows up in her Tennessee town.

Julia suspects there's more to Eli Donovan's past than his motherless son, Alex. But with the chance discovery of a dusty stack of love letters, the long-dead ghosts of a Civil War romance envelop Julia and Eli, connecting them to the inn's violent history and challenging them both to risk facing yesterday's darkness for a future bright with hope and healing.

New women's fiction from Linda Goodnight.
Please visit lindagoodnight.com for more information.

Pick up your copy today!

Be sure to connect with us at:
Harlequin.com/Newsletters
Facebook.com/HarlequinBooks
Twitter.com/HQNBooks

www.HQNBooks.com

PHLG964R2

LISA JACKSON

77877	PROOF OF INNOCENCE	___ $7.99 U.S.	___ $8.99 CAN.
77876	MEMORIES	___ $7.99 U.S.	___ $8.99 CAN.
77728	CONFESSIONS	___ $7.99 U.S.	___ $9.99 CAN.
77578	STRANGERS	___ $7.99 U.S.	___ $9.99 CAN.

(limited quantities available)

TOTAL AMOUNT	$ _____
POSTAGE & HANDLING	$ _____
($1.00 FOR 1 BOOK, 50¢ for each additional)	
APPLICABLE TAXES*	$ _____
TOTAL PAYABLE	$ _____

(check or money order—please do not send cash)

To order, complete this form and send it, along with a check or money order for the total above, payable to Harlequin HQN, to: **In the U.S.:** 3010 Walden Avenue, P.O. Box 9077, Buffalo, NY 14269-9077; **In Canada:** P.O. Box 636, Fort Erie, Ontario, L2A 5X3.

Name: _____

Address: _____ City: _____

State/Prov.: _____ Zip/Postal Code: _____

Account Number (if applicable): _____

075 CSAS

*New York residents remit applicable sales taxes.
*Canadian residents remit applicable GST and provincial taxes.

HQN™

www.HQNBooks.com

PHLJ0115BL